THE WORD

Jasper, this month, is the Word.

Jasper is the pass/code/warning that the Singers of the Cities (who, last month, sang "Opal" from their divine injuries; and on Mars I'd heard the Word and used it thrice, along with devious imitations, to fix possession of what was not rightfully my own; and even there I pondered Singers and their wounds) relay by word of mouth for that loose and roguish fraternity with which I have been involved (in various guises) these nine years. It goes out new every thirty days; and within hours every brother knows it, throughout six worlds and worldlets. Usually it's grunted at you by some blood-soaked bastard staggering into your arms from a dark doorway; hissed at you as you pass a shadowed alley; scrawled on a paper scrap pressed into your palm by some nasty-grimy moving too fast through the crowd. And this month it was: Jasper.

from: "Time Considered as a Helix of Semi-Precious Stones," just one of the wonder-filled award-winning tales by Samuel R. Delany together for the first time in this volume.

Bantam Books by Samuel R. Delany
Ask your bookseller for the ones you have missed.

THE COMPLETE NEBULA AWARD-WINNING FICTION
of
Samuel R. Delany

BANTAM BOOKS
TORONTO · NEW YORK · LONDON · SYDNEY · AUCKLAND

THE COMPLETE NEBULA AWARD-WINNING FICTION

A Bantam Spectra Book / February 1986

PRINTING HISTORY

Babel-17 *copyright* © *1966 by Ace Books, Inc.*
A Fabulous, Formless Darkness, *formerly published under the title* The
Einstein Intersection, *copyright* © *1967 by Samuel R. Delany.* "Aye, and
Gomorrah . . ." *copyright* © *1967 by Samuel R. Delany.* "Time Con-
sidered as a Helix of Semi-Precious Stones" *copyright* © *1969 by
Samuel R. Delany.*

All epigraphs in Babel-17 *are from poems by Marilyn Hacker. Most of
those excerpted were later included in her collections* Presentation
Piece *(by Marilyn Hacker, Viking Press: New York, 1974) and* Separations *(by Marilyn Hacker, Alfred A. Knopf: New York, 1976). A few
lines are earlier versions of those to be found in the volume collections.*

ISBN 0-553-25610-6

Published simultaneously in the United States and Canada

Bantam Books are published by Bantam Books, Inc. Its trademark,
consisting of the words "Bantam Books" and the portrayal of a
rooster, is Registered in U.S. Patent and Trademark Office and in
other countries. Marca Registrada. Bantam Books, Inc., 666 Fifth
Avenue, New York, New York 10103.

PRINTED IN THE UNITED STATES OF AMERICA

H   0 9 8 7 6 5 4 3 2 1

Contents

BABEL-17

—this one, now, is
for Bob Folsom,
to explain just a little of
the past year—

NOTE

All epigraphs in *Babel-17* are from the poems of Marilyn Hacker. Most were excerpted from poems later included in *Presentation Piece* (by Marilyn Hacker, Viking Press: New York, 1974) and *Separations* (by Marilyn Hacker, Alfred A. Knopf: New York, 1976). A few lines here are earlier versions of those to be found in the volume collections.

—S. R. D.

PART ONE

~~~~~~

Rydra Wong

...Here is the hub of ambiguity.
Electric spectra splash across the street.
Equivocation knots the shadowed features
of boys who are not boys; a quirk of darkness
shrivels a full mouth to senility
or pares it to a razor-edge, pours acid
across an amber cheek, fingers
a crotch, or smashes in the pelvic arch
and wells a dark clot oozing in a chest
dispelled with motion or a flare of light
that swells the lips and dribbles them with blood.
They say the hustlers paint their lips with blood.
They say the same crowd surges up the street
and surges down again, like driftwood borne
tidewise ashore and sucked away with backwash,
only to slap into the sand again,
only to be jerked out and spun away.
Driftwood; the narrow hips, the liquid eyes,
the wideflung shoulders and the rough-cast hands,
the gray-faced jackals kneeling to their prey.

*The colors disappear at break of day
when stragglers toward the west riverdocks meet
young sailors ambling shipward on the street . . .*

—from *Prism and Lens.*

1

It's a port city.

Here fumes rust the sky, the General thought. Industrial gases flushed the evening with oranges, salmons, purples with too much red. West, ascending and descending transports, shuttling cargoes to stellarcenters and satellites, lacerated the clouds. It's a rotten poor city too, thought the General, turning the corner by the garbage-strewn curb.

Since the Invasion six ruinous embargoes for months apiece had strangled this city whose lifeline must pulse with interstellar commerce to survive. Sequestered, how could this city exist? Six times in twenty years he'd asked himself that. Answer? It couldn't.

Panics, riots, burnings, twice cannibalism—

The General looked from the silhouetted loading-towers that jutted behind the rickety monorail to the grimy buildings. The streets were smaller here, cluttered with transport workers, loaders, a few stellarmen in green uniforms, and the hoard of pale, proper men and women who managed the intricate sprawl of customs operations. They are quiet now, intent on home or work, the General thought. Yet all these people have lived for two decades under the Invasion. They've starved during the embargoes, broken windows, looted, run screaming before firehoses, torn flesh from a corpse's arm with decalcified teeth.

Who is this animal man? He asked himself the abstract question to blur the lines of memory. It was easier, being a general, to ask about the "animal man" than about the woman who had sat in the middle of the sidewalk during the last

7

embargo holding her skeletal baby by one leg, or the three scrawny teen-age girls who had attacked him on the street with razors (—she had hissed through brown teeth, the bar of metal glistening towards his chest, "Come here, Beefsteak! Come get me, Lunch-meat . . ." He had used karate—) or the blind man who had walked up the avenue, screaming.

Pale and proper men and women now, who spoke softly, who always hesitated before they let an expression fix their faces, with pale, proper, patriotic ideas: work for victory over the Invaders; Alona Star and Kip Rhyak were great in "Stellar Holliday" but Ronald Quar was the best serious actor around. They listened to Hi Lite's music (or did they listen, wondered the General, during those slow dances where no one touched). A position in Customs was a good secure job.

Working directly in Transport was probably more exciting and fun to watch in the movies; but really, such strange people—

Those with more intelligence and sophistication discussed Rydra Wong's poetry.

They spoke of the Invasion often, with some hundred phrases consecrated by twenty years' repetition on newscasts and in the papers. They referred to the embargoes seldom, and only by the one word.

Take any of them, take any million. Who are they? What do they want? What would they say if given a chance to say anything?

Rydra Wong has become this age's voice. The General recalled the glib line from a hyperbolic review. Paradoxical: a military leader with a military goal, he was going to meet Rydra Wong now.

The street lights came on and his image glazed on the plate glass window of the bar. That's right, I'm not wearing my uniform now. He saw a tall, muscular man with the authority of half a century in his craggy face. He was uncomfortable in the gray civilian suit. Till age thirty, the physical impression he had left with people was "big and bumbling." Afterwards—the change had coincided with the Invasion—it was "massive and authoritarian."

Had Rydra Wong come to see him at Administrative

Alliance Headquarters, he would have felt secure. But he was in civvies, not in stellarman-green. The bar was new to him. And she was the most famous poet in five explored galaxies. For the first time in a long while he felt bumbling again.

He went inside.

And whispered, "My God, she's beautiful," without even having to pick her from among the other women. "I didn't know she was so beautiful, not from the pictures. . . ."

She turned to him (as the figure in the mirror behind the counter caught sight of him and turned away), stood up from the stool, smiled.

He walked forward, took her hand, the words *Good evening, Miss Wong,* tumbling on his tongue till he swallowed them unspoken. And now she was about to speak.

She wore copper lipstick, and the pupils of her eyes were beaten disks of copper—

"Babel-17," she said. "I haven't solved it yet, General Forester."

A knitted indigo dress, and her hair like fast water at night spilling one shoulder; he said, "That doesn't really surprise us, Miss Wong."

Surprise, he thought. She puts her hand on the bar, she leans back on the stool, hip moving in knitted blue, and with each movement, I am amazed, surprised, bewildered. Can I be this off guard, or can she really be that—

"But I've gotten further than you people at Military have been able to." The gentle line of her mouth bowed with gentler laughter.

"From what I've been led to expect of you, Miss Wong, that doesn't surprise me either." Who is she? he thought. He had asked the question of the abstract population. He had asked it of his own reflected image. He asked it of her now, thinking, No one else matters, but I must know about her. That's important. I have to know.

"First of all, General," she was saying, "Babel-17 isn't a code."

His mind skidded back to the subject and arrived teetering. "Not a code? But I thought Cryptography had at least established——" He stopped, because he wasn't sure what Cryptography had established, and because he needed another moment to haul himself down from the ledges of her high cheekbones, to retreat from the caves of her eyes. Tightening the muscles of his face, he marshaled his thoughts to Babel -17. The Invasion: Babel-17 might be one key to ending this twenty-year scourge. "You mean we've just been trying to decipher a lot of nonsense?"

"It's not a code," she repeated. "It's a language."

The General frowned. "Well, whatever you call it, code or language, we still have to figure out what it says. As long as we don't understand it, we're a hell of a way from where we should be." The exhaustion and pressure of the last months homed in his belly, a secret beast to strike the back of his tongue, harshening his words.

Her smile had left, and both hands were on the counter. He wanted to retract the harshness. She said, "You're not directly connected with the Cryptography Department." The voice was even, calming.

He shook his head.

"Then let me tell you this. Basically, General Forester, there are two types of codes, ciphers, and true codes. In the first, letters, or symbols that stand for letters, are shuffled and juggled according to a pattern. In the second, letters, words, or groups of words are replaced by other letters, symbols, or words. A code can be one type or the other, or a combination. But both have this in common: once you find the key, you just plug it in and out come logical sentences. A language, however, has its own internal logic, its own grammar, its own way of putting thoughts together with words that span various spectra of meaning. There is no key you can plug in to unlock the exact meaning. At best you can get a close approximation."

"Do you mean that Babel-17 decodes into some other language?"

"Not at all. That's the first thing I checked. We can take a probability scan on various elements and see if they are congruent with other language patterns, even if these elements are in the wrong order. No. Babel-17 is a language itself which we do not understand."

"I think"—General Forester tried to smile—"what you're trying to tell me is that because it isn't a code, but rather an alien language, we might as well give up." If this were defeat, receiving it from her was almost relief.

But she shook her head. "I'm afraid that's not what I'm saying at all. Unknown languages have been deciphered without translations, Linear B and Hittite for example. But if I'm to get further with Babel-17, I'll have to know a great deal more."

The General raised his eyebrows. "What more do you need to know? We've given you all our samples. When we get more, we'll certainly——"

"General, I have to know everything you know about Babel-17; where you got it, when, under what circumstances, anything that might give me a clue to the subject matter."

"We've released all the information that we——"

"You gave me ten pages of double-spaced typewritten garble with the code name Babel-17 and asked me what it meant. With just that I can't tell you. With more, I might. It's that simple."

He thought: If it were that simple, if it were only that simple, we would never have called you in about it, Rydra Wong.

She said: "If it were that simple, if it were only that simple, you would never have called me in about it, General Forester."

He started, for one absurd moment convinced she had read his mind. But of course, she would know that. Wouldn't she?

"General Forester, has your Cryptography Department even discovered it's a language?"

"If they have, they haven't told me."

"I'm fairly sure they don't know. I've made a few structural inroads on the grammar. Have they done that?"

"No."

"General, although they know a hell of a lot about codes, they know nothing of the nature of language. That sort of idiotic specialization is one of the reasons I haven't worked with them for the past six years."

Who is she? he thought again. A security dossier had been handed him that morning, but he had passed it to his aide and merely noted, later, that it had been marked "approved." He heard himself say, "Perhaps if you could tell me a little about yourself, Miss Wong, I could speak more freely with you." Illogical, yet he'd spoken it with measured calm and surety. Was her expression quizzical?

"What do you want to know?"

"What I already know is only this: your name, and that some time ago you worked for Military Cryptography. I know that even though you left when very young, you had enough of a reputation so that, six years laer, the people who remembered you said unanimously—after they had struggled with Babel-17 for a month—'Send it to Rydra Wong.'" He paused. "And you tell me you have gotten someplace with it. So they were right."

"Let's have drinks," she said.

The bartender drifted forward, drifted back, leaving two small glasses of smoky green. She sipped, watching him. Her eyes, he thought, slant like astounded wings.

"I'm not from Earth," she said. "My father was a Communications engineer at Stellarcenter X-11-B just beyond Uranus. My mother was a translator for the Court of Outer Worlds. Until I was seven I was the spoiled brat of the Stellarcenter. There weren't many children. We moved rock-side to Uranus-XXVII in '52. By the time I was twelve, I knew seven Earth languages and could make myself understood in five extra-terrestrial tongues. I pick up languages like most people pick up the lyrics to popular songs. I lost both parents during the second embargo."

"You were on Uranus during the embargo?"

"You know what happened?"

"I know the Outer Planets were hit a lot harder than the Inner."

"You don't know. But yes, they were." She drew a breath as memory surprised her. "One drink isn't enough to make me talk about it, though. When I came out of the hospital, there was a chance I may have had brain damage."

"Brain damage——?"

"Malnutrition you know about. Add neuro-sciatic plague."

"I know about plague, too."

"Anyway, I came to Earth to stay with an aunt and uncle here and receive neuro-therapy. Only I didn't need it. And I don't know whether it was psychological or physiological, but I came out of the whole business with total verbal recall. I'd been bordering on it all my life so it wasn't too odd. But I also had perfect pitch."

"Doesn't that usually go along with lightning calculation and eidetic memory? I can see how all of them would be of use to a cryptographer."

"I'm a good mathematician, but no lightning calculator. I test high on visual conception and special relations—dream in technicolor and all that—but the total recall is strictly verbal. I had already begun writing. During the summer I got a job translating with the government and began to bone up on codes. In a little while I discovered that I had a certain knack. I'm not a good cryptographer. I don't have the patience to work that hard on anything written down that I didn't write myself. Neurotic as hell; that's another reason I gave it up for poetry. But the 'knack' was sort of frightening. Somehow, when I had too much work to do, and somewhere else I really wanted to be, and was scared my supervisor would start getting on my neck, suddenly everything I knew about communication would come together in my head, and it was easier to read the thing in front of me and say what it said than to be that scared and tired and miserable."

She glanced at her drink.

"Eventually the knack almost got to where I could control it. By then I was nineteen and had a reputation as the little girl who could crack anything. I guess it was knowing something about language that did it, being more facile at recognizing patterns—like distinguishing grammatical order from random rearrangement by feel, which is what I did with Babel-17."

"Why did you leave?"

"I've given you two reasons. A third is simply that when I mastered the knack, I wanted to use it for my own purposes. At nineteen, I quit the Military and, well, got . . . married, and started writing seriously. Three years later my first book came out." She shrugged, smiled. "For anything after that, read the poems. It's all there."

"And on the worlds of five galaxies, now, people delve your imagery and meaning for the answers to the riddles of language, love, and isolation." The three words jumped his sentence like vagabonds on a boxcar. She was before him, and was talking; here, divorced from the military, he felt desperately isolated; and he was desperately in——No!

That was impossible and ridiculous and too simple to explain what coursed and pulsed behind his eyes, inside his hands. "Another drink?" Automatic defense. But she will take it for automatic politeness. Will she? The bartender came, left.

"The worlds of five galaxies," she repeated. "That's so strange. I'm only twenty-six." Her eyes fixed somewhere behind the mirror. She was only half through her first drink.

"By the time Keats was your age, he was dead."

She shrugged. "This is an odd epoch. It takes heroes very suddenly, very young, then drops them as quickly."

He nodded, recalling half a dozen singers, actors, even writers in their late teens or early twenties who had been named genius for a year, two, three, only to disappear. Her reputation was only a phenomenon of three years' duration.

"I'm part of my times," she said. "I'd like to transcend my times, but the times themselves have a good deal to do with who I am." Her hand retreated across the mahogany from her glass. "You in Military, it must be much the same." She raised her head. "Have I given you what you want?"

He nodded. It was easier to lie with a gesture than a word.

"Good. Now, General Forester, what's Babel-17?"

He looked around for the bartender, but a glow brought his eyes back to her face: the glow was simply her smile, but from the corner of his eye he had actually mistaken it for a light. "Here," she said, pushing her second drink, untouched, to him. "I won't finish this."

He took it, sipped. "The Invasion, Miss Wong . . . it's got to be involved with the Invasion."

She leaned on one arm, listening with narrowing eyes.

"It started with a series of accidents—well, at first they seemed like accidents. Now we're sure it's sabotage. They've occurred all over the Alliance regularly since December '68. Some on warships, some in Space Navy Yards, usually involving the failure of some important equipment. Twice, explosions have caused the death of important officials. Several times these 'accidents' have happened in industrial plants producing essential war products.''

"What connects all these 'accidents', other than that they touched on the war? With our economy working this way, it would be difficult for any major industrial accident not to affect the war.''

"The thing that connects them all, Miss Wong, is Babel-17.''

He watched her finish her drink and set the glass precisely on the wet circle.

"Just before, during, and immediately after each accident, the area is flooded with radio exchanges back and forth from indefinite sources; most of them only have a carrying power of a couple of hundred yards. But there are occasional bursts through hyperstatic channels that blanket a few light-years. We have transcribed the stuff during the last three 'accidents' and given it the working title Babel-17. Now. Does that tell you anything you can use?''

"Yes. There's a good chance you're receiving radio instructions for the sabotage back and forth between whatever is directing the 'accidents'——''

"——But we can't find a thing!'' Exasperation struck. "There's nothing but that blasted gobbledy-gook, piping away at double speed! Finally someone noticed certain repetitions in the pattern that suggested a code. Cryptography seemed to think it was a good lead but couldn't crack it for a month; so they called you.''

As he talked, he watched her think. Now she said, "General Forester, I'd like the original monitors of these radio exchanges, plus a thorough report, second by second if it's available, of those accidents timed to the tapes.''

"I don't know if——''

"If you don't have such a report, make one during the next 'accident' that occurs. If this radio garbage is a conversation, I have to be able to follow what's being talked about. You may not have noticed, but, in the copy Cryptography gave me, there was no distinction as to which voice was which. In short, what I'm working with now is a transcription of a highly technical exchange run together without punctuation, or even word breaks.''

''I can probably get you everything you want except the original recordings——''

''You have to. I must make my own transcription, carefully, and on my own equipment.''

''We'll make a new one to your specifications.''

She shook her head. ''I have to do it myself, or I can't promise a thing. There's the whole problem of phonemic and allophonic distinctions. Your people didn't even realize it was a language, so it didn't occur to them——''

Now he interrupted her. *''What* sort of distinctions?''

''You know the way some Orientals confuse the sounds of R and L when they speak a Western language? That's because R and L in many Eastern languages are allophones, that is, considered the same sound, written and even heard the same—just like the *th* at the beginning of *they* and at the beginning of *theater.''*

''What's different about the sound of *th*eatre and *th*ey?''

''Say them again and listen. One's voiced and the other's unvoiced, they're as distinct as V and F; only they're allophones—at least in British English; so Britishers are used to hearing them as though they were the same phoneme. Now Americans, of course, have the minimal pair 'ether/either,' where the voicing alone marks the semantic difference—''

''Oh . . .''

''But you see the problem a 'foreigner' has transcribing a language he doesn't speak; he may come out with too many distinctions of sound, or not enough.''

''How do you propose to do it?''

''By what I know about the sound systems of a lot of other languages and by feel.''

''The 'knack' again?''

She smiled. ''I suppose.''

She waited for him to grant approval. What wouldn't he have granted her? For a moment he had been distracted by her voice through subtleties of sound. ''Of course, Miss Wong,'' he said, ''you're our expert. Come to Cryptography tomorrow and you can have access to whatever you need.''

"Thank you, General Forester. I'll bring my official report in then."

He stood in the static beam of her smile. I must go now, he thought desperately. Oh, let me say something more— "Fine, Miss Wong. I'll speak to you then." Something more, something—

He wrenched his body away. (I must turn from her.) Say one thing more, thank you, be you, love you. He walked to the door, his thoughts quieting: who is she? Oh, the things that should have been said. I have been brusque, military, efficient. But the luxurience of thought and word I would have given her. The door swung open and evening brushed blue fingers on his eyes.

My god, he thought, as coolness struck his face, all that inside me and she doesn't know! I didn't communicate a thing! Somewhere in the depths the words, *not a thing, you're still safe*. But stronger on the surface was the outrage at his own silence. Didn't communicate a thing at all——

Rydra stood up, her hands on the edge of the counter, looking at the mirror. The bartender came to remove the glasses at her fingertips. As he reached for them, he frowned.

"Miss Wong?"

Her face was fixed.

"Miss Wong, are you——"

Her knuckles were white, and as the bartender watched, the whiteness crept along her hands till they looked like shaking wax.

"Is there something wrong, Miss Wong?"

She snapped her face toward him. "You noticed?" Her voice was a hoarse whisper, harsh, sarcastic, strained. She whirled from the bar and started toward the door, stopped once to cough, then hurried on.

II

~~~~~~

"Mocky, help me!"

"Rydra?" Dr. Markus T'mwarba pushed himself from
the pillow in the darkness. Her face sprung in smoky light
above the bed. "Where are you?"

"Downstairs, Mocky. Please, I've got to talk to you."
Her agitated features moved right, left, trying to avoid his
look. He squinched his eyes against the glare, then opened
them slowly. "Come on up."

Her face disappeared.

He waved his hand across the control board, and soft
light filled the sumptuous bedroom. He shoved back the gold
quilt, stood on the fur rug, took a black silk robe from a
gnarled bronze column, and as he swung it across his back
the automatic contour wires wrapped the panels across his
chest and straightened the shoulders. He brushed the induc-
tion bank in the rococo frame again, and aluminium flaps fell
back on the sideboard. A steaming carafe and liquor decant-
ers rolled forward.

Another gesture started bubble chairs inflating from the
floor. As Dr. T'mwarba turned to the entrance cabinet,
it creaked, mica wings slid out, and Rydra caught her
breath.

"Coffee?" He pushed the carafe and the force-field
caught it and carried it gently toward her. "What've you been
doing?"

"Mocky, it . . . I . . . ?"

"Drink your coffee."

18

She poured a cup, lifted it halfway to her mouth. "No sedatives?"

"Crème de cacao or crème de cafe?" He held up two small glasses. "Unless you think alcohol is cheating, too. Oh, and there're some franks and beans left over from dinner. I had company."

She shook her head. "Just cacao."

The tiny glass followed the coffee across the beam. "I've had a perfectly dreadful day." He folded his hands. "No work all afternoon, dinner guests who wanted to argue, and then deluged with calls from the moment they left. Just got to sleep ten minutes ago." He smiled. "How was your evening?"

"Mocky, it . . . it was terrible."

Dr. T'mwarba sipped his liqueur. "Good. Otherwise I'd never forgive you for waking me up."

In spite of herself she smiled. "I can . . . can always c-c-count on you for s-sympathy, Mocky."

"You can count on me for good sense and cogent psychiatric advice. Sympathy? I'm sorry, not after eleven-thirty. Sit down. What happened?" A final sweep of his hand brought a chair up behind her. The edge tapped the back of her knees and she sat. "Now stop stuttering and talk to me. You got over that when you were fifteen." His voice had become very gentle and very sure.

She took another sip of coffee. "The code, you remember the code I was working on?"

Dr. T'mwarba lowered himself to a wide leather hammock and brushed back his white hair, still awry from sleep. "I remember you were asked to work on something for the government. You were rather scornful of the business."

"Yes. And . . . well, it's not the code—which is a language, by the way—but just this evening, I-I talked to the General in charge, General Forester, and it happened . . . I mean again, it happened, and I knew!"

"Knew what?"

"Just like last time, knew what he was thinking!"

"You read his mind?"

"No. No, it was just like last time! I could tell, from what he was doing, what he was saying . . ."

"You've tried to explain this to me before, but I still don't understand, unless you're talking about some sort of telepathy."

She shook her head, shook it again.

Dr. T'mwarba locked his fingers and leaned back. Suddenly Rydra said in an even voice: *"Now I do have some idea of what you're trying to say, dear, but you'll have to put it in words yourself.* That's what you were about to say, Mocky, wasn't it?"

T'mwarba raised the white hedges of his eyebrows. "Yes. It was. You say you didn't read my mind? You've demonstrated this to me a dozen times———"

"I know what *you're* trying not to say; and you don't know what *I'm* trying to say. It's not fair!" She nearly rose from her seat.

They said in unison: "That's why you're such a fine poet." Rydra went on, "I know, Mocky. I have to work things out carefully in my head and put them in my poems so people will understand. But that's not what I've been doing for the past ten years. You know what I do? I listen to other people, stumbling about with their half thoughts and half sentences and their clumsy feelings that they can't express, and it hurts me. So I go home and burnish it and polish it and weld it to a rhythmic frame, make the dull colors gleam, mute the garish artificiality to pastels, so it doesn't hurt any more: that's my poem. I know what they want to say, and I say it for them."

"The voice of your age," said T'mwarba.

She said something unprintable. When she finished there were tears starting on her lower lids. "What *I* want to say, what I want to express, *I* just . . ." Again she shook her head. "I can't say it."

"If you want to keep growing as a poet, you'll have to."

She nodded. "Mocky, up till a year ago, I didn't even realize I was just saying other people's ideas. I thought they were my own."

"Every young writer who's worth anything goes through that. That's when you learn your craft."

"And now I have things to say that are all my own. They're not what other people have said before, put in an original way. And they're not just violent contradictions of what other people have said, which amounts to the same thing. They're new, and I'm scared to death."

"Every young writer who becomes a mature writer has to go through that."

"It's easy to repeat; it's hard to speak, Mocky."

"Good, if you're learning that now. Why don't you start by telling me exactly how this . . . this business of your understanding works?"

She was silent for five, stretching to ten, seconds. "All right. I'll try again. Just before I left the bar, I was standing there, looking in the mirror, and the bartender came up and asked me what was wrong."

"Could he sense you were upset?"

"He didn't 'sense' anything. He looked at my hands. They were clenched on the edge of the bar and they were turning white. He didn't have to be a genius to figure out something odd was going on in my head."

"Bartenders are pretty sensitive to that sort of signal. It's part of their job." He finished his coffee. "Your fingers were turning white? All right, what was this General saying to you, or not saying to you, that he wanted to say?"

A muscle in her cheek jumped twice, and Dr. T'mwarba thought, Should I be able to interpret that more specifically than just her nervousness?

"He was a brisk, ramrod efficient man," she explained, "probably unmarried, with a military career, and all the insecurity that implies. He was in his fifties, and feeling odd about it. He walked into the bar where we were supposed to meet; his eyes narrowed, then opened, his hand was resting against his leg, and the fingers suddenly curled, then straightened, his pace slowed as he came in, but quickened by the time he was three steps toward me, and he shook my hand like he was afraid it would break."

T'mwarba's smile turned into laughter. "He fell in love with you!"

She nodded.

"But why in the world should that upset you? I think you should be flattered."

"Oh, I was!" She leaned forward. "I *was* flattered. And I could follow the whole thing through his head. Once, when he was trying to get his mind back on the code, Babel-17, I said exactly what he was thinking, just to let him know I was so close to him. I watched the thought go by that perhaps I was reading his mind——"

"Wait a minute. This is the part I don't understand. How did you know *exactly* what he was thinking?"

She raised her hand to her jaw. "He told me, here. I said something about needing more information to crack the language. He didn't want to give it to me. I said I had to have it or I couldn't get any farther, it was that simple. He raised his head just a fraction—to avoid shaking it. If he had shaken his head, with a slight pursing of the lips, what do you think he would have been saying?"

Dr. T'mwarba shrugged. "That it wasn't as simple as you thought?"

"Yes. Now he made one gesture to avoid making that one. What does that mean?"

T'mwarba shook his head.

"He avoided the gesture because he connected its not being that simple with my being there. So he raised his head instead."

"Something like: If it were that simple, we wouldn't need you," T'mwarba suggested.

"Exactly. Now, while he raised his head, there was a slight pause halfway up. Don't you see what that adds?"

"No."

"If it were that simple—now the pause—if *only* it were that simple, we wouldn't have called you in about it." She turned her hands up in her lap. "And I said it back to him; then his jaw clenched——"

"In surprise?"

"—Yes. That's when he wondered for a second if I could read his mind."

Dr. T'mwarba shook his head. "It's too exact, Rydra. What you're describing is muscle-reading, which can be pretty accurate, especially if you know the logical area the person's thoughts are centred on. But it's still too exact. Get back to why you were upset by the business. Your modesty was offended by the attention of this . . . uncouth stellarman?"

She came back with something neither modest nor couth.

Dr. T'mwarba bit the inside of his lip and wondered if she saw.

"I'm not a little girl," she said. "Besides, he wasn't thinking anything uncouth. As I said, I was flattered by the whole thing. When I pulled my little joke, I was just trying to let him know how much in key we were. I thought he was charming. And if he had been able to see as clearly as I could he would have known I had nothing but good feeling for him. Only when he left——"

Dr. T'mwarba heard roughness work back into her voice.

"—when he left, the last thing he thought was, 'She doesn't know; I haven't communicated a thing to her.' "

Her eyes darkened—no, she bent slightly forward and half dropped her upper lids so that her eyes looked darker. He had watched that happen thousands of times since the scrawny near-autistic twelve-year-old girl had been sent to him for neurotherapy, which had developed into psychotherapy, and then into friendship. This was the first time he'd understood the mechanics of the effect. Her precision of observation had inspired him before to look more closely at others. Only since therapy had officially ended had it come full circle and made him look more closely at her. What did the darkening signify other than change? He knew there were myriad marks of personality about him that she read with a microscope. Wealthy, worldly, he had known many people equal to her in reputation. The reputation did not awe him. Often she did.

"He thought I didn't understand. He thought nothing had been communicated. And I was angry. I was hurt. All the misunderstandings that tie the world up and keep people apart were quivering before me at once, waiting for me to untangle them, explain them, and I couldn't. I didn't know the words, the grammar, the syntax. And—"

Something else was happening in her Oriental face, and he strained to catch it. "Yes?"

"—Babel-17."

"The language?"

"Yes. You know what I used to call my 'knack'?"

"You mean you suddenly understood the language?"

"Well, General Forester had just told me what I had was not a monologue, but a dialogue, which I hadn't known before. That fitted in with some other things I had in the back of my mind. I realized I could tell where the voices changed myself. And then——"

"Do you understand it?"

"I understand some of it better than I did this afternoon. There's something about the language itself that scares me even more than General Forester."

Puzzlement fixed itself to T'mwarba's face. "About the language itself?"

She nodded.

"What?"

The muscle in her cheek jumped again. "For one thing, I think I know where the next accident is going to be."

"Accident?"

"Yes. The next sabotage that the Invaders are planning, if it is the Invaders, which I'm not sure of. But the language itself—it's . . . it's strange."

"How?"

"Small," she said. "Tight. Close together— That doesn't mean anything to you, does it? In a language, I mean?"

"Compactness?" asked Dr. T'mwarba. "I would think it's a good quality in a spoken language."

"Yes," and the sibilant became a breath. "Mocky, I am scared!"

"Why?"

"Because I'm going to try to do something, and I don't know if I can or not."

"If it's worth trying, you should be a little afraid. What is it?"

"I decided it back in the bar, and I figured out I'd better talk to somebody first. That usually means you."

"Give."

"I'm going to solve this whole Babel-17 business myself."

T'mwarba leaned his head to the right.

"Because I have to find out who speaks this language, where it comes from, and what it's trying to say."

His head went left.

"Why? Well, most textbooks say language is a mechanism for expressing thought, Mocky. But language *is* thought. Thought is information given form. The form is language. The form of this language is . . . amazing."

"What amazes you?"

"Mocky, when you learn another tongue, you learn the way another people see the world, the universe."

He nodded.

"And as I see into this language, I begin to see . . . too much."

"It sounds very poetical."

She laughed. "You always say that to me to bring me back to earth."

"Which I don't have to do too often. Good poets tend to be practical and abhor mysticism."

"Something about trying to hit reality; you figure it out," she said. "Only, as poetry tries to touch something real, maybe this is poetical."

"All right. I still don't understand. But how do you propose to solve the Babel-17 mystery?"

"You really want to know?" Her hands fell to her knees. "I'm going to get a spaceship, get a crew together, and get to the scene of the next accident."

"That's right, you do have Interstellar Captain's papers. Can you afford it?"

"The government's going to subsidize it."

"Oh, fine. But why?"

"I'm familiar with a half-dozen languages of the Invaders. Babel-17 isn't one of them. It isn't a language of the Alliance. I want to find out who speaks this language— because I want to find out who, or what, in the Universe thinks that way. Do you think I can, Mocky?"

"Have another cup of coffee." He reached back over his shoulder and sailed the carafe across to her again. "That's a good question. There's a lot to consider. You're not the most stable person in the world. Managing a spaceship crew takes a special sort of psychology which—you have. Your papers, if I remember, were the result of that odd—eh, marriage of yours, a couple of years ago. But you only used an automatic crew. For a trip this length, won't you be managing Transport people?''

She nodded.

"Most of my dealings have been with Customs persons. You're more or less Customs."

"Both parents were Transport. I was Transport up till the time of the Embargo."

"That's true. Suppose I say, 'yes, I think you can'?"

"I'd say, 'thanks,' and leave tomorrow."

"Suppose I said I'd like a week to check over your psyche-indices with a microscope, while you took a vacation at my place, taught no classes, gave no public readings, avoided cocktail parties?"

"I'd say, 'thanks'. And leave tomorrow."

He grinned. "Then why are you bothering me?"

"Because——" She shrugged. "Because tomorrow I'm going to be busy as the devil . . . and I won't have time to say good-bye."

"Oh." The wryness of his grin relaxed into a smile.

And he thought about the myna bird again.

Rydra, thin, thirteen, and gawky, had broken through the triple doors of the conservatory with the new thing called laughter she had just discovered how to make in her mouth. And he was parental proud that the near corpse, who had been given into his charge six months ago, was now a girl again, with boy-cropped hair and sulks and tantrums and questions and caresses for the two guinea pigs she had named Lump and Lumpkin. The air-conditioning pressed back the shrubbery to the glass wall and sun struck through the transparent roof. She had said, "What's that, Mocky?"

And he, smiling at her, sun-spotted in white shorts and superfluous halter, said, "It's a myna bird. It'll talk to you. Say hello."

The black eye was dead as a raisin with a pinhead of live light jammed in the corner. The feathers glistened and the needle beak lazed over a thick tongue. She cocked her head as the bird head cocked, and whispered, "Hello?"

Dr. T'mwarba had trained it for two weeks with fresh-dug earthworms to surprise her. The bird looked over its left shoulder and droned, *"Hello, Rydra, it's a fine day out and I'm happy."*

Screaming.

As unexpected as that.

He'd thought she'd started to laugh. But her face was contorted, she began to beat at something with her arms, stagger backwards, fall. The scream rasped in near collapsed lungs, choked, rasped again. He ran to gather up her flailing, hysterical figure, while the drone of the bird's voice undercut her wailing: *"It's a fine day out and I'm happy."*

He'd seen acute anxiety attacks before. But this shook him. When she could talk about it later, she simply said— tensely, with white lips, "It frightened me!"

Which would have been it, had the damn bird not gotten loose three days later and flown up into the antenna net he and Rydra had put up together for her amateur radio stasis-crafter with which she could listen to the hyperstatic communications of the transport ships in this arm of the galaxy. A wing and a leg got caught, and it began to beat against one of the hot lines so that you could see the sparks even in the sunlight. "We've got to get him out of there!" Rydra had cried. Her fingertips were over her mouth, but as she looked at the bird, he could see the color draining from under her tan. "I'll take care of it, honey," he said. "You just forget about him."

"If he hits that wire a couple of more times he'll be dead!"

But he had already started inside for the ladder. When he came out, he stopped. She had shinnied four-fifths up the guy wire on the leaning catalpa tree that shaded the corner of the house. Fifteen seconds later he was watching her reach out, draw back, reach out again toward the wild feathers. He knew damn well she wasn't afraid of the hot line, either; she'd strung it up herself. Sparks again. So she made up her mind and grabbed. A minute later she was coming across the yard, holding the rumpled bird at arm's length. Her face looked as if it had been blown across with powdered lime.

"Take it, Mocky," she said, with no voice behind her trembling lips, "before it says something and I start hollering again."

So now, thirteen years later, something else was speaking to her, and she said she was scared. He knew how scared she could be; he also knew with what bravery she could face down her fears.

He said, "Good-bye. I'm glad you woke me up. I'd be mad as a damp rooster if you hadn't come. Thank you."

"The thanks is yours, Mocky," she said. "I'm still frightened."

III

Daniel D. Appleby, who seldom thought of himself by his name—he was a Customs Officer—stared at the order through wire-framed glasses and rubbed his hand across his crew-cut red hair. "Well, it says you can, if you want to."

"And——?"

"And it is signed by General Forester."

"Then I expect you to cooperate."

"But I have to approve——"

"Then you'll come along and approve on the spot. I don't have time to send the reports in and wait for processing."

"But there's no way——"

"Yes, there is. Come with me."

"But Miss Wong, I don't walk around Transport town at night."

"I enjoy it. Scared?"

"Not exactly. But——"

"I have to get a ship and a crew by the morning. And it's General Forester's signature. All right?"

"I suppose so."

"Then come on. I have to get my crew approved."

Insistent and protesting respectively, Rydra and the officer left the bronze and glass building.

They waited for the monorail nearly six minutes. When

they came down, the streets were smaller, and a continuous whine of transport ships fell across the sky. Warehouses and repair and supply shops sandwiched rickety apartments and rooming houses. A larger street cut past, rumbling with traffic, busy loaders, stellarmen. They passed neon entertainments, restaurants of many worlds, bars, and brothels. In the crush the Customs Officer pulled his shoulders in, walked more quickly to keep up with Rydra's long-legged stride.

"Where do you intend to find—?"

"My pilot? That's who I want to pick up first." She stopped on the corner, shoved her hands into the pockets of her leather pants, and looked around.

"Do you have someone in mind?"

"I'm thinking of several people. This way." They turned on a narrower street, more cluttered, more brightly lit.

"Where are we going? Do you know this section?"

But she laughed, slipped her arm through his, and, like a dancer leading without pressure, she turned him toward an iron stairway.

"In here?"

"Have you ever been to this place before?" she asked with an innocent eagerness that made him feel for a moment he was escorting her.

He shook his head.

Up from the basement cafe black burst—a man, ebony-skinned, with red and green jewels set into his chest, face, arms, and thighs. Moist membranes, also jeweled, fell from his arms, billowing on slender tines as he hurried up the steps.

Rydra caught his shoulder. "Hey, Lome!"

"Captain Wong!" The voice was high, the white teeth needle-filed. He whirled to her with extending sails. Pointed ears shifted forward. "What you here for?"

"Lome, Brass is wrestling tonight?"

"You want to see him? Aye, Skipper, with the Silver Dragon, and it's an even match. Hey, I look for you on Deneb. I buy your book too. Can't read much, but I buy. And I no find you. Where you been a' six months?"

"Earthside, teaching at the University. But I'm going out again."

"You ask Brass for pilot? You heading out Specelli way?"

"That's right."

Lome dropped his black arm around her shoulder and the sail cloaked her, shimmering. "You go out Caesar, you call Lome for pilot, ever you do. Know Caesar——" He screwed his face and shook his head. "Nobody know it better."

"When I do, I will. But now it's Specelli."

"Then you do good with Brass. Work with him before?"

"We got drunk together when we were both quarantined for a week on one of the Cygnet planetoids. He seemed to know what he was talking about."

"Talk, talk, talk," Lome derided. "Yeah, I remember you, Captain who talk. You go watch that son of a dog wrestle; then you know what sort of pilot he make."

"That's what I came to do." Rydra turned to the Customs Officer, who shrank against the iron banister. (God, he thought, she's going to introduce me!) But she cocked her head with a half smile and turned back. "I'll see you again, Lome, when I get home."

"Yeah, yeah, you say that and say that twice. But I no in six months see you." He laughed. "But I like you, lady Captain. Take me to Caesar some day, I show you."

"When I go, you go, Lome."

A needle leer. "Go, go, you say. I got go now. Bye-bye, lady Captain"—he bowed and touched his head in salute—"Captain Wong." And was gone.

"You shouldn't be afraid of him," Rydra told the Officer,

"But he's——" During his search for a word, he wondered, How did she know? "Where in five hells did he come from?"

"He's an Earthman. Though I believe he was born en route from Arcturus to one of the Centauris. His mother was a Slug, I think, if he wasn't lying about that too. Lome tells tall tales."

"You mean all that getup is cosmetisurgery?"

"Um-hm." Rydra started down the stairs.

"But why the devil do they do that to themselves?

They're all so weird. That's why decent people won't have anything to do with them."

"Sailors used to get tattoos. Besides, Lome has nothing else to do. I doubt he's had a pilot's job in forty years."

"He's not a good pilot? What was all that about the Caesar nebula?"

"I'm sure he knows it. But he's at least a hundred and twenty years old. After eighty, your reflexes start to go, and that's the end of a pilot's career. He just shuttle-bums from port city to port city, knows everything that happens to everybody, stays good for gossip and advice."

They entered the cafe on a ramp that swerved above the heads of the customers drinking at bar and table thirty feet below. Above and to the side of them, a fifty-foot sphere hovered like smoke, under spotlights, Rydra looked from the globe to the Customs Officer. "They haven't started the games yet."

"Is this where they hold those *fights?*"

"That's right."

"But that's supposed to be illegal!"

"Never passed the bill. After they debated, it got shelved."

"Oh."

As they descended among the jovial transport workers, the Officer blinked. Most were ordinary men and women, but the results of cosmetisurgery were numerous enough to keep his eyes leaping. "I've never *been* in a place like this before!" he whispered. Amphibian or reptilian creatures argued and laughed with griffins and metallic-skinned sphinxes.

"Leave your clothing here?" smiled the check girl. Her naked skin was candy green, her immense coif piled like pink cotton. Her breasts, navel, and lips flashed.

"I don't believe so," the Customs Officer said quickly.

"At least take your shoes and shirt off," Rydra said, slipping off her blouse. "People will think you're strange." She bent, rose and handed her sandals over the counter. She had begun to unbuckle her waist cinch when she caught his desperate look, smiled, and fastened the buckle again.

Carefully he removed jacket, vest, shirt, and undershirt. He was about to untie his shoes when someone grabbed his arm. "Hey Customs!"

He stood up before a huge, naked man with a frown on his pocked face like a burst in rotten rind. His only ornaments were mechanical beetle lights that swarmed in patterns over his chest, shoulders, legs, and arms.

"Eh, pardon me?"

"What you doing here, Customs?"

"Sir, I am not bothering you."

"And I'm not bothering you. Have a drink, Customs. I'm being friendly."

"Thank you very much, but I'd rather——"

"I'm being friendly. You're not. If you're not gonna be friendly, Customs, I'm not gonna be friendly either."

"Well, I'm with some——" He looked helplessly at Rydra.

"Come on. Then you both have a drink. On me. Real friendly, damn it." His other hand fell toward Rydra's shoulder, but she caught his wrist. The fingers opened from the many scaled stellarimeter grafted onto his palm. "Navigator?"

He nodded, and she let the hand go, which landed.

"Why *are* you so 'friendly' tonight?"

The intoxicated man shook his head. His hair was knotted in a stubby black braid over his left ear. "I'm just friendly with Customs here. I like you."

"Thanks. Buy us that drink and I'll buy you one back."

As he nodded heavily, his green eyes narrowed. He reached between her breasts and fingered up the gold disk that hung from the chain around her neck. "*Captain* Wong?"

She nodded.

"Better not mess with you, then." He laughed. "Come on, Captain, and I'll buy you and Customs here something to make you happy." They pushed their way to the bar.

What was green and came in small glasses at more respectable establishments, here was served in mugs.

"Who you betting on in the Dragon/Brass skirmish, and if you say the Dragon, I'll throw this in your face. Joking, of course, Captain."

"I'm not betting," Rydra said. "I'm hiring. You know Brass?"

"Was a navigator on his last trip. Got in a week ago."

"You're friendly for the same reason he's wrestling?"

"You might say that."

The Customs Officer scratched his collarbone and looked puzzled.

"Last trip Brass made went bust," Rydra explained to him. "The crew is out of work. Brass is on exhibit tonight." She turned again to the Navigator. "Will there be many captains bidding for him?"

He put his tongue under his upper lip, squinted one eye and dropped his head. He shrugged.

"I'm the only one you've run into?"

A nod, a large swallow of liquor.

"What's your name?"

"Calli, Navigator-Two."

"Where are your One and Three?"

"Three's over there somewhere getting drunk. One was a sweet girl named Cathy O'Higgin's. She's dead." He finished the drink and reached over for another one.

"My treat," Rydra said. "Why's she dead?"

"Ran into Invaders. Only people who ain't dead, Brass, me, and Three, and our Eye. Lost the whole platoon, our Slug. Damn good Slug too. Captain, that was a bad trip. The Eye, he cracked up without the Ear and Nose. They'd been discorporate for ten years together. Ron, Cathy, and me, we'd only been tripled for a couple of months. But even so . . ." He shook his head. "It's bad."

"Call your Three over," Rydra said.

"Why?"

"I'm looking for a full crew."

Calli wrinkled his forehead. "We don't got no One anymore."

"You're going to mope around here forever? Go to the Morgue."

Calli *humphed*. "You wanna see my Three, you come on."

Rydra shrugged in aquiescence, and the Customs Officer followed behind them.

"Hey, stupid, swing around."

The kid who turned on the bar stool was maybe nineteen. The Customs Officer thought of a snarl of metal bands. Calli was a large, comfortable man—

"Captain Wong, this is Ron, best Three to come out of the Solar System."

—but Ron was small, thin, with uncannily sharp muscular definition: pectorals like scored metal plates beneath drawn wax skin; stomach like ridged hosing, arms like braided cables. Even the facial muscles stood at the back of the jaw and jammed against the separate columns of his neck. He was unkempt and towheaded and sapphire eyed, but the only cosmetisurgery evident was the bright rose growing on his shoulder. He flung out a quick smile and touched his forehead with a forefinger in salute. His nails were nub-gnawed on fingers like knotted lengths of white rope.

"Captain Wong is looking for a crew."

Ron shifted on the stool, raising his head a little; every other muscle in his body moved too, like snakes under milk.

The Customs Officer saw Rydra's eyes widen. Not understanding her reaction, he ignored it.

"Don't got no One," Ron said. His smile was quick and sad again.

"Suppose I found a One for you?"

The Navigators looked at each other.

Calli turned to Rydra and rubbed the side of his nose with his thumb. "You know the thing about a triple like us——"

Rydra's left hand caught her right. "Like this, you have to be. My choice is subject to your approval, of course."

"Well, it's pretty difficult for someone else——"

"It's impossible. But it's your choice. I just make suggestions. But my suggestions are damn good ones. What do you say?"

Calli's thumb moved from his nose to his earlobe. He shrugged. "You can't make an offer much better than that."

Rydra looked at Ron.

The kid put one foot up on the stool, hugged his knee, and peered across his patella. "I say, let's see who you suggest."

She nodded. "Fair."

"You know, jobs for broken triples aren't that easy to come by." Calli put his hand on Ron's shoulder.

"Yeah, but——"

Rydra looked up. "Let's watch the wrestling."

Along the counter people raised their heads. At the tables, patrons released the catch in their chair arms so that the backs swung to half recline.

Calli's mug clinked on the counter, and Ron raised both feet to the stool and leaned back against the bar.

"What are they looking at?" the Customs Officer asked. "Where's everybody——" Rydra put her hand on the back of his neck and did something so that he laughed and swung his head up. Then he sucked a great breath and let it out slowly.

The smoky, null-grav globe, hung in the vault, was shot with colored light. The room had gone dim. Thousands of watts of floodlights struck the plastic surface and gleamed on the faces below as smoke in the bright sphere faded.

"What's going to happen?" the Customs Officer asked. "Is that where they wrestle . . . ?"

Rydra brushed her hand over his mouth and he nearly swallowed his tongue: but was quiet.

And the Silver Dragon came, wings working in the smoke, silver feathers like clashed blades, scales on the grand haunches shaking; she rippled her ten-foot body and squirmed in the antigravity field, green lips leering, silver lids batting over green. "It's a woman!" breathed the Customs Officer.

An appreciative tattoo of finger snapping scattered through the audience.

Smoke rolled in the globe—

"That's our Brass!" whispered Calli.

—and Brass yawned and shook his head, ivory saber teeth glistening with spittle, muscles humped on shoulders and arms; brass claws unsheathed six inches from yellow plush paws. Bunched bands on his belly bent above them. The barbed tail beat on the globe's wall. His mane, sheared to prevent handholds, ran like water.

Calli grabbed the Customs Officer's shoulder. "Snap your fingers, man! That's *our* Brass!"

The Customs Officer, who had never been able to, nearly broke his hand trying.

The globe flared red. The two pilots turned to one another across the sphere's diameter. Voices quieted. The

Customs Officer glanced from the ceiling to the people around him. Every other face was up. The Navigator, Three, was hunched in a foetal knot on the bar stool. Copper shifting; Rydra too dropped her eyes to glance at the lean bunched arms and straited thighs of the rose-shouldered boy.

Above, the opponents flexed and stretched, drifting. A sudden movement from the Dragon, and Brass drew back, then launched from the wall.

The Customs Officer grabbed something.

The two forms struck, grappled, spun against a wall and ricocheted. People began to stamp. Arm reached over arm, leg wrapped around leg, till Brass whirled loose from her and was hurled to the upper wall of the arena. Shaking his head, he righted. Below, alert, the Dragon twisted and writhed, anticipation jerked her wings. Brass leapt from the ceiling, reversed suddenly, and caught the Dragon with his hind feet. She staggered back, flailing. Saber teeth came together and missed.

"What are they trying to do?" the Customs Officer whispered. "How can you tell who's winning?" He looked down again: what he'd grabbed was Calli's shoulder.

"When one can throw the other against the wall and only touch the far wall himself with one limb on the ricochet," Calli explained, not looking down, "that's a fall."

The Silver Dragon snapped her body like bent metal released, and Brass shot away and spread-eagled against the globe. But as she floated back to take the shock on one hind leg, she lost her balance and the second leg touched, too.

An anticipatory breath loosed in the audience. Encouraging snapping; Brass recovered, leaped, pushed her to the wall, but his rebound was too sharp and he, too, staggered on three limbs.

A twist in the center again. The Dragon snarled, stretched, shook her scales. Brass glowered, peered with eyes like gold coins hooded, spun back quaking, then leapt forward.

Silver whirled beneath his shoulder blow, hit the globe. She looked for the world as if she were trying to climb the wall. Brass rebounded lightly, caught himself on one paw, then pushed away.

The globe flashed green, and Calli pounded the bar. "Look at him show that tinsel bitch!"

Grappling limbs braided one another, and claw caught claw till the stifled arms shook, broke apart. Two more falls that went to neither side; then the Silver Dragon came head first into Brass' chest, knocked him back, and recovered on tail alone. Below the crowd stamped.

"That's a foul!" Calli exclaimed, shaking the Customs Officer away. "Damn it, that's a foul!" But the globe flashed green again. Officially the second fall was hers.

Warily now they swam in the sphere. Twice the Dragon feinted, and Brass jerked aside his claws or sucked in his belly to avoid hers.

"Why don't she lay off him?" Calli demanded of the sky. "She's nagging him to death. Grapple and fight!"

As if in answer, Brass sprang, swiping her shoulder; what would have been a perfect fall got messed up because the Dragon caught his arm and he swerved off, smashing clumsily against the plastic.

"She can't do that!" This time it was the Customs Officer. He grabbed Calli again. "Can she do that? I don't think they should allow——" And he bit his tongue because Brass swung back, hauled her from the wall, flipped her between his legs, and as she scrambled off the plastic, he bounced on his forearm and hovered centrally, flexing for the crowd.

"That's it!" cried Calli. "Two out of three!"

The globe flashed green again. Snapping broke into applause. "Did he win?" demanded the Customs Officer. "Did he win?"

"Listen! Of course he won! Hey, let's go see him. Come on, Captain!"

Rydra had already started through the crowd. Ron sprang behind her, and Calli, dragging the Customs Officer, came after. A flight of black tile steps took them into a room with couches where a few groups of men and women stood around Condor, a great gold and crimson creature, who was being made ready to fight Ebony who waited alone in the corner. The arena exit opened and Brass came in sweating.

"Hey," Calli called. "Hey, that was great, boy. And the Captain here wants to talk to you."

Brass stretched, then dropped to all fours, a low rumble in his chest. He shook his mane, then his gold eyes widened in recognition. "Ca'tain Wong!" The mouth, distended through cosmetisurgically implanted fangs, could not deal with a plosive labial unless it was voiced. "How you'd like me tonight?"

"Well enough to want you to pilot me through the Specelli." She roughed a tuft of yellow behind his ear. "You said sometime ago you'd like to show me what you could do."

"Yeah," Brass nodded. "I just think I'm dreaming." He pulled away his loin rag and swabbed his neck and arms with the bunched cloth, then caught the Customs Officer's amazed expression. "Just cosmetisurgery." He kept on swabbing.

"Hand him your psyche-rating," Rydra said, "and he'll approve you."

"That means we leave tomorrow, Ca'tain?"

"At dawn."

From his belt pouch Brass drew a thin metal card. "Here you go, Customs."

The Customs Officer scanned the runic marking. On a metal tracing plate from his back pocket, he noted the shift in stability index, but decided to integrate for the exact summation later on. Practice told him it was well above acceptable. "Miss Wong, I mean Captain Wong, what about their cards?" He turned to Calli and Ron.

Ron reached behind his neck and rubbed his scapula. "You don't worry about us till you get a Navigator-One." The hard, adolescent face held an engaging belligerence.

"We'll check them later," Rydra said. "We've got more people to find first."

"You're looking for a full crew?" asked Brass.

Rydra nodded. "What about the Eye that came back with you?"

Brass shook his head. "Lost his Ear and Nose. They were a real close tri'le, Ca'tain. He hung around maybe six hours before he went back to the Morgue."

"I see. Can you recommend anyone?"

"No one in 'articular. Just hang around the Discor'orate Sector and see what turns u'."

"If you want a crew by morning, we better start now," said Calli.

"Let's go," said Rydra.

As they walked to the ramp's foot, the Customs Officer asked "The Discorporate Sector?"

"What about it?" Rydra was at the rear of the group.

"That's so—well, I don't like the idea."

Rydra laughed. "Because of the dead men? They won't hurt you."

"And I know *that's* illegal, for bodily persons to be in the Discorporate Sector."

"In certain parts," Rydra corrected, and the other men laughed now. "We'll stay out of the illegal sections—if we can."

"Would you like your clothes back?" the check-girl asked.

People had been stopping to congratulate Brass, pounding at his hip with appreciative fists and snapping their fingers. Now he swung his contour cape over his head. It fell to his shoulders, clasped his neck, draped under his arms and around his thick hams. Brass waved to the crowd and started up the ramp.

"You can really judge a pilot by watching him wrestle?" the officer inquired of Rydra.

She nodded. "In the ship, the pilot's nervous system is connected directly with the controls. The whole hyperstasis transit consists of him literally wrestling the stasis shifts. You judge by his reflexes, his ability to control his artificial body. An experienced Transporter can tell exactly how he'll work with hyperstasis currents."

"I'd heard about it, of course. But this was the first time I've seen it. I mean in person. It was . . . exciting."

"Yes," Rydra said, "isn't it?"

As they reached the ramp's head, lights again pierced the globe. Ebony and Condor circled in the fighting sphere.

On the sidewalk Brass dropped back, loping on all fours, to Rydra's side. "What about a Slug and a 'latoon?"

The platoon was a group of twelve who did all the mechanical jobs on the ship. Such simple work was done by the very young, so they usually needed a nursemaid: that was the Slug.

"I'd like to get a one-trip platoon if I can."

"Why so green?"

"1 want to train them my way. The older groups tend to be too set."

"A one-tri' grou' can be a hell of a 'roblem to disci'line. And inefficient as 'iss, so I've heard. Never been with one myself."

"As long as there're no out and out nuts, I don't care. Besides, if I want one now, I can be surer of getting one by morning if I put my order in at Navy."

Brass nodded. "Your request in yet?"

"I want to check with my pilot first and see if you had any preferences."

They were passing a street phone on the corner lamppost. Rydra ducked beneath the plastic hood. A minute later she was saying, "—a platoon for a run toward Specelli scheduled at dawn tomorrow. I know that it's short notice, but I don't need a particularly seasoned group. Even a one trip will do." She looked from under the hood and winked at them. "Fine. I'll call later to get their psyche-indices for Customs approval. Yes, I have an Officer with me. Thank you."

She came from under the hood. "Closest way to the Discorporate Sector is through there."

The streets narrowed about them, twisting through one another, deserted. Then a stretch of concrete where metal turrets rose. Crossed, and recrossed, wires webbed them. Pylons of bluish light dropped half shadows.

"Is this . . . ?" the Customs Officer began. Then he was quiet. Walking out, they slowed their steps. Against the darkness red light shot between towers.

"What . . . ?"

"Just a transfer. They go on all night," Calli explained. Green lightning crackled to their left.

"Transfer?"

"It's a quick exchange of energies resulting from the relocation of discorporate states," the Navigator-Two volunteered glibly.

"But I still don't..."

They had moved between the pylons now when a flickering coalesced. Silver latticed with red fire glimmered through industrial smog. Three figures formed: the women's sequined skeletons glittered toward them, casting hollow eyes.

Kittens clawed the Customs Officer's back, for strut work pylons gleamed behind the apparitional bellies.

"The faces," he whispered. "As soon as you look away, you can't remember what they look like. When you look at them, they look like people, but when you look away——"
He caught his breath as another passed. "You can't remember!" He stared after them. "Dead?" He shook his head. "You know I've been approving psyche-indices on Transport workers corporate and discorporate for ten years. And I've never been close enough to speak to a discorporate soul. Oh, I've seen pictures and occasionally passed one of the less fantastic on the street. But this..."

"There're some jobs"—Calli's voice was as heavy with alcohol as his shoulders with muscle—"some jobs on a Transport Ship you just can't give to a live human being."

"I know, I know," said the Customs Officer. "So you use dead ones."

"That's right." Calli nodded. "Like the Eye, Ear, and Nose. A live human scanning all that goes on in those hyperstasis frequencies would—well, die first, and go crazy second."

"I do know the theory," the Customs Officer stated sharply.

Calli suddenly cupped the Officer's cheek in his hand and pulled him close to his own pocked face. "You don't know anything, Customs." The tone was of their first exchange in the cafe. "Aw, you hide in your Customs cage, cage hid in the safe gravity of Earth, Earth held firm by the sun, sun fixed headlong toward Vega, all in the predicted tide of this spiral arm——" He gestured across night where the Milky Way would run over a less bright city. "And you never break free!" Suddenly he pushed the little spectacled red head away. "Ehhh! You have nothing to say to me!"

The bereaved navigator caught a guy cable slanting from support to concrete. It *twanged*. The low note set something loose in the Officer's throat which reached his mouth with the metal taste of outrage.

He would have spat it, but Rydra's copper eyes were now as close to his face as the hostile, pitted visage had been.

She said: "He was part," the words lean, calm, her eyes intent on not losing his, "of a triple, a close, precarious, emotional, and sexual relation with two other people. And one of them has just died."

The edge of her tone hued away the bulk of the Officer's anger; but a sliver escaped him: "Perverts!"

Ron put his head to the side, his musculature showing clear the double of hurt and bewilderment. "There're some jobs," he echoed Calli's syntax, "some jobs on a Transport Ship you just can't give to two people alone. The jobs are too complicated."

"I *know.*" Then he thought, I've hurt the boy, too. Calli leaned on a girder. Something else was working in the Officer's mouth.

"You have something to say," Rydra said.

Surprise that she knew prized his lips. He looked from Calli to Ron, back. "I'm sorry for you."

Calli's brows raised, then returned, his expression settling. "I'm sorry for you too."

Brass reared. "There's a transfer conclave about a quarter of a mile down in the medium energy states. That would attract the sort of Eye, Ear, and Nose you want for Specelli." He grinned at the Officer through his fangs. "That's one of your illegal sections. The hallucination count goes way u', and some cor'orate egos can't handle it. But most sane 'eo'le don't have any 'roblem."

"If it's illegal, I'd just as soon wait here," the Customs Officer said. "You can just come back and pick me up. I'll approve their indices then."

Rydra nodded. Calli threw one arm around the waist of the ten-foot pilot, the other around Ron's shoulder. "Come on, Captain, if you want to get your crew by morning."

"If we don't find what we want in an hour, we'll be back anyway," she said.

The Customs Officer watched them move away between the slim towers.

IV

~~~~~~

—recall from broken banks and color of earth breaking into clear pool water her eyes; the figure blinking her eyes and speaking.

He said: "An Officer, ma'am. A Customs Officer."

Surprise at her witty return, at first hurt, then amusement following. He answered: "About ten years. How long have you been discorporate?"

And she moved closer to him, her hair holding the recalled odor of. And the sharp transparent features reminding him of. More words from her, now, making him laugh.

"Yes, this is all very new to me. Doesn't the whole vagueness with which everything seems to happen get you, too?"

Again her answer, both coaxing and witty.

"Well, yes," he smiled. "For you I guess it wouldn't be."

Her ease infected him; and either she reached playfully to take his hand or he amazed himself by taking hers, and the apparition was real beneath his fingers with skin as smooth as.

"You're so forward. I mean I'm not used to young women just coming up and . . . behaving like this."

Her charming logic again explained it away, making him feel her near, nearer, nearing, and her banter made music, a phrase from.

"Well, yes, you're discorporate, so it doesn't matter. But——"

43

And her interruption was a word or a kiss or a frown or a smile, sending not humor through him now, but luminous amazement, fear, excitement; and the feel of her shape against his completely new. He fought to retain it, pattern of pressure and pressure, fading as the pressure itself faded. She was going away. She was laughing like, as though, as if. He stood, losing her laughter, replaced by whirled bewilderment in the tides of his consciousness fading—

V

When they returned, Brass called, "Good news! We got who we wanted."

"Crew's coming along," commented Calli.

Rydra handed him the three index cards. "They'll report to the ship discorporate two hours before—what's wrong?"

Danil D. Appleby reached to take the cards. "I . . . she . . ." and couldn't say anything else.

"Who?" Rydra asked. The concern on her face was driving away even his remaining memories, and he resented it, memories of, of.

Calli laughed. "A succubus! While we were gone, he got hustled by a succubus!"

"Yeah!" from Brass. "Look at him!" Ron laughed, too.

"It was a woman . . . I think. I can remember what *I* said——"

"How much did she take you for?" Brass asked.

"Take me?"

Ron said, "I don't think he knows."

Calli grinned at the Navigator-Three and then at the Officer. "Take a look in your billfold."

"Huh?"

"Take a look."

Incredulously he reached in his pocket. The metallic envelope flipped apart in his hands. "Ten . . . twenty . . . But I had *fifty* in here when I left the cafe!"

Calli slapped his thighs laughing. He loped over and encircled the Customs Officer's shoulder. "You'll end up a Transport man after that happens a couple of more times."

"But she . . . I . . ." The emptiness of his thefted recollections was real as any love loss. The rifled wallet seemed trivial. Tears banked his eyes. "But she was——" Confusion snarled the sentence's end.

"What was she, friend?" Calli asked.

"She . . . was." That was the sad entirety.

"Since discor'oration, you *can* take it with you," said Brass. "They try for it with some 'retty shady methods, too. I'd be embarrassed to tell you how many times that's ha"ened to me."

"She left you enough to get home with," Rydra said. "I'll reimburse you."

"No, I . . ."

"Come on, Captain. He paid for it, and he got his money's worth, aye, Customs?"

Choking on the embarrassment, he nodded.

"Then . . . check these ratings," Rydra said. "We still have a Slug to pick up, and a Navigator-One."

At a public phone, Rydra called back to Navy. Yes, a platoon had turned up. A Slug had been recommended along with them. "Fine," Rydra said, and handed the phone to the officer. He took the psyche-indices from the clerk and incorporated them for final integration with the Eye, Ear, and Nose cards that Rydra had given him. The Slug looked particularly favorable. "Seems to be a talented coordinator," he ventured.

"Can't have too good a Slug. Es'ecially with a new 'latoon." Brass shook his mane. "He's got to keep those kids in line."

"This one should do it. Highest compatibility index I've seen in a long while."

"What's the hostility on him?" asked Calli. "Compatibility, hell! Can he give your butt a good kick when you need it?"

The Officer shrugged. "He weighs two hundred and seventy pounds and he's only five nine. Have you met a fat person yet who wasn't mean as a rat underneath it all?"

"There you go!" Calli laughed.

"Where do we go to fix the wound?" Brass asked Rydra.

She raised her brows questioningly.

"To get a first navigator," he explained.

"To the Morgue."

Ron frowned. Calli looked puzzled. The flashing bugs collared his neck, then spilled his chest, scattering. "You know our first navigator's got to be a girl who will——"

"She will be," Rydra said.

They left the Discorporate Sector and took the monorail through the tortuous remains of Transport Town, then along the edge of the space-field. Blackness beyond the windows was flung with blue signal lights. Ships rose with a white flare, blued through distance, became bloody stars in the rusted air.

They joked for the first twenty minutes over the humming runners. The fluorescent ceiling dropped greenish light on their faces, in their laps. One by one, the Customs Officer watched them go silent while the side-to-side inertia became a headlong drive. He had not spoken at all, still trying to regain her face, her words, her shape. But it stayed away, frustrating as the imperative comment that leaves your mind as speech begins, and the mouth is left empty, a lost referent to love.

When they stepped onto the open platform at Thule Station, warm wind flushed the east. The clouds had shattered under an ivory moon. Gravel and granite silvered the broken edges. Behind was the city's red mist. Before, on broken night, rose the black Morgue.

They went down the steps and walked quietly through the stone park. The garden of water and rock was eerie. Nothing grew here.

At the door slabbed metal without external light blotted the darkness. "How do you get in?" the Officer asked, as they climbed the shallow steps.

Rydra lifted the Captain's pendant from her neck and

placed it against a small disk. Something hummed, and light divided the entrance as the doors slid back. Rydra stepped through, the rest followed.

Calli stared at the metallic vaults overhead. "You know there's enough transport meat deep-frozen in this place to service a hundred stars and all their planets."

"And Customs people too," said the Officer.

"Does anybody ever bother to call back a Customs who decided to take a rest?" Ron asked with candid ingenuousness.

"Don't know what for," said Calli.

"It's been known to happen," responded the Officer dryly. "Occasionally."

"More rarely than with Transport," Rydra said. "As of yet, the Customs work involved in getting ships from star to star is a science. The transport work maneuvering through hyperstasis levels is still an art. In a hundred years they may both be sciences. Fine. But today a person who learns the rules of art well is a little rarer than the person who learns the rules of science. Also, there's a tradition involved. Transport people are used to dying and getting called back, working with dead men or live. This is still a little hard for Customs to take. Over here to the Suicides."

They left the main lobby for the labeled corridor that sloped up through the storage chamber. It emptied them onto a platform in an indirectly lighted room, racked up its hundred-foot height with glass cases, catwalked and laddered like a spider's den. In the coffins, dark shapes were rigid beneath frost shot glass.

"What I don't understand about this whole business," the Officer whispered, "is the calling back. Can anybody who dies be made corporate again? You're right, Captain Wong, in Customs it's almost impolite to talk about things like . . . this."

"Any suicide who discorporates through regular Morgue channels can be called back. But a violent death where the Morgue just retrieves the body afterward, or the run of the mill senile ending that most of us hit at a hundred and fifty or so, then you're dead forever; although there, if you pass through regular channels, your brain pattern is recorded and your thinking ability can be tapped if anyone wants it, though your consciousness is gone wherever consciousness goes.''

Beside them, a twelve-foot filing crystal glowed like pink quartz. "Ron," said Rydra. "No, Ron and Calli too."

The Navigators stepped up, puzzled.

"You know some first navigator who suicided recently that you think we might——"

Rydra shook her head. She passed her hand before the filing crystal. In the concaved screen at the base, words flashed. She stilled her fingers. "Navigator-Two. . . ." She turned her hand. "Navigator-One. . . ." She paused and ran her hand in a different direction. ". . . male, male, male, female. Now, you talk to me, Calli, Ron."

"Huh? About what?"

"About yourselves, about what you want."

Rydra's eyes moved back and forth between the screen and the man and boy beside her.

"Well, huh . . . ?" Calli scratched his head.

"Pretty," said Ron. "I want her to be pretty." He leaned forward, an intense light in his blue eyes.

"Oh, yes," said Calli, "but she can't be a sweet, plump Irish girl with black hair and agate eyes and freckles that come out after four days of sun. She can't have the slightest lisp that makes you tingle even when she reels off her calculations quicker and more accurate than a computer voice, yet still lisping, or makes you tingle when she holds your head in her lap and tells you about how much she needs to feel——"

"Calli!" from Ron.

And the big man stopped with his fist against his stomach, breathing hard.

Rydra watched, her hand drifting through centimeters over the crystal's face. The names on the screen flashed back and forth.

"But pretty," Ron repeated. "And likes sports, to wrestle, I think, when we're planet side. Cathy wasn't very athletic. I always thought it would have been better, for me, if she was, see. I can talk better to people I can wrestle with. Serious though, I mean about working. And quick like Cathy could think. Only . . ."

Rydra's hand drifted down, then made a jerk motion to the left.

"Only," said Calli, his hand falling from his belly, his breath more easy, "she's got be a whole person, a new person, not somebody who is half what we remember about somebody else."

"Yes," said Ron. "I mean if she's a good navigator, and she loves us."

". . . could love us," said Calli.

"If she was all you wanted and herself besides," asked Rydra, her head shaking between two names on the screen, "could you love her?"

The hesitation, the nod slow from the big man, quick from the boy.

Rydra's hand came down on the crystal face, and the name glowed on the screen. "Mollya Twa, Navigator-One." Her coordinate numbers followed. Rydra dialed them at the desk.

Seventy-five feet overhead something glittered. One among hundreds of thousands of glass coffins was tracking from the wall above them on an inductor beam.

The recall-stage jutted up a pattern of lugs, the tips glowing. The coffin dropped, its contents obscured by streaks and hexagonal bursts of frost inside the glass. The lugs caught the template on the coffin's base. It rocked a moment, settled, clicked.

The frost melted of a sudden, and the inside surface fogged, then ran with droplets. They stepped forward to see.

Dark band on dark. A movement beneath the glaring glass; then the glass parted, melting back from her dark, warm skin and beating, terrified eyes.

"It's all right," Calli said, touching her shoulder. She raised her head to look at his hand, then dropped back to the pillow. Ron crowded the Navigator-Two. "Hello?"

"Eh . . . Miss Twa?" Calli said. "You're alive now. Will you love us?"

"Ninyi ni nani?" Her face was puzzled. *"Nino wapi hapa?"*

Ron looked up amazed. "I don't think she speaks English."

"Yes. I know," Rydra grinned. "But other than that she's perfect. This way you'll have to get to know each other before you can say anything really foolish. She likes to wrestle, Ron."

Ron looked at the young woman in the case. Her graphite colored hair was natural, her dark lips purpled with chili. "You wrestle?"

"Ninyi ni nani?" she asked again.

Calli lifted his hand from her shoulder and stepped back. Ron scratched his head and frowned.

"Well?" said Rydra.

Calli shrugged. "Well, we don't know."

"Navigation Instruments are standard gear. There won't be any trouble communicating there."

"She is pretty," Ron said. "You are pretty. Don't be frightened. You're alive now."

"Ninaogapa!" She seized Calli's hand. *"Jee, ni usiku au mchana?"* Her eyes were wide.

"Please don't be frightened!" Ron took the wrist of the hand that had seized Calli's.

"Sielewi lugha yenu." She shook her head, a gesture containing no negation, only bewilderment. *"Sikujuweni ninyi nani. Ninaogapa."*

And with bereavement-born urgency, both Ron and Calli nodded in affirmative reassurance.

Rydra stepped between them and spoke.

After a long silence, the woman nodded slowly.

"She says she'll go with you. She lost two-thirds of her triple seven years ago, also killed through the Invasion. That's why she came to the Morgue and killed herself. She says she will go with you. Will you take her?"

"She's still afraid," Ron said. "Please don't be. I won't hurt you. Calli won't hurt."

"If she'll come with us," Calli said, "we'll take her."

The Customs Officer coughed. "Where do I get her psyche rating?"

"Right on the screen under the filing crystal. That's how they're arranged within the larger categories."

The Officer walked back to the crystal. "Well"—He took out his pad and began to record the indices. "It's taken a while but you've got just about everybody."

"Integrate," Rydra said.

He did, and looked up, surprised in spite of himself. "Captain Wong, I think you've got your crew!"

VI

Dear Mocky,

When you get this I'll have taken off two hours ago. It's a half hour before dawn and I want to talk to you, but I won't wake you up again.

I am, nostalgically enough, taking out Fobo's old ship, the Rimbaud (the name was Muels' idea, remember). At least, I'm familiar with it; lots of good memories here. I leave in twenty minutes.

Present location: I'm sitting in a folding chair in the freight lock looking over the field. The sky is star speckled to the west, and gray to the east. Black needles of ships pattern around me. Lines of blue signal lights fade toward the south. It is calm now. Subject of my thinking: a hectic night of crew hunting that took me all over Transport Town and out to the Morgue, through dives and glittering byways, etc. Loud and noisy at the beginning, calming to this at the end.

To get a good pilot you watch him wrestle. A trained captain can tell exactly what sort of a pilot a person will make by observing his reflexes in the arena. Only I am not that well trained.

Remember what you said about muscle-reading? Maybe you were righter than you thought. Last night I ran into a kid, a Navigator, who looks like Brancusi's graduation offering, or maybe what Michelangelo wished the human body was. He was born in Transport and knows pilot wrestling inside out, apparently. So I watched him watch my pilot wrestle, and just looking at his quivers and jerks I got a complete analysis of what was going on over my head.

You know De Faure's theory that psychic indices have their corresponding muscular tensions (a restatement of the old Wilhelm Reich hypothesis of muscular armature): I was thinking about it last night. The kid I was telling you about was part of a broken triple, two guys and a girl and the girl got it from the Invaders. The boys made me want to cry. But I didn't. Instead I took them to the Morgue and found them a replacement. Weird business. I'm sure they'll think it was magic for the rest of their lives. The basic requirements, however, were all on file: a female Navigator-One who lacks two men. How to adjust the indices? I read Ron's and Calli's from watching them move while they talked. The corpses are filed under psyche-indices so I just had to feel out when they were congruent. The final choice was a stroke of genius, if I do say so. I had it down to six young ladies who would do. But it needed to be more precise than that, and I couldn't play it more precise, at least not by ear. One young lady was from N'gonda Province in Pan Africa. She'd suicided seven years ago. Lost two husbands in an Invasion attack, and returned to earth in the middle of an embargo. You remember what the politics were like then between Pan Africa and Americasia; I was sure she didn't speak English. We woke her, and she didn't. Now, at this point, their indices may be a mite jarring. But, by the time they fight through learning to understand each other—and they will, because they need to—they'll graph out congruent a foot down the logarithmic grid. Clever?

And Babel-17, the real reason for this letter. Told you I had deciphered it enough to know where the next attack will be. The Alliance War Yards at Armsedge. Wanted to let you know that's where I'm going, just in case. Talk and talk and talk: what sort of mind can talk like that language talks? And *why? Still scared—like a kid at a spelling bee—but having fun. My platoon reported an hour ago. Crazy, lazy lovable kids all. In just a few minutes I'll be going to see my Slug (fat galoof with black eyes, hair, beard; moves slow and thinks fast). You know, Mocky, getting this crew together I was interested in one thing (above competency, and they are all competent): they had to be people I could talk to. And I can.*

Love, Rydra.

VII

Light but no shadow. The General stood up on the saucer-sled, looking at the black ship, the paling sky. At the base he stepped from the gliding two-foot diameter disk, climbed onto the lift, and rose a hundred feet toward the lock. She wasn't in the captain's cabin. He ran into a fat bearded man who directed him up the corridor to the freight lock. He climbed to the top of the ladder and took hold of his breath because it was about to run away.

She dropped her feet from the wall, sat up in the canvas chair and smiled. "General Forester, I thought I might see you this morning." She folded a piece of message tissue and sealed the edge.

"I wanted see you . . ." and his breath was gone and had to be caught once more, "before you left."

"I wanted to see you, too."

"You told me if I gave you license to conduct this expedition, you would inform me where you——"

"My report, which you should find satisfactory, was mailed last night and is on your desk at Administrative Alliance Headquarters—or will be in an hour."

"Oh. I see."

She smiled. "You'll have to go shortly. We take off in a few minutes."

'Yes. Actually, I'm taking off for Administrative Alliance Headquarters myself this morning, so I was here at the field, and I'd already gotten a synopsis of your report by stellarphone a few minutes ago, and I just wanted to say——" and he said nothing.

"General Forester, once I wrote a poem I'm reminded of. It was called 'Advice to Those Who Would Love Poets'."

The General opened his teeth without separating his lips.

"It started something like:

Young man, she will gnaw out your tongue. Lady,
he will steal your hands . . .

You can read the rest. It's in my second book. If you're not willing to lose a poet seven times a day, it's frustrating as hell."

He said simply: "You knew I . . ."

"I knew and I know. And I'm glad."

The lost breath returned and an unfamiliar thing was happening to his face: he smiled. "When I was a private, Miss Wong, and we'd be confined to barracks, we'd talk about girls and girls and girls. And somebody would say about one: she was so pretty she didn't have to give me any, just promise me some." He let the stiffness leave his shoulders a moment, and though they actually fell half an inch, the effect was that they seemed broader by two. "That's what I was feeling."

"Thank you for telling me," she said. "I like you, General. And I promise I'll still like you the next time I see you."

"I . . . thank you. I guess that's all. Just thank you . . . for knowing and promising." Then he said, "I have to go now, don't I?"

"We'll be taking off in ten minutes."

"Your letter," he said, "I'll mail it for you."

"Thanks." She handed it to him, he took her hand, and for the slightest moment with the slightest pressure, held her. Then he turned, left. Minutes later she watched his saucer-sled glide across the concrete, its sun-side flaring suddenly as light blistered the east.

PART TWO

~~~~~~

Ver Dorco

If words are paramount I am afraid
that words are all my hands have ever seen ...

—from *Quartet*

1

~~~~~~

The retranscribed material passed on the sorting screen.
By the computer console lay the four pages of definitions she
had amassed and a *cuaderno* full of grammatical speculations.
Chewing her lower lip, she ran through the frequency tabulation
of depressed diphthongs. On the wall she had tacked three
charts labeled:

Possible Phonemic Structure . . .

Possible Phonetic Structure . . .

Semiotic, Semantic, and Syntactic Ambiguities . . .

The last contained the problems to be solved. The
questions, formulated and answered, were transferred as cer-
tainties to the first two.

"Captain?"

She turned on the bubble seat.

Hanging from the entrance hatch by his knees was
Diavalo.

"Yes?"

"What you want for dinner?" The little platoon cook
was a boy of seventeen. Two cosmetisurgical horns jutted
from shocked albino hair. He was scratching one ear with the
tip of his tail.

Rydra shrugged. "No preferences. Check around with
the rest of the platoon."

"Those guys'll eat liquified organic waste if I give it to
them. No imagination, Captain. What about pheasant under
glass, or maybe rock Cornish game hen?"

"You're in the mood for poultry?"

"Well——" He released the bar with one knee and kicked the wall so he swung back and forth. "I could go for something birdy."

"If nobody objects, try coq au vin, baked Idahos, and broiled beefsteak tomatoes."

"Now you're cookin'!"

"Strawberry shortcake for dessert?"

Diavalo snapped his fingers and swung up toward the hatch. Rydra laughed and turned back to the console.

"Macon on the coq, May wine with the meal!" The pink-eyed face was gone.

Rydra had discovered the third example of what might have been syncope when the bubble chair sagged back. The cuaderno slammed against the edge of the desk. Her shoulders wrenched. Behind her the skin of the bubble chair split and showered suspended silicon.

The cabin stilled and she turned to see Diavalo spin through the hatch and crack his hip as he grabbed at the transparent wall.

Jerk.

She slipped on the wet, deflated skin of the bubble chair. The Slug's face jounced on the intercom. "Captain!"

"What the hell . . . !" she demanded.

The blinker from Drive Maintenance was flashing. Something jarred the ship again.

"Are we still breathing?"

"Just a . . ." The Slug's face, heavy and rimmed with a thin black beard, got an unpleasant expression. "Yes. Air: all right. Drive Maintenance has the problem."

"If those damn kids have . . ." She clicked them on.

Flip, the platoon Maintenance Foreman, said, "Jesus, Captain, something blew."

"What?"

"I don't know." Flop's face appeared over his shoulder. "A and B shifters are all right. C's glittering like a Fourth of July sparkler. Where the hell are we, anyway?"

"On the first hour shift between Earth and Luna. We haven't even got free of Stellarcenter-9. Navigation?" Another click.

Mollya's dark face popped up.

"Wie gehts?" demanded Rydra.

The first Navigator reeled off their probability curve and located them between two vague logarithmic spirals. "We're orbiting Earth so far," Ron's voice cut over. "Something knocked us way off course. We don't have any drive power and we're just drifting."

"How high up and how fast?"

"Calli's trying to find out now."

"I'm going to take a look around outside." She called down to the Sensory Detail. "Nose, what does it smell like out there?"

"It stinks. Nothing in this range. We've hit soup."

"Can you hear anything, Ear?"

"Not a peep, Captain. All the stasis currents in this area are at a standstill. We're too near a large gravitational mass. There's a faint ethric undertow about fifty spectres K-ward. But I don't think it will take us anywhere except around in a circle. We're riding in momentum from the last stiff wind from Earth's magnosphere."

"What's it look like, Eyes?"

"Inside of a coal scuttle. Whatever happened to us, we picked a dead spot to have it happen in. In my range that undertow is a little stronger and might move us into a good tide."

Brass cut in. "But I'd like to know where it's going before I went jum'ing off into it. That means I gotta know where we are, first."

"Navigation?"

Silence for a moment. Then the three faces appeared. Calli said, "We don't know, Captain."

The gravity field had stabilized a few degrees off. The silicon suspension collected in one corner. Little Diavalo shook his head and blinked. Through the contortion of pain on his face he whispered, "What happened, Captain?"

"Damned if I know," Rydra said. "But I'm going to find out."

Dinner was eaten silently. The platoon, all kids under twenty-one, made as little noise as possible. At the officers' table the Navigators sat across from the apparitional figures of the discorporate Sensory Observers. The hefty Slug at the table's head poured wine for the silent crew. Rydra dined with Brass.

"I don't know." He shook his maned head, turning his glass in gleaming claws. "It was smooth sailing with nothing in the way. Whatever ha"ened, ha"ened inside the shi'."

Diavalo, hip in a pressure bandage, dourfully brought in the shortcake, served Rydra and Brass, then retired to his seat at the platoon table.

"So," Rydra said, "we're orbiting Earth with all our instruments knocked out and can't even tell where we are."

"The hy'erstasis instruments are good," he reminded her. "We just don't know where we are on this side of the jum'."

"And we can't jump if we don't know where we're jumping from." She looked over the dining room. "Do you think they're expecting to get out of this, Brass?"

"They're ho'ing you can get them out, Ca'tain."

She touched the rim of her glass to her lower lip.

"If somebody doesn't, we'll sit here eating Diavalo's good food for six months, then suffocate. We can't even get a signal out until after we lea' for hy'erstasis with the regular communicator shorted. I asked the Navigators to see if they could im'rovise something, but no go. They just had time to see that we were launched in a great circle."

"We should have windows," Rydra said. "At least we could look out at the stars and time our orbit. It can't be more than a couple of hours."

Brass nodded. "Shows you what modern conveniences mean. A 'orthole and an old-fashioned sextant could set us right, but we're electronicized to the gills, and here we sit, with a neatly insoluble 'roblem."

"Circling——" Rydra put down her wine.

"What is it?"

"Der Kreis," said Rydra. She frowned.

"What's that?" asked Brass.

"Ratas, orbis, il cerchio." She put her palms flat on the table top and pressed. "Circles," she said. "Circles in different languages!"

Brass' confusion was terrifying through his fangs. The glinting fleece above his eyes bristled.

"Sphere," she said, "il globo, gumlas." She stood up, "Kule, kuglet, kring!"

"Does it matter what language it's in? A circle is a cir——"

But she was laughing, running from the dining room.

In her cabin she grabbed up her translation. Her eyes fled down the pages. She banged the button for the Navigators. Ron, wiping whipped-cream from his mouth, said, "Yes, Captain? What do you want?"

"A watch," said Rydra, "and a—bag of marbles!"

"Huh?" asked Calli.

"You can finish your shortcake later. Meet me in G-center right now."

"Mar-bles?" articulated Mollya wonderingly. "Marbles?"

"One of the kids in the platoon must have brought along a bag of marbles. Get it and meet me in G-center."

She jumped over the ruined skin of the bubble seat and leapt up the hatchway, turned off at the radial shaft seven, and launched down the cylindrical corridor toward the hollow spherical chamber of G-center. The calculated center of gravity of the ship, it was a chamber thirty feet in diameter in constant free fall where certain gravity-sensitive instruments took their readings. A moment later the three Navigators appeared through triametric entrances. Ron held up a mesh bag of glass balls. "Lizzy asks you to try and get these back to her by tomorrow afternoon because she's been challenged by the kids in Drive and she wants to keep her championship."

"If this works she can probably have them back tonight."

"Work?" Mollya wanted to know. "Idea you?"

"I do. Only it's not really my idea."

"Whose is it, and what is it?" Ron asked.

"I suppose it belongs to somebody who speaks another language. What we've got to do is arrange the marbles around the wall of the room in a perfect sphere, and then sit back with the clock and keep tabs on the second hand."

"What for?" asked Calli.

"To see where they go and how long it takes them to get there."

"I don't get it," said Ron.

"Our orbit tends toward a great circle about the Earth, right? That means everything in the ship is also tending to orbit in a great circle, and, if left free of influence, will automatically seek out such a path."

"Right. So what?"

"Help me get these marbles in place," Rydra said. "These things have iron cores. Magnetize the walls, will you, to hold them in place, so they can all be released at once." Ron, confused, went to power the metal walls of the spherical chamber. "You still don't see? You're mathematicians, tell me about great circles."

Calli took a handful of marbles and started to space them—tiny click after click—over the wall. "A great circle is the largest circle you can cut through a sphere."

"The diameter of the great circle equals the diameter of the sphere," from Ron, as he came back from the power switch.

"The summation of the angles of intersection of any three great circles within one topologically contained shape approaches five hundred and forty degrees. The summation of the angles of N great circles approaches N times one hundred and eighty degrees." Mollya intoned the definitions, which she had begun memorizing in English with the help of a personafix that morning, with her musically inflected voice. "Marble here, yes?"

"All over, yes. Evenly as you can space them, but they don't have to be exact. Tell me some more about the intersections."

"Well," said Ron, "on any given sphere all great circles intersect each other—or lie congruent."

Rydra laughed. "Just like that, hey? Are there any other circles on a sphere that have to intersect no matter how you maneuver them?"

"I think you can push around any other circles so that they're equidistant at all points and don't touch. All great circles have to have at least two points in common."

"Think about that for a minute and look at these marbles, all being pulled along great circles."

Mollya suddenly floated back from the wall with an expression of recognition and brought her hands together. She blurted something in Kiswahili, and Rydra laughed. "That's right," she said. To Ron's and Calli's bewilderment she translated: "They'll move toward each other and their paths'll intersect."

Calli's eyes widened. "That's right, at exactly a quarter of the way around our orbit, they should have flattened out to a circular plane."

"Lying along the plane of our orbit," Ron finished.

Mollya frowned and made a stretching motion with her hands. "Yeah," Ron said, "a distorted circular plain with a tail at each end, from which we can compute which way the earth lies."

"Clever, huh?" Rydra moved back into the corridor opening. "I figure we can do this once, then fire our rockets enough to blast us maybe seventy or eighty miles either up or down without hurting anything. From that we can get the length of our orbits, as well as our speed. That'll be all the information we need to locate ourselves in relation to the nearest major gravitational influence. From there we can jump stasis. All our communications instruments for stasis are in working order. We can signal for help and pull in some replacements from a stasis station."

The amazed Navigators joined her in the corridor. "Count down," Rydra said.

At zero Ron released the magnetic walls. Slowly the marbles began to drift, lining up slowly.

"Guess you learn something every day," Calli said. "If you'd asked me, I would have said we were stuck here forever. And knowing things like this is supposed to be my job. Where did you get the idea?"

"From the word for 'great circle' in . . . another language."

"Language speaking tongue?" Mollya asked. "You mean?"

"Well," Rydra took out a metal tracing plate and a stylus. "I'm simplifying it a little, but let me show you." She marked the plate. "Let's say the word for circle is: O. This language has a melody system to illustrate comparatives. We'll represent this by the diacritical marks: ˇ, ˉ, and ˆ, respectively, mean smallest, ordinary, and biggest. So what would Ō mean?"

"Smallest possible circle?" said Calli. "That's a single point."

Rydra nodded. "Now, when referring to a circle on a sphere, suppose the word for just an ordinary circle is Ō followed by either of two symbols, one of which means not touching anything else, the other of which means crossing —11 or X. What would ŌX mean?"

"Ordinary circle that intersects," said Ron.

"And because all great circles intersect, in this language the word for great circle is always ÔX. It carries the information right in the word. Just like *busstop* or *foxhole* carry information in English that *la gare* or *le terrier*— comparable words in French—lack. "Great Circle" carries some information with it, but not the right information to get us out of the jam we're in. We have to go to another language in order to think about the problem clearly without going through all sorts of roundabout paths for the proper aspects of what we want to deal with."

"What language is this?" asked Calli.

"I don't know its real name. For now it's called Babel-17. From what little I know about it already, most of its words carry more information about the things they refer to than any four or five languages I know put together, and in less space." She gave a brief translation for Mollya.

"Who speak?" Mollya asked, determined to stick to her minimal English.

Rydra bit the inside of her lip. When she asked herself that question, her stomach would tighten, her hands start toward something and the yearning for an answer grow nearly to pain in the back of her throat. It happened now; it faded. "I don't know. But I wish I did. That's what the main reason for this trip is, to find out."

"Babel-17," Ron repeated.

One of the platoon tube-boys coughed behind them.

"What is it, Carlos?"

Squat, taurine, with a lot of curly black hair, Carlos had

big, loose muscles, and a slight lisp. "Captain, could I show you something?" He shifted from side to side in adolescent awkwardness, scuffing his bare soles, heat-calloused from climbing over the drive tubes, against the door sill. "Something down in the tubes. I think you should take a look at it yourself."

"Did Slug tell you to get me?"

Carlos prodded behind his ear with a gnawed thumbnail. "Um-hm."

"You three can take care of this business, can't you?"

"Sure, Captain." Calli looked at the closing marbles.

Rydra ducked after Carlos. They rode down the ladder-lift and hunched through the low ceilinged causeway.

"Down here," Carlos said, hesitantly taking the lead beneath arched bus bars. At a mesh platform he stopped and opened a component cabinet in the wall. "See." He removed a board of printed circuits. "There." A thin crack ran across the plastic surface. "It's been broken."

"How?" Rydra asked.

"Like this." He took the plate in both hands and made a bending gesture.

"Sure it didn't crack by itself?"

"It can't," Carlos said. "When it's in place, it's supported too well. You couldn't crack it with a sledge hammer. This panel carries all the communication circuits."

Rydra nodded.

"The gyroscopic field deflectors for all our regular space maneuvering . . ." He opened another door and took out another panel. "Here."

Rydra ran her fingernail along the crack in the second plate. "Someone in the ship broke these," she said. "Take them to the shop. Tell Lizzy when she finishes reprinting them to bring them to me and I'll put them in. I'll give her the marbles back then."

II

Drop a gem in thick oil. The brilliance yellows slowly, ambers, goes red at last, dies. That was the leap into hyperstatic space.

At the computer console, Rydra pondered the charts. The dictionary had doubled since the trip began. Satisfaction filled one side of her mind like a good meal. Words, and their easy patterning, facile always on her tongue, in her fingers, ordered themselves for her, revealing, defining, and revealing.

And there was a traitor. The question, a vacuum where no information would come to answer who or what or why, made an emptiness on the other side of her brain, agonizing to collapse. Someone had deliberately broken those plates. Lizzy said so, too. What words for this? The names of the entire crew, and by each, a question mark.

Fling a jewel into a glut of jewels. This is the leap out of hyperstasis into the area of the Alliance War Yards at Armsedge.

At the communication board, she put on the Sensory Helmet. "Do you want to translate for me?"

The indicator light blinked acceptance. Each discorporate observer perceived the details of the gravitational and electromagnetic flux of the stasis currents for a certain frequency with all his senses, each in his separate range. Those details were myriad, and the pilot sailed the ship through those currents as sailing ships winded the liquid ocean. But the helmet made a condensation that the captain could view for a general survey of the matrix, reduced to terms that would leave the corporate viewer sane.

She opened the helmet, covering her eyes, ears, and nose.

Flung through loops of blue and wrung with indigo, drifted the complex of stations and planetoids making up the War Yards. A musical hum punctured with bursts of static sounded over the earphones. The olfactory emitters gave a confused odor of perfumes and hot oil charged with the bitter smell of burning citrus peel. With three of her senses filled, she was loosed from the reality of the cabin to drift through sensory abstractions. It took nearly a minute to collect her sensations, to begin their interpretation.

"All right. What am I looking at?"

"The lights are the various planetoids and ring stations that make up the War Yards," the Eye explained to her. "That bluish color to the left is a radar net they have spread out toward Stellarcenter Forty-two. Those red flashes in the upper right hand corner are just a reflection of Bellatrix from a half-glazed solar-disk rotating four degrees outside your field of vision."

"What's that low humming?" Rydra asked.

"The ship's drive," the Ear explained. "Just ignore it. I'll block it out if you want."

Rydra nodded, and the hum ceased.

"That clicking——" the Ear began.

"——is morse code," Rydra finished. "I recognize that. It must be two radio amateurs that want to keep off the visual circuits."

"That's right," the Ear confirmed.

"What stinks like that?"

"The overall smell is just Bellatrix's gravitational field. You can't receive the olfactory sensations in stereo, but the burnt lemon peel is the power plant that's located in that green glare right ahead of you."

"Where do we dock?"

"In the sound of the E-minor triad."

"In the hot oil you can smell bubbling to your left."

"Home in on that white circle."

Rydra switched to the pilot. "O.K., Brass, take her in."

The saucer-disk slid down the ramp as she balanced easily in the four-fifths gravity. A breeze through the artificial twilight pushed her hair back from her shoulders. Around her stretched the major arsenal of the Alliance. Momentarily she pondered the accident of birth that had seated her firmly inside the Alliance's realm. Born a galaxy away, she might as easily have been an Invader. Her poems were popular on both sides. That was upsetting. She put the thought away. Here, gliding the Alliance War Yards, it was not clever to be upset over that.

"Captain Wong, you come under the auspices of General Forester."

She nodded as her saucer stopped.

"He forwarded us information that you are at present the expert on Babel-17."

She nodded once more. Now the other saucer paused before hers.

"I'm very happy then, to meet you, and for any assistance I can offer, please ask."

She extended her hand. "Thank you, Baron Ver Dorco."

Black eyebrows raised and the slash of mouth curved in the dark face. "You read heraldry?" He raised long fingers to the shield on his chest.

"I do."

"An accomplishment, Captain. We live in a world of isolated communities, each hardly touching its neighbor, each speaking, as it were, a different language."

"I speak many."

The Baron nodded. "Sometimes I believe, Captain Wong, that without the Invasion, something for the Alliance to focus its energies upon, our society would disintegrate. Captain Wong——" He stopped, and the fine lines of his face shifted, contracted to concentration, then a sudden opening. "Rydra Wong . . . ?"

She nodded, smiling at his smile, yet wary before what the recognition would mean.

"I didn't realize——" He extended his hand as though he were meeting her all over again. "But, of course——" The surface of his manner shaled away, and had she never seen this transformation before she would have warmed to his warmth. "Your books, I want you to know——" The sentence trailed in a slight shaking of the head. Dark eyes too wide; lips, in their humor, too close to a leer; hands seeking one another: it all spoke to her of a disquieting appetite for her presence, a hunger for something she was or might be, a ravenous—"Dinner at my house is served at seven." He interrupted her thought with unsettling appropriateness. "You will dine with the Baroness and myself this evening."

"Thank you. But I wanted to discuss with my crew——"

"I extend the invitation to your entire entourage. We have a spacious house, conference rooms at your disposal, as well as entertainment, certainly less confined than your ship." The tongue, purplish and flickering behind white, white teeth; the brown lines of his lips, she thought, form words as languidly as the slow mandibles of the cannibal mantis.

"Please come a little early so we can prepare you——"

She caught her breath, then felt foolish; a faint narrowing of his eyes told her he had registered, though not understood, her start.

"—for your tour through the yards. General Forester has suggested you be made privy to all our efforts against the Invaders. That is quite an honor, Madam. There are many well-seasoned officers at the yards who have not seen some of the things you will be shown. A good deal of it will probably be tedious, I dare say. In my opinion, it's stuffing you with a lot of trivial tidbits. But some of our attempts have been rather ingenious. We keep our imaginations simmering."

This man brings out the paranoid in me, she thought. I don't like him. "I'd prefer not to impose on you, Baron. There are some matters on my ship that I must——"

"Do come. Your work here will be much facilitated if you accept my hospitality, I assure you. A woman of your talent and accomplishment would be an honor to my house. And recently I have been starved"—dark lips slid together over gleaming teeth—"for intelligent conversation."

She felt her jaw clamp involuntarily on a third ceremonious refusal. But the Baron was saying: "I will expect you, and your crew, leisurely, before seven."

The saucer-disk slid away over the concourse. Rydra looked back at the ramp where her ship waited, silhouetted against the false evening. Her disk began to negotiate the slope back to the *Rimbaud*.

"Well," she said to the little albino cook who had just come out of his pressure bandage the day before, "you're off tonight. Slug, the crew's going out to dinner. See if you can brush the kids up on their table manners—make sure every one knows which knife to eat his peas with, and all that."

"The salad fork is the little one on the outside," the Slug announced suavely, turning to the platoon.

"And what about the little one outside that?" Allegra asked.

"That's for oysters."

"But suppose they don't serve oysters?"

Flop rubbed his underlip with the knuckle of his thumb. "I guess you could pick your teeth with it."

Brass dropped a paw on Rydra's shoulder. "How you feel, Ca'tain?"

"Like a pig over a barbecue pit."

"You look sort of done——" Calli began.

"Done?" she asked.

"—in," he finished, quizzically.

"Maybe I've been working too hard. We're guests at the Baron Ver Dorco's this evening. I suppose we can all relax a bit there."

"Ver Dorco?" asked Mollya.

"He's in charge of coordinating the various research projects against the Invaders."

"This is where they make all the bigger and better secret weapons?" Ron asked.

"They also make smaller, more deadly ones. I imagine it should be an education."

"These sabotage attem'ts," Brass said. She had given them a rough idea of what was going on. "A successful one here at the War Yards could be 'retty bad to our efforts against the Invaders."

"It's about as central a hit as they could try, next to planting a bomb in Administrative Alliance Headquarters itself."

"Will you be able to stop it?" Slug asked.

Rydra shrugged, turning to the simmering absences of

the discorporate crew. "I've got a couple of ideas. Look, I'm
going to ask you guys to be sort of unhospitable this evening
and do some spying. Eyes, I want you to stay on the ship and
make sure you're the only one here. Ears, once we leave for
the Baron's, go invisible and from then on, don't get more
than six feet away from me until we're all back to the ship.
Nose, you run messages back and forth. There's something
going on that I don't like. I don't know whether it's my
imagination or what."

The Eye spoke something ominous. Ordinarily the corporate could only converse with the discorporate—and remember the conversation—over special equipment. Rydra
solved the problem by immediately translating whatever they
spoke to her into Basque before the weak synapses broke.
Though the original words were lost, the translation remained:
Those broken circuit plates weren't your imagination, was the
gist of the Basque she retained.

She looked over the crew with gnawing discomfort. If
one of the kids or officers was merely psychotically destructive, it would show up on his psyche index. There was,
among them, a consciously destructive one. It hurt, like an
unlocateable splinter in the sole of her foot that jabbed
occasionally with the pressure of walking. She remembered
how she had searched them from the night. Pride. Warm
pride in the way their functions meshed as they moved her
ship through the stars. The warmth was the relieved anticipation for all that could go wrong with the machine-called-the-
ship, if the machine-called-the-crew were not interlocked and
precise. Cool pride in another part of her mind, at the ease
with which they moved by one another: the kids, inexperienced
both in living and working; the adults, so near pressure
situations that might have scarred their polished efficiency
and made psychic burrs to snag one another. But she had
chosen them; and the ship, her world, was a beautiful place
to walk, work, live, for a journey's length.

But there was a traitor.

That shorted something. *Somewhere in Eden, now* . . . she
recalled, again looking over the crew. *Somewhere in Eden,
now, a worm, a worm.* Those cracked plates told her: the
worm wanted to destroy not just her, but the ship, its crew,

and contents, slowly. No blades plunged in the night, no shots from around a corner, no cord looped on the throat as she entered a dark cabin. Babel-17, how good a language would it be to argue with for your life?

"Slug, the Baron wants me to come soon and see some of his latest methods of slaughter. Have the kids there decently early, will you? I'm leaving now. Eye and Ear, hop aboard."

"Righto, Captain," from Slug.

The discorporate crew deperceptualized.

She leaned her sled over the ramp again and slid away from the milling youngsters and officers, curious at the source of her apprehension.

III

"Gross, uncivilized weapons." The Baron gestured toward the row of plastic cylinders increasing in size along the rack. "It's a shame to waste time on such clumsy contraptions. The little one there can demolish an area of about fifty square miles. The big ones leave a crater twenty-seven miles deep and a hundred and fifty across. Barbaric. I frown on their use. That one on the left is more subtle: it explodes once with enough force to demolish a good size building, but the bomb casing itself is hidden and unhurt under the rubble. Six hours later it explodes again and does the damage of a fair-sized atomic bomb. This leaves the victims enough time to concentrate their reclamation forces, all sorts of reconstruction workers, Red Cross nurses, or whatever the Invaders call them, lots of experts determining the size of the damage. Then *poof*. A delayed hydrogen explosion, and a good thirty or forty miles crater. It doesn't do as much physical damage as even the smallest of these others, but it gets rid of a lot of equipment and busybody do-gooders. Still, a schoolboy's weapon. I keep them in my own personal collection just to show them we have standard fare."

She followed him through the archway into the next hall. There were filing cabinets along the wall and a single display case in the center of the room.

"Now here is one I'm justly proud of." The Baron walked to the case and the transparent walls fell apart.

"What," Rydra asked, "exactly is it?"

"What does it look like?"

"A . . . piece of rock."

"A chunk of metal," corrected the Baron.

"Is it explosive, or particularly hard?"

"It won't go bang," he assured her. "Its tensile strength is a bit over titanium steel, but we have much harder plastics."

Rydra started to extend her hand, then thought to ask, "May I pick it up and examine it?"

"I doubt it," the Baron said. "Try."

"What will happen?"

"See for yourself."

She reached out to take the dull chunk. Her hand closed on air two inches above the surface. She moved her fingers down to touch it, but they came together inches to the side. Rydra frowned.

She moved her hand to the left, but it was on the other side of the strange shard.

"Just a moment." The Baron smiled, picked up the fragment. "Now if you saw this just lying on the ground, you wouldn't look twice, would you?"

"Poisonous?" Rydra suggested. "Is it a component of something else?"

"No." The Baron turned the shape about thoughtfully. "Just highly selective. And obliging." He raised his hand. "Suppose you needed a gun"—in the Baron's hand now was a sleek vibra-gun of a model later than she had ever seen—"or a crescent wrench." Now he held a foot long wrench. He adjusted the opening. "Or a machete." The blade glistened as he waved his arm back. "Or a small crossbow." It had a pistol grip and a bow length of not quite ten inches. The spring, however, was doubled back on itself and held with quarter inch bolts. The Baron pulled the trigger—there was no arrow—and the *thump* of the release, followed by the continuous *pinnnnnng* of the vibrating tensile bar, set her teeth against one another.

"It's some sort of illusion," Rydra said. "That's why I couldn't touch it."

"A metal punch," said the Baron. It appeared in his hand, a hammer with a particularly thick head. He swung it against the floor of the case that had held the "weapon" with a strident clang. "There."

Rydra saw the circular indentation left by the hammer-head. Raised in the middle was the faint shape of the Ver Dorco shield. She moved the tips of her fingers over the bossed metal, still warm from impact.

"No illusion," said the Baron. "That crossbow will put a six inch shaft completely through three inches of oak at forty yards. And the vibra-gun—I'm sure you know what it can do."

He held the—it was a chunk of metal again—above its stand in the case. "Put it back for me."

She stretched her hand beneath his, and he dropped the chunk. Her fingers closed to grab it. But it was on the stand again.

"No hocus-pocus. Merely selective and . . . obliging."

He touched the edge of the case and the plastic sides closed over the display. "A clever plaything. Let's look at something else."

"But how does it work?"

Ver Dorco smiled. "We've managed to polarize alloys of the heavier elements so that they exist only on certain percep-tual matrices. Otherwise, they deflect. That means that, besides visually—and we can blank that out as well—it's undetectable. No weight, no volume; all it has is inertia. Which means simply by carrying it aboard any hyperstasis craft, you'll put its drive controls out of commission. Two or three grams of this anywhere near the inertia-stasis system will create all sorts of unaccounted-for strain. That's its major function right there. Smuggle that on board the Invaders' ships and we can stop worrying about them. The rest—that's child's play. An unexpected property of polarized matter is tensile-memory." They moved toward an archway into the next room. "Annealed in any shape for a time, and codified, the structure of that shape is retained down to the molecules. At any angle to the direction that the matter has been polarized in, each molecule has completely free movement. Just jar it, and it falls into that structure like a rubber figure returning to shape." The Baron glanced back at the case. "Simple, really. There"—he motioned toward the filing cabinets along the wall—"is the real weapon: approximately three thousand individual plans incorporating that little polarized chunk. The 'weapon' is the knowledge of what to do with what you have. In hand-to-hand combat, a six-inch length of vanadium wire can be deadly. Inserted directly into the inner corner of the eye, piercing diagonally across the frontal lobes, then brought quickly down, it punctures the cerebellum, causing general paralysis; thrust completely in, and it will mangle the joint of spinal cord and the medulla: Death. You can use the same piece of wire to short out a Type 27-QX communications unit, which is the sort currently employed in the Invaders' stasis systems."

Rydra felt the muscles along her spine tighten. The repulsion which she had quelled till now came flooding back.

"This next display is from the Borgia. The Borgia," he laughed, "my nickname for our toxicology department. Again, some terribly gross products." He picked a sealed glass phial from a wall rack. "Pure diphtheria toxin. Enough here to make the reservoir of a good-sized city fatal."

"But standard vaccination procedure——" Rydra began.

"Diphtheria toxin, my dear. Toxin! Back when contagious diseases were a problem, you know, they would examine the corpses of diphtheria victims and discover nothing but a few hundred thousand baccilli, all in the victim's throat. Nowhere else. With any other sort of bacillis, that's enough of an infection to cause a minor cough. It took years to discover what was going on. That tiny number of bacilli produced an even tinier bit of a substance that is still the most deadly natural organic compound we know of. The amount required to kill a man—oh, I'd even say thirty or forty men—is, for all practical purposes, undetectable. Up till now, even with all our advances, the only way you could obtain it was from an obliging diphtheria bacillus. The Borgia has changed that." He pointed to another bottle. "Cyanide, the old war horse! But then, the telltale smell of almonds—are you hungry? We can go up for cocktails any time you wish."

She shook her head, quickly and firmly.

"Now these are delicious. Catalytics." He moved his hand from one phial to the next. "Color blindness, total blindness, tone deafness, complete deafness, ataxia, amnesia, and on and on." He dropped his hand and smiled like a hungry rodent. "And they're all controlled by this. You see, the problem with anything of such a specific effect is that you have to introduce comparatively huge amounts of it. All these require at least a tenth of a gram or more. So, catalytics. None of what I've shown you would have any effect at all even if you swallowed the whole vial." He lifted the last container he had pointed to and pressed a stud at the end and there was a faint hiss of escaping gas. "Until now. A perfectly harmless atomized steroid."

"Only it activates the poisons here to produce . . . these effects?"

"Exactly," smiled the Baron. "And the catalyst can be in doses nearly as microscopic as the diphtheria toxin. The contents of that blue jar will give you a mild stomach ache and minor head pains for half an hour. Nothing more. The green one beside it: total cerebral atrophy over a period of a week. The victim becomes a living vegetable the rest of his life. The purple one: death." He raised his hands, palms up, and laughed. "I'm famished." The hands dropped. "Shall we go up to dinner?"

Ask him what's in that room over there, she said to herself, and would have dismissed the passing curiosity, but she was thinking in Basque: it was a message from her discorporate bodyguard, invisible beside her.

"When I was a child, Baron"—she moved toward the door—"soon after I came to Earth, I was taken to the circus. It was the first time I had ever seen so many things so close together that were so fascinating. I wouldn't go home till almost an hour after they had intended to leave. What do you have in this room?"

Surprise in the little movement in the muscles of his forehead.

"Show me."

He bowed his head in mocking, semi-formal aquiescence. "Modern warfare can be fought on so many delightfully different levels," he continued, walking back to her side as if no interruption of the tour had been suggested. "One wins a battle by making sure one's troops have enough blunderbusses and battle axes like the ones you saw in the first room; or by the well-placed six-inch length of vanadium wire in a Type 27-QX communications unit. With the proper orders delayed, the encounter never takes place. Hand-to-hand weapons, survival kit, plus training, room, and board: three thousand credits per enlisted stellarman over a period of two years active duty. For a garrison of fifteen hundred men that's an outlay of four million, five hundred credits. That same garrison will live in and fight from three hyperstasis battle-ships which, fully-equipped, run about a million and a half credits apiece—a total outlay of nine million credits. We have spent, on occasion, perhaps as much as a million on the preparation of a single spy or saboteur. That is rather higher than usual. And I can't believe a six-inch length of vanadium wire costs a third of a cent. War is costly. And although it has taken some time, Administrative Alliance Headquarters is beginning to realize subtlety pays. This way, Miss—Captain Wong."

Again they were in a room with only a single display case, but it was seven feet high.

A statue, Rydra thought. No, real flesh, with detail of muscle and joint; no, it must be a statue because a human body, dead or in suspended animation, doesn't look that—alive. Only art could produce that vibrancy.

"So you see, the proper spy is very important." Though the door had opened automatically, the Baron held it with his hand in vestigial politeness. "This is one of our more expensive models. Still well under a million credits, but one of my favourites—though in practice he has his faults.

With a few minor alterations I would like to make him a permanent part of our arsenal.''

"A model of a spy?" Rydra asked. "Some sort of robot or android?"

"Not at all." They approached the display case. "We made half a dozen TW-55's. It took the most exacting genetic search. Medical science has progressed so that all sorts of hopeless human refuse lives and reproduces at a frightening rate—inferior creatures that would have been too weak to survive a handful of centuries ago. We chose our parents carefully, and then with artificial insemination we got our half dozen zygotes, three male, three female. We raised them in, oh, such a carefully controlled nutrient environment, speeding the growth rate by hormones and other things. But the beauty of it was the experiential imprinting. Gorgeously healthy creatures; you have no idea how much care they received.''

"I once spent a summer on a cattle farm," Rydra said shortly.

The Baron's nod was brisk. "We'd used the experiential imprints before, so we knew what we were doing. But never to synthesize completely the life situation of, say, a sixteen-year-old human. Sixteen was the physiological age we brought them to in six months. Look for yourself what a splendid specimen it is. The reflexes are fifty percent above the human aged normally. The human musculature is beautifully engineered: a three-day-starved, six-month-atrophied myasthenia gravis case, can, with the proper stimulant drugs, overturn a ton and a half automobile. It will kill him—but that's still remarkable efficiency. Think what the biologically perfect body, operating, at all times at point nine-nine efficiency, could accomplish in physical strength alone.''

"I thought hormone growth incentive had been outlawed. Doesn't it reduce the life span some drastic amount?"

"To the extent we used it, the life span reduction is seventy-five percent and over." He might have smiled the same way watching some odd animal at its incomprehensible antics. "But, Madam, we are making weapons. If TW-55 can function twenty years at peak efficiency, then it will have outlasted the average battle cruiser by five years. But the experiential imprinting! To find among ordinary men someone who can function as a spy, is *willing* to function as a spy, you must search the fringes of neurosis, often psychosis. Though such deviations might mean strength in a particular area, it always means an overall weakness in the personality. Functioning in any but that particular area, a spy may be dangerously inefficient. And the Invaders have psyche-indices too, which will keep the average spy out of any place we might want to put him. Captured, a good spy is a dozen times as dangerous as a bad one. Post-hypnotic suicide suggestions and the like are easily gotten around with drugs; and are wasteful. TW-55 here will register perfectly normal on a psyche integration. He has about six hours of social conversation, plot synopses of the latest novels, political situations, music, and art criticism—I believe in the course of an evening he is programmed to drop your name twice, an honor you share only with Ronald Quar. He has one subject on which he can expound with scholarly acumen for an hour and a half—this one is 'haptoglobin grouping among the marsupials,' I believe. Put him in formal wear and he will be perfectly at home at an ambassadorial ball or a coffee break at a high level government conference. He is a crack assassin, expert with all the weapons you have seen up till now, and more. TW-55 has twelve hours' worth of episodes in fourteen different dialects, accents, or jargons concerning sexual conquests, gambling experiences, fisticuff encounters, and humorous anecdotes of semi-illegal enterprises, all of which failed miserably. Tear his shirt, smear grease on his face and slip a pair of overalls on him, and he could be a service mechanic on any one of a hundred spaceyards or stellarcenters on the other side of the Snap. He can disable any space drive system, communications components, radar works, or alarm system used by the Invaders in the past twenty years with little more than——"

"Six inches of vanadium wire?"

The Baron smiled. "His fingerprints and retina pattern, he can alter at will. A little neural surgery has made all the muscles of his face voluntary, which means he can alter his facial structure drastically. Chemical dies and hormone banks beneath the scalp enable him to color his hair in seconds, or, if necessary, shed it completely and grow a new batch in half an hour. He's a past master in the psychology and physiology of coercion.''

"Torture?"

"If you will. He is totally obedient to the people whom he has been conditioned to regard as his superiors; totally destructive toward what he has been ordered to destroy. There is nothing in that beautiful head even akin to a super-ego.''

"He is..." and she wondered at herself speaking, "beautiful." The dark lashed eyes with lids about to quiver open, the broad hands hung at the naked thighs, fingers half-curled, about to straighten or become a fist. The display light was misty on the tanned, yet near translucent skin. "You say this isn't a model, but really alive?"

"Oh, more or less. But it's rather firmly fixed in something like a yoga trance, or a lizard's hibernation. I could activate it for you—but it's ten to seven. We don't want to keep the others waiting at the table now, do we?"

She looked away from the figure in glass to the dull, taut skin of the Baron's face. His jaw, beneath his faintly concave cheek, was involuntarily working on its hinge.

"Like the circus," Rydra said. "But, I'm older now. Come." It was an act of will to offer her arm. His hand was paper dry, and so light she had to strain to keep from flinching.

IV

"Captain Wong! I am delighted."

The Baroness extended her plump hand, of a pink and gray hue suggesting something parboiled. Her puffy freckled shoulders heaved beneath the straps of an evening dress tasteful enough over her distended figure, still grotesque.

"We have so little excitement here at the Yards that when someone as distinguished as yourself pays us a visit . . ."

She let the sentence end in what would have been an ecstatic smile, but the weight of her doughy cheeks distorted it into a porcine pastiche of itself.

Rydra held the soft, malleable fingers as short a time as politeness allowed and returned the smile. She remembered, as a little girl, being obliged not to cry through punishment. Having the smile was worse. The Baroness seemed a muffled, vast, vacuous silence. The small muscle shifts, those counter communications that she was used to in direct conversation, were blunted in the Baroness under the fat. Even though the voice came from the heavy lips in strident little screeches, it was as though they talked through blankets.

"But your crew! We intended them all to be present. twenty-one, now I know that's what a full crew consists of." She shook her finger in patronizing disapproval. "I read up on these things, you know. And there are only eighteen of you here."

"I thought the discorporate members might remain on the ship," Rydra explained. "You need special equipment to talk with them and I thought they might upset your other guests. They're really more content with themselves for company and they don't eat."

They're having barbecued lamb for dinner and you'll go to hell for lying, she commented to herself—in Basque.

"Discorporate?" The Baroness patted the lacquered intricacies of her high-coifed hair. "You mean dead? Oh, of course. Now I hadn't thought of that at all. You see how cut off we are from one another in this world? I'll have their places removed." Rydra wondered whether the Baron had discorporate detecting equipment operating, as the Baroness leaned toward her and whispered confidentially, "Your crew has enchanted everybody! Shall we go on?"

With the Baron on her left—his palm a parchment sling for her forearm—and the Baroness leaning on her right—breathy and damp—they walked from the white stone foyer into the hall.

"Hey, Captain!" Calli bellowed, striding toward them from a quarter of the way across the room. "This is a pretty fine place, huh?" With his elbows he gestured around at the crowded hall, then held up his glass to show the size of his drink. He pursed his lips and nodded approvingly. "Let me get you some of these, Captain." Now he raised a handful of tiny sandwiches, olives stuffed with liver, and bacon-wrapped prunes. "There's a guy with a whole tray full running around over there." He pointed again with his elbow. "Ma'am, sir"—he looked from the Baroness to the Baron—"can I get you some, too?" He put one of the sandwiches in his mouth and followed it with a gulp from his glass. "Uhmpmnle."

"I'll wait till he brings them over here," the Baroness said.

Amused, Rydra glanced at her hostess, but there was a smile, much more the proper size, winding through her fleshy features. "I hope you like them."

Calli swallowed. "I do." Then he screwed up his face, set his teeth, opened his lips, and shook his head. "*Except* those real salty ones with the fish. I didn't like those at all, ma'am. But the rest are O.K."

"I'll tell you"—the Baroness leaned forward, the smile crumbling into a chesty chuckle—"I never really liked the salty ones either!"

She looked from Rydra to the Baron with a shrug of mock surrender. "But one is so tyrannized by one's caterer nowadays, what can one do?"

"If I didn't like them," Calli said, jerking his head aside in determination, "I'd tell him don't bring none!"

The Baronness looked back with raised eyebrows. "You know, you're perfectly right! That's exactly what I'm going to do!" She peered across Rydra to her husband. "That's just what I'm going to do, Felix, next time."

A waiter with a tray of glasses said, "Would you care for a drink?"

"She don't want one of them little tiny ones," Calli said, gesturing toward Rydra. "Get her a big one like I got."

Rydra laughed. "I'm afraid I have to be a lady tonight, Calli."

"Nonsense!" cried the Baroness. "I want a big one, too. Now let's see, I put the bar somewhere over there, didn't I?"

"That's where it was when I saw it last," Calli said.

"We're here to have fun this evening, and nobody is

going to have fun with one of *those*." She seized Rydra's arm
and called back to her husband, "Felix, be sociable," and led
Rydra away. "That's Dr. Keebling. The woman with the
bleached hair is Dr. Crane, and that's my brother-in-law,
Albert. I'll introduce you on the way back. They're all my
husband's colleagues. They work with him on those dreadful
things he was showing you in the cellar. I wish he wouldn't
keep his private collection in the house. It's gruesome. I'm
always afraid one of them will crawl up here in the middle of
the night and chop our heads off. I think he's trying to make
up for his son. You know we lost our little boy, Nyles—I think
it's been eight years. Felix has thrown himself totally into his
work since. But that's a terribly glib explanation, isn't it?
Captain Wong, do you find us dreadfully provincial?"

"Not at all."

"You should. But then, you don't know any of us well,
do you. Oh, the bright young people who come here, with
their bright, lively imaginations. They do nothing all day long
but think of ways to kill. It's a terribly placid society, really.
But, why shouldn't it be? All its aggressions are vented from
nine to five. Still, I think it does something to our minds.
Imagination should be used for something other than pondering
murder, don't you think?"

"I do." Concern grew for the weighty woman.

Just then they were stopped by clotted guests.

"What's going on here?" demanded the Baroness. "Sam,
what are they doing in there?"

Sam smiled, stepped back, and the Baroness wedged
herself into the space, still clutching Rydra's arm.

"Hold 'em back some!"

Rydra recognized Lizzy's voice. Someone else moved
and she could see. The kids from Drive had cleared a space
ten feet across, and were guarding it like junior police. Lizzy
crouched with three boys, who, from their dress, were local
gentry of Armsedge. "What you have to understand," she
was saying, "is that it's all in the wrist." She flipped a
marble with her thumbnail: it struck first one, then another,
and one of the struck ones struck a third.

"Hey, do that again!"

Lizzy picked up another marble. "Only one knuckle on

the floor, now, so you can pivot. But it's mostly from the wrist."

The marble darted out, struck, struck, and struck. Five or six people applauded. Rydra was one.

The Baroness touched her breast. "Lovely shot! Perfectly lovely!" She remembered herself and glanced back. "Oh, you must want to watch this, Sam. You're the ballistics expert, anyway." With polite embarrassment she relinquished her place and turned to Rydra as they continued across the floor. "There. There, that is why I'm so glad you and your crew came to see us this evening. You bring something so cool and pleasing, so fresh, so crisp."

"You speak about us as though we were a salad." Rydra laughed. In the Baroness the "appetite' was not so menacing.

"I dare say if you stayed here long enough we would devour you, if you let us. What you bring we are very hungry for."

"What is it?"

They arrived at the bar, then turned with their drinks. The Baroness' face strained toward hardness. "Well, you . . . you come to us and immediately we start to learn things, things about you, and ultimately about ourselves."

"I don't understand."

"Take your Navigator. He likes his drinks big and all the hors d'oeuvres except the anchovies. That's more than I know about the likes and dislikes of anyone else in the room. You offer Scotch, they drink Scotch. You offer tequila, tequila they then down by the gallon. And just a moment ago I discovered"—she shook her supine hand—"that it's all in the wrist. I never knew *that* before."

"We're used to talking to each other."

"Yes, but you tell the important things. What you like, what you don't like, how you do things. Do you really want to be introduced to all those stuffy men and women who kill people?"

"Not really."

"Didn't think so. And I don't want to bother myself. Oh, there are three or four who I think you would like. But I'll see that you meet them before you leave." She barreled into the crowd.

Tides, Rydra thought. Oceans. Hyperstasis currents. Or the movement of people in a large room. She drifted along the least resistant ways that pulsed open, then closed as someone moved to meet someone, to get a drink, to leave a conversation.

Then there was a corner, a spiral stair. She climbed, pausing as she came around the second turn to watch the crowd beneath. There was a double door ajar at the top, a breeze. She stepped outside.

Violet had been replaced by artful, cloud-streaked purple. Soon the planetoid's chromadome would simulate night. Moist vegetation lipped the railing. At one end, the vines had completely covered the white stone.

"Captain?"

Ron, shadowed and brushed with leaves, sat in the corner of the balcony, hugging his knees. Skin is not silver, she thought, yet whenever I see him that way, curled up in himself, I picture a knot of white metal. He lifted his chin from his kneecaps and put his back against the verdant hedge so there were leaves in his corn-silk hair.

"What're you doing?"

"Too many people."

She nodded, watching him press his shoulders downward, watching his triceps leap on the bone, then still. With each breath in the young, gnarled body the tiny movements sang to her. She listened to the singing for nearly half a minute while he watched her, sitting still, yet always the tiny entrancements. The rose on his shoulder whispered against the leaves. When she had listened to the muscular music a while, she asked:

"Trouble between you, Mollya, and Calli?"

"No. I mean . . . just . . ."

"Just what?" She smiled and leaned on the balcony edge.

He lowered his chin to his knees again. "I guess they're fine. But, I'm the youngest . . . and . . ." Suddenly the shoulders raised. "How the hell would you understand! Sure, you know about things like this, but you don't really know. You write what you see. Not what you do." It came out in little explosions of half whispered sound. She heard the words and watched the jaw muscle jerk and beat and pop, a small beast inside his cheek. "Perverts," he said. "That's what you Customs all really think. The Baron and the Baroness, all those people in there staring at us, who can't understand why you could want more than two. And you can't understand either."

"Ron?"

He snapped his teeth on a leaf and yanked it from the stem.

"Five years ago, Ron, I was . . . tripled."

The face turned to her as if pulling against a spring, then yanked back. He spit the leaf. "You're Customs, Captain. You circle Transport, but just the way you let them eat you up with their eyes, the way they turn and watch to see who you are when you walk by: you're a Queen, yeah. But a Queen in Customs. You're not Transport."

"Ron, I'm public. That's why they look. I write books. Customs people read them, yes, but they look because they want to know who the hell wrote them. Customs didn't write them. I talk to Customs and Customs looks at me and says: 'You're Transport.'" She shrugged. "I'm neither. But even so, I was tripled. I know about that."

"Customs don't triple," he said.

"Two guys and myself. If I ever do it again it'll be with a girl and a guy. For me that would be easier, I think. But I was tripled for three years. That's over twice as long as you've been."

"Yours didn't stick, then. Ours did. At least it was sticking together with Cathy."

"One was killed," Rydra said. "One is in suspended animation at Hippocrates General waiting for them to discover a cure for Caulder's disease. I don't think it will be in my lifetime, but if it is——" In the silence he turned to her. "What is it?" she asked.

"Who were they?"

"Customs or Transport?" She shrugged. "Like me, neither really. Fobo Lombs, he was captain of an interstellar transport; he was the one who made me go through and get my Captain's papers. Also he worked planetside doing hydroponics research, working on storage methods for hyperstatic hauls. Who was he? He was slim and blond and wonderfully affectionate and drank too much sometimes, and would come back from a trip and get drunk and in a fight and in jail, and we'd bail him out—really it only happened twice—but we teased him with it for a year. And he didn't like to sleep in the middle of the bed because he always wanted to let one arm hang over."

Ron laughed, and his hands, grasping high on his forearms, slid to his wrists.

"He was killed in a cave-in exploring the Ganymede Catacombs during the second summer that the three of us worked together on the Jovian Geological Survey."

"Like Cathy," Ron said, after a moment.

"Muels Aranlyde was——"

"Empire Star!" Ron said, his eyes widening, "and the 'Comet Jo' books! You were tripled with Muels Aranlyde?"

She nodded. "Those books were a lot of fun, weren't they?"

"Hell, I must've read all of them," Ron said. His knees came apart. "What sort of a guy was he? Was he anything like Comet?"

"As a matter of fact, Comet Jo started out to be Fobo. Fobo would get involved in something or other, I'd get upset, and Muels would start another novel."

"You mean they're like true stories?"

She shook her head. "Most of the books are just all the fantastic things that could have happened, or that we worried might have happened. Muels himself? In the books he always disguises himself as a computer. He was dark, and withdrawn, and incredibly patient and incredibly kind. He showed me all about sentences and paragraphs—did you know the emotional unit in writing is the paragraph?—and how to separate what you can say from what you can imply, and when to do one or the other——" She stopped. "Then he'd give me a manuscript and say, 'Now you tell me what's wrong with the words.' The only thing I could ever find was that there were too many of them. It was just after Fobo was killed that I really got down to my poetry. Muels used to tell me if I ever would, I'd be great because I knew so much about its elements to start. I had to get down something then, because Fobo was . . . but you know about that, though. Muels caught Caulder's disease about four months later. Neither one of them saw my first book, though they'd seen most of the poems. Maybe someday Muels will read them. He might even write some more of Comet's adventures—and maybe even go to the Morgue and call back my thinking pattern and ask, 'Now tell me what's wrong with the words'; and I'll be able to tell him so much more, so much. But there won't be any consciousness left . . ." She felt herself drift toward the dangerous emotions, let them get as close as they would. Dangerous or not, it had been three years since her emotions had scared her too much to watch them. ". . . so much more."

Ron sat cross-legged now, forearms on his knees, hands hanging.

"*Empire Star* and Comet Jo; we had so much fun with those stories, whether it was arguing about them all night over coffee, or correcting galleys, or sneaking into bookshops and pulling them out from behind the other books."

"I used to do that, too," Ron said. "But just 'cause I liked them."

"We even had fun arguing about who was going to sleep in the middle."

It was like a cue. Ron began to pull back together, knees rising, arms locking around them, chin down. "I got both of mine, at least," he said. "I guess I should be pretty happy."

"Maybe you should. Maybe you shouldn't. Do they love you?"

"They said so."

"Do you love them?"

"Christ, yes. I talk to Mollya and she's trying to explain something to me and she still don't talk so good yet, but suddenly I figure out what she means, and . . ." He straightened his body and looked up as though the word he was searching for was someplace high.

"It's wonderful," she supplied.

"Yeah, it's——" He looked at her. "It's wonderful."

"You and Calli?"

"Hell, Calli's just a big old bear and I can tumble him around and play with him. But it's him and Mollya. He still can't understand her so well. And because I'm the youngest, he thinks he should learn quicker than me. And he doesn't, so he keeps away from both of us. Now like I say, when he gets in a mood, I can always handle him. But she's new, and thinks he's mad at her.''

''Want to know what to do?'' Rydra asked, after a moment.

''Do you know?''

She nodded. ''It hurts more when there's something wrong between them because there doesn't seem to be anything you can do. But it's easier to fix.''

''Why?''

''Because they love you.''

He was waiting now.

''Calli gets into one of his moods, and Mollya doesn't know how to get through to him.''

Ron nodded.

''Mollya speaks another language, and Calli can't get through that.''

He nodded again.

''Now you can communicate with both of them. You can't act as a go-between; that never works. But you can teach each of them how to do what you know already.''

''Teach?''

''What do you do with Calli when he gets moody?''

''I pull his ears,'' Ron said. ''He tells me to cut it out until he starts laughing, and then I roll him around on the floor.''

Rydra made a face. ''It's unorthodox, but if it works, fine. Now show Mollya how. She's athletic. Let her practice on you till she gets it right, if you have to.''

''I don't like to get *my* ears pulled,'' Ron said.

''Sometimes you have to make sacrifices.'' She tried not to smile; and smiled anyway.

Ron rubbed his left earlobe with the ham of his thumb. ''I guess so.''

''And you have to teach Calli the words to get through to Mollya.''

''But I don't know the words myself, sometimes. I can just guess better than he can.''

"If he knew the words, would it help?"

"Sure."

"I've got Kiswahili grammar books in my cabin. Pick them up when we get back to the ship."

"Hey, that would be fine——" He stopped, withdrawing just a bit into the leaves. "Only Calli don't read much or anything."

"You'll help him."

"Teach him," Ron said.

"That's right."

"Do you think he'll do it?" Ron asked.

"To get closer to Mollya?" asked Rydra. "Do you think so?"

"He will." Like metal unbending, Ron suddenly stood. "He will."

"Are you going inside now?" she asked. "We'll be eating in a few minutes."

Ron turned to the rail and looked at the vivid sky. "They keep a beautiful shield up here."

"To keep from being burned up by Bellatrix," Rydra said.

"So they don't have to think about what they're doing."

Rydra raised her eyebrows. Still the concern over right and wrong, even amidst domestic confusion. "That, too," she said and wondered about the war.

His tensing back told her he would come later, wanted to think some more. She went through the double doors and started down the staircase.

"I saw you go out, and I thought I'd wait for you to come back in."

Déja vu, she thought. But she couldn't have seen him before in her life. Blue-black hair over a face craggy for its age in the late twenties. He stepped back to make way for her on the stairway with an incredible economy of movement. She looked from hands to face for a gesture revealing something. He watched her back, giving nothing; then he turned and nodded toward the people below. He indicated the Baron, who stood alone toward the middle of the room. "Yon Cassius has a lean and hungry look."

"I wonder how hungry he is?" Rydra said, and felt strange again.

The Baroness was churning toward her husband through the crowd, to ask advice about whether to begin dinner or wait another five minutes, or some other equally desperate decision.

"What must a marriage between two people like that be?" the stranger asked with austerely patronizing amusement.

"Comparatively simple, I suppose," Rydra said. "They've just got each other to worry about."

A polite look of inquiry. When she offered no elucidation, the stranger turned back to the crowd. "They make such odd faces when they glance up here to see if it's you, Miss Wong."

"They leer," she said, shortly.

"Bandicoots. That's what they look like. A pack of them."

"I wonder if their artificial sky makes them seem so sickly?" She felt herself leaking a controlled hostility.

He laughed. "Bandicoots with thalassanemia!"

"I guess so. You're not from the Yards?" His complexion had a life that would have faded under the artificial sky.

"As a matter of fact, I am."

Surprised, she would have asked him more, but the loudspeakers suddenly announced: "Ladies and Gentlemen, dinner is served."

He accompanied her down the stairs, but two or three steps into the crowd she discovered he had disappeared. She continued toward the dining room alone.

Under the arch the Baron and Baroness waited for her. As the Baroness took her arm, the chamber orchestra on the dais fell to their instruments.

"Come, we're down this way."

She kept near the puffy matron through the people milling about the serpentine table that curved and twisted back on itself.

"We're over there."

And the Basque message: Captain, on your transcriber,

something's coming over back on the ship. The small explosion in her mind stopped her.

"Babel-17!"

The Baron turned to her. "Yes, Captain Wong?" She watched uncertainty score tense lines on his face.

"Is there any place in the yards with particularly important materials or research going on that might be unguarded now?"

"That's all done automatically. Why?"

"Baron, there's a sabotage attack about to take place, or taking place right now."

"But how did you——"

"I can't explain now, but you'd better make sure everything is all right."

And the tension turned.

The Baroness touched her husband's arm, and said with sudden coolness. "Felix, there's your seat."

The Baron pulled out his chair, sat down, and unceremoniously pushed aside his place setting. There was a control panel beneath the doily. As people seated themselves, Rydra saw Brass, twenty feet away, lower himself on the special hammock that had been set up for his glittering, gigantic bulk.

"You sit here, my dear. We'll simply go on with the party as if nothing was happening. I think that's best."

Rydra seated herself next to the Baron, and the Baroness lowered herself carefully to the chair on her left. The Baron was whispering into a throat microphone. Pictures, which she was at the wrong angle to see clearly, flashed on the eight inch screen. He looked up long enough to say, "Nothing yet, Captain Wong."

"Ignore what he's doing," the Baroness said. "This is much more interesting over here."

Into her lap she swung out a small console from where it had hung beneath the table edge.

"Ingenious little thing," the Baroness continued, looking around. "I think we're ready. There!" Her pudgy forefinger struck at one of the buttons, and lights about the room began to lower. "I control the whole meal just by pressing the right one at the right time. Watch!" She struck at another one.

Along the center of the table now, under the gentled light, panels opened and great platters of fruit, candied apples and sugared grapes, halved melons filled with honeyed nuts, rose up before the guests.

"And wine!" said the Baroness, reaching down again.

Along the hundreds of feet of table, basins rose. Sparkling froth foamed the brim as the fountain mechanism began. Spurting liquid streamed.

"Fill your glass, dear. Drink up," prompted the Baroness, raising her own beneath a jet; the crystal splashed with purple.

On her right the Baron said: "The Arsenal seems to be all right. I'm alerting all the special projects. You're sure this sabotage attack is going on right now?"

"Either right now," she told him, "or within the next two or three minutes. It might be an explosion, or some major piece of equipment may fail."

"That doesn't leave me much to go on. Though communications has picked up your Babel-17. I've been alerted to how these attempts run."

"Try one of these, Captain Wong." The Baroness handed her a quartered mango which Rydra discovered, when she tasted it, had been marinated in Kirsch.

Nearly all the guests were seated now. She watched a platoon kid, named Mike, searching for his name-card halfway across the hall. And down the table length she saw the stranger who had stopped her on the spiral stair hurrying toward them behind the seated guests.

"The wine is not grape, but plum," the Baroness said. "A little heavy to start with, but so good with fruit. I'm particularly proud of the strawberries. The legumes are a hydroponicist's nightmare, you know, but this year we were able to get such lovely ones."

Mike found his seat and reached both hands into the fruit bowl. The stranger rounded the last loop of table. Calli was holding a goblet of wine in each hand, looking from one to the other, trying to determine the larger.

"I could be a tease," the Baroness said, "and bring out

the sherbets first. Or do you think I ought best go on to the caldo verde? The way I prepare it, it's very light. I can never decide——"

The stranger reached the Baron, leaned over his shoulder to watch the screen, and whispered something. The Baron turned to him, turned back slowly with both hands on the table—and fell forward! A trickle of blood wormed from beneath his face.

Rydra jerked back in her chair. Murder. A mosaic came together in her head, and when it was together, it said: murder. She leapt up.

The Baroness exhaled hoarse breath and rose, overturning her chair. She flapped her hands hysterically toward her husband and shook her head.

Rydra whirled to see the stranger snatch a vibra-gun from beneath his jacket. She yanked the Baroness out of the way. The shot was low and struck the console.

Once moved, the Baroness staggered to her husband and grasped him. Her breathy moan took voice and became a wail. The hulking form, like a blimp deflating, sank and pulled Felix Ver Dorco's body from the table, till she was kneeling on the floor, holding him in her arms, rocking him gently, screaming.

Guests had risen now; talking became roaring.

With the console smashed, along the table the fruit platters were pushed aside by emerging peacocks, cooked, dressed, and reassembled with sugared heads, tail feathers swaying. None of the clearing mechanisms were operating. Tureens of caldo verde crowded the wine basins till both overturned, flooding the table. Fruit rolled over the edge.

Through the voices, the vibra-gun hissed on her left, left again, then right. People ran from their chairs, blocked her view. She heard the gun once more and saw Dr. Crane double over, to be caught by a surprised neighbor as her bleached hair came undone and tumbled her face.

Spitted lambs rose to upset the peacocks. Feathers swept the floor. Wine fountains spurted the glistening amber skins which hissed and steamed. Food fell back into the opening and struck red heating coils. Rydra smelled burning.

She darted forward, caught the arm of the fat, black-bearded man. "Slug, get the kids out of here!"

"What do you think I'm doing, Captain?"

She darted away, came up against a length of table, and vaulted the steaming pit. The intricate, oriental dessert—sizzling bananas dipped first in honey then rolled to the plate over a ramp of crushed ice—was emerging as she sprang. The sparkling confections shot across the ramp and dropped to the floor, honey crystallized to glittering thorns. They rolled among the guests, cracked underfoot. People slipped and flailed and fell.

"Snazzy way to slide on a banana, huh, Captain?" commented Calli. "What's going on?"

"Get Mollya and Ron back to the ship!"

Urns rose now, struck the rotisserie arrangement, overturned, and grounds and boiling coffee splattered. A woman shrieked, clutching her scalded arm.

"This ain't no fun anymore," Calli said. "I'll round them up."

He started away as Slug hurried back the other way. "Slug, what's a bandicoot?" She caught his arm again.

"Vicious little animal. Marsupial, I think. Why?"

"That's right. I remember now. And thalassanemia?"

"Funny time to ask. Some sort of anemia."

"I know that. *What* sort? You're the medic on the ship."

"Let me see." He closed his eyes a moment. "I got all this once in a hypno-course. Yeah, I remember. It's hereditary, the Caucasian equivalent of sickle cell anemia, where the red blood cells collapse because the haptoglobins break down——"

"—and allow the hemoglobins to leak out and the cell gets crushed by osmotic pressure. I've figured it out. Get the hell out of here."

Puzzled, the Slug started toward the arch.

Rydra started after him, slipped in wine sherbet, and grabbed Brass, who now gleamed above her. "Take it easy, Ca'tain!"

"Out of here, baby," she demanded. "And fast."

"Ho' a ride?" Grinning, he hooked his arms at his hip, and she climbed to his back, clutching his sides with her knees and holding his shoulders. The great muscles that had defeated the Silver Dragon bunched beneath her, and he leapt, clearing the table and landing on all fours. Before the fanged, golden beast, guests scattered. They made for the arched door.

V

〜〜〜〜〜〜〜〜〜〜〜〜〜〜〜〜〜〜〜〜〜〜〜〜〜〜〜〜〜〜

Hysterical exhaustion frothed.

She smashed through it, into the *Rimbaud*'s cabin, and punched the intercom. "Slug, is every——"

"All present and accounted for, Captain,"

"The discorporate——"

"Safe aboard, all three."

Brass, panting, filled the entrance hatch behind her.

She switched to another channel, and a near musical sound filled the room. "Good. It's still going."

"That's it?" asked Brass.

She nodded. "Babel-17. It's been automatically transcribed so I can study it later. Anyway, here goes nothing." She threw a switch.

"What you doing?"

"I prerecorded some messages and I'm sending them out now. Maybe they'll get through." She stopped the first take and started a second. "I don't know it well, yet. I know a little, but not enough. I feel like someone at a performance of Shakespeare shouting catcalls in pidgin English."

An outside line signaled for her attention. "Captain Wong, this is Albert Ver Dorco." The voice was perturbed. "We've had a terrible catastrophe, and we're in total confusion here. I could not find you at my brother's, but flight clearance just told me you had requested immediate take off for hyperstasis jump."

"I requested nothing of the kind. I just wanted to get my

crew out of there. Have you found out what's going on?''

"But, Captain, they said you were in the process of clearing for flight. You have top priority, so I can't very well countermand your order. But I called to request that you please stay until this matter is cleared up, unless you are acting on some imformation that——''

"We're not taking off," Rydra said.

"We better not be," interjected Brass. "I'm not wired into the ship yet."

"Apparently your automatic James Bond ran berserk," Rydra told Ver Dorco.

". . . Bond?"

"A mythological reference. Forgive me. TW-55 flipped."

"Oh, yes. I know. It assassinated my brother, and four extremely important officials. It couldn't have picked out four more key figures if it had been planned."

"It was. TW-55 was sabotaged. And no, I don't know how. I suggest you contact General Forester back at——''

"Captain, flight clearance says you're still signaling for take off! I have no official authority here, but you must——''

"Slug! Are we taking off?"

"Why, yes. Didn't you just issue orders down here for emergency hyperstasis exit?''

"Brass isn't even at his station yet, you idiot!"

"But I just received clearance from you thirty seconds ago. Of course he's hooked in. I just spoke——''

Brass lumbered across the floor and bellowed into the microphone. "I'm standing right behind her, numbskull! What are you gonna do, dive into the middle of Bellatrix? Or maybe come out inside some nova? These things head for the biggest mass around when they drift!''

"But you just——''

A grinding started somewhere below them. And a sudden surge.

Over the loudspeaker from Albert Ver Dorco: "Captain Wong!''

Rydra shouted again, "Idiot, cut the stasis gen——''

But the generators were already whistling over the roar.

And surge again; she jerked against her hands holding the desk edge, saw Brass flail one claw in the air. And—

PART THREE

Jebel Tarik

Real, grimy, and exiled, he
eludes us.
I would show him books and bridges.
I would make a language we could all speak.
No blond fantasy
Mother has sent to plague us in the Spring,
he has his own bad dreams, needs work, gets drunk,
maybe would not have chosen to be beautiful.

—from *The Navigators*

You have imposed upon me a treaty of silence.

—from *The Song of Liadan*

1

‿‿‿

Abstract thoughts in a blue room: Nominative, genitive, elative, accusative one, accusative two, ablative, partitive, illative, instructive, abessive, adessive, inessive, essive, allative, translative, comitative. Sixteen cases to the Finnish noun. Odd, some languages get by with only singular and plural. The North American Indian languages even failed to distinguish number. Except Sioux, in which there was a plural only for animate objects. The blue room was round and warm and smooth. No way to say *warm* in French. There was only *hot* and *tepid*. If there's no word for it, how do you think about it? And, if there isn't the proper form, you don't have the how even if you have the words. Imagine, in Spanish having to assign a gender to every object: dog, table, tree, can-opener. Imagine, in Hungarian, not being able to assign a gender to anything: *he, she, it* all the same word. Thou art my friend, but you are my king; thus the distinctions of Elizabeth the First's English. But with some oriental languages, which all but dispense with gender and number, you are my friend, *you* are my parent, and YOU are my priest, and *YOU* are my king, and You are my servant, and *You* are my servant whom I'm going to fire tomorrow if *You* don't watch it, and YOU are my king whose policies I totally disagree with and have sawdust in YOUR head instead of brains, YOUR highness, and YOU may be my friend, but I'm still gonna smack YOU up side the head if YOU ever say that to me again: and who the hell are you anyway ... ?

What's your name? she thought in a round warm blue room.

Thoughts without a name in a blue room: Ursula, Priscilla, Barbara, Mary, Mona, and Natica: respectively, Bear, Old Lady, Chatterbox, Bitter, Monkey, and Buttock. Name. Names? What's in a name? What name am I in? In my father's father's land, his name would come first, Wong Rydra. In Mollya's home, I would not bear my father's name at all, but my mother's. Words are names for things. In Plato's time things were names for ideas—what better description of the Platonic Ideal? But were words names for things, or was that just a bit of semantic confusion? Words were symbols for *whole* categories of things, where a name was put to a single object: a name on something that requires a symbol jars, making humor. A symbol on something that takes a name jars, too: a memory that contained a torn window shade, his liquored breath, her outrage, and crumpled clothing wedged behind a chipped, cheap night table, "All right, *woman,* come here!" and she had whispered, with her hands achingly tight on the brass bar, "My *name* is *Rydra!*" An individual, a thing apart from its environment, and apart from all things in that environment; an individual was a type of thing for which symbols were inadequate, and so names were invented. I am invented. I am not a round warm blue room. I am someone in that room, I am—

Her lids had been half-closed on her eyeballs. She opened them and came up suddenly against a restraining web. It knocked her breath out, and she fell back, turning about to look at the room.

No.

She didn't "look at the room."

She *"something*ed at the *something.*" The first something was a tiny vocable that implied an immediate, but passive, perception that could be aural or olfactory as well as visual. The second something was three equally tiny phonemes that blended at different musical pitches: one, an indicator that fixed the size of the chamber at roughly twenty-five feet cubical, the second identifying the color and probable substance of the walls—some blue metal—while the third was at once a place holder for particles that should denote the room's function when she discovered it, and a sort of grammatical tag by which she could refer to the whole experience with only the one symbol for as long as she needed. All four sounds took less time on her tongue and in her mind than the one clumsy diphthong in *'room'*. Babel-17; she had felt it before with other languages, the opening, the widening, the mind forced to sudden growth. But this, this was like the sudden focusing of a lens blurry for years.

She sat up again. Function?

What was the room used for? She rose slowly, and the web caught her around the chest. Some sort of infirmary. She looked down at the—not 'webbing', but rather a three particle vowel differential, each particle of which defined one stress of the three-way tie, so that the weakest points in the mesh were identified when the total sound of the differential reached its lowest point. By breaking the threads at these points, she realized, the whole web would unravel. Had she flailed at it, and not named it in this new language, it would have been more than secure enough to hold her. The transition from 'memorized' to 'known' had taken place while she had been——

Where had she been? Anticipation, excitement, fear! She pulled her mind back into English. Thinking in Babel-17 was like suddenly seeing through water at the bottom of a well that a moment ago you thought had only gone down a few feet. She reeled with vertigo.

It took her a blink to register the others. Brass hung in the large hammock at the far wall—she saw the tines of one yellow claw over the rim. The two smaller hammocks on the other side must have been platoon kids. Above one edge she saw shiny black hair as a head turned in sleep: Carlos. She couldn't see the third. Curiosity made a small, unfriendly fist on something important in her lower abdomen.

Then the wall faded.

She had been about to try and fix herself, if not in place and hour, at least in some set of possibilities. With the fading wall, the attempt stopped. She watched.

It happened in the upper part of the wall to her left. It glowed, grew transparent, and a tongue of metal formed in the air, sloped gently toward her.

Three men:

The closest, at the ramp's head, had a face like brown

rock cut roughly and put together fast. He wore an outdated garment, the sort that had preceded contour capes. It automatically formed to the body, but was made of porous plastic and looked rather like armor. A black, deep piled material cloaked one shoulder and arm. His worn sandals were laced high on his calves. Tufts of fur beneath the thongs prevented chafing. His only cosmetisurgery was false silver hair and upswept metallic eyebrows. From one distended earlobe hung a thick silver ring. He touched his vibra-gun holster resting on his stomach as he looked from hammock to hammock.

The second man stepped in front. He was a slim, fantastic concoction of cosmetisurgical invention, sort of a griffin, sort of a monkey, sort of a sea horse: scales, feathers, claws, and beak had been grafted to a body she was sure had originally resembled a cat's. He crouched at the first man's side, squatting on surgically distended haunches, brushing his knuckles on the metal flooring. He glanced up as the first man absently reached down to scratch his head.

Rydra waited for them to speak. A word would release identification: Alliance or Invader. Her mind was ready to spring on whatever tongue they spoke, to extract what she knew of its thinking habits, tendencies toward logical ambiguities, absence or presence of verbal rigor, in whatever areas she might take advantage of—

The second man moved back and she saw the third who still stood at the rear. Taller, and more powerfully built than the others, he wore only a breech, was mildly round-shouldered. Grafted onto his wrists and heels were cocks' spurs—they were sometimes sported by the lower elements of the transport underworld, and bore the same significance as brass knuckles or blackjacks of centuries past. His head had been recently shaved and the hair had started back in a dark, Elektra brush. Around one knotty bicep was a band of red flesh, like a blood bruise or inflamed scar. The brand had become so common on characters in mystery novels five years back that now it had been nearly dropped as a hopeless cliché. It was a convict's mark from the penal caves of Titin. Something about him was brutal enough to make her glance away. Something was graceful enough to make her look back.

The two on the head of the ramp turned to the third. She

waited for words, to define, fix, identify. They looked at her, then walked into the wall. The ramp began to retract.

She pushed herself up. "Please," she called out. "Where are we?"

The silver-haired man said, "Jebel Tarik." The wall solidified.

Rydra looked down at the web (which was something else in another language) popped one cord, popped another. The tension gave, till it unraveled and she jumped to the floor. As she stood she saw the other platoon kid was Kile, who worked with Lizzy in Repair. Brass had started struggling. "Keep still a second." She began to pop cords.

"What did he say to you?" Brass wanted to know. "Was that his name, or was he telling you to lie down and shut u'?"

She shrugged and broke another. "Jebel, that's *mountain* in Old Moorish. Tarik's Mountain, maybe."

Brass sat up as the frayed string fell. "How do you do that?" he asked. "I pushed against the thing for ten minutes and it wouldn't give."

"Tell you some other time. Tarik could be somebody's name."

Brass looked back at the broken web, clawed behind one tufted ear, then shook his puzzled head and reared.

"At least they're not Invaders," Rydra said.

"Who says?"

"I doubt that many humans on the other side of the axis have even heard of Old Moorish. The Earthmen who migrated there all came from North and South America before Americasia was formed and Pan Africa swallowed up Europe. Besides, the Titin penal caves are inside Caesar."

"Oh yea," Brass said. "Him. But that don't mean one of its alumni has to be."

She looked at where the wall had opened. Grasping their situation seemed as futile as grasping that blue metal.

"What the hell ha''ened anyway?"

"We took off without a pilot," Rydra said. "I guess whoever broadcast in Babel-17 can also broadcast English."

"I don't think we took off without a 'ilot. Who did Slug talk to just before we shot? If we didn't have a 'ilot, we wouldn't be here. We'd be a grease s'ot on the nearest, biggest sun.''

"Probably whoever cracked those circuit boards." Rydra cast her mind into the past as the plaster of unconsciousness crumbled. "I guess the saboteur doesn't want to kill me. TW-55 could have picked me off as easily as he picked off the Baron."

"I wonder if the s'y on the shi' s'eaks Babel-17 too?"

Rydra nodded. "So do I."

Brass looked around. "Is this all there is? Where's the rest of the crew?"

"Sir, Ma'am?"

They turned.

Another opening in the wall. A skinny girl, with a green scarf binding back brown hair, held out a bowl.

"The master said you were about, so I brought this." Her eyes were dark and large, and the lids beat like bird wings. She gestured with the bowl.

Rydra responded to her openness, yet also detected a fear of strangers. But the thin fingers grasped surely on the bowl's edge. "You're kind to bring this."

The girl bowed slightly and smiled.

"You're frightened of us, I know," Rydra said. "You shouldn't be."

The fear was leaving; bony shoulders relaxed.

"What's your master's name?" Rydra asked.

"Tarik."

Rydra looked back and nodded to Brass.

"And we're in Tarik's Mountain?" She took the bowl from the girl. "How did we get here?"

"He hooked your ship up from the center of the Cygnus-42 nova just before your stasis generators failed this side of the jump."

Brass hissed, his substitute for a whistle. "No wonder we went unconscious. We did some fast drifting."

The thought pulled the plug from Rydra's stomach. "Then we did drift into a nova area. Maybe we didn't have a pilot after all."

Brass removed the white napkin from the bowl. "Have some chicken, Ca'tain." It was roasted and still hot.

"In a minute," she said. "I have to think about that one some more." She turned back to the girl. "Tarik's Mountain is a ship, then. And we're on it?"

The girl put her hands behind her back and nodded. "And it's a good ship, too."

"I'm sure you don't take passengers. What cargo do you haul?"

She had asked the wrong question. Fear again; not a personal distrust of strangers, something formal and pervasive. "We carry no cargo, ma'am." Then she blurted, "I'm not supposed to talk to you none. You have to speak with Tarik." She backed into the wall.

"Brass," Rydra said, turning and scratching her head, "there're no space-pirates any more, are there?"

"There haven't been any hi-jacks on transport ships for seventy years."

"That's what I thought. So what sort of ship are we on?"

"Beats me." Then the burnished planes of his cheeks shifted in the blue light. Silken brows pulled down over the deep disks of his eyes. *"Hooked* the *Rimbaud* out of the Cygnus-42? I guess I know why they call it Tarik's Mountain. This thing must be big as a damn battleshi'."

"If it is a warship, Tarik doesn't look like any stellarman I ever saw."

"And they don't allow ex-convicts in the army, anyway. What do you think we've stumbled on, Ca'tain?"

She took a drumstick from the bowl. "I guess we wait till we speak to Tarik." There was movement in the other hammocks. "I hope the kids are all right. Why didn't I ask that girl if the rest of the crew was aboard?" She strode to Carlos' hammock. "How do *you* feel this morning?" she asked brightly. For the first time she saw the snaps that held the webbing to the underside of the sling.

"My head," Carlos said, grinning. "I got a hangover, I think."

"Not with that leer on your face. What do you know about hangovers, anyway?" The snaps took three times as long to undo as breaking the net.

"The wine," Carlos said, "at the party. I had a lot. Hey, what happened?"

"Tell you when I find out. Upsy-daisy." She tipped the hammock and he rolled to his feet.

Carlos pushed the hair out of his eyes. "Where's everybody else?"

"Kile's over there. That's all of us in this room."

Brass had freed Kile, who sat on the hammock edge now, trying to put his knuckles up his nose.

"Hey, baby," Carlos said. "You all right?"

Kile ran his toes up and down his Achilles tendon, yawned, and said something unintelligible at the same time.

"You did not," Carlos said, "because I checked it just as soon as I got in."

Oh well, she thought, there were still languages left at which she might gain more fluency.

Kile was scratching his elbow now. Suddenly he stuck his tongue in the corner of his mouth and looked up.

So did Rydra.

The ramp was extending from the wall again. This time it joined the floor.

"Will you come with me, Rydra Wong?"

Tarik, holstered and silver-haired, stood in the dark opening.

"The rest of my crew," Rydra said, "are they all right?"

"They are all in other wards. If you wish to see them——"

"Are they all right?"

Tarik nodded.

Rydra thumped Carlos on his head. "I'll see you later," she whispered.

The commons was arched and balconied, the walls dull as rock. The expanses were hung with green and crimson zodiac signs or representations of battles. And the stars—at first, she thought the light flecked void beyond the gallery columns was an actual view-port; but it was only a great hundred-foot long projection of the night beyond their ship.

Men and women sat and talked around wooden tables, or lounged by the walls. Down a broad set of steps was a wide counter filled with food and pitchers. The opening hung with pots, pans, and platters, and behind it she saw the aluminium and white recess of the galley where aproned men and women prepared dinner.

The company turned when they entered. Those nearest touched their foreheads in salute. She followed Tarik to the raised steps and walked to the cushioned benches at the top.

The griffin man came scurrying up. "Master, this is she?" Tarik turned to Rydra, his rocky face softening. "This is my amusement, my distraction, my ease of ire, Captain Wong. In him I keep the sense of humor that all around will tell you I lack. Hey, Klik, leap up and straighten the seats for conference."

The feathered head ducked brightly, black eye winking, and Klik whacked the cushions puffy. A moment later Tarik and Rydra sank into them.

"Tarik," asked Rydra, "what route does your ship run?"

"We stay in the Specelli Snap." He pushed his cape back from his three-knobbed shoulder. "What was your original position before you were caught up in the noval tide?"

"We . . . took off from the War Yards at Armsedge."

Tarik nodded. "You are fortunate. Most shadow-ships would have left you to emerge in the nova when your generators gave out. It would have been a rather final discorporation."

"I guess so." Rydra felt her stomach sink at the memory. Then she asked, "Shadow-ships?"

"Yes. That's Jebel Tarik."

"I'm afraid I don't know what a shadow-ship is."

Tarik laughed, a soft, rough sound in the back of his throat. "Perhaps it's just as well. I hope you never have occasion to wish I had not told you."

"Go ahead," Rydra said. "I'm listening."

"The Specelli Snap is radio-dense. A ship, even a mountain like Tarik, over any long-range is undetectable. It also runs across the stasis side of Cancer."

"That galaxy lies under the Invaders," Rydra said, with conditioned apprehension.

"The Snap is the boundary along Cancer's edge. We . . .

patrol the area and keep the Invader ships . . . in their place.''

Rydra watched the hesitation in his face. "But not officially?"

Again he laughed. "How could we, Captain Wong?" He stroked a ruff of feathers between Klik's shoulder blades. The jester arched his back. "Even official warships cannot receive their orders and directions in the Snap because of the radio-density. So Administrative Alliance Headquarters is lenient with us. We do our job well; they look the other way. They cannot give us orders; neither can they supply us with weapons or provisions. Therefore we ignore certain salvage conventions and capture regulations. Stellarmen call us looters." He searched her for a reaction. "We are staunch defenders of the Alliance, Captain Wong, but . . ." He raised his hand, made a fist and brought the fist against his belly. "But if we are hungry, and no Invader ship has come by—well, we take what comes past.''

"I see," Rydra said. "Do I understand I am taken?" She recalled the Baron, the rapaciousness implicit in his lean figure.

Tarik's fingers opened on his stomach. "Do I look hungry?''

Rydra grinned. "You look very well fed.''

He nodded. "This has been a prosperous month. Were it not, we would not be sitting together so amiably. You are our guests for now.''

"Then you will help us repair the burned-out generators?"

Tarik raised his hand again, signaling her to halt. ". . . for now," he repeated.

Rydra had moved forward on her seat; she sat back again.

Tarik spoke to Klik: "Bring the books." The jester stepped quickly away and delved into a stand beside the couches. "We live dangerously," Tarik went on. "Perhaps that is why we live well. We are civilized—when we have time. The name of your ship convinced me to heed the Butcher's suggestion to hook you out. Here on the *rim* we are seldom visited by a *Bard*." Rydra smiled as politely as she could at the pun.

Klik returned with three volumes. The covers were black with silver edging. Tarik held them up. "My favorite is the second. I was particularly struck with the long narrative *Exiles in Mist*. You tell me you have never heard of shadow-ships, yet you do know the feelings 'that loop night to bind you'—that is the line, isn't it? I confess, your third book I do not understand. But there are many references and humorous allusions to current events. We here are out of the main-stream." He shrugged. "We . . . salvaged the first from the collection of the captain of an Invader transport tramp that had wandered off course. The second—well, it came from an Alliance destroyer. I believe there's an inscription on the inside cover." He opened it and read: 'For Joey on the first flight; she says so well what I have always wanted to say so much. With so much, much love, Lenia.' " He closed the cover. "Touching. The third I only acquired a month ago. I will read it several times more before I speak of it to you again. I am astounded at the coincidence that brings us together." He placed the books in his lap. "How long has the third one been out?"

"A little under a year."

"There is a fourth?"

She shook her head.

"May I inquire what literary work you are engaged in now?"

"Now, nothing. I've done some short poems that my publisher wants to put out in a collection, but I want to wait until I have another large, sustained work to balance them."

Tarik nodded. "I see. But your reticence deprives us of great pleasure. Should you be moved to write, I will be honored. At meals we have music, some dramatic or comic entertainment, directed by clever Klik. If you would give us prologue or epilogue with what fancy you choose, you will have an appreciative audience." He extended his brown, hard hand. Appreciation is not a warm feeling, Rydra realized, but cool, and makes your back relax at the same time that you smile. She took his hand.

"Thank you, Tarik," she said.

"I thank you," Tarik returned. "Having your good will, I shall release your crew. They are free to wander Jebel as my own men are." His brown gaze shifted and she released his hand. "The Butcher." He nodded and she turned.

The convict who had been with him on the ramp now stood on the step below.

"What was that blot that lay toward Rigel?" Tarik asked.

"Alliance running, Invader tracking."

Tarik's face furrowed, then relaxed. "No, let them both pass. We eat well enough this month. Why upset our guests with violence? This is Rydra——"

The Butcher brought his right fist cracking into his left palm. People below turned. She jumped at the sound, and with her eyes she tried to strip meaning from the faintly quivering muscles, the fixed, full-lipped face: lancing but inarticulate hostility; an outrage at stillness, a fear of motion halted, safety in silence furious with movement—

Now Tarik spoke again, voice lower, slower, harsh. "You're right. But what whole man is not of two minds on any matter of moment, eh, Captain Wong?" He rose. "Butcher, pull us closer to their trajectory. Are they an hour out? Good. We will watch a while, then trounce"—he paused and smiled at Rydra—"the Invaders."

The Butcher's hands came apart, and Rydra saw relief (or release) ease his arms. He breathed again.

"Ready Jebel, and I will escort our guest to where she may watch."

Without response, the Butcher strode to the bottom of the steps. Those nearest had overheard, and the information saturated the room. Men and women rose from their benches. One upset his drinking horn. Rydra saw the girl who had served them in the infirmary run with a towel to sop the drink.

At the head of the gallery stairs she looked over the balcony rail at the commons below, empty now.

"Come." Tarik motioned her through the columns toward the darkness and the stars. "The Alliance ship is coming through there." He pointed to a bluish cloud. "We have equipment that can penetrate a good deal of this mist, but I doubt the Alliance ship even knows it is being tracked by Invaders." He moved to a desk and pressed a raised disk. Two dots of light flashed in the mist. "Red for Invaders," Tarik explained. "Blue for Alliance. Our little spider-boats will be yellow. You can follow the progress of the encounter from here. All our sensory evaluations and sensory perceptors and navigators remain on Jebel and direct the major strategy by remote control, so formations remain consistent. But within a limited range, each spider-boat battles for itself. It's fine sport for the men."

"What sort of ships are these you hunt?" She was amused that the slight archaic tone that perfused Tarik's speech had begun to affect hers.

"The Alliance ship is a military supply ship. The Invader is tracking her with a small destroyer."

"How far apart are they?"

"They should engage each other in about twenty minutes."

"And you are going to wait sixty minutes before you . . . trounce the Invaders?"

Tarik smiled. "A supply ship doesn't have much chance against a destroyer."

"I know." She could see him waiting, behind the smile, for her to object. She looked for objection in herself, but it was blocked by a clot of tiny singing sounds on an area of her tongue smaller than a coin: Babel-17. They defined a concept of exactingly necessary expedient curiosity that became in any other language a clumsy string of polysyllables. "I've never watched a stellar skirmish," she said.

"I would have you come in my flagship, but I know that the little danger there is, is danger enough. From here you can follow the whole battle much more clearly."

Excitement caught her up. "I'd like to go with you." She hoped he might change his mind.

"Stay here," Tarik said. "The Butcher rides with me this time. Here's a sensory helmet if you wish to view the stasis currents. Though with combat weapons, there's so much electromagnetic confusion I doubt that even a reduction would mean much." A run of lights flashed across the desk top. "Excuse me. I go to review my men and check my cruiser." He bowed shortly. "Your crew has revived. They will be directed up here and you may explain their status as my guests however you see fit.''

As Tarik walked to the steps, she looked back to the glittering view-screen and a few moments later thought: What an amazing graveyard they have on this hulk; it must take fifty discorporate souls to do all the sensory reading for Tarik and its spider-boats—in Basque again. She looked back and saw the translucent shapes of her Eye, Ear, and Nose across the gallery.

"Am I glad to see you!" she said. "I didn't know whether Tarik had discorporate facilities!"

"Does it!" Came the Basque response. "We'll take you on a trip through the Underworld here. Captain. They treat you like the lords of Hades.''

From the speaker came Tarik's voice: "Hear this: the strategy is Asylum. Asylum. Repeat a third time, Asylum. Inmates gather to face Caesar. Psychotics ready at the K-ward gate. Neurotics gather before the R-ward gate. Criminally insane prepare for discharge at the T-ward gate. All right, drop your straitjackets.''

At the bottom of the hundred-foot screen appeared three groups of yellow lights—the three groups of spider-boats that would attack the Invader once it had overtaken the Alliance supply ship. "Neurotics advance. Maintain contact to avoid separation anxiety.'' The middle group began to move slowly forward. On the under-speakers now, punctuated with static, Rydra heard lower voices as the men began to report back to the Navigators on Jebel:

Keep us on course, now, Kippi, and don't get shook.

Sure thing. Hawk, will you get your reports back on time?

Ease up. My caper-unit keeps sticking.

Who told you to leave without getting overhauled?

Come on, ladies, be kind to us for once.

Hey, Pigfoot, you want to be lobbed in high or low?

Low, hard, and fast. Don't hang me up.

You just get your reports in, honeybunch.

Over the main speaker Tarik said: "The Hunter and the Hunted have engaged———'' The red light and the blue light started blinking on the screen. Calli, Ron, and Mollya came from the head of the steps.

"What's going . . . ?" Calli started, but silenced at a gesture from Rydra.

"That red light's an Invader ship. We're attacking it in a few moments. We're the yellow lights down here." She left the explanation at that.

"Good luck, us," Mollya said, dryly.

In five minutes there was only the red light left. By now Brass had clanked up the steps to join them. Tarik announced: "The Hunter has become the Hunted. Let the criminally-insane schiz out." The yellow group on the left started forward, spreading apart.

That Invader looks pretty big, there, Hawk.

Don't worry. She'll run us out tough.

Hell. I don't like hard work. Got my reports yet?

Right-o. Pigfoot, stop jamming Ladybird's beam!

Okay, okay, okay. Did anyone check out tractor's nine and ten?

You think of everything at the right time, don't you?

Just curious. Don't the spiral look pretty back there?

"Neurotics proceed with delusions of grandeur. Napoleon Bonaparte take the lead. Jesus Christ bring up the rear." The ships on the right moved forward now in diamond formation. "Stimulate severe depression, non-comunicative, with repressed hostility."

Behind her she heard young voices. The Slug herded the platoon up the steps. Arriving, they quieted before the vast representation of night. The explanation of the battle filtered back among the children in whispers.

"Commence the first psychotic episode." Yellow lights ran forward into the darkness.

The Invader must have spotted them at last, for it began to move away. The gross bulk could not outrun the spiders unless it jumped currents. And there was not enough leeway to check out. The three groups of yellow lights—formed, unformed, and dispersed—drew closer. After three minutes, the Invader stopped running. On the screen there was a sudden shower of red lights. It had released its own barrage of cruisers which also separated into the three standard attack groups.

"The life goal has become dispersed," Tarik announced. "Do not become despondent."

Come on, let them babies try and get us!
Remember, Kippi, low, fast, and hard!
If we scare them into offensive, we got it made!

"Prepare to penetrate hostile defense mechanisms. All right. Administer medication!"

The formation of the Invader's cruiser, however, was not offensive. A third of them fanned horizontally across the stars, the second group combed over their paths at a sixty degree angle, and the third group moved through another rotation of sixty degrees so they made a three-way defensive grid before the mother ship. The red cruisers doubled back on themselves at the end of their run and swept out again, netting the space before the Invader with small ships.

"Take heed. The enemy has tightened its defense mechanisms."

What's with this new formation, anyway?
We'll get through. You worried——?
Static chopped out one speaker.
Damn, they strafed Pigfoot!
Pull me back, Kippi. There you go. Pigfoot?
Did you see how they got him? Hey, let's go.

"Administer active therapy to the right. Be as directive as you can. Let the center enjoy the pleasure principle. And the left go hang."

Rydra watched, fascinated, as yellow lights engaged the red which still swept hynotically along their grid, net, web—

Webbing! The picture flipped over in her mind and the other side had all the missing lines. The grid was identical to the three-way web she had torn off the hammock hours before, with the added factor of timing, because the strands were the paths of ships, not strings; but it worked the same way. She snatched up a microphone from the desk. "Tarik!" The word took forever to slide from post-dental, to palital stop, beside the sounds that danced through her brain now. She barked at the Navigators beside her: "Calli, Mollya, Ron, coordinate the battle area for me."

"Huh?" said Calli. "All right." He began to adjust the dial of the stellarimeter in his palm. Slow motion, she thought. They're all moving in slow motion. She knew what should be done, must be done, and watched the situation changing.

"Rydra Wong, Tarik is occupied," came the Butcher's gravelly voice.

Calli said over his shoulder: "Coordinates 3-B, 41-F, and 9-K. Pretty quick, huh?"

It seemed she'd asked for them an hour ago. "Butcher, did you get those coordinates down? Now look, in . . . twenty-seven seconds a cruiser will pass through——" She gave a three number location. "Hit it with your closest neurotics." While she waited for a response, she saw where the next hit must lie, "Forty seconds off, starting—eight, nine, ten, *now,* an Invader cruiser will pass through——" another location. "—Get it with whatever's nearest. Is the first ship out of commission?"

"Yes, Captain Wong."

Her amazement and relief took no breath. At least the Butcher was listening; she gave the coordinates of three more ships in the 'web.' "Now hit them straight on and watch things fall apart!"

As she put the microphone down, Tarik's voice announced: "Advance for group therapy!"

The yellow spider-boats surged into the darkness again. Where there should have been Invaders, there were empty holes; where there should have been reinforcements, there was confusion. First one, then another, red cruiser fled its position.

The yellow lights were through. The flare of a vibra-blast shattered the red glow of the Invader ship.

Ratt jumped up and down, holding on to Carlos' and Flop's shoulder. "Hey, we won!" the midget Reconversion Engineer cried out. "We won!"

The platoon murmured to one another. Rydra felt oddly far away. They talked so slowly, taking such impossible time to say what could be so quickly delineated by a few simple—

"Are you all right, Ca'tain?" Brass put his yellow paw around her shoulder.

She tried to speak, but it came out a grunt. She staggered against his arm.

The Slug had turned now. "You feel well?" he asked.

"Sssssss," and realized that she didn't know how to say it in Babel-17. Her mouth bit into the shape and feel of English. "Sick," she said. "Jesus, I feel sick."

As she said it, the dizziness passed.

"Maybe you better lie down?" suggested the Slug.

She shook her head. The tenseness in her shoulders and back, the nausea was leaving. "No. I'm all right. I just got a little too excited, I think."

"Sit down a minute," Brass said, letting her lean against the desk. But she pushed herself upright.

"Really, I'm O.K. now." She took a deep breath. "See?" She pulled from under Brass' arm. "I'm going to take a walk. I'll feel better then." Still unsteady, she started away. She felt their wariness to let her go, but suddenly she wanted to be somewhere else. She continued across the gallery floor.

Her breath got back to normal when she reached the upper levels. Then, from six different directions, hallways joined with rolling ramps to descend toward other floors. She stopped, confused over which way to take, then turned at a sound.

A group of Tarik's crew was crossing the corridor. The Butcher, among them, paused to lean against the door frame. He grinned at her, seeing her confusion, and pointed to the right. She didn't feel like speaking, so merely smiled and touched her forehead in salute. As she started toward the righthand ramp, the meaning behind his grin surprised her. There was the pride of their joint success (which had allowed her to remain silent), yes; and a direct pleasure at offering her his wordless aid. But that was all. The expected amusement over someone who had lost her way was missing. Its presence would not have annoyed her. But its absence charmed. Also it fit the angular brutality she had watched before, as well as the great animal grace of him.

She was still smiling when she reached the commons.

II

~~~~~~

She leaned on the catwalk railing to watch the activity in the cradle of the loading dock curving below. "Slug, take the kids down to give a hand with those carter-winches. Tarik said they could use some help."

Slug guided the platoon to the chair-lift that dropped into Jebel's pit:

". . . all right, when you get down there, go over to that man in the red shirt and ask him to put you to work. Yeah, work. Don't look so surprised, stupid. Kile, strap yourself in, will you. It's two hundred and fifty feet down and a little hard on your head if you fall. Hey, you two, cut it out. I know he started first. Just get down there and be constructive . . ."

Rydra watched machinery, organic supplies—Alliance and Invader—handed in from the dismantling crews that worked over the ruins of the two ships, and their swarm of cruisers; the stacked, sorted crates were piled along the loading area.

"We'll be jettisonning the cruiser ships shortly. I'm afraid *Rimbaud* will have to go, too. Is there anything you'd like to salvage before we dump it, Captain?" She turned at Tarik's voice.

"There are some important papers and recordings I have to get. I'll leave my platoon here and take my officers with me."

"Very well." Tarik joined her at the railing. "As soon as we finish here, I'll send a work-crew with you in case there's anything large you want to bring back."

119

"That won't be . . ." she began. "Oh, I see. You need fuel, don't you."

Tarik nodded. "And stasis components, also spare parts for our own spider-boats. We will not touch the *Rimbaud* until you have finished with it."

"I see. I guess that's only fair."

"I'm impressed," Tarik went on to change the subject, "with your method of breaking the Invader's defense net. That particular formation has always given us some trouble. The Butcher tells me you tore it apart in less than five minutes, and we only lost one spider. That's a record. I didn't know you were a master strategist as well as a poet. You have many talents. It is lucky that Butcher took your call, though. I would not have had sense enough to follow your instructions just on the spur of the moment. Had the results not been so praiseworthy, I would have been put out with him. But then his decisions have never yet brought me less than profit." He looked across the pit.

On a suspended platform in the center, the ex-convict lounged, silent overseer to the operations below.

"He's a curious man," Rydra said. "What was he in prison for?"

"I have never asked," Tarik said, raising his chin. "He has never told me. There are many curious persons on Jebel. And privacy is important in so small a space. Oh, yes. In a month's time you will learn how tiny the Mountain is."

"I forgot myself," Rydra apologized. "I shouldn't have inquired."

An entire foresection of a blasted Invader's cruiser was being dragged through the funnel on a twenty-foot wide, pronged conveyor. Dismantlers swarmed up the side with bolt punches and laser spots. Gig-cranes caught on the smooth hull and began to turn it slowly.

A workman at the port-disk suddenly cried out and swung hastily aside. His tools clattered down the bulkhead. The port-disk swung up and a figure in a silver skin suit dropped the twenty-five feet to the conveyor belt, rolled between two prongs, regained footing, leaped down the next ten-foot drop to the floor, and ran. The hood slipped from her head to release shoulder-length brown hair which swung wildly as she changed her course to avoid a trundling sludge. She moved fast, yet with a certain awkwardness. Then Rydra recognized that what she had taken for paunchiness in the fleeing Invader was at least a seven months' pregnancy. A mechanic flung a wrench at her, but she dodged so that it deflected off her hip. She was running toward an open space between the stacked supplies.

Then the air was cut by a vibrant hiss: the Invader stopped, sat down hard on the floor as the hiss repeated; she pitched to the side, kicked out one leg, kicked again.

On the tower, the Butcher put his vibra-gun back in the holster.

"That was unnecessary," Tarik said, with shocking softness.

"Couldn't we have . . ." and there seemed to be nothing to suggest. On Tarik's face was pain and curiosity. The pain, she realized, was not at the double death on the deck below, but the chagrin of a gentleman caught at something ugly. His curiosity was at her reaction. And it might be worth her life to react to the twisting in her stomach. She watched him preparing to speak: he was going to say—and so she said it for him—: "They will use pregnant women as pilots on fighting ships. Their reflexes are faster." She watched for him to relax, saw the relaxation begin.

The Butcher was already stepping from the chair-lift onto the catwalk. He came toward them, banging his fist against his corded thigh with impatience. "They should ray everything before they take it on. They won't listen. Second time in two months now." He grunted.

Below, Jebel's men and her platoon mingled over the body.

"They will next time." Tarik's voice was still soft and cool. "Butcher, you seemed to have pricked Captain Wong's interest. She was wondering what sort of a fellow you were, and I really couldn't tell her. Perhaps you can explain why you had to——"

"Tarik," Rydra said. Her eyes, seeking him, snagged on the Butcher's dark gaze. "I'd like to go to my ship now and see to it before you start salvaging."

Tarik exhaled the rest of the breath he'd held since the hiss of the vibra-gun. "Of course."

"No, not a monster, Brass." She unlocked the door to the captain's cabin of the *Rimbaud* and stepped through. "Just expedient. It's just like . . ." And she said a lot more to him till his fang-distended mouth sneered and he shook his head.

"Talk to me in English, Ca'tain. I don't understand you."

She took the dictionary from the console and placed it on top of the charts. "I'm sorry," she said. "This stuff is wicked. Once you learn it, it makes everything so easy. Get those tapes out of the playback. I want to run through them again."

"What are they?" Brass brought them over.

"Transcriptions of the last Babel-17 dialogues at the War Yards just before we took off." She put them on the spindle and started the first playing.

A melodious torrent rippled through the room, caught her up in ten and twenty second bursts she could understand. The plot to undermine TW-55 was delineated with hallucinatory vividness. When she reached a section she could not understand, she was left shaking against the wall of non-communication. While she listened, while she understood, she moved through psychedelic perceptions. When understanding left, her breath left her lungs with shock, and she had to blink, shake her head, once accidentally bit her tongue, before she was free again to comprehend.

"Captain Wong?"

It was Ron. She turned her head, aching slightly now, to face him.

"Captain Wong, I don't want to disturb you."

"That's all right," she said. "What is it?"

"I found this in the Pilot's Den." He held up a small spool of tape.

Brass was still standing by the door. "What was it doing in my part of the shi'?"

Ron's features fought with each other for an expression. "I just played it back with Slug. It's Captain Wong's—or somebody's—request to Flight Clearance back at the War Yards for take off, and the all clear signal to Slug to get ready to blast.''

"I see," Rydra said. She took the spool. Then she frowned. "This reel is from my cabin. I use the three-lobed spools I brought with me from the University. All the other machines on the ship are supplied with four-lobed ones. That tape came from this machine here.''

"So," Brass said, "a''arently somebody snuck in and made it when you were out.''

"When I'm out, this place is locked so tight a discorporate flea couldn't crawl under the door." She shook her head. "I don't like this. I don't know where I'll be fouled up next. Well"—she stood up—"at least I know what I have to do about Babel-17 now.''

"What's that?" Brass asked. Slug had come to the door and was looking over Ron's flowered shoulder.

Rydra looked over the crew. Discomfort or distrust, which was worst? "I really can't tell you now, can I?" she said. "It's that simple." She walked to the door. "I wish I could. But it would be a little silly after this whole business.''

"But I would rather speak to Tarik!''

Klik ruffled his feathers and shrugged. "Lady, I would honor your desire above all others' on the mountain, save Tarik's. And it is Tarik's desire that you now counter. He wishes not to be disturbed. He is plotting Jebel's destination over the next time-cycle. He must judge the currents carefully, and weigh even the weights of the stars about us. It is an arduous task, and——''

"Then where's the Butcher? I'll ask him, but I would prefer to talk directly with——''

The jester pointed with a green talon. "He is in the biology theatre. Go down through the commons and take the first lift to level twelve. It is directly to your left.''

"Thank you." She headed toward the gallery steps.

At the top of the lift she found the huge iris door, and pressed the entrance disk. Leaves folded, and she blinked in green light.

His round head and mildly humped shoulders were silhouetted before a bubbling tank in which a tiny figure floated: the spray of bubbles that rose about the form deflated on the feet, caught in the crossed curved hands like sparks, frothed the bent head, and foamed in the brush of birth-hair that swirled up in the miniature currents.

The Butcher turned, saw her, and said, "It died." He nodded with vigorous belligerence. "It was alive until five minutes ago. Seven and a half months. It should have lived. It was strong enough!" His left fist cracked against his right palm, as she had seen him do in the commons. Shaking muscles stilled. He thumbed toward an operating table where the Invader's body lay—sectioned. "Badly hurt before she got out. Internal organs messed up. A lot of abdominal necrosis all the way through." He turned his hand so the thumb now pointed over his shoulder to the drifting homunculus, and the gesture that had seemed rough took on an economical grace. "Still—it should have lived."

He switched off the light in the tank and the bubbles ceased. He stepped from behind the laboratory table. "What the Lady want?"

"Tarik is planning Jebel's route for the next months. Could you ask him . . ." She stopped. Then she asked, "Why."

Ron's muscles, she thought, were living cords that snapped and sang out their messages. On this man, muscles were shields to hold the world out, the man in. And something inside was leaping up again and again, striking the shield from behind. The scored belly shifted, the chest contracted over a let breath; the brow smoothed, then creased again.

"Why?" she repeated. "Why did you try to save the child?"

He twisted his face for answer, and his left hand circled the convict's mark on his other bicep as though it had started to sting. Then he gave up with disgust. "Died. No good any more. What the Lady want?"

What leaped and leaped retreated now, and so did she. "I want to know if Tarik will take me to Administrative Alliance Headquarters. I have to deliver some important information concerning the Invasion. My pilot tells me the Specelli Snap runs within ten hyperstatic units, which a spider-boat could make, so Jebel could remain in radio-dense space all the way. If Tarik will escort me to Headquarters, I will guarantee his protection and a safe return to the denser part of the Snap."

He eyed her. "All the way down the Dragon's Tongue?"

"Yes. That's what Brass told me the tip of the Snap was called."

"Protection guaranteed?"

"That's right. I'll show you my credentials from General Forester of the Alliance if you . . ."

But he waved for her silence. "Tarik." He spoke into the wall intercom.

The speaker was directional so she couldn't hear the answer.

"Make Jebel go down the Dragon's Tongue during the first cycle."

There was either questioning or objection.

"Go down the Tongue and it'll be good."

He nodded to the unintelligible whisper, then said, "It died," and switched off. "All right. Tarik will take Jebel to Headquarters."

Amazement undercut her initial disbelief. It was an amazement she would have felt before when he responded so unquestioningly to her plan to destroy the Invader's defense, had not Babel-17 precluded such feelings. "Well, thanks," she began, "but you haven't even asked me . . ." Then she decided to phrase the whole thing another way.

But the Butcher made a fist:

"Knowing what ships to destroy, and ships are destroyed." He banged his fist against his chest. "Now to go down the Dragon's Tongue, Jebel go down the Dragon's Tongue." He banged his chest again.

She wanted to question, but looked at the dead fetus turning in dark liquid behind him and said instead, "Thank you, Butcher." As she stepped through the iris door, she mulled over what he had said to her, trying to frame some explanation of his actions. Even the rough way in which his words fell—

His *words!*
It struck her at once, and she hurried down the corridor.

III

~~~~~~

"Brass, he can't say 'I'!" She leaned across the table, surprised curiosity impelling her excitement.

The pilot locked his claws around his drinking horn. The wooden tables across the commons were being set up for the evening meal.

"Me, my, mine, myself. I don't think he can say any of those either. Or think them. I wonder where the hell he's from."

"You know any language where there's no word for 'I'?"

"I can think of a couple where it isn't used often, but no one that doesn't even have the concept, if only hanging around in a verb ending."

"Which all means what?"

"A strange man with a strange way of thinking. I don't know why, but he's aligned himself with me, sort of my ally on this trip and a go-between with Tarik. I'd like to understand, so I won't hurt him."

She looked around the commons at the bustle of preparation. The girl who had brought them chicken was glancing at her now, wondering, still afraid, fear melting to curiosity which brought her two tables nearer, then curiosity evaporating to indifference, and she was off for more spoons from the wall drawer.

She wondered what would happen if she translated her perceptions of people's movement and muscle tics into Babel-17. It was not only a language, she understood now, but a flexible matrix of analytical possibilities where the same 'word' defined the stresses in a webbing of medical bandage, or a defensive grid of spaceships. What would it do with the tensions and yearnings in a human face? Perhaps the flicker of eyelids and fingers would become mathematics, without meaning. Or perhaps— While she thought, her mind changed gears into the headlong compactness of Babel-17. And she swept her eyes around the—voices.

Expanding and defining through one another, not the voices themselves, but the minds making the voices, braiding with one another, so that the man entering the hall now she knew to be the grieving brother *She sat in the great commons while men and women filed in for the evening meal, and was aware of so much more.* of Pigfoot, and the girl who'd served them was in love, so in love with the dead youth from the discorporate sector who tickled her dreams turning about the general hunger, a belly beast with teeth in one man, a lazy pool in another, now the familiar rush of adolescent confusion as the *Rimbaud*'s platoon came pummeling in, driven by the deep concern of Slug, and further over amidst ebullience, hunger, and love, a *fear!* It gonged in the hall, flashed red in the indigo tide, and she searched for Tarik or the Butcher because their names were in the fear, but found neither in the room; instead, a thin man named Geoffry Cord in whose brain crossed wires sparked and sputtered *Make death with the knife I have sheathed to my leg,* and again *With my steel tongue make me a place in an eyrie high on Jebel,* and the minds about him, groping and hungering, *They set her place, brought first a flagon, then bread, which she saw and smiled at but was seeing so much else.* mumbling over humor and hurt, loving a little and groping for more, all crosshatched with relaxation one way at the coming meal, and in others anticipation at what clever Klik would present that evening, the minds of the actors of the pantomime keyed to performance while they perused the spectators whom, at an earlier hour, they had worked and slept with, one elderly navigator with a geometrical head hurrying to give the girl, who was to play in the play at being in love, a silver clasp he had melted and scribed himself to see if she would play at loving him, yet through all this her mind circled back to the alarm of Geoffry Cord, *I must act this evening as the actors close,* and unable to focus on anything but his urgency, she watched him roil and ravel through his plotting, to hurry forward when the pantomime began as if he wanted to get a closer look as many would do, slip beside the table where Tarik would be sitting, then blade between Tarik's ribs with his serpent fang, grooved metal ran with paralytic poison, then chomp down on his hollow tooth that was filled with hypnotic drugs so that when he was taken prisoner they would think he

Around her people were sitting, relaxing, while the serving people hurried to the food counter where the roasts and fried fruit steamed.

was under somebody else's control, and at last he would release a wild story, implanted below the level of the hypnotics by many painful hours under the personafix, that he was under the Butcher's control; then somehow he would contrive to be alone with the Butcher and bite the Butcher's hand or wrist or leg, injecting the same hypnotic drugs that poisoned his own mouth and rend the hulking convict helpless, and he would control him, and when the Butcher ultimately became Jebel's ruler after the assassination, Geoffry Cord would become the Butcher's lieutenant as the Butcher was now Tarik's, and when Tarik's Jebel was the Butcher's Jebel, Geoffry would control the Butcher the same way he suspected the Butcher controlled Tarik, and there would be a reign of harshness and all strangers expelled from the berg to death by vacuum, and they would fall mightily on all ships, Invader, Alliance, or Shadow in the Snap, and Rydra tore her mind from his and swept the brief surface of

She saw so much more than the little demonic jester on the stage saying, "Before our evening's entertainment I wish to ask our guest, Captain Wong, if she would speak some few words or perhaps recite for us." And she knew with a very small part of her mind —but it took no more—that she must use this chance to denounce him.

Tarik and the Butcher, and saw no hypnotics, but also that they suspected no treachery and her own delayed fear, taking

The realisation momentarily blotted everything else, but then returned to its proper size, for she knew she could not let Cord stop her from getting to Headquarters, so she stood up and walked to the stage at the end of the commons, picking from Cord's mind as she walked a deadly blade so quickly to fit into the cracks of Geoffrey Cord. her from what she felt in her slipping and lapping with doubled and halved voice and no yes, she was able, even as she walked to pick the words and images that would drive and push him to her betrayal and no yes, once struck by his fear and rebounding, she brought herself back to a single line that scribed through both perception and action, speech and communication, both one now, picking down

sounds that would persuade with the deliberation this lengthened time lent and she reached the platform beside the gorgeous beast, Klik, and

mounted, hearing the voices that sang in the hall's silence, and tossed her words now from the sling of her vibrant voice, so that they hung outside her, and she watched them and watched his watch- *Her fear broke from her vast ship-picture while she felt schismic rages of him and still would survive it and found his fear as porous, porous as a sponge.*

ing: the rhythm which was barely intricate to most ears in the commons was to him painful because it was timed to the processes of his body, to jar and strike against them . . . and she was surprised he had held up this long.

"All right, Cord,
to be lord of this black barrick,
Tarik's, you need more than jackal lore,
or a belly full of murder and jelly knees.
Open your mouth and your hands. To understand
power, use your wit, please.
Ambition like a liquid ruby stains
your brain, birthed in the cervixed will

to kill, swung in the arc of death's again,
you name yourself victim each time you fill
with swill the skull's cup lipping murder. It
predicts your fingers' movement toward the blade
long laid against the leather sheath cord-fixed
to pick the plan your paling fingers made;
you stayed in safety, missing worlds of wonder,
under the lithe hiss of the personafix
inflicting false memories to make them blunder
while thunder cracks the change of Tarik.
You stick pins in peaches, place your strange
blade, ranged with a grooved tooth, while the long
and strong lines of my meaning make your mind change
from fulgent to frangent. Now you hear the wrong
cord-song, to instruct you. Assassin,
pass in . . ."

She looked directly at Geoffry Cord. Geoffry Cord looked directly at her and shrieked.

The scream snapped something. She had been thinking in Babel-17 and choosing her English words with it. But now she was thinking in English again.

Geoffry Cord jerked his head sideways, black hair shaking, flung his table over, and ran, raging, toward her. The drugged knife which she had seen only through his mind was out and aimed at her stomach.

She jumped back, kicked at his wrist as he vaulted the platform edge, missed, but struck his face. He fell backwards, rolling on the floor.

Gold, silver, amber: Brass was running from his side of the room. Silver-haired Tarik was coming from the other, his cloak billowing. And the Butcher had already reached her, was between her and the uncoiling Cord.

"What is this?" Tarik demanded.

Cord was on one knee, knife still poised. His black eyes went from vibra-gun muzzle to vibra-gun muzzle, then to Brass' unsheathed claws. He froze.

"I don't appreciate attacks on my guests."

"That knife is meant for you, Tarik," she panted.

"Check the records of Jebel's personafix. He was going to kill you and get the Butcher under hypnotic control, and take over Jebel."

"Oh," Tarik said. "One of those." He turned to the Butcher. "It was time for another one, wasn't it? About once every six months. I'm again grateful to you, Captain Wong."

The Butcher stepped forward and took the knife from Cord, whose body seemed frozen, whose eyes danced. Rydra listened to Cord's breath measure out the silence, while the Butcher, holding the knife by the blade, examined it. The blade itself, in the Butcher's heavy fingers, was printed steel. The handle, a seven inch length of bone, was rigid, runneled, and stained with walnut dye.

With his free hand, the Butcher caught his fingers in Cord's black hair. Then, not particularly quickly, he pushed the knife to the hilt into Cord's right eye, handle first.

The scream became a gurgle. The flailing hands fell from the Butcher's shoulders. Those sitting close stood.

Rydra's heart banged twice to break her ribs. "But you didn't even check.... Suppose I was wrong ... Maybe there was more to it than ..." Her tongue wagged through the meaningless protests. And maybe her heart had stopped.

The Butcher, both hands bloody, looked at her coldly. "He moved with a knife on Jebel toward Tarik or Lady and he dies." Right fist ground on left palm, now soundless with red lubricant.

"Miss Wong," Tarik said, "from what I've seen, there's little doubt in my mind that Cord was certainly dangerous. I'm sure there's not much in yours, either. You are highly useful. I am highly obliged. I hope this trip down the Dragon's Tongue proves propitious. The Butcher had just told me it was at your request that we are going."

"Thank you, but ..." Her heart was pounding again. She tried to form some clause to hang from the hook of 'but' still hesitant in her mouth. Instead she got very sick, pitched forward, half blinded. The Butcher caught her on red palms.

The round, warm, blue room again. But alone, and she

was at last able to think about what had happened in the commons. It was not what she'd repeatedly tried to describe to Mocky. It was what Mocky had repeatedly insisted to her: telepathy. But, apparently, telepathy was the nexus of old talent and a new way of thinking. It opened worlds of perception, of action. Then why was she sick? She recalled how time slowed when her mind worked under Babel-17, how her mental processes speeded up. If there was a corresponding increase in her physiological functions, her body might not be up to the strain.

The tapes from the *Rimbaud* had told her the next 'sabotage' attempt would be at Administrative Alliance Headquarters. She wanted to get there with the language, the vocabulary and grammar, give it to them, and retire. She was almost ready to hand over the search for this mysterious speaker. But no, not quite, there was still something, something to be heard and spoken. . . .

Sick and falling, she snagged on bloody finger, woke starting. The Butcher's egoless brutality, hammered linear by what she could not know, less than primitive, was for all its horror, still human. Though bloody handed, he was safer than the precision of the world linguistically corrected. What could you say to a man who could not say 'I'? What could he say to her? Tarik's cruelties, kindnesses, existed at the articulate limits of civilization. But this red bestiality fascinated her!

IV

She rose from the hammock, this time unsnapping the bandage. She'd felt better nearly an hour, but she had lain still thinking most of the time. The ramp tilted to her feet.

When the infirmary wall solidified behind her, she paused in the corridor. The airflow pulsed like breath. Her translucent slacks brushed the tops of her bare feet. The neckline of her black silk blouse lay loose on her shoulders.

She had rested well into Jebel's night shift. During a period of high activity, the sleeping time was staggered, but when they merely moved from location to location, there were hours when nearly the whole population slept.

Rather than head toward the commons, she turned down an unfamiliar sloping tunnel. White light diffused from the floor, became amber fifty feet on, then amber became orange— she stopped and looked at her hands in orange light—and forty feet further, the orange light was red. Then . . .

Blue.

The space opened around her, the walls slanting back, the ceiling rising into darkness too high for her to see. The air flickered and blotted with the after-image from the change in color. Insubstantial mists plus her unsettled eyes made her turn to orient herself.

A man was silhouetted against the red entrance to the hall. "Butcher?"

He walked toward her, blue light fogging his features as he neared. He stopped, nodded.

"I decided to take a walk when I felt better," she explained. "What part of the ship is that?"

"Discorporate quarters."

"I should have known." They fell in step with one another. "Are you just wandering around, too?"

He shook his heavy head. "An alien ship passes close to Jebel and Tarik wants its sensory vectors."

"Alliance or Invader?"

The Butcher shrugged. "Only to know that it is not a human ship."

There were nine species among the five explored galaxies with interstellar travel. Three had allied themselves definitely with the Alliance. Four had sided with the Invaders. Two were not committed.

They had gone so far into the discorporate sector, nothing seemed solid. The walls were blue mist without corners. The echoing crackle of transference energies caused distant lightning, and her eyes were deviled by half-remembered ghosts, who had always passed moments ago, yet were never there.

"How far do we go?" she asked, having decided to walk with him, thinking as she spoke: If he doesn't know the word for 'I', how can he understand 'we'?

Understanding or not, he answered, "Soon." Then he looked directly at her with dark, heavy ridged eyes and asked, "Why?"

The tone of his voice was so different, she knew he was not referring to anything in their exchange during the past few minutes. She cast in her mind for anything she had done that might strike him as perplexing.

He repeated, "Why?"

"Why what, Butcher?"

"Why the saving of Tarik from Cord?"

There was no objection in his question, only ethical curiosity. "Because I like him and because I need him to get me to Headquarters and I would feel sort of funny if I'd let him . . ." She stopped. "Do you know who 'I' am?"

He shook his head.

"Where do you come from, Butcher? What planet were you born on?"

He shrugged. "The head," he said, after a moment, "they said there was something wrong with the brain."

"Who?"

"The doctors."

Blue fog drifted between them.

"The doctors on Titin?" she hazarded.

The Butcher nodded.

"Then why didn't they put you in a hospital instead of a prison?"

"The brain is not crazy, they said. This hand"—he held up his left—"kill four people in three days. This hand"—he raised the other—"kill seven. Blow up four buildings with thermite. The foot"—he slapped his left leg—"kicked in the head of the guard at the Telechron Bank. There's a lot of money there, too much to carry. Carry maybe four hundred thousand credits. Not much."

"You robbed the Telechron Bank of four hundred thousand credits!"

"Three days, eleven people, four buildings: all for four

hundred thousand credits. But Titin"—his face twisted—
"was not fun at all."

"So I'd heard. How long did it take for them to catch
you?"

"Six months."

Rydra whistled. "I take my hat off to you, if you could
keep out of their hands that long, after a bank robbery. And you
know enough biotics to perform a difficult Caesarean section
and keep the fetus alive. There's something in that head."

"The doctors say the brain not stupid."

"Look, you and I are going to talk to each other. But
first I have to teach"—she stopped—"the brain something."

"What?"

"About *you* and *I*. You must hear the words a hundred
times a day. Don't you ever wonder what they mean?"

"Why? Most things make sense without them."

"Hey, speak in whatever language you grew up with."

"No."

"Why not? I want to see if it's one I know anything
about."

"The doctors say there's something wrong with the
brain."

"All right. What did they say was wrong?"

"Aphasia, alexia, amnesia."

"Then you were pretty messed up." She frowned. "Was
that before or after the bank robbery?"

"Before."

She tried to order what she had learned. "Something
happened to you that left you with no memory, unable to
speak or read, and so the first thing you did was rob the
Telechron bank—which Telechron Bank?"

"On Rhea-IV."

"Oh, a small one. But, still—and you stayed free for six
months. Any idea what happened to you before you lost your
memory?"

The Butcher shrugged.

"I suppose they went through all the possibilities that
you were working for somebody else under hypnotics. You
don't know what language you spoke before you lost your

memory? Well, your speech patterns now must be based on your old language or you would have learned about *I* and *you* just from picking up new words.''

''Why must these sounds mean something?''

''Because you asked a question just now that I can't answer if you don't understand them.''

''No.'' Discomfort shadowed his voice. ''No. There is an answer. The words of the answer must be simpler, that's all.''

''Butcher, there are certain ideas which have words for them. If you don't know the words, you can't know the ideas. And if you don't have the idea, you don't have the answer.''

''The word *you* four times, yes? Still nothing unclear, and *you* means nothing.''

She sighed. ''That's because I was using the word phatically—ritually, without regard for its real meaning . . . as a figure of speech. Look, I asked you a question that you couldn't answer.''

The Butcher frowned.

''See, you have to know what they mean to make sense out of what I just said. The best way to learn a language is by listening to it. So listen. When you''—she pointed to him—''said to me,'' and she pointed to herself, *''Knowing what ships to destroy, and ships are destroyed. Now to go down the Dragon's Tongue, Jebel go down the Dragon's Tongue,* twice the fist''—she touched his left hand—''banged the chest.'' She raised his hand to his chest. The skin was cool and smooth under her palm. ''The fist was trying to tell something. And if you had used the word 'I', you wouldn't have had to use your fist. What you wanted to say was: 'You knew what ships to destroy and I destroyed the ships. You want to go down the Dragon's Tongue, I will get Jebel down the Dragon's Tongue.' ''

The Butcher frowned. ''Yes, the fist to tell something.''

''Don't you see, sometimes you want to say things, and you're missing an idea to make them with, and missing a word to make the idea with. In the beginning was the word. That's how somebody tried to explain it once. Until something is named, it doesn't exist. And it's something the brain needs to have exist, otherwise you wouldn't have to beat your chest, or strike your fist on your palm. The brain wants it to exist; let me teach it the word."

The frown cut deeper into his face.

Just then mist blew away before them. In star-flecked blackness something drifted, flimsy and flickering. They had reached a sensory port, but it was transmitting over frequencies close to regular light. "There," said the Butcher, "there is the alien ship."

"It's from Çiribia-IV," Rydra said. "They're friendly to the Alliance."

The Butcher was surprised she'd recognized it. "A very odd ship."

"It does look funny to us, doesn't it."

"Tarik did not know where it came from." He shook his head.

"I haven't seen one since I was a kid. We had to entertain delegates from Çiribia to the Court of Outer Worlds. My mother was a translator there." She leaned on the railing and gazed at the ship. "You wouldn't think something that's so flimsy and shakes around like that would fly or make stasis jumps. But it does."

"Do they have this word, *I?*"

"As a matter of fact they have three forms of it: I-below-a-temperature-of-six-degrees-centigrade, I-between-six-and-ninety-three-degrees-centigrade, and I-above-ninety-three."

The Butcher looked confused.

"It has to do with their reproductive process," Rydra explained. "When the temperature is below six degrees they're sterile. They can only conceive when the temperature is between six and ninety-three, but to actually give birth, they have to be above ninety-three."

The Çiribian ship moved like floppy feathers across the screen.

"Maybe I can explain something to you this way; with all nine species of galaxy-hopping life forms, each as widespread as our own, each as technically intelligent, with as complicated an economy, seven of them engaged in the same war we are, still we hardly ever run into them; and they run into us or each other about as frequently: so infrequently, that

even when an experienced spaceman like Tarik passes along-
side one of their ships, he can't identify it. Wonder why?"

"Why?"

"Because compatibility factors for communication are
incredibly low. Take the Çiribians, who have enough knowledge to sail their triple-yoked poached eggs from star to star:
they have no word for 'house', 'home', or 'dwelling.' 'We
must protect our families and our homes.' When we were
preparing the treaty between the Çiribians and ourselves at
the Court of Outer Worlds, I remember that sentence took
forty-five minutes to say in Çiribian. Their whole culture is
based on heat and changes in temperature. We're just lucky
that they do know what a 'family' is, because they're the only
ones besides humans who have them. But for 'house' you
have to end up describing '. . . an enclosure that creates a
temperature discrepancy with the outside environment of so
many degrees, capable of keeping comfortable a creature with
a uniform body temperature of ninety-eight-point-six, the
same enclosure being able to lower the temperature during the
months of the warm season and raise it during the cold
season, providing a location where organic sustenance can be
refrigerated in order to be preserved, or warmed well above
the boiling point of water to pamper the taste mechanism of
the indigenous habitants who, through customs that go back
through millions of hot and cold seasons, have habitually
sought out this temperature changing device . . .' and so forth
and so on. At the end you have given them some idea of what
a 'home' is and why it is worth protecting. Give them a
schematic of the air-conditioning and central heating system,
and things begin to get through. Now: there is a huge
solar-energy conversion plant that supplies all the electrical
energy for the Court. The heat amplifying and reducing
components take up an area a little bigger than Jebel. One
Çiribian can slither through that plant and then go describe it
to another Çiribian who never saw it before so that the
second can build an exact duplicate, even to the color the
walls are painted—and this actually happened, because they
thought we'd done something ingenious with one of the
circuits and wanted to try it themselves—where each piece is

located, how big it is, in short completely describe the whole business, in nine words. Nine very small words, too."

The Butcher shook his head. "No. A solar-heat conversion system is too complicated. These hands dismantle one, not too long ago. Too big. Not——"

"Yep, Butcher, nine words. In English it would take a couple of books full of schematics and electrical and architectural specifications. They have the proper nine words. We don't."

"Impossible."

"So's that." She pointed toward the Çiribian ship. "But it's there and flying." She watched the brain, both intelligent and injured, thinking. "If you have the right words," she said, "it saves a lot of time and makes things easier."

After a while he asked, "What is *I?*"

She grinned. "First of all it's very important. A good deal more important than anything else. The brain will let any number of things go to pot as long as 'I' stay alive. That's because the brain is part of I. A book is, a ship is, Tarik is, the universe is, but, as you must have noticed, I am."

The Butcher nodded. "Yes. But I am what?"

Fog closed over the view-port, misting stars and the Çiribian ship. "That's a question only you can answer."

"You must be important too," the Butcher mused, "because the brain has overheard that you are."

"Good boy!"

Suddenly he put his hand on her cheek. The cock's spur rested lightly on her lower lip. "You and I," the Butcher said. He moved his face close to hers. "Nobody else is here. Just you and I. But which is which?"

She nodded, cheek moving on his fingers. "You're getting the idea." His chest had been cool; his hand was warm. She put her hand on top of his. "Sometimes you frighten me."

"I and me," the Butcher said. "Only a morphological distinction, yes? The brain figure that out before. Why does you frighten me sometimes?"

"*Do* frighten. A morphological correction. You frighten

me because you rob banks and put knife handles in people's heads, Butcher!''

"You do?" Then his surprise left. "Yes, you do, don't you. You forgot."

"But I didn't," Rydra said.

"Why does that frighten I? . . . correction, me. Overhear that too."

"Because it's something I've never done, never wanted to do, never could do. And I like you, I like your hand on my cheek, so that if you suddenly decided to put a knife handle in *my* eye, well . . ."

"Oh. You never would put a knife handle in my eye," the Butcher said. "I don't have to worry."

"You could change your mind."

"You won't." He looked at her closely. "I don't really think you're going to kill me. You know that. I know that. It's something else. Why don't I tell you something else that frightened me? Maybe you can see some pattern and you will understand then. The brain is not stupid."

His hand slid to her neck, and there was concern in his puzzled eyes. She had seen it before the moment he'd turned from the dead fetus in the biology theater. "Once . . ." she began slowly, ". . . well, there was a bird."

"Birds frighten me?"

"No. But this bird did. I was just a kid. You don't remember being a kid, do you? In most people what you were as a kid has a lot to do with what you are now."

"And what I am too?"

"Yes, me too. My doctor had gotten this bird for me as a present. It was a myna bird, which can talk. But it doesn't know what it's saying. It just repeats like a tape recorder. Only I didn't know that. A lot of times I know what people are trying to say to me, Butcher. I never understood it before, but since I've been on Jebel, I've realized it's got something to do with telepathy. Anyway, this myna bird had been trained to talk by feeding it earthworms when it said the right thing. Do you know how big an earthworm is?"

"Like so?"

"That's right. And some of them even run a few inches longer. And a myna bird is about eight or nine inches long. In other words a earthworm can be about five-sixths as long as a myna bird, which is what's important. The bird had been trained to say: Hello, Rydra, it's a fine day out and I'm happy. But the only thing this meant in the bird's mind was a rough combination of visual and olfactory sensations that translated loosely, *There's another earthworm coming*. So when I walked into the greenhouse and said hello to this myna bird, and it replied, 'Hello, Rydra, it's a fine day and I'm happy,' I knew immediately it was lying. There was another earthworm coming, that I could see and smell, and it was this thick and five-sixths as long as I was tall. And I was supposed to eat it. I got a little hysterical. I never told my doctor, because I never could figure exactly what happened until now. But when I remember, I still get shaky.''

The Butcher nodded. ''When you left Rhea with the money, you eventually holed up in a cave in the ice-hell of Dis. You were attacked by worms, twelve foot ones. They burrowed up out of the rocks with acid slime on their skins. You were scared, but you killed them. You rigged up an electric net from your hop-sled power source. You killed them, and when you knew you could beat them, you weren't afraid any more. The only reason you didn't eat them was because the acid made their flesh toxic. But you hadn't eaten anything for three days.''

''I did? I mean . . . you did?''

''You are not frightened of the things I am frightened of. I am not frightened of the things you are frightened of. That's good, isn't it?''

''I guess so.''

Gently he leaned his face against hers, then pulled away, and searched her face for a response.

''What is it that you're frightened of?'' she asked.

He shook his head, not in negation but in confusion, as she saw him trying to articulate. ''The baby, the baby that died,'' he said. ''The brain afraid, afraid for you, that you would be alone.''

''How afraid that you would be alone, Butcher?''

He shook his head again.

''Loneliness is not good.''

She nodded.

"The brain knows that. For a long time it didn't know, but after a while it learned. Lonely on Rhea, you were, even with all the money. Lonelier on Dis; and in Titin, even with the other prisoners, you were loneliest of all. No one really understood you when you spoke to them. You did not really understand them. Maybe because they said *I* and *you* so much, and you just now are beginning to learn how important you are and I am."

"You wanted to raise the baby yourself so he would grow up and . . . speak the same language you speak? Or at any rate speak English the same way you speak it?"

"Then both not be alone."

"I see."

"It died," Butcher said. He grunted once again. "But now you are not quite so alone. I teach you to understand the others, a little. You're not stupid, and you learn fast." Now he turned fully toward her, rested his fists on her shoulder and spoke gravely. "You like me. Even when I first came on Jebel, there was something about me that you liked. I saw you do things I thought were bad, but you liked me. I told you how to destroy the Invaders defensive net, and you destroyed it, for me. I told you I wanted to go to the tip of the Dragon's Tongue, and you saw that I get there. You will do anything I ask. It's important that I know that."

"Thank you, Butcher," she said wonderingly.

"If you ever rob another bank, you will give me all the money."

Rydra laughed. "Why, thank you. Nobody ever wanted to do that for me. But I hope you don't have to rob——"

"You will kill anyone that tries to hurt me, kill them a lot worse than you ever killed anyone before."

"But you don't have to——"

'You will kill all of Jebel if it tries to take you and me apart and keep us alone."

"Oh, Butcher——" She turned from him and put her fist against her mouth. "One hell of a teacher I am! You don't understand a thing—I—*I* am talking about."

The voice, astonished and slow: "I don't understand you, you think."

She turned back to him. "But I do, Butcher! I do

understand you. Please believe that. But trust me that you have a little more to learn.''

''You trust me,'' he said firmly.

''Then listen. Right now we've met each other halfway. I haven't really taught you about *I* and *you*. We've made up our own language, and that's what we're talking now.''

''But—''

''Look, every time you've said *you* in the last ten minutes, you should have said *I*. Every time you've said *I*, you meant *you*.''

He dropped his eyes to the floor, then raised them again, still without answer.

''What I talk about as I, you must speak of as you. And the other way around, don't you see?''

''Are they the same word for the same thing, that they are interchangeable?''

''No, just . . . yes! They both mean the same sort of thing. In a way they're the same.''

''Then you and I are the same.''

Risking confusion, she nodded.

''I suspect it. But you''—he pointed to her—''have taught me.'' He touched himself.

''And that's why you can't go around killing people. At least you better do a hell of a lot of thinking before you do. When you talk to Tarik, I and you still exist. With anyone you look at on the ship, or even through a view-screen, I and you are still there.''

''The brain must think about that.''

''You must think about that, with more than your brain.''

''If I must then I will. But we are one, more than others.'' He touched her face again. ''Because you taught me. Because with me you do not have to be afraid of anything. I have just learned, and I may make mistakes with other people; for an *I* to kill a *you* without a lot of thought is a mistake, isn't it? Do I use the words correctly now?''

She nodded.

''I will make no mistakes with you. That would be too terrible. I will make as few mistakes as I possibly can. And someday I will learn completely.'' Then he smiled. ''Let's hope nobody tries to make any mistakes with me, though. I am sorry for them if they do, because I will probably make a mistake with them very quickly and with very little thought.''

"That's fair enough for now, I guess," Rydra said. She took his arms in her hands. "I'm glad you and I are together, Butcher." Then his arms came up and caught her against his body, and she pressed her face on his shoulder.

"I thank you," he whispered. "I thank you and thank you."

"You're warm," she said into his shoulder. "Don't let go for a little while."

When he did, she blinked up at his face through blue mist and turned all cold. "What *is* it, Butcher!"

He took her face between his hands and bent his head till amber hair brushed her forehead.

"Butcher, remember I told you I can tell what people are thinking? Well, I can tell something's wrong now, and you said I didn't have to be afraid of you, but you're scaring me now."

She raised his face. There were tears on it.

"Look, just the way something wrong with me would scare you, one thing that's going to scare hell out of me for a long time is something wrong with you. Tell me what it is."

"I can't," he said hoarsely. "*I* can't. *I* can't tell *you*." And the one thing she understood immediately was that it was the most horrible thing he could conceive with his new knowledge.

She watched him fight, and fought herself: "Maybe I can help, Butcher! There's a way I can go into the brain and find out what it is."

He backed away and shook his head. "*You* mustn't. *You* mustn't do that to *me*. Please."

"Butcher, I w-won't." She was confused. "Th-then I . . . I won't." Confusion hurt. "Butcher . . . I-I won't!" Her adolescent stutter staggered in her mouth.

"I——" he began, breath hard, but becoming softer, "I have been alone and not I for a long time. I must be alone for a little while longer."

"I s-see." Suspicion, very small and easily dealt with, came now. When he had backed away, it entered the space between them. But that was human, too. "Butcher? Can you read my mind?"

He looked surprised. "No. I don't even understand how you can read mine."

"All right. I thought maybe there was something in my head that you might be picking up that makes you afraid of me."

He shook his head.

"That's good. Hell, I wouldn't want somebody prying under my scalp. I think I understand."

"I tell you now," he said, coming toward her again, "I and you are one; but I and you are very different. I have seen a lot you will never know. You know of things that I will never see. You have made me not alone, a little. There is a lot in the brain, my brain, about hurting and running and fighting and, even though I was in Titin, a lot about winning. If you are ever in danger, but a real danger where someone might make a mistake with you, then go into the brain, see what is there. Use whatever you need. I ask you, only, to wait until you have done everything else first."

"I'll wait, Butcher," she said.

He held out his hand. "Come."

She took his hand, avoiding the cock spurs.

"No need to see the stasis currents about the alien ship if it is friendly to the Alliance. You and I will stay together a while."

She walked with her shoulder against his arm. "Friend or enemy," she said as they passed through the twilight, heavy with ghosts. "This whole Invasion—sometimes it seems so stupid. That's something they don't allow you to think back where I come from. Here on Jebel Tarik you more or less avoid the question. I envy you that."

"You are going to Administrative Alliance Headquarters because of the Invasion, yes?"

"That's right. But after I go, don't be surprised if I come back." Steps later she looked up again. "That's another thing I wish I could get straight in my head. The Invaders killed my parents, and the second embargo almost killed me. Two of my Navigators lost their wife to the Invaders. Still,

Ron could wonder about just how right the War Yards were. Nobody likes the Invasion, but it goes on. It's so big I never really thought about trying to get out of it before. It's funny to see a whole bunch of people in their odd, and maybe destructive, way doing just that. Maybe I should simply not bother to go to Headquarters, tell Tarik to turn around and head toward the densest part of the Snap.''

"The Invaders," the Butcher said, almost musingly, "they hurt lots of people, you, me. They hurt me too."

"They did?"

"The brain sick, I told you. Invaders did that."

"What did they do?"

The Butcher shrugged. "First thing I remember is escaping from Nueva-nueva York."

"That's the huge port terminal for the Cancer cluster?"

"That's right."

"The Invaders had captured you?"

He nodded. "And did something. Maybe experiment, maybe torture." He shrugged. "It doesn't matter. I can't remember. But when I escaped, I escaped with nothing: no memory, voice, words, name."

"Perhaps you were a prisoner of war, or maybe even somebody important before they captured you——"

He bent and put his cheek against her lips to stop her talking. When he rose, he smiled, sadly she saw. "There are some things the brain may not know, but it can guess: I was always a thief, a murderer, a criminal. And I was no I. The Invaders caught me once. I escaped. The Alliance caught me later at Titin. I escaped——"

"You *escaped* from Titin?"

He nodded. "I will probably be caught again, because that's what happens to criminals in this universe. And maybe I will escape once more." He shrugged. "Maybe I will not be caught again, though." He looked at her, surprised not at her but at something in himself. "I was no I before, but now there is a reason to stay free. I will not be caught again. There is a reason."

"What is it, Butcher?"

"Because I am," he said softly, "and you are."

V

"You finishing u' your dictionary?" Brass asked.

"Finished it yesterday. This is a poem." She closed the notebook. "We should be at the tip of the Tongue soon. Butcher just told me this morning that the Çiribians have been keeping us company for four days. Brass, do you have any idea what they——"

Magnified by the loudspeakers, Tarik's voice: "Ready Jebel for immediate defense. Repeat, immediate defense."

"What the hell is going on now?" Rydra asked. Around them the commons rose in unified activity. "Look, hunt up the crew and get them down to ejection gates."

"That's where the s'ider-boats leave from?"

"Right." Rydra stood.

"We gonna mix it u' some, Ca'tain?"

"If we have to," Rydra said, and started across the floor.

She beat the crew by a minute and caught the Butcher at the ejection hatch. Jebel's fighting crew hurried along the corridor in ordered confusion.

"What's going on? Did the Çiribians get hostile?"

He shook his head. "Invaders twelve degrees off galactic center."

"This close to Administrative Alliance?"

"Yes. And if Jebel Tarik doesn't attack first, Jebel's had it. They're bigger than Jebel, and Jebel's going to bump right into them."

"Tarik's going to attack them?"

147

"Yes."

"Then come on, let's attack."

"You are going with me?"

"I'm a master strategist, remember?"

"Jebel is in danger," the Butcher said. "This will be a greater battle than you saw before."

"The better to use my talents on, my dear. Is your boat equipped to hold a full crew?"

"Yes. But we use the Navigation and Sensory detail of Jebel by remote control."

"Let's take a crew, anyway, just in case we want to break strategy in a hurry. Is Tarik riding with you this time?"

"No."

Up the hall Slug turned the corner, followed by Brass, the Navigators, the insubstantial figures of the discorporate trio, and the platoon.

The Butcher looked from them to Rydra. "All right. Come inside. Get in, gang!"

She kissed his shoulder because she couldn't reach his cheek; the Butcher opened the ejection hatch, and motioned them on.

Allegra, as she started up the ladder, caught Rydra's arm. "Are we gonna fight this time, Captain?" There was an excited smile on her freckled face.

"There's a good chance. Scared?"

"Yep," Allegra said, still grinning, and scurried into the dark tunnel. Rydra and the Butcher brought up the rear.

"They won't have any trouble with this equipment if they have to take over from remote control, will they?"

"This spider-boat is ten feet shorter than the *Rimbaud*. Things are more cramped in discorporate quarters, but everything else is the same."

Rydra thought: We've worked the sensory details on a forty-foot one-generator sloop; this is a breeze, Captain— Basque.

"The captain's cabin is different," he added. "That's where the weapon controls are. We're going to make some mistakes."

"Moralize later," she said. "We'll fight like hell for Jebel Tarik. But on the chance fighting like hell won't do any good, I want to be able to get out of here. No matter what happens, I've got to get back to Administrative Alliance Headquarters."

"Tarik wanted to know if the Çiribian ship will fight beside us. They're still hanging T-ward."

"They'll probably watch the whole business and not understand what's going on, unless they're directly attacked. If they are, they can pretty well take care of themselves. But I doubt they'll join us in an offensive."

"That's bad," the Butcher said. "Because we'll need help."

"Strategy Workshop. Strategy Workshop," Tarik's voice came over the speaker. "Repeat, Strategy Workshop."

Where language charts had hung in her cabin, a viewing screen—replica of the hundred-foot projection in Jebel's gallery—spread over the wall. Where her console had been were ranged and banked assortments of bomb and vibra-blast controls. "Gross, uncivilized weapons," she commented as she sat down on one of the curved shock-boards where her bubble seat had been. "But effective as hell, I would imagine, if you know what you're doing."

"What?" The Butcher strapped himself beside her.

"I was misquoting the late Weapons Master of Armsedge."

The Butcher nodded. "You see to your crew. I'll go over the check list up here."

She switched on the intercom. "Brass, you wired in place?"

"Right."

"Eye, Ear, Nose?"

"It's dusty down here, Captain. When's the last time they swept out this graveyard?"

"I don't care about the dust. Does everything work?"

"Oh, everything works all right . . ." The sentence ended with a ghostly sneeze.

"Gesundheit. Slug, what's happening?"

"All in place, Captain." Then muffled: "Will you put those marbles away!'

"Navigation?"

"We're fine. Móllya is teaching Calli judo. But I'm right here and'll call them soon as something happens."

"Keep alert."

The Butcher bent toward her, stroked her hair, and laughed.

"I like them too," she told him. "I just hope we don't have to use them. One of them is a traitor who's tried to get me twice now. I'd rather not give him a third chance. Though if I have to, I think I can handle him this time."

Tarik's voice over the speaker: "Carpenters gather to face thirty-two degrees off galactic center. Hacksaws at the K-ward gate. Ripsaws make ready at the R-ward gate. Crosscut blades ready at T-ward gate."

The ejectors clicked open. The cabin went black and the view-screen flickered with stars and distant gases. Controls gleamed with red and yellow signal lights along the weapon board. Through the underspeakers the chatter of the crews, back with the Navigation department of Jebel, began.

This is gonna be a rough one. Can you see her, Jehosaphat? She's right in front of me. A big mother.

I just hope she ain't seen us yet. Keep cool, Kippi.

"Drill presses, Bandsaws, and Lathes: make sure your components are oiled and your power-lines plugged in."

"That's us," the Butcher said. His hands leapt in the half-dark among the weapon controls.

What's the three ping-pong balls in the mosquito netting?

Tarik says it's a Çiribian ship.

Long as it's on our side, baby, it's fine with me.

"Power tools commence operations. Hand tools mark out for finishing work."

"Zero," the Butcher whispered. Rydra felt the ship jump. The stars began to move. Ten seconds later she saw the snub-snouted Invader rooting toward them.

"Ugly, isn't it," Rydra said.

"Jebel looks about the same size, only smaller. And when we come home, it will be beautiful. There's no way to enlist the Çiribians' help? Tarik will have to attack the Invader directly at her ports and smash as many as he can, which won't be a lot. Then they'll attack, and if they still outnumber Jebel's spider-boats, and surprise doesn't play heavily on Tarik's side, then that's''—she heard fist strike palm in the darkness—''it.''

''You can't just lob a gross, uncivilized atom bomb at them?''

''They have deflectors that would explode it in Tarik's hands.''

''I'm glad I brought the crew then. We may have to make a quick exit to Administrative Alliance Headquarters.''

''If they let us,'' the Butcher said, grimly. ''What strategies then to win?''

''Tell you soon as the attack starts. I have a method, but if I use it too much I pay high.'' She recalled the illness after the incident with Geoffry Cord.

While Tarik continued to set up formations, the men chatted with Jebel and the spider-boats slipped ahead in the night.

It started so fast she nearly missed it. Five hacksaws had slipped within a hundred yards of the Invader. Simultaneously they blasted at the ejector ports, and red beetles scurried from the sides of the black hog. It took four and a half seconds for the remaining twenty-seven ejectors to open and shoot their first barrage of cruisers. But Rydra was already thinking in Babel-17.

Through her distended time sense she saw they did need help. And the articulation of their need was also the answer.

''Break strategy, Butcher. Follow me with ten ships. My crew is taking over.''

The maddening feeling that her English words took so long on her tongue! The Butcher's request—''Kippi, put hacksaws on trail and leave them there!''—seemed like a tape played at quarter speed. But her crew was already in control of the spider-boat. She hissed their trajectory into the mike.

Brass flung them at right angles to the tide, and for a moment she saw the hacksaws behind her. Now a hairpin turn and they drove behind the first sheet of Invader cruisers.

''Warm their behinds!''

The Butcher's hand hesitated at a weapon. ''Drive them toward Jebel?''

"The hell I will. Fire, sweetheart!"

He fired, and the hacksaws followed suit.

In ten seconds it was clear she was right. Tarik lay R-ward. Ahead were the poached eggs, the mosquito netting, the flimsy, feathery vessel of Çiribia. Çiribia was Alliance, and at least one of the Invaders knew it because he fired at the weird contraption hung up on the sky. Rydra saw the Invader's gun-port cough green fire, but the fire never reached the Çiribians. The Invader cruiser turned into white-hot smoke that blackened and dispersed. Then another cruiser went, then three more, then three more.

"Out of here, Brass!" and they swung up and away.

"What was——" the Butcher started.

"A Çiribian heat ray. But they won't use it unless they're attacked. Part of the treaty signed at the Court in '47. So we make the Invaders attack. Want to do it again?"

Brass' voice over the speaker: "We already are, Ca'tain."

She was thinking in English again, waiting for the nausea to hit, but excitement held it back.

"Butcher," came from Tarik now, "what are you doing?"

"It's working, isn't it?"

"Yes. But you've left a hole in our defenses ten miles across."

"Tell him we'll plug it up in a minute as soon as we drive the next batch through."

Tarik must have heard her. "And what do we do for the next sixty seconds, young lady?"

"Fight like hell." And the next batch of herded cruisers disappeared before the Çiribian heat ray. Then from the underspeakers:

Hey, Butcher, they're out for you.

They got the idea you're spearheading this thing.

Butcher, six on your tail. Shake 'em fast.

"I can dodge them easy, Ca'tain," Brass called up. "They're all on remote control. I've got more freedom."

"One more and we can really put the odds on Tarik's side."

"Tarik outnumbers them already," the Butcher said. "This spider-boat has got to shake those burrs." He called into the mike, "Hacksaws disperse and break up the cruisers behind."

Will do. Hold onto your heads, fellows.

Hey, Butcher, one of them's not giving up.

Tarik said: "I thank you for my hacksaws back, but there's something following you that may be out for a hand-to-hand."

Rydra questioned him with a look.

"Heroes," the Butcher grunted disgustedly. "They'll try to grapple, board, and fight."

"Not with these kids on this ship! Brass, turn around and ram them, or come close enough to make them think we're crazy."

"May break a cou'le ribs . . ." The ship swung and they were flung hard against the straps of the shock-boards.

A youngster's voice through the intercom: "Wheeeee . . ."

On the view-screen the Invader cruiser swerved to the side.

"Good chance if they grapple," the Butcher said. "They don't know there's a full crew aboard. They have no more than two——"

"Watch out, Ca'tain!"

The Invader cruiser filled the screen. *Clunnnggg* sang the bones of the spider-boat.

The Butcher yanked at the straps of the shock-board and grinned. "Now to fighting hand-to-hand. Where are *you* going?"

"With you."

"You have a vibra-gun?" He tightened the holster on his stomach.

"Sure do." She pushed aside a panel of her loose blouse. "And this, too. Vanadium wire, six inches. Wicked thing."

"Come." He slapped the lever on a gravity inductor down to full field.

"What's that for?"

They were already in the corridor.

"To fight in a space suit out there is no good. False gravity field released around both ships will keep a breatheable atmosphere to about twenty feet from the surface and keep some heat in . . . more or less.''

''What's less?'' She swung behind him into the lift.

''It's about ten degrees below zero out there.''

He had abandoned even his breech since the evening they had met in Jebel's graveyard. All he wore was the holster. ''I guess we won't be out there long enough to need overcoats.''

''I guarantee you, whoever is out there more than a minute will be dead, and not from overexposure.'' His voice suddenly deepened as they ducked into the hatchway. ''If you don't know what you're doing, stay back.'' Then he bent to brush her cheek with amber hair. ''But you know, and I know. We must do it well.''

In the same motion that he raised his head, he released the hatch. Cold came in for them. She didn't feel it. The increased metabolic rate that accompanied Babel-17 wrapped her in a shield of physical indifference. Something went flying overhead. They knew what to do and both did it; they ducked. Whatever it was exploded—the explosion identifying it as a grenade that had just missed coming into the hatch—and light bleached the Butcher's face. He leaped and the fading glow slid down his body.

She followed him, reassured by the slow motion effect of Babel-17. She spun as she jumped. Someone ducked behind the ten foot bulge of an outrigger. She fired at him, the slow motion giving her time to take careful aim. She didn't wait to see if she hit, but kept turning. The Butcher was making for the ten foot wide column of the Invader's grapple.

Like a triple clawed crab, the enemy boat angled away into the night. K-ward rose the flattened spiral of the home galaxy. Shadows were carbon-paper black on the smooth hulls. From the K-ward side nobody could see her, unless her movement blotted a fugitive star or passed into the direct light of Specelli arm itself.

She jumped again—at the surface of the Invader cruiser now. For a moment it got much colder. Then she struck, near the grappler base, and rolled to her knees as, below, someone heaved another grenade at the hatch. They hadn't realized she and the Butcher were out yet. Good. She fired. And another hiss sounded from where the Butcher must be.

In the darkness below, figures moved. Then a vibra-blast stung the metal hatch beneath her hand. It came from her own ship's hatch and she wasted a quarter of a second analyzing and disregarding the idea that the spy she had been afraid of from her own crew had joined the Invaders. Rather, the Invader's tactic had been to keep them from leaving their ship and blow them up in the hatch. It had failed, so now they had taken cover in the hatch itself for safety and were firing from there. She fired, fired again. From his hiding place behind the other grapple, the Butcher was doing the same.

A section of the hatch rim began to glow from the repeated blasts. Then a familiar voice was calling, "All right, all right already, Butcher! You got them, Ca'tain!"

Rydra monkeyed down the grapple, as Brass turned the hatch light on and stood up in the glow that fanned across the bulkhead. The Butcher, gun down, came from his hiding place.

The underlighting distorted Brass' demon features still further. He held a limp figure in each claw.

"Actually this one's mine." He shook the right one, "He was trying to crawl back into the shi', so I ste''ed on his head." The pilot heaved the limp bodies onto the hullplates. "I don't know about you folks, but I'm cold. Reason I came up here in the first 'lace was Diavalo told me to tell you when you were ready for a coffee break, he'd fixed u' some Irish whiskey. Or maybe you'd 'refer hot buttered rum? Come on, come on! You're blue!"

At the lift her mind got back to English and she began to shiver. The frost on the Butcher's hair had started to melt to shiny droplets along his hairline. Her hand stung where she had just missed a burning.

"Hey," she said, as they stepped into the corridor, "if you're up here, Brass, who's watching the store?"

"Ki''i. We went back on remote control."

"Rum," the Butcher said. "No butter and not hot. Just rum."

"Man after my own heart," nodded Brass. He dropped

one arm around Rydra's shoulder, the other around the Butcher's. Friendly, but also, she realized, he was half-carrying both of them.

Something went *clang* through the ship.

The pilot glanced at the ceiling. "Maintenance just cut those grapples loose." He edged them into the captain's cabin. As they collapsed on the shock-boards, he called into the intercom: "Hey, Diavalo, come u' here and get these 'eo'le drunk, huh? They deserve it."

"Brass!" She caught his arm as he started back out. "Can you get us from here to Administrative Alliance Headquarters?"

He scratched his ear. "We're right at the ti' of the Tongue. I only know the inside of the Sna' by chart. But Sensory tells me we're right in something that must be the beginning of Natal-beta Current. I know it flows out of the Sna' and we can take it down to Atlas-run and then into Administrative Alliance's front door. We're about eighteen, twenty hours away."

"Let's go." She looked at the Butcher. He made no objection.

"Good idea," Brass said. "About half of Tarik is . . . eh, discor'orate."

"The Invaders won?"

"No'e. The Çiribians finally got the idea, roasted that big 'ig, and took off. But only after Tarik got a hole in its side large enough to 'ut three s'ider-boats through, sideways. Ki''i tells me everyone who's still alive is sealed off in one quarter of the shi', but they have no running 'ower."

"What about Tarik?" the Butcher asked.

"Dead," Brass said.

Diavalo poked his white head down the entrance hatch. "Here you go."

Brass took the bottle and the glasses.

Then static on the speaker: "Butcher, we just saw you cast off the Invaders' cruiser. So, you got out alive."

Butcher leaned forward and picked up the mike. "Butcher alive, chief."

"Some people have all the luck. Captain Wong, I expect you to write me an elegy."

"Tarik?" She sat down next to the Butcher. "We're going to Administrative Alliance Headquarters now. We'll come back with help."

"At your convenience, Captain. We're just a trifle crowded, though."

"We're leaving now."

Brass was already out the door.

"Slug, are the kids all right?"

"Present and accounted for. Captain, you didn't give anyone permission to bring firecrackers aboard, did you?"

"Not that I remember."

"That's all I wanted to know. Ratt, come back here . . ."

Rydra laughed. "Navigation?"

"Ready when you are," Ron said. In the background she heard Mollya's voice: *"Nilitaka kulala, nilale milele——"*

"You can't go to sleep forever," Rydra said. "We're taking off!"

"Mollya's teaching us a poem in Swahili," Ron explained.

"Oh. Sensory?"

"*Ka*chuuu! I always said, Captain, keep your graveyard clean. You might need it some day. Tarik's a case in point. We're ready."

"Get Slug to send one of the kids down with a dust mop. All wired in, Brass?"

"Checked out and ready, Ca'tain."

The stasis generators cut in and she leaned back on the shock-board. Inside something at last relaxed. "I didn't think we were going to get out of there." She turned to the Butcher, who sat on the edge of his board watching her. "You know I'm nervous as a cat. And I don't feel too well. Oh, hell, it's starting." With the relaxation the sickness which she had put off for so long began to climb her body. "This whole thing makes me feel like I'm about to fly apart. You know when you doubt everything, mistrust all your feelings, I begin to think I'm not me anymore . . ." Her breath got painful in her throat.

"I am," he said softly, "and you are."

"Don't ever let me doubt it, Butcher. But I even have to wonder about that. There's a spy among my crew. I told you that, didn't I? Maybe it's Brass and he's going to hurl us into another nova!'' Within the sickness was a blister of hysteria. The blister broke, and she smacked the bottle from the Butcher's hand. "Don't drink that! D-D-Diavalo, he might poison us!" She rose unsteadily. There was a red haze over everything. ". . . Or one of the d-d-dead. How . . . how can I f-f-f . . . fight a ghost?" Then pain hit her stomach, and she staggered back as away from a blow. Fear came with the pain. The emotions were moving behind his face, and even they blurred in her attempt to see them clearly. ". . . to kill . . . k-k-kill *us*!" she whispered, ". . . s-s-something to kill . . . s-s-so no y-*you*, n-n-no *I* . . ."

It was to get away from the pain which meant danger and the danger which meant silence that she did it. He had said, *If you are ever in danger . . . then go into my brain, see what is there, and use what you need.*

An image in her mind without words: once she, Muels, and Fobo had been in a barroom brawl on Tantor. She had caught a punch in the jaw and staggered back, shocked and turning, just as somebody picked the bar mirror from behind the counter and flung it at her. Her own terrified face had come screaming toward her, smashed over her outstretched hand. As she stared at the Butcher's face, through pain and Babel-17, it happened all over—

PART FOUR

~~~~~~

The Butcher

. . . turning in the brain to wake
with wires behind his eyes, forking the joints
akimbo. He wakes, wired,
forked fingers crackling, gagging on his tongue.
We wake, turning.
   Spined against the floor,
his spine turning, chest hollowed,
air in the wires, sparks
glint from the wired ceiling, tapping
his sparking fingernails. Coughs, cries.
The twin behind the eyes coughs, cries.
The dark twin doubles on the floor, swallows his tongue.
Splashed to the dark pole circuited behind
the eyes, the dark twin snaps his spine free, slaps
his palms against the ceiling. Charged beads fly.
The ceiling, polarized, batters his cheek with metal.
Tears free skin. Tears ribs,
torn pectorals off metal curved away
black, behind the cracks, dried,
that are his torn lips. More.

Buttocks and shoulderblades grind on the floor
gritty and green with brine.
  They wake.
We wake, turning.
  He, gargling blood, turns,
born, on the wet floor . . .

—from *The Dark Twin*

1

~~~~~~

"We just left the Sna', Ca'tain. You two drunk yet?"

Rydra's voice: "No."

"How do you like that. I guess you're all right, though."

Rydra's voice: "The brain fine. The body fine."

"Huh? Hey, Butcher, she didn't have one of her s'ells again?"

The Butcher's yoice: "No."

"Both of you sound funny as hell. Shall I send the Slug u' there to take a look at you?"

The Butcher's voice: "No."

"All right. It's clear sailing now, and I can 'ut a cou'le of hours off. What do you say?"

The Butcher's voice: "What is to say?"

"Try 'thanks'. You know, I'm flying my tail off down here."

Rydra's voice: "Thanks."

"You're welcome, I guess. I'll leave you two alone. Hey, I'm sorry if I interru'ted something."

II

~~~~~~

Butcher, I didn't know! I couldn't have known!

And in the echo their minds fused a cry, Couldn't have—couldn't. This light—

I told Brass, told him you must speak a language without the word 'I' and I said I didn't know of one; but there was one, the obvious one, Babel-17 . . . !

Congruent synapses quivered sympathetically till images locked, and out of herself she created, saw him—

—In the solitary confinement box of Titin, he scratched a map on the green wall paint with his spur over the palimpsestic obscenities of two centuries' prisoners, a map that they would follow on his escape and would take them in the wrong direction; she watched him pace that four-foot space for three months till his six and a half-foot frame was starved to a hundred and one pounds and he collapsed in the chains of starvation.

On a triple rope of words she climbed from the pit: starve, stave, stake; collapse, collate, collect; chains, change, chance.

He collected his winnings from the cashier and was about to stride across the maroon carpet of *Casino Cosmica* to the door when the black croupier blocked his way, smiling at the thick money case. "Would you like to take one more chance, sir? Something to challenge a player of your skill?" He was taken to a magnificent 3-D chessboard with glazed ceramic pieces. "You play against the house computer. Against each piece you lose, you stake a thousand credits. Each piece you win gains you the same. Checks win or lose you five

162

hundred. Checkmate gains the winner one hundred times the rest of the game's earnings, for either you or the house.'' It was a game to even out his exorbitant winnings—and he had been winning exorbitantly. "Going home and take this money now," he said to the croupier. The croupier smiled and said, "The house insists you play." She watched, fascinated, while the Butcher shrugged, turned to the board—and checkmated the computer in a seven move fool's mate. They gave him his million credits—and tried to kill him three times before he got to the mouth of the casino. They did not succeed, but the sport was better than the gambling.

Watching him function and react in these situations, her mind shook inside his, curving to his pain or pleasure, strange emotions because they were ego-less and inarticulate, magic, seductive, mythical. *Butcher*—

She managed to interrupt the headlong circling.

—*if you understood Babel-17 all along,* her questions hurled in her own storming brain, *why did you only use it gratuitously for yourself, an evening of gambling, a bank robbery, when a day later you would lose everything and make no attempt to keep things for yourself?*

What "self"? There was no "I".

She had entered him in some bewildering reversed sexuality. Enclosing her, he was in agony. *The light—you make! You make!* his crying in terror.

Butcher, she asked, more familiar in patterning words about emotional turbulences than he, *what does my mind in yours look like?*

Bright, bright moving, he howled, the analytical precision of Babel-17, crude as stone to articulate their melding, making so many patterns, reforming them.

That's just being a poet, she explained, the oblique connection momentarily cutting the flood through. *Poet in Greek means* maker *or* builder.

There's one! There's a pattern now. Ahhhh!—so bright, bright!

Just that simple semantic connection? She was astounded.

But the Greeks were poets three thousand years ago and you are a poet now. You snatch words together over such distance and their wakes blind me. Your thoughts are all fire, over shapes I cannot catch. They sound like music too deep, that shakes me.

That's because you were never shaken before. But I'm flattered.

You are so big inside me I will break. I see the pattern named The Criminal *and artistic consciousness meeting in the same head with one language between them . . .*

· *Yes, I had started to think something like—*

Flanking it, shapes called Baudelaire—*Ahhh!—and* Villon. *They were ancient French po—*

Too bright! Too bright! The "I" in me is not strong enough to hold them. Rydra, when I look at the night and stars, it is only a passive act, but you are active even watching, and halo the stars with more luminous flame.

What you perceive you change, Butcher. But you must *perceive it.*

I must—the light; central in you I see mirror and motion fused, and the pictures are meshed, rotating, and everything is choice.

My poems! It was the embarrassment of nakedness.

Definitions of "I" each great and precise.

She thought: I/Aye/Eye, the self, a sailor's *yes*, the organ of visual perception.

He began, *You—*

You/Ewe/Yew, the other self, a female sheep, the Celtic vegetative symbol for death.

—you ignite my words with meanings I can only glimpse. What am I surrounding? What am I, surrounding you?

Still watching, she saw him commit robbery, murder, mayhem, because the semantic validity of *mine* and *thine* were ruined in a snarl of frayed synapses. *Butcher, I heard it ringing in your muscles, that loneliness, that made you make Tarik hook up the* Rimbaud *just to have someone near you who could speak this analytical tongue, the same reason you tried to save the baby,* she whispered.

Images locked on her brain.

Long grass whispered by the weir. Alleppo's moons fogged the evening. The plainsmobile hummed, and with measured impatience he flicked the ruby emblem on the steering wheel with the tip of his left spur. Lill twisted against him, laughing. "You know, Butcher, if Mr. Big thought you'd driven out here with me on such a romantic night he'd get very hostile. You're really gonna take me to Paris when you finish here?" Unnamed warmth mixed in him with unnamed impatience. Her shoulder was damp under his hand, her lips red. She had coiled her champagne colored hair high over one ear. Her body beside his moved in a rippling motion that had the excuse of her turning to face him. "If you're kidding me, about Paris, I'll tell Mr. Big. If I were a smart girl, I'd wait till after you took me there before I let us get . . . friendly." Her breath was perfumed in the sweltering night. He moved his other hand up her arm. "Butcher, get me off this hot, dead world. Swamps, caves, rain! Mr. Big scares me, Butcher! Take me away from him, to Paris. Don't just be pretending. I want to go with you so bad." She made another laughing sound with only her lips. "I guess I'm . . . I'm not a smart girl after all." He placed his mouth against her mouth—and broke her neck with one thrust of his hands. Her eyes still open, she sagged backwards. The hypodermic ampule she had been about to plunge into his shoulder fell from her hand, rolled across the dashboard, and dropped among the foot pedals. He carried her into the weir, and came back muddy to mid-thigh. In the seat he flipped on the radio. "It's finished, Mr. Big."

"Very good. I was listening. You can pick up your money in the morning. It was very silly of her to try and double cross me out of that fifty thousand."

The plainsmobile was rolling, the warm breeze drying the mud on his arms, the long grass hissing against the runners.

Butcher . . . !

But that's me, Rydra.

I know. But I . . .

I had to do the same thing to Mr. Big himself two weeks later.

Where did you promise to take him?

The gambling caves of Minos. And once I had to crouch—

—though it was his body crouching under the green light of Kreto, breathing with wide open mouth to stop all sound, it was her anticipation, her fear controlled to calm. The loader in his red uniform halts and wipes his forehead with a bandanna. Step out quickly, taps his shoulder. The loader turns, surprised, and the hands come up leading with the heel, cock spurs opening the loader's belly, which spills all over the platform, and then running, while the alarms start, vaulting the sandbags, snatching up the hawser chain and swinging it down on the amazed face of the guard standing on the other side who turned to see him with arms surprised open—

—*broke into the open and got away,* he told her. *The trail disguise worked and the Tracers couldn't follow me past the lava pits.*

Opening you up, Butcher. All the running, opening me? Does it hurt, does it help? I didn't know.

But there were no words in your mind. Even Babel-17 was like the brain noise of a computer engaged in a purely synaptical analysis.

Yes. Now do you begin to understand—

—standing, shivering in the roaring caves of Dis where he had been wombed nine months, eaten all the food, Lonny's pet dog, then Lonny who had frozen to death trying to climb over the mounded ice—till suddenly the planetoid swung out from the shadow of Cyclops and blazing Ceres flared in the sky so that in forty minutes the cave was flooded with ice water to his waist. When he finally freed his hop-sled, the water was warm and he was slimy with sweat. He ran at top speed for the two mile twilight strip, setting the automatic pilot a moment before he collapsed, dizzy with heat. He fainted two minutes before he pulled into Gotter-dammerung.

Faint in the darkness of your lost memory, Butcher, I must find you. Who were you before Nueva-nueva York?

And he turned to her in gentleness. *You're afraid, Rydra? Like before . . .*

No, not like before. You're teaching me something, and it's shaking my whole picture of the world and myself. I thought I was afraid before because I couldn't do what you could do, Butcher. The white flame went blue, protective, and trembled. *But I was afraid because I could do all those things, and for my own reasons, not your lack of reasons, because I am, and you are. I'm a lot bigger than I thought I was, Butcher, and I don't know whether to thank you or damn you for showing me.* And something inside was crying, stuttering, was still. She turned in the silences she had taken from him, fearfully, and in the silences something waited for her to speak, alone, for the first time.

Look at yourself, Rydra.

Mirrored in him, she saw growing in the light of her, a darkness without words, only noise—growing! And cried out at its name and shape. The broken circuit boards! *Butcher, those tapes that could only have been made on my console when I was there! Of course—!*

Rydra, we can control them if we can name them.

How can we, now? We have to name ourselves first. And you don't know who you are.

Your words, Rydra, can we somehow use your words to find out who I am?

Not my words, Butcher. But maybe yours, maybe Babel-17. No . . .

I am, she whispered, *believe me, Butcher, and you are.*

III

"Headquarters, Captain. Take a look through the sensory helmet. Those radio nets look like fireworks, and corporate souls tell me it smells like cornedbeef hash and fried eggs. Hey, thanks for getting us dusted out. Had a tendency toward hayfever when I was alive that I never did shake."

Rydra's voice: "The crew will debark with the Captain and the Butcher. The crew will take them to General Forester, together, and not let them be separated."

The Butcher's voice: "There is a tape recording in the Captain's cabin on the console containing a grammar of Babel-17. The Slug will send that tape immediately to Dr.

Markus T'mwarba on Earth by special delivery. Then inform Dr. T'mwarba by stellarphone that the tape was sent, at what time, and its contents.''

"Brass, Slug! Something's wrong up there!" Ron's voice overcut the Captain's signal. "You ever heard them talk like that? Hey, Captain Wong, what's the matter . . . ?"

PART FIVE

~~~~~~

Markus T'mwarba

Growing older I descend November.
The asymptotic cycle of the year
plummets to now. In crystal reveries
I pass beneath a fixed white line of trees
where dry leaves lie for footsteps to dismember.
They crackle with a muted sound like fear.
That and the wind is all that I can hear.
I ask cold air, "What is the word that frees?"
The wind says, "Change," and the white sun, "Remem-
    ber."

                            —from *Electra*

1

The spool of tape, the imperative directive from General Forester, and the infuriated Dr. T'mwarba reached Danil D. Appleby's office within thirty seconds of each other.

He was opening the flat box when the noise outside the partition made him look up. "Michael," he asked the intercom. "What's that?"

"Some madman who says he's a psychiatrist!"

"I am not mad!" Dr. T'mwarba said loudly. "But I know how long it takes a package to get from Administrative Alliance Headquarters to Earth, and it should have reached my door with this morning's mail. It didn't, which means it's been held up, and this is where you do things like that. Let me in."

Then the door crashed back against the wall and he was.

Michael craned around T'mwarba's hip: "Hey, Dan, I'm sorry. I'll call the——"

Dr. T'mwarba pointed to the desk and said, "That's mine. Gimme."

"Don't bother, Michael," the Customs Officer said before the door was slammed again. "Good afternoon, Dr. T'mwarba. Won't you sit down. This is addressed to you, isn't it? Don't look so surprised that I know you. I also handle security psyche-index integration, and all of us in the department know your brilliant work in schizoid-differentiation. I'm so glad to meet you."

"Why can't I have my package?"

"One moment and I'll find out." As he picked up the

171

directive, Dr. T'mwarba picked up the box and stuck it in his pocket:

"Now you can explain."

The Customs Officer opened the letter. "It seems," he said, pressing his knee against the desk to release some of the hostility that had built up in very little time, "that you may have . . . eh, keep the tape on condition you leave for Administrative Alliance Headquarters this evening on the *Midnight Falcon* and bring the tape with you. Passage has been booked, thanking you in advance for your cooperation, sincerely, General X. J. Forester."

"Why?"

"He doesn't say. I'm afraid, doctor, that unless you agree to go, I won't be able to let you keep that. And we can get it back."

"That's what you think. Have you any idea what they want?"

The officer shrugged. "You were expecting it. Who's it from?"

"Rydra Wong."

"Wong?" The Customs Officer had put both knees against the desk. He dropped them. "The poet, Rydra Wong? You know Rydra, too?"

"I've been her psychiatric advisor since she was twelve. Who are you?"

"I'm Danil D. Appleby. Had I known you were Rydra's friend, I would have ushered you up here myself!" The hostility had acted as a take off from which to spring into ebullient camaraderie. "If you're leaving on the *Falcon*, you've got time to step out a little while with me, haven't you? I was going to leave work early anyway. I have to stop off at . . . well, someplace in Transport Town. Why didn't you say you knew her before? There's a delightfully ethnic place right near where I'm going. Get a reasonable meal and a good drink there; do you follow the wrestling? Most people think it's illegal, but you can watch it there. Ruby and Python are on display this evening. If you'll just make that one stop with me first, I know you'll find it fascinating. And I'll get you to the *Falcon* on time."

"I think I know the place."

"You go downstairs and they have this big bubble on the ceiling, where they fight . . . ?" Effervescent, he leaned forward. "As a matter of fact, Rydra first took me there."

Dr. T'mwarba began to smile.

The Customs Officer slapped the desk top. "We had a wild time that night! Simply wild!" He narrowed his eyes. "Ever been picked up by one of those . . ." He snapped his fingers three times. ". . . in the discorporate sector? Now that still *is* illegal. But take a walk out there some evening."

"Come," laughed the doctor. "Dinner and a drink; best idea I've heard all day. I'm starved and I haven't seen a good match in four months."

"I've never been inside *this* place before," the Officer said, as they stepped from the monorail. "I called to make an appointment but they told me I didn't need one, just to come in; they were open till six. I figured what the hell, I'd take off from work." They crossed the street and passed the newsstand where frayed, unshaven loaders were picking up schedule sheets for incoming flights. Three stellarmen in green uniforms lurched along the sidewalk, arms about each other's shoulders. "You know," the Customs Officer was saying, "I've had quite a battle with myself; I've wanted to do it ever since I first came down here—hell, ever since I first went to the movies and saw pictures. But anything really bizarre just wouldn't go at the office. Then I said to myself, it could be something simple, covered up when I was wearing clothes. Here we are."

The Officer pushed open the door of Plastiplasm Plus ("Addendums, Superscripts, and Footnotes to the Beautiful Body").

"You know I always meant to ask someone who was an authority; do you think there's anything psychologically off about wanting something like this?"

"Not at all."

A young lady with blue eyes, lips, hair and wings said, "You can go right in. Unless you want to check our catalogue first."

"Oh, I know exactly what I want," the Customs Officer assured her. "This way?"

"That's right."

"Actually," Dr. T'mwarba went on, "it's psychologically important to feel in control of your body, that you can change it, shape it. Going on a six month diet or a successful muscle building program can give quite a sense of satisfaction. So can a new nose, chin, or set of scales and feathers."

They were in a room with white operating tables. "Can I help you?" asked a smiling, Polynesian cosmetisurgeon in a blue smock. "Why don't you lie down here?"

"I'm just watching," Dr. T'mwarba said.

"It's listed in your catalogue as 5463," the Customs Officer declared. "I want it there." He clapped his left hand to his right shoulder.

"Oh yes. I rather like that one myself. Just a moment." He opened the top of a stand by the table. Instruments glittered.

The surgeon went off to the glass-faced refrigeration unit at the far wall where behind the glass doors intricate plastiplasm shapes were blurred by frost. He returned with a tray full of various fragments. The only recognizable one was the front half of a miniature dragon with jeweled eyes, glittering scales, and opalescent wings: it was less than two inches long.

"When he's connected up to your nervous system, you'll be able to make him whistle, hiss, roar, flap his wings and spit sparks, though it may take a few days to assimilate him into your body picture. Don't be surprised if at first he just burps and looks seasick. Take your shirt off, please."

The Officer opened his collar.

"We'll just block off all sensation from your shoulder on . . . there, that didn't really hurt. This? Oh, it's a local venal and arterial constrictant; we want to keep things clean. Now, we'll just cut you along the —well, if it upsets you, don't look. Talk to your friend there. It'll just take a few minutes. Oh, that must have tickled all down in your tummy! Never mind. Just once more. Fine. That's your shoulder joint. I know; your arm does look sort of funny hanging there without it. We'll just stick in this transparent plastiplasm cage now. Exact same articulation as your shoulder joint, and it holds your muscles out of the way. See, it's got grooves for your arteries. Move your chin, please. If you want to watch, look in the mirror. Now we'll just crimp it around the edges. Keep this vivatape around the rim of the cage for a couple of days until things grow together. There's not much chance of its pulling apart unless you strain your arm suddenly, but you ought to be safe. Now I'll just connect the little fellow in there to the nerve. This will hurt——"

"Gnnnnn!" The Customs Officer half rose.

"—Sit! Sit! All right, the little catch here—look in the mirror—is to open the cage. You'll learn how to make him come out and do tricks, but don't be impatient. It takes a bit of time. Let me turn the feeling back on in your arm."

The surgeon removed the electrodes and the Officer whistled.

"Stings a little. It will for about an hour. If there's any redness or inflammation, please don't hesitate to come back. Everything that comes through that doorway gets perfectly sterilized, but every five or six years somebody comes down with an infection. You can put your shirt on now."

As they walked into the street, the Customs Officer flexed his shoulder. "You know they claim it should make absolutely no difference." He made a face. "My fingers feel funny. Do you think he might have bruised a nerve?"

'I doubt it," Dr. T'mwarba said, "but you will if you keep twisting like that. You'll pull the vivatape loose. Let's go eat."

The Officer fingered his shoulder. "It feels odd to have a three inch hole there and your arm still working."

"So," Dr. T'mwarba said over his mug, "Rydra first brought you to Transport Town."

"Yes. Actually—well, I only met her that once. She was getting a crew together for a government sponsored trip. I was just along to approve indices. But something happened that evening."

"What was it?"

"I saw a bunch of the weirdest, oddest people I had ever met in my life, who thought different, and acted different, and even made love different. And they made me laugh, and get angry, and be happy, and be sad, and excited, and even fall in love a little myself.'' He glanced up at the sphere of the wrestling arena aloft in the bar. ''And they didn't seem to be so weird or strange anymore.''

''Communication was working that night?''

''I guess so. It's presumptuous my calling her by her first name. But I feel like she's my . . . friend. I'm a lonely man, in a city of lonely men. And when you find some place where—communications are working, you come back to see if it will happen again.''

''Has it?''

Danil D. Appleby looked down from the ceiling and began to unbutton his shirt. ''Let's have dinner.'' He shrugged his shirt over the back of the chair and glanced down at the dragon caged in his shoulder. ''You come back anyway.'' Turning in his seat, he picked his shirt up, folded it neatly, and put it down again. ''Dr. T'mwarba, have you any idea why they want you to come to Administrative Alliance Headquarters?''

''I assume it concerns Rydra and this tape.''

''Because you said you were her doctor. I just hope it isn't a medical reason. If anything happened to her, it would be terrible. For me, I mean. She managed to say so much to me in that one evening, so very simply.'' He laughed and ran his finger around the rim of the cage. The beast inside gurgled. ''And half the time she wasn't even looking in my direction when she said it.''

''I hope she's all right,'' Dr. T'mwarba said. ''She'd better be.''

II

Before the *Midnight Falcon* landed, he inveigled the captain into letting him speak with Flight Control. ''I want to know when the *Rimbaud* came in.''

"Just a moment, sir. I don't believe it has. Certainly not within the past six months. It would take a little time to check back further than——"

"No. It would be more like the past few days. Are you sure the *Rimbaud* did not land here recently under Captain Rydra Wong?"

"Wong? I believe she did land yesterday, but not in the *Rimbaud*. It was an unmarked fighter ship. There was some mixup because the serial numbers had been filed off the tubes and there was a possibility it might have been stolen."

"Was Captain Wong all right when she disembarked?"

"She'd apparently relinquished command to her——" The voice stopped.

"Well?"

"Excuse me, sir. This has been all marked classified. I didn't see the sticker, and it was accidentally put back in the regular file. I can't give you any more information. It's only cleared to authorized persons."

"I'm Dr. Markus T'mwarba," the doctor said, with authority and no idea whether it would do any good.

"Oh, there is a notation concerning you, sir. But you're not on the cleared list."

"Then what the hell does it say, young lady?"

"Just that if you requested information, to refer you directly to General Forester."

An hour later he walked into General Forester's office. "All right, what's the matter with Rydra?"

"Where's the tape?"

"If Rydra wanted me to have it, she had good reason. If she'd wanted you to have it, she would have given it to you. Believe me, you won't get your hands on it unless I give it to you."

"I'd expected more cooperation, Doctor."

"I am cooperating. I'm here, General. But you must want me to do something, and unless I know exactly what's going on, I can't."

"It's a very unmilitary attitude," General Forester said, coming around the desk. "It's one I'm having to deal with more and more, recently. I don't know whether I like it. But I don't know whether I dislike it either." The green-suited stellarman sat on the desk's edge, touched the stars on his collar, looked pensive. "Miss Wong was the first person I've met in a long time to whom I could not say: do this, do that, and be damned if you inquire about the consequences. The first time I spoke to her about Babel-17, I thought I could just hand her the transcription, and she would hand it back to me in English. She told me flatly: No; I would have to tell her more. That's the first time anyone's told me I *had* to do anything in fourteen years. I may not like it; I sure as hell respect it." His hands dropped protectively to his lap. (Protective? Was it Rydra who had taught him to interpret that movement, T'mwarba wondered briefly.) "It's so easy to get caught in your fragment of the world. When a voice comes cutting through, it's important. Rydra Wong..." and the General stopped, an expression settling on his features that made T'mwarba chill as he looked at it with what Rydra had taught him.

"Is she all right, General Forester? Is this something medical?"

"I don't know," the General said. "There's a woman in my inner office—and a man. I can't tell you whether the woman is Rydra Wong or not. It certainly isn't the same woman I talked to that evening on Earth about Babel-17."

But T'mwarba, already at the door, shoved it open.

A man and a woman looked up. The man was massively graceful, amber-haired—a convict, the doctor realized from the mark on his arm. The woman—

He put both fists on his hips: "All right, what am I about to say to you?"

She said: "Non comprehension."

Breathing pattern, curl of hands in lap, carriage of shoulders, the details whose import she had demonstrated to him a thousand times: he learned in the horrifying length of a breath just how much they identified. For a moment he wished she had never taught him, because they were all gone, and their absence in her familiar body were worse than scars and disfigurements. He began in a voice that was habitually for her, the one he had praised or chastened her with, "I was going to say—if this is a joke, sweetheart, I'll ... paddle

you." It ended with the voice for strangers, for salesmen and
wrong numbers, and he felt unsteadied. "If you're not
Rydra, who are you?"

She said: "Non comprehension of the question. General
Forester, is this man Doctor Markus T'mwarba?"

"Yes, he is."

"Look." Dr. T'mwarba turned to the General. "I'm
sure you've gone over fingerprints, metabolic rates, retina
patterns, that sort of identification."

"That's Rydra Wong's body, Doctor."

"All right: hypnotics, experiential imprinting, graft of
presynapsed cortical matter—can you think of any other way
to get one mind into another head?"

"Yes. Seventeen. There's no evidence of any of them."
The General stepped from the door. "She's made it clear she
wants to speak to you alone. I'll be right outside." He closed
the door.

"I'm pretty sure who you're not," Doctor T'mwarba
said after a moment.

The woman blinked and said: "Message from Rydra
Wong, delivered verbatim, non comprehension of its significance." Suddenly the face took on its familiar animation. Her
hands grasped each other, and she leaned slightly forward:
"Mocky, am I glad you got here. I can't sustain this very
long, so here goes. Babel-17 is more or less like Onoff,
Algol, Fortran. I am telepathic after all, only I've just learned
how to control it. I . . . we've taken care of the Babel-17
sabotage attempts. Only we're prisoners, and if you want to
get us out, forget about who I am. Use what's on the end of
the tape, and find out who he is!" She pointed to the Butcher.

The animation left, the rigidity returned to her face. The
whole transformation left T'mwarba holding his breath. He
shook his head, started breathing again. After a moment he
went back into the General's office. "Who's the jailbird?" he
asked matter-of-factly.

"We're tracking that down now. I hoped to have the
report this morning." Something on the desk flashed. "Here
it is now." He flipped up a slot in the desk top and pulled out a
folder. As he slit the seal, he paused. "Would you like to tell
me what Onoff, Algol, and Fortran are?"

"To be sure, listening at keyholes." T'mwarba sighed and sat down in a bubble chair in front of the desk. "They're ancient, twentieth century languages—artificial languages that were used to program computers, designed especially for machines. Onoff was the simplest. It reduced everything to a combination of two words, *on* and *off*, or the binary number system. The others were more, complicated."

The General nodded, and finished opening the folder. "That guy came from the swiped spider-boat with her. The crew got very upset when we wanted to put them in separate quarters." He shrugged. "It's something psychic. Why take chances? We leave them together."

"Where is the crew? Were they able to help you?"

"Them? It's like trying to talk to something out of your bad dreams. Transport. Who can talk to people like that?"

"Rydra could," Doctor T'mwarba said. "I'd like to see if I might."

"If you wish. We're keeping them at Headquarters." He opened the folder, then made a face. "Odd. There's a fairly detailed account of his existence for a five year period that started with some petty thievery, strong arm work, then graduates to a couple of rub-outs. A bank robbery——" The General pursed his lips and nodded appreciatively. "He served two years in the penal caves of Titin, escaped—this boy *is* something. Disappeared into the Specelli Snap where he either died, or perhaps got into a shadow-ship. He certainly didn't die. But before December '61, he doesn't seem to have existed. He's usually called the Butcher."

Suddenly the General dived into a drawer and came up with another folder. "Kreto, Earth, Minos, Callisto," he read, then slapped the folder with the back of his hand. "Aleppo, Rhea, Olympia, Paradise, Dis!"

"What's that, the Butcher's itinerary until he went into Titin?"

"It just so happens it is. But it's also the locations of a series of accidents that began in December '61. We'd just gotten around to connecting them up with Babel-17. We'd only been working with recent 'accidents', but then this pattern from a few years ago turned up. Reports of the same sort of radio exchange. Do you think Miss Wong has brought home our saboteur?"

"Could be. Only that isn't Rydra in there."

"Well, yes. I guess you could say that."

"For similar reasons I would gather that the gentleman with her is not the Butcher."

"Who do you think he is?"

"Right now I don't know. I'd say it's fairly important we found out." He stood up. "Where can I get hold of Rydra's crew?"

III

"A pretty snazzy place!" Calli said as they stepped from the lift at the top floor of Alliance Towers.

"Nice now," said Mollya, "to be able to walk about."

A headwaiter in white formal wear came across the civet rug, looked just a trifle askance at Brass, then said, "This is your party, Dr. T'mwarba?"

"That's right. We have an alcove by the window. You can bring us a round of drinks right away. I've ordered already."

The waiter nodded, turned, and led them toward a high, arched window that looked over Alliance Plaza. A few people turned to watch them.

"Administrative Headquarters can be a very pleasant place." Dr. T'mwarba smiled.

"If you got the money," Ron said. He craned to look at the blue-black ceiling, where the lights were arranged to simulate the constellations seen from Rymik, and whistled softly. "I read about places like this but I never thought I'd be in one."

"Wish I could have brought the kids," the Slug mused. "They thought the Baron's was something."

At the alcove the waiter held Mollya's chair.

"Was that Baron Ver Dorco of the War Yards?"

"Yeah," said Calli. "Barbequed lamb, plum wine, the best looking peacocks I've seen in two years. Never got to eat 'em." He shook his head.

"One of the annoying habits of aristocracy," T'mwarba laughed, "they'll go ethnic at the slightest provocation. But there're only a few of us left, and most of us have the good manners to drop our titles."

"Late weapons master of Armsedge," the Slug corrected.

"I read the report of his death. Rydra was there?"

"We all were. It was a 'retty wild evening."

"What exactly happened?"

Brass shook his head. "Well, Ca'tain went early . . ." When he had finished recounting the incidents, with the others adding details, Dr. T'mwarba sat back in his chair.

"The papers didn't give it that way. But they wouldn't. What was this TW-55 anyway?"

Brass shrugged.

There was a click as the discorporaphone in the doctor's ear went on: "It's a human being who's been worked over and over from birth till it isn't human anymore," the Eye said. "I was with Captain Wong when the Baron first showed it to her."

Dr. T'mwarba nodded. "Is there anything else you can tell me?"

Slug, who had been trying to get comfortable in the hardbacked chair, now leaned his stomach against the table edge. "Why?"

The others got still, quickly.

The fat man looked at the rest of the crew. "Why are we telling him all this? He's going back and give it to the stellarmen."

"That's right," Dr. T'mwarba said. "Any of it that might help Rydra."

Ron put down his glass of iced cola. "The stellarmen haven't been what you'd call nice to us, Doc," he explained.

"They don't take us to no fancy restaurants." Calli tucked his napkin into the zircon necklace he'd worn for the occasion. A waiter placed a bowl of french fried potatoes on the table, turned away, and came back with a platter of hamburgers.

Across the table Mollya picked up the tall, red flask and looked at it questioningly.

"Ketchup," Dr. T'mwarba said.

"Ohhh," breathed Mollya and returned it to the damask table cloth.

"Diavalo should be here now." The Slug sat back slowly and stopped looking at the doctor. "He's an artist with a carbo-synth, and he's got a feel for a protein-dispenser that's fine for good solid meals like nut stuffed pheasant, fillet of snapper-meyonaise, and good stick-to-your-ribs food for a hungry spaceship crew. But this fancy stuff"—he spread mustard carefully across his bun—"give him a pound of real chopped meat, and I bet he'd run out of the galley 'cause it might bite him."

Brass said: "What's wrong with Ca'tain Wong? That's what nobody wants to ask."

"I don't know. But if you'll tell me all you can, I'll have a lot better chance of doing something."

"The other thing nobody wants to say," Brass went on, "is that *one* of us don't want you to do anything for her. But we don't know which."

The others silenced again.

"There was a s'y on the shi'. We all knew about it. It tried to destroy the shi' twice. I think it's res'onsible for whatever ha''ened to Ca'tain Wong and the Butcher."

"We all think so," the Slug said.

"This is what you didn't want to tell the stellarmen?" Brass nodded.

"Tell him about the circuit boards and the phony take off before we got to Tarik," Ron said.

Brass explained.

"If it hadn't been for the Butcher," the discorporaphone clicked again, "we would have reentered normal space in the Cygnus Nova. The Butcher convinced Tarik to hook us out and take us aboard."

"So." Dr. T'mwarba looked around the table. "One of you is a spy."

"It could be one of the kids," the Slug said. "It doesn't have to be someone at this table."

"If it is," Dr. T'mwarba said, "I'm talking to the rest of you. General Forester couldn't get anything out of you. Rydra needs somebody's help. It's that simple."

Brass broke the lengthening silence. "I'd just lost a shi' to the Invaders, Doc; a whole 'latoon of kids, more than half the officers. Even though I could wrestle well and was a good 'ilot, to any other trans'ort ca'tain, that run-in with the Invaders made me a stiff jinx. Ca'tain Wong's not from our world. But wherever she came from, she brought a set of values with her that said, 'I like your work and I want to hire you.' I'm grateful."

"She knows about so much," Calli said. "This is the wildest trip I've ever been on. Worlds. That's it, Doc. She cuts through worlds and don't mind taking you along. When's the last time somebody took me to a Baron's for dinner and espionage? Next day I'm eating with pirates. And here I am now. Sure I want to help."

"Calli's too mixed up with his stomach," Ron interrupted. "What it is, is she gets you thinking, Doc. She made me think about Mollya and Calli. You know, she was tripled with Muels Aranlyde, the guy who wrote *Empire Star*. But I guess you must, if you're her doctor. Anyway, you start thinking that maybe those people who live in other worlds—like Calli says—where people write books or make weapons, are real. If you believe in them, you're a little more ready to believe in yourself. And when somebody who can do that needs help, you help."

"Doctor," Mollya said, "I was dead. She made me alive. What can I do?"

"You can tell me everything you know"—he leaned across the table and locked his fingers—"about the Butcher."

"The Butcher?" Brass asked. The others were surprised. "What about him? We don't know anything exce't that Ca'tain and him got to be real close."

"You were on the same ship with him for three weeks. Tell me everything you saw him do."

They looked at one another, silence questioning.

"Was there anything that might have indicated where he was from?"

"Titin," Calli said. "The mark on his arm."

"Before Titin, at least five years before. The problem is that the Butcher doesn't know either."

They looked even more perplexed. Then Brass said, "His language. Ca'tain said he originally had s'oken a language where there was no word for 'I'."

Dr. T'mwarba frowned more deeply as the discorporaphone clicked again. "She taught him how to say *I* and *you*. They wandered through the graveyard in evening, and we hovered over them while they taught each other who they were."

"The 'I'," T'mwarba said, "that's something to go on." He sat back. "It's funny. I suppose I know everything about Rydra there is to know. And I know just that little about _____"

The discorporaphone clicked a third time. "You don't know about the myna bird."

T'mwarba was surprised. "Of course I do. I was there."

The discorporate crew laughed softly. "But she never told you why she was so frightened."

"It was a hysterical onset brought about by her previous condition——"

Ghostly laughter again. "The worm, Dr. T'mwarba. She wasn't afraid of the bird at all. She was afraid of the telepathic impression of a huge worm crawling toward her, the worm that the bird was picturing."

"She told you this——" and never told me, was the ending of what had begun in minor outrage and ceased in wonder.

"Worlds," the ghost reiterated. "Sometimes worlds exist under your eyes and you never see. This room might be filled with phantoms; you never know. Even the rest of the crew can't be sure what we're saying now. But Captain Wong, she never used a discorporaphone. She found a way to talk with us without one. She cut through worlds, and joined them—that's the important part—so that both became bigger."

"Then somebody's got to figure out where in the world,

yours, or mine, or hers, the Butcher came from." A memory resolved like a cadence closing, and he laughed. The others looked puzzled. "A worm. *Somewhere in Eden now, a worm, a worm . . .* That was one of her earliest poems. And it never occurred to me."

IV

~~~~~~

"Am I supposed to be happy?" Dr. T'mwarba asked.

"You're supposed to be interested," said General Forester.

"You've looked at a hyperstatic map and discovered that though the sabotage attempts over the last year and a half lie all over a galaxy in regular space, they're within cruiser distance of the Specelli Snap across the jump. Also, you've discovered that during the time the Butcher was in Titin, there were no 'accidents' at all. In other words, you have discovered that the Butcher could be responsible for the whole business, just from physical proximity. No, I am not happy at all."

"Why not?"

"Because he's an important person."

"Important?"

"I know he's . . . important to Rydra. The crew told me that."

"Him?" Then comprehension struck. *"Him?* Oh, no. Anything else. He's the lowest form of . . . Not that. Treason, sabotage, how many murders . . . I mean he's———"

"You don't know what he is. And if he's responsible for the Babel-17 attacks, in his own right he's as extraordinary as Rydra." The Doctor stood from his bubble seat. "Now will you give me a chance to try out my idea? I've been listening to yours all morning. Mine will probably work."

"I still don't understand what you want, though."

Dr. T'mwarba sighed. "First I want to get Rydra and the Butcher and us in the most heavily guarded, deepest, darkest, impenetrable dungeon Administrative Alliance Headquarters has——"

"But we don't have a dun——"

"Don't put me on," Dr. T'mwarba said evenly. "You're fighting a war, remember?"

The General made a face. "Why all this security?"

"Because of the mayhem this guy has caused up till now. He's not going to enjoy what I plan to do. I'd just be happier if there was something, like the entire military force of the Alliance, on my side. Then I'd feel I had a chance."

Rydra sat on one side of the cell, the Butcher on the other, both strapped to plastic coated chair forms that were part of the walls. Dr. T'mwarba looked after the equipment that was being rolled from the room. "No dungeons and torture chambers, eh, General?" He glanced at a spot of red-brown that had dried on the stone floor by his foot, and shook his head. "I'd be happier if the place was swabbed out with acid and disinfected first. But, I suppose on short order——"

"Do you have all your equipment here, Doctor?" the General asked, ignoring the Doctor's goad. "If you change your mind I can have a barrage of specialists here inside of fifteen minutes."

"The place isn't big enough," Dr. T'mwarba said. "I've got nine specialists right here." He rested his hand on a medium-sized computer that had been placed in the corner beside the rest. "I'd just as soon you weren't here, either. But since you won't go, just watch quietly."

"You say," General Forester said, "you want maximum security. I can have a few two hundred and fifty pound akido masters in here also."

"I have a black belt in akido, General. I think the two of us will do."

The General raised his eyebrows. "I'm karate myself. Akido is one martial art I've never really understood. And you have a black belt?"

Dr. T'mwarba adjusted a larger piece of equipment and nodded. "So does Rydra. I don't know what the Butcher can do, so I'm keeping everybody strapped good and tight."

"Very well." The General touched something at the corner of the door jamb. The metal slab lowered slowly. "We'll be in here five minutes." The slab reached the floor and the line along the edge of the door disappeared. "We're welded in now. We're at the center of twelve layers of defense, all impenetrable. Nobody even knows the location of the place, including myself."

"After those labyrinths we came through, I certainly don't," T'mwarba said.

"Just in case somebody managed to map it, we're moved automatically every fifteen seconds. He's not going to get out." The General gestured toward the Butcher.

"I'm just assuming no one can get in." T'mwarba pressed a switch.

"Go over this once more."

"The Butcher has amnesia, say the doctors on Titin. That means his consciousness is restricted to the section of his brain with synapse connections dating from '61. His consciousness is, in effect, restricted to one segment of his cortex. What this does"—the doctor lifted a metal helmet and put it on the Butcher's head, glancing at Rydra—"is create a series of 'unpleasantnesses' in that segment until he is driven out of that part of the brain back into the rest."

"What if there simply are no connections from one part of the cortex to the other?"

"If it gets unpleasant enough, he will make new ones."

"With the sort of life he's led," commented the General, "I wonder what would be unpleasant enough to drive him out of his head."

"Onoff, Algol, Fortran," said Dr. T'mwarba.

The General watched the doctor make further adjustments. "Ordinarily this would create a snake pit situation in the brain. However, with a mind that doesn't know the word 'I', or hasn't known it for long, fear tactics won't work."

"What will?"

"Algol, Onoff, and Fortran, with the help of a barber and the fact that it's Wednesday."

"Dr. T'mwarba, I didn't bother with more than a precursory check on your psyche-index——"

"I know what I'm doing. None of those computer languages have the word for 'I' either. This prevents such statements as 'I can't solve the problem.' Or, 'I'm really not interested.' Or 'I've got better things to waste my time with.' General, in a little town on the Spanish side of the Pyrenees there is only one barber. This barber shaves all the men in the town who do not shave themselves. Does the barber shave himself or not?"

The General frowned.

'You don't believe me? But General, I always tell the truth. Except Wednesdays; on Wednesday every statement I make is a lie."

"But today's Wednesday!" the General exclaimed, beginning to fluster.

"How convenient. Now, now, General, don't hold your breath until you're blue in the face."

"I'm not holding my breath!"

"I didn't say you were. But just answer yes or no: have you stopped beating your wife?"

"Damn it, I can't answer a question like . . ."

"Well, while you think about your wife, decide whether to hold your breath, bearing in mind that it's Wednesday, tell me: who shaves the barber?"

The General's confusion broke open into laughter. "Paradoxes! You mean you're going to feed him paradoxes he's got to contend with."

"When you do it to a computer, they burn out unless they've been programmed to turn off when confronted with them."

"Suppose he decides to discorporate?"

"Let a little thing like discorporation stop me?" He pointed to another machine. "That's what this is for."

"Just one more thing. How do you know what paradoxes to give him? Surely the ones you told me wouldn't—"

"They wouldn't. Besides, they only exist in English and a few other analytically clumsy languages. Paradoxes break down into linguistic manifestations of the language in which they're expressed. For the Spanish barber, and Wednesday, it's the words 'every' and 'all' that hold contradictory meanings. The construction 'don't until' has a similar ambiguity. The same with the word 'stop.' The tape Rydra sent me was a grammar and vocabulary of Babel-17. Fascinating. It's the most analytically exact language imaginable. But that's because everything is flexible, and ideas come in huge numbers of congruent sets, governed by the same words. This just means that the number of paradoxes you can come up with is staggering. Rydra had filled the whole last half of the tape up with some of the more ingenious. If a mind limited to Babel-17 got caught up in them, it would burn itself out, or break down———"

"Or escape to the other side of the brain. I see. Well, go ahead. Start."

"I did two minutes ago."

The General looked at the Butcher. "I don't see anything."

"You won't for another minute." He made a further adjustment. "The paradoxical system I've set up has to worm itself through the entire conscious part of his brain. There are a lot of synapses to start clicking on and off."

Suddenly the lips of the hard muscled face pulled back from the teeth.

"Here we go," Dr. T'mwarba said.

"What's happening to Miss Wong?"

Rydra's face underwent the same contortion.

"I'd hoped that wouldn't happen," Dr. T'mwarba sighed, "but I suspected it would. They're in telepathic union."

A *crack* from the Butcher's chair. The headstrap had been slightly loose and his skull struck the back of his chair.

A sound from Rydra, opening into a full-throated wail that suddenly choked off. Her startled eyes blinked twice, and she cried, "Oh, Mocky, it hurts!"

One of the armstraps gave on the Butcher's chair, and the fist flew up.

Then a light by Dr. T'mwarba's thumb went from white to amber, and the thumb jammed down on the switch. Something happened in the Butcher's body; he relaxed.

General Forester started, "He discor———"

But the Butcher was panting.

"Let me out of here, Mocky," came from Rydra.

Dr. T'mwarba brushed his hand across a micro-switch and the bands that had bound her forehead, calves, wrists, and arms came loose with popping sounds. She rushed across the cell to the Butcher. "Him too?"

She nodded.

He pushed the second micro-switch and the Butcher fell forward into her arms. She went down to the floor with his weight, at the same time began working her knuckles along the stiffened muscles on his back.

General Forester was holding a vibra-gun on them. "Now who the hell is he and where is he from?" he demanded.

The Butcher started to collapse again, but his hands slapped the floor and he held himself up. "Ny . . ." he began. "I . . . I'm Nyles Ver Dorco." His voice had lost the grating mineral quality. The pitch was nearly a fourth higher and a slight aristocratic drawl suffused his words. "Armsedge. I was born at Armsedge. And I've . . . I've killed my father!"

The door slab raised into the wall. There was an inrush of smoke and the odor of hot metal. "Now what the devil is that smell?" General Forester said. "That's not supposed to happen."

"I would guess," Dr. T'mwarba said, "the first half dozen layers of defenses for this security chamber have been broken through. Had it taken a few minutes longer, chances are we wouldn't be here."

A rush of footsteps. A soot-streaked stellarman staggered through the door. "General Forester, are you all right? The outer wall exploded, and somehow the radio-locks on the double-gates were shorted out. Something cut halfway through the ceramic walls. It looks like lasers or something."

The General got very pale. "What was trying to get in here?"

Dr. T'mwarba looked at Rydra.

The Butcher got to his feet, holding on to her shoulder. "A couple of my father's more ingenious models, first cousins to TW-55. There are maybe six in inconspicuous, but effective, positions through the staff here at Administrative Alliance Headquarters. But you don't have to worry about them any more.''

"Then I'd appreciate it,'' General Forester said measuredly, "if you would all get the hell up to my office and explain what's going on.''

"No. My father wasn't a traitor, General. He simply wanted to make me into the Alliance's most powerful secret agent. But the weapon is not the tool; rather the knowledge of how to use it. And the Invaders had that, and that knowledge is Babel-17.''

"All right. You could be Nyles Ver Dorco. But that just makes a few things I thought I understood an hour ago more confusing.''

"I don't want him to talk too much,'' Dr. T'mwarba said. "The strain his whole nervous system has just been through——''

"I'm all right, Doctor. I've got a complete spare set. My reflexes are quite above normal and I've got control of my whole autonomic layout, down to how fast my toenails grow. My father was a very thorough man.''

General Forester swung his boot heel against the front of his desk. "Better let him go on. Because if I don't understand this whole business in five minutes, I'll put you all away.''

"My father had just begun his work on custom tailored spies when he got the idea. He had me doctored up into the most perfect human he could devise. Then he sent me into Invader territory with the hope I would wreak as much confusion among them as I could. And I did a lot of damage too, before they captured me. Another thing Dad realized was that he would be making rapid progress with the new spies, and eventually they would far outstrip me—which was quite true. I didn't hold a candle to TW-55 for example. But because of—I guess it was family pride, he wanted to keep control of their operations in the family. Every spy from Armsedge can receive radio commands through a pre-established key. Grafted under my medula is a hyperstasis transmitter most of whose parts are electroplastiplasms. No matter how complexed the future spies became, I was still in primary control of the whole fleet of them. Over the past years, several thousand have been released into Invader territory. Up until the time I was captured, we made a very effective force."

"Why weren't you killed?" the General asked. "Or did they find out and manage to turn that entire army of spies back on us?"

"They did discover that I was an Alliance weapon. But that hyperstasis transmitter breaks down under certain conditions and flushes out with my body's waste matter. It takes me about three weeks to grow a new one. So they never learned I was in control of the rest. But they had just come up with their own secret weapon, Babel-17. They gave me a thorough case of amnesia, left me with no communication facilities save Babel-17, then let me escape from Nueva-nueva York back into Alliance territory. I didn't get any instructions to sabotage you. The powers I had, the contact with the other spies dawned on me very painfully and very slowly. And my whole life as a saboteur masquerading as a criminal just grew up. How, or why, I still don't know."

"I think I can explain that, General," Rydra said. "You can program a computer to make mistakes, and you do it not by crossing wires, but by manipulating the 'language' you teach it to 'think' in. The lack of an 'I' precludes any self-critical process. In fact it cuts out any awareness of the symbolic process at all—which is the way we distinguish between reality and our expression of reality."

"Come again?"

"Chimpanzees," Dr. T'mwarba interrupted, "are quite coordinated enough to learn to drive cars, and smart enough to distinguish between red and green lights. But once they learn, they still can't be turned loose, because when the light goes green, they will drive through a brick wall if it's in front of them, and if the light turns red, they will stop in the middle of an intersection even if a truck is bearing down on top of them. They don't have the symbolic process. For them, red *is* stop, and green *is* go."

"Anyway," Rydra went on. "Babel-17 as a language contains a pre-set program for the Butcher to become a criminal and saboteur. If you turn somebody with no memory loose in a foreign country with only the words for tools and machine parts, don't be surprised if he ends up a mechanic. By manipulating his vocabulary properly you can just as easily make him a sailor, or an artist. Also, Babel-17 is such an exact analytical language, it almost assures you technical mastery of any situation you look at. And the lack of an 'I' blinds you to the fact that though it's a highly useful way to look at things, it isn't the only way."

"But you mean that this language could even turn you against the Alliance?" the General asked.

"Well," said Rydra, "to start off with, the word for Alliance in Babel-17 translates literally into English as: one-who-has-invaded. You take it from there. It has all sorts of little diabolisms programmed into it. While thinking in Babel-17 it becomes perfectly logical to try and destroy your own ship and then blot out the fact with self-hypnosis so you won't discover what you're doing and try and stop yourself."

"That's your spy!" Dr. T'mwarba interrupted.

Rydra nodded. "It 'programs' a self-contained schizoid personality into the mind of whoever learns it, reinforced by self-hypnosis—which seems the sensible thing to do since everything else in the language is 'right', whereas any other tongue seems so clumsy. This 'personality' has the general desire to destroy the Alliance at any cost, and at the same time remain hidden from the rest of the consciousness until it's strong enough to take over. That's what happened to us. Without the Butcher's pre-capture experience, we weren't strong enough to keep complete control, although we could stop them from doing anything destructive."

"Why didn't they completely dominate you?" Dr. T'mwarba asked.

"They didn't count on my 'talent', Mocky," Rydra said. "I analyzed it with Babel-17 and it's very simple. The human nervous system puts out radio noise. But you'd have to have an antenna of several thousand miles surface area to tune in anything fine enough to make sense out of that noise. In fact, the only thing with that sort of area is another human nervous system. It happens to an extent in everybody. A few people like me just happen to have better control of it. The schizoid personalities aren't all that strong, and I've also got some control of the noise I send out. I've just been jamming them.''

"And what am I supposed to do with these schizy espionage agents each of you is housing in your head? Lobotomize you?''

"No," Rydra said. "The way you fix your computer isn't to hack out half the wires. You correct the language, introduce the missing elements and compensate for ambiguities.''

"We introduced the main elements," the Butcher said, "back in Tarik's graveyard. We're well on the way to the rest.''

The General stood up slowly. "It won't do." He shook his head. "T'mwarba, where's that tape?''

"Right in my pocket where it's been since this afternoon," Dr. T'mwarba said, pulling out the spool.

"I'm taking this right down to cryptography, then we're going to start all over again." He walked to the door. "Oh, yes, and I'm locking you in." He left, and the three looked at each other.

V

"... yes, of course I should have known that somebody who could get halfway through to our maximum security room and sabotage the war effort over one whole arm of the galaxy could escape from my locked office! ... I am *not* a nit-wit, but I thought— I know you don't care what I think, but they— No, it didn't occur to me that they were going to steal a ship. Well, yes, I— No. Of course I didn't assume— Yes, it was one of our largest battleships. But they left a— No, they're not going to attack our— I have *no* way of knowing except that they left a note saying— Yes, on my desk, they left a note. . . . Well, of course I'll read it to you. That's what I've been trying to do for the last . . .''

VI

〜〜〜〜〜〜〜〜〜〜〜〜〜〜〜〜〜〜〜〜〜〜〜〜〜〜〜〜

Rydra stepped into the spacious cabin of the battleship *Chronos*. Ratt was riding her piggyback.

As she lowered him to the floor, the Butcher turned from the control panel. "How's everybody doing down there?"

"Anybody really confused with the new controls?" Rydra asked.

The platoon boy pulled his ear. "I don't know, Captain. This here is a lot of ship for us to run."

"We just have to get back to the Snap and give this ship to Tarik and the others on Jebel. Brass says he can get us there if you kids keep everything moving smooth."

"We're trying. But there're so many orders all coming through from all over the place at once. I should be down there now."

"You can get down there in a minute," Rydra said. "Suppose I make you honorary quipucamayocuna?"

"Who?"

"That's the guy who reads all the orders as they come through and interprets them and hands them out. Your great grandparents were Indian, weren't they?"

"Yeah. Seminoles."

Rydra shrugged. "Quipucamayocuna is Mayan. Same difference. They gave orders by tying knots in rope; we use punch cards. Scoot, and just keep us flying."

Ratt touched his forehead and scooted.

"What do you think the General made of your note?" the Butcher asked her.

196

"It doesn't really matter. It will make its round of all the top officials; and they'll ponder over it and the possibility will be semantically imprinted in their minds, which is a good bit of the job. And we have Babel-17 corrected—perhaps I should call it Babel-18—which is the best tool conceivable to build it into truth."

"Plus my battery of assistants," the Butcher said. "I think six months should do it. You're lucky those sickness attacks weren't from the speeded up metabolic rates after all. That sounded a little odd to me. You should have collapsed before you came out of Babel-17, if that was the case."

"It was the schiz-configuration trying to force its way into dominance. Well, as soon as we finish with Tarik, we have a message to leave on the desk of Invader Commander Meihlow at Nueva-nueva York."

"This war will end within six months," she quoted. "Best prose sentence I ever wrote. But now we have to work "

"We have the tools to do it no one else has," the Butcher said. He moved over as she sat beside him. "And with the right tools it shouldn't be too difficult. What are we going to do with our spare time?"

"I'm going to write a poem, I think. But it may be a novel. I have a lot to say."

"But I'm still a criminal. Canceling out bad deeds with good is a linguistic fallacy that's gotten people in trouble more than once. Especially if the good deed is in the offing. I'm still responsible for a lot ot murders. To end this war I may have to use dad's spies to make a lot more . . . mistakes. I'll just try to keep them down."

"The whole mechanism of guilt as a deterrent to right action is just as much a linguistic fault. If it bothers you, go back, get tried, be acquitted, then go on about your business. Let me be your business for a while."

"Sure. But who says I get acquitted at this trial?"

Rydra began to laugh. She stopped before him, took his hands, and laid her face against them, still laughing. "But I'll be your defense! And even without Babel-17, you should know by now, I can talk my way out of anything."

—New York,
Dec '64—Sept '65

A FABULOUS, FORMLESS
DARKNESS

For Don Wollheim,
a responsible man in all meanings
to and for what is within,
and Jack Gaughan,
for what is without.

It darkles, (tinct, tint) all this our funanimal world.
James Joyce/*Finnegans Wake*

I do not say, however, that every delusion or wandering of the mind should be called madness.
Erasmus of Rotterdam/*The Praise of Folly*

There is a hollow, holey cylinder running from hilt to point in my machete. When I blow across the mouthpiece in the handle, I make music with my blade. When all the holes are covered, the sound is sad—as rough as rough can be and be called smooth. When all the holes are open, the sound pipes about, bringing to the eye flakes of sun on water, crushed metal. There are twenty holes. And since I've been playing music I've been called all different kinds of fool—more times than Lobey, which is my name.

What I look like?

Ugly and grinning most of the time. That's a whole lot of big nose and gray eyes and wide mouth crammed on a small brown face proper for a fox. That, all scratched around with spun brass for hair. I hack most of it off every two months or so with my machete. Grows back fast. Which is odd, because I'm twenty-three and no beard yet. I have a figure like a bowling pin, thighs, calves, and feet of a man (gorilla?) twice my size (which is about five-nine) and hips to match. There was a rash of hermaphrodites the year I was born, which doctors thought I might be. Somehow I doubt it.

Like I say, ugly. My feet have toes almost as long as my fingers, and the big ones are semi-opposable. But don't knock it; once I saved Little Jon's life.

We were climbing the Beryl Face, slipping around on all that glassy rock, when Little Jon lost his footing and was dangling by one hand. I was hanging by *my* hands, but I stuck my foot down, grabbed him up by the wrist, and pulled him back where he could step on something.

At this point Lo Hawk folds his arms over his leather shirt, nods sagely so that his beard bobs on his ropy neck, says: "And just what were you two young Lo men doing on Beryl Face in the first place? It's dangerous, and we avoid danger, you know. The birthrate is going down, down all the time. We can't afford to lose our productive youth in foolishness." Of course it isn't going down. That's just Lo Hawk. What he means is that the number of *total norms* is going down. But there's plenty of births. Lo Hawk is from the generation where the number of non-functionals, idiots, mongoloids, and cretins was well over fifty percent. (We hadn't adjusted to your images yet. Ah, well.) But now there are noticeably more functionals than non-functionals; so no great concern.

Anyway, not only do I bite my fingernails disgracefully, I also bite my toenails.

And at this point I recall sitting at the entrance of the source-cave where the stream comes from the darkness and makes a sickle of light into the trees, and a blood spider big as my fist suns himself on the rock beside me, belly pulsing out from the sides of him, leaves flicking each other above. Then La Carol walks by with a sling of fruit over her shoulder and the kid under her arm (we had an argument once whether it was mine or not. One day it had

my eyes, my nose, my ears. The next, "Can't you see it's
Lo Easy's boy? Look how strong he is!" Then we both
fell in love with other people and now we're friends again)
and she makes a face and says, "Lo Lobey, what *are* you
doing?"

"Biting my toenails. What does it look like?"

"Oh, really!" and she shakes her head and goes into the
woods towards the village.

But right now I prefer to sit on the flat rock, sleep,
think, gnaw, or sharpen my machete. It's my privilege, so
La Dire tells me.

Until a little while ago, Lo Little Jon, Lo Easy, and Lo
me herded goats together (which is what we were doing on
the Beryl Face: looking for pasture). We made quite a trio.
Little Jon, though a year older than me, will till death look
like a small black fourteen-year-old with skin smooth as
volcanic glass. He sweats through his palms, the soles of
his feet, and his tongue (no real sweat glands: piddles like a
diabetic on the first day of winter, or a very nervous dog).
He's got silver mesh for hair—not white, silver. The
pigment's based on the metal pure; the black skin comes
from a protein formed around the oxide. None of that rusty
iron brown of melanin that suntans you and me. He sings,
being a little simple, running and jumping around the
rocks and goats, flashing from head and groin and armpits,
then stops to cock his leg (like a nervous dog, yeah)
against a tree-trunk, glancing around with embarrassed
black eyes. Smiling, those eyes fling as much light, on a
different frequency, as his glittering head. He's got claws.
Hard, sharp horny ones where I have nubs. He's not a
good Lo to have mad at you.

Easy, on the other hand, is large (about eight feet tall),
furry (umber hair curls all down the small of his back,
makes ringlets on his belly), strong (that three hundred and

twenty-six pounds of Easy is really a lot of rock jammed jagged into his pelt: his muscles have corners), and gentle. Once I got angry at him when one of the fertile nannies fell down a rock chimney.

I saw it coming. The ewe was the big blind one who had been giving us perfect norm triplets for eight years. I stood on one foot and threw rocks and sticks with the other three limbs. It takes a rock on the head to get Easy's attention; he was much closer than I was.

"Watch it, you non-functional, lost-Lo mongoloid! She's gonna fall in the—" At which point she did.

Easy stopped looking at me with his what-are-you-throwing-stones-at-me-for? face, saw her scrabbling at the edge, dove for her, missed, and both of them started bleating. I put my all behind the rock that caught him on the hip and almost cried. Easy did.

He crouched at the chimney edge, tears wetting the fur on his cheeks. The ewe had broken her neck at the bottom of the chimney. Easy looked up and said, "Don't hurt me no more, Lobey. That"—he knuckled his blue eyes, then pointed down—"hurts too much already." What can you do with a Lo like that? Easy has claws too. All he ever uses them for is to climb the titan palms and tear down mangoes for the children.

Generally we did a good job with the goats, though. Once Little Jon leaped from the branch of an oak to the back of a lion and tore out its throat before it got to the herd (and rose from the carcass, shook himself, and went behind a rock, glancing over his shoulder). And as gentle as he is, Easy crushed a blackbear's head with a log. And I got my machete, all ambidextrous, left footed, right handed, or vice versa. Yeah, we did a good job.

Not no more.

What happened was Friza.

"Friza" or "La Friza" was always a point of debate

with the older folk-doctors and the elders who have to pass on titles. She looked normal: slim, brown, full mouth, wide nose, brass-colored eyes. I think she may have been born with six fingers on one hand, but the odd one was non-functional, so a travelling doctor amputated it. Her hair was tight, springy, and black. She kept it short, though once she found some red cord and wove it through. That day she wore bracelets and copper beads, strings and strings. She was beautiful.

And silent. When she was a baby, she was put in the kage with the other non-functionals because she didn't move. No La. Then a keeper discovered she didn't move because she already knew how; she was agile as a squirrel's shadow. She was taken out of the kage. Got back her La. But she never spoke. So at age eight, when it was obvious that the beautiful orphan was mute, away went her La. They couldn't very well put her back in the kage. Functional she was, making baskets, plowing, an expert huntress with the bolas. That's when there was all the debate.

Lo Hawk upheld, "In my day, La and Lo were reserved for total norms. We've been very lax, giving this title of purity to any functional who happens to have the misfortune to be born in these confusing times."

To which La Dire replied, "Times change, and it has been an unspoken precedent for thirty years that La and Lo be bestowed on any functional creature born in this our new home. The question is merely how far to extend the definition of functionality. Is the ability to communicate verbally its *sine qua non*? She is intelligent and she learns quickly and thoroughly. I move for *La Friza*."

The girl sat and played with white pebbles by the fire while they discussed her social standing.

"The beginning of the end, the beginning of the end," muttered Lo Hawk. "We must preserve something."

"The end of the beginning," sighed La Dire. "Everything must change." Which had been their standing exchange as long as I remember.

Once, before I was born, so goes the story, Lo Hawk grew disgruntled with village life and left. Rumors came back: he'd gone to a moon of Jupiter to dig out some metal that wormed in blue veins through the rock. Later: he'd left the Jovian satellite to sail a steaming sea on some world where three suns cast his shadows on the doffing deck of a ship bigger than our whole village. Still later: he was reported chopping away through a substance that melted to poisonous fumes someplace so far there were no stars at all during the year-long nights. When he had been away seven years, La Dire apparently decided it was time he came back. She left the village and returned a week later—with Lo Hawk. They say he hadn't changed much, so nobody asked him about where he'd been. But from his return dated the quiet argument that joined La Dire and Lo Hawk faster than love.

". . . must preserve," Lo Hawk.

". . . must change," La Dire.

Usually Lo Hawk gave in, for La Dire was a woman of wide reading, great culture, and wit; Lo Hawk had been a fine hunter in his youth and a fine warrior when there was need. And he was wise enough to admit in action, if not words, that such need had gone. But this time Lo Hawk was adamant:

"Communication is vital, if we are ever to become human beings. I would sooner allow some short-faced dog who comes from the hills and can approximate forty or fifty of our words to make known his wishes, than a mute child. Oh, the battles my youth has seen! When we fought off the giant spiders, or when the wave of fungus swept from the jungle, or when we destroyed with lime and salt the twenty-foot slugs that pushed up from the ground, we won these battles because we could speak to one another, shout instructions, bellow a warning, whisper plans in the twilit darkness of the source-caves. Yes, I would sooner give La or Lo to a talking dog!''

Somebody made a nasty comment: "Well, you couldn't very well give her a Le!" People snickered. But the older folk are very good at ignoring that sort of irreverence. Everybody ignores a Le anyway. Anyway, the business never did get settled. Towards moondown people wandered off, when somebody suggested adjournment. Everyone creaked and groaned to his feet. Friza, dark and beautiful, was still playing with the pebbles.

Friza didn't move when a baby because she knew how already. Watching her in the flicker (I was only eight myself) I got the first hint why she didn't talk: she picked up one of the pebbles and hurled it, viciously, at the head of the guy who'd made the remark about "Le." Even at eight she was sensitive. She missed, and I alone saw. But I saw too the snarl that twisted her face, the effort in her shoulders, the way her toes curled—she was sitting crosslegged—as she threw it. Both fists were knotted in her lap. You see, she didn't use her hands or feet. The pebble just rose from the dirt, shot through the air, missed its target, and chattered away through low leaves. But I saw: she *threw* it.

Each night for a week I have lingered on the wild flags of the waterfront, palaces crowding to the left, brittle light crackling over the harbor in the warm autumn. FFD goes strangely. Tonight when I turned back into the great trapezoid of the Piazza, fog hid the tops of the red flágpoles. I sat on the base of one nearest the tower and màde notes on Lobey's hungers. Later I left the decaying gold and indigo of the Basilica and wandered through the back alleys of the city till well after midnight. Once I stopped on a bridge to watch the small canal drift through the close walls beneath the nightlamps and clotheslines. At a sudden shrieking I whirled: half a dozen wailing cats hurled themselves about my feet and fled after a brown rat. Chills snarled the nerves along my vertebrae. I looked back at the water: six flowers—roses— floated from beneath the bridge, crawling over the oil. I watched them till a motorboat puttering on some larger waterway nearby sent water slapping the foundations. I made my way over the small bridges to the Grand Canal and caught the Vaporetto back to Ferovia. It turned windy as we floated beneath the black wood arch of the Ponte Academia; I was trying to assimilate the flowers, the vicious animals, with Lobey's adventure—each applies, but as yet I don't quite know how. Orion straddled the water. Lights from the

shore shook in the canal as we passed beneath the
dripping stones of the Rialto.

Writer's Journal/Venice, October 1965

In a few lines I shall establish how Maldoror was
virtuous during his first years, virtuous and happy.
Later he became aware he was born evil. Strange
fatality!

Isidore Ducasse (Comte de Lautreamont)/
The Songs of Maldoror

All prologue to why Lo Easy, Lo Little John, and Lo me don't herd goats no more.

Friza started tagging along, dark and ambiguous, running and jumping with Little Jon in a double dance to his single song and my music, play-wrestling with Easy, and walking with me up the brambly meadow holding my hand—whoever heard of La-ing or Lo-ing somebody you're herding goats with, or laughing with, or making love with. All of which I did with Friza. She would turn on a rock to stare at me with leaves shaking beside her face. Or come tearing towards me through the stones; between her graceful gait and her shadow in the rocks all suspended and real motion was. And was released when she was in my arms laughing—the one sound she did make, loving it in her mouth.

She brought me beautiful things. And kept the dangerous away. I think she did it the same way she threw the pebble. One day I noticed that ugly and harmful things just weren't happening; no lions, no condor bats. The goats stayed together; the kids didn't get lost and kept from cliffs.

"Little Jon, you don't have to come up this morning."

"Well, Lobey, if you don't think—"

"Go on, stay home."

So Easy, Friza, and me went out with the goats.

The beautiful things were like the flock of albino hawks that moved to the meadow. Or the mother woodchuck who brought her babies for us to see.

"Easy, there isn't enough work for all of us here. Why don't you find something else to do?"

"But I like coming up here, Lobey."

·"Friza and me can take care of the herd."

"But I don't mi—"

"Get lost, Easy."

He said something else and I picked up a stone in my foot and hefted it. He looked confused, then lumbered away. Imagine, coming on like that with Easy.

Friza and I had the field and the herd to ourselves alone. It stayed good and beautiful with unremembered flowers beyond rises when we ran. If there were poisonous snakes, they turned off in lengths of scarlet, never coiling. And, ah! did I make music.

Something killed her.

She was hiding under a grove of lazy willows, the trees that droop lower than weeping, and I was searching and calling and grinning—she shrieked. That's the only sound I ever heard her make other than laughter. The goats began to bleat.

I found her under the tree, face in the dirt.

As the goats bleated, the meadow went to pieces on their rasping noise. I was silent, confused, amazed by my despair.

I carried her back to the village. I remember La Dire's face as I walked into the village square with the limber body in my arms.

"Lobey, what in the world . . . How did she . . . Oh, no! Lobey, no!"

So Easy and Little Jon took the herd again. I went and sat at the entrance to the source-cave, sharpened my blade, gnawed my nails, slept and thought alone on the flat rock. Which is where we began.

Once Easy came to talk to me.

"Hey, Lobey, help us with the goats. The lions are back. Not a lot of them, but we could still use you." He squatted, still towering me by a foot, shook his head. "Poor Lobey." he ran his hairy fingers over my neck. "We need you. You need us. Help us hunt for the two missing kids?"

"Go away."

"Poor Lobey." But he went.

Later Little Jon came. He stood around for a minute thinking of something to say. But by the time he did, he had to go behind a bush, got embarrassed, and didn't come back.

Lo Hawk came too. "Come hunting, Lo Lobey. There's a bull been seen a mile south. Horns as long as your arm, they say."

"I feel rather non-functional today," I said. Which is not the sort of thing to joke about with Lo Hawk. He retired, humphing. But I just wasn't up to his archaic manner.

When La Dire came, though, it was different. As I said, she has great wit and learning. She came and sat with a book on the other side of the flat rock, and ignored me for an hour. Till I got mad. "What are you doing here?" I asked at last.

"Probably the same thing you are."

"What's that?"

She looked serious. "Why don't you tell me?"

I went back to my knife. "Sharpening my machete."

"I'm sharpening my mind," she said. "There is something to be done that will require an edge on both."

"Huh?"

"Is that an inarticulate way of asking what it is?"

"Huh?" I said again. "Yeah. What is it?"

"To kill whatever killed Friza." She closed her book. "Will you help?"

I leaned forward, feet and hands knotting, opened my mouth—then La Dire wavered behind tears. I cried. After all that time it surprised me. I put my forehead on the rock and bawled.

"Lo Lobey," she said, the way Lo Hawk had, only it was different. Then she stroked my hair, like Easy. Only different. As I gained control again I sensed both her compassion and embarrassment. Like Little Jon's; different.

I lay on my side, feet and hands clutching each other, sobbing towards the cavity of me. La Dire rubbed my shoulder, my bunched, distended hip, opening me with gentleness and words:

"Let's talk about mythology, Lobey. Or let's you listen. We've had quite·a time assuming the rationale of this world. The irrational presents just as much of a problem. You remember the legend of the Beatles? You remember the Beatle Ringo left his Maureen love even though she treated him tender. He was the one Beatle who did not sing, so the earliest forms of the legend go. After a hard day's night he and the rest of the Beatles were torn apart by screaming girls, and he and the other Beatles returned, finally at one, with the great rock and the great roll." I put my head in La Dire's lap. She went on. "Well, that myth is a version of a much older story that is not so well known. There are no 45's or 33's from the time of this older story. There are only a few written versions, and reading is rapidly losing its interest for the young. In the older story Ringo was called Orpheus. He too was torn apart by screaming girls. But the details are different. He lost his love—in this version Eurydice—and she went straight to the great rock and the great roll, where Orpheus had to go to get her back. He went singing, for in this version Orpheus was the greatest singer, instead of the silent one. In myths things always turn into their opposites as one version supersedes the next."

I said, "How could he go into the great rock and the great roll? That's all death and all life."

"He did."

"Did he bring her back?"

"No."

I looked from La Dire's old face and turned my head in her lap to the trees. "He lied, then. He didn't really go. He probably went off into the woods for a while and just made up some story when he came back."

"Perhaps," La Dire said.

I looked up again. "He wanted her back," I said. "I know he wanted her back. But if he had gone any place where there was even a chance of getting her, he wouldn't have come back unless she was with him. That's how I know he must have been lying. About going to the great rock and the great roll, I mean."

"All life is a rhythm," she said as I sat up. "All death is rhythm suspended, a syncopation before life resumes." She picked up my machete. "Play something." She held the handle out. "Make music."

I put the blade to my mouth, rolled over on my back, curled around the bright, dangerous length, and licked the sounds. I didn't want to but it formed in the hollow of my tongue, and breathing carried it into the knife.

Low; first slow; I closed my eyes, feeling each note in the quadrangle of shoulder blades and buttocks pressed on the rock. Notes came with only the meter of my own breathing, and from beneath that, there was the quickening of the muscles of my fingers and toes that began to cramp for the faster, closer dance of the heart's time. The mourning hymn began to quake.

"Lobey, when you were a boy, you used to beat the rock with your feet, making a rhythm, a dance, a drum. Drum, Lobey!"

I let the melody speed, then flailed it up an octave so I could handle it. That means only fingers.

"Drum, Lobey!"

I rocked to my feet and began to slap my soles against the stone.

"Drum!"

I opened my eyes long enough to see the blood spider scurry. The music laughed. Pound and pound, trill and warble, and La Dire laughed for me too, to play, hunched down while sweat quivered on my nape, threw up my head and it dribbled into the small of my back, while I, immobile above the waist, flung my hips, beating cross rhythms with toes and heels, blade up to prick the sun, new sweat trickling behind my ears, rolling the crevices of my corded neck.

"Drum, my Lo Ringo; play, my Lo Orpheus," La Dire cried. "Oh, Lobey!" She clapped and clapped.

Then, when the only sound was my own breath, the leaves and the stream, she nodded, smiling. "Now you've mourned properly."

I looked down. My chest glistened, my stomach wrinkled and smoothed and wrinkled. Dust on the tops of my feet had become tan mud.

"Now you're almost ready to do what must be done. Go now, hunt, herd goats, play more. Soon Le Dorik will come for you."

All sound from me stopped. Breath and heart too, I think, a syncopation before the rhythm resumed. "*Le* Dorik?"

"Go. Enjoy yourself before you begin your journey."

Frightened, I shook my head, turned, fled from the cave mouth.

Le—

> Suddenly the wandering little beast fled, leaving in
> my lap—O horror—a monster and misshapen maggot
> with a human head.
> "Where is your soul that I may ride it!"
>   Aloysius Bertrand/*The Dwarf*

> *Come ALIVE! You're in the PEPSI generation!*
>   Current catchphrase/*(Commercial)*

—Dorik!

An hour later I was crouching, hidden, by the kage. But the kage-keeper, Le Dorik, wasn't around. A white thing (I remember when the woman who was Easy's mother flung it from her womb before dying) had crawled to the electrified fence to slobber. It would probably die soon. Out of sight I heard Griga's laughter; he had been Lo Griga till he was sixteen. But something—nobody knew if it was genetic or not—rotted his mind inside his head, and laughter began to gush from his gums and lips. He lost his Lo and was placed in the kage. Le Dorik was probably inside now, putting out food, doctoring where doctoring would do some good, killing when there was some person beyond doctoring. So much sadness and horror penned up there; it was hard to remember they were people. They bore no title of purity, but they were people. Even Lo Hawk would get as offended over a joke about the kaged ones as he would

216

about some titled citizen. "You don't *know* what they did to them when I was a boy, young Lo man. You never saw them dragged back from the jungle when a few did manage to survive. You didn't see the barbaric way complete norms acted, their reason shattered bloody by fear. Many people we call Lo and La today would not have been allowed to live had they been born fifty years ago. Be glad *you* are a child of more civilized times." Yes, they were people. But this is not the first time I had wondered what•it feels like to keep such people—Le Dorik?

I went back to the village.

Lo Hawk looked up from re-thonging his cross-bow. He'd piled the power cartridges on the ground in front of the door to check the caps. "How you be, Lo Lobey?"

I picked a cartridge out with my foot, turned it over. "Catch that bull yet?"

"No."

I pried the clip back with the tip of my machete. It was good. "Let's go," I said.

"Check the rest first.".

While I did, he finished stringing the bow, went in and got a second one for me; then we went down to the river.

Silt stained the water yellow. The current was high and fast, bending ferns and long grass down, combing them from the shore like hair. We kept to the soggy bank for about two miles.

"What killed Friza?" I asked at last.

Lo Hawk squatted to examine a scarred log: tusk marks. "You were there. You saw. La Dire only guesses."

We turned from the river. Brambles scratched against Lo Hawk's leggings. I don't need leggings. My skin is tough and tight. Neither does Easy or Little Jon.

"I didn't see anything," I said. "What does she guess?"

An albino hawk burst from a tree and gyred away. Friza hadn't needed leggings either.

"Something killed Friza that was non-functional, something about her that was non-functional."

"Friza was functional," I said. "She was!"

"Keep your voice down, boy."

"She kept the herd together," I said more softly. "She could make the animals do what she wanted. She could move the dangerous things away and bring the beautiful ones nearer."

"Bosh," said Lo Hawk, stepping over ooze.

"Without a gesture or a word, she could move the animals anywhere she wanted, or I wanted."

"That's La Dire's nonsense you've been listening to."

"No. I saw it. She could move the animals just like the pebble."

Lo Hawk started to say something else. Then I saw his thoughts backtrack. "What pebble?"

"The pebble she picked up and threw."

"*What* pebble, Lobey?"

So I told him the story. "And it was functional," I concluded. "She kept the herd safe, didn't she? She could have kept it even without me."

"Only she couldn't keep herself alive," Lo Hawk said. He started walking again.

We kept silent through the whispering growth, while I mulled. Then:

"*Yaaaaaa—*" on three different tones.

The leaves whipped back and the Bloi triplets scooted out. One of them leaped at me and I had an armful of hysterical, redheaded ten-year-old.

"*Hey* there now," I said sagely.

"Lo Hawk, Lobey! Back there—"

"Watch it, will you?" I added, avoiding an elbow.

"—back there! It was stamping, and pawing the rocks—"
This from one of them at my hip.

"Back where?" Lo Hawk asked. "What happened?"

"Back there by the—"

"—by the old house near the place where the cave roof
falls in—"

"—the bull came up and—"

"—and he was awful big and he stepped—"

"—he stepped on the old house that—"

"—we was playing inside—"

"Hold up," I said and put Bloi-3 down. "Now where
was all this?"

They turned together and pointed through the woods.

Hawk swung down his crossbow. "That's fine," he
said. "You boys get back up to the village."

"Say—" I caught Bloi-2's shoulder. "Just how big was
he?"

Inarticulate blinking now.

"Never mind," I said. "Just get going."

They looked at me, at Lo Hawk, at the woods. Then
they got.

In silent consensus we turned from the river through the
break in the leaves from which the children had tumbled.

A board, shattered at one end, lay on the path just
before us as we reached the clearing. We stepped over it,
stepped out between the sumac branches.

And there were a lot of other smashed boards scattered
across the ground.

A five-foot section of the foundation had been kicked in,
and only one of the four supporting beams was upright.

Thatch bits were shucked over the yard. A long time
ago Carol had planted a few more flowers in this garden,
when, wanting to get away from the it-all of the village,
we had moved down here to the old thatched house that

used to be so cozy, that used to be . . . she had planted the hedge with the fuzzy orange blooms. You know that kind?

I stopped by one cloven print where petals and leaves had been ground in a dark mandala on the mud. My foot fit inside the print easily. A couple of trees had been uprooted. A couple more had been broken off above my head.

It was easy to see which way he had come into the clearing. Bushes, vines and leaves had erupted inward. Where he had left, everything sort of sagged out.

Lo Hawk ambled into the clearing swinging his cross-bow nonchalantly.

"You're not really that nonchalant, are you?" I asked. I looked around again at the signs of destruction. "It must be huge."

Lo Hawk threw me a glance full of quartz and gristle. "You've been hunting with me before."

"True. It can't have been gone very long if it just scared the kids away," I added.

Hawk stalked towards the place where things were sagging.

I hurried after.

Ten steps into the woods, we heard seven trees crash somewhere: three—pause—then four more.

"Of course, if he's that big he can probably move pretty far pretty fast," I said.

Another three trees.

Then a roar:

An unmusical sound with much that was metallic in it, neither rage nor pathos, but noise, heaved from lungs bigger than smelting bellows, a long sound, then echoing while the leaves turned up beneath a breeze.

Under green and silver we started again through the cool, dangerous glades.

And step and breathe and step.

Then in the trees to our left—

He came leaping, and that leap rained us with shadow and twigs and bits of leaf.

Turning his haunch with one foreleg over here and a hindleg *way* the hell over there, he looked down at us with an eye bloodshot, brown, and thickly oystered in the corners. His eyeball must have been big as my head.

The wet, black nostrils steamed.

He was very noble.

Then he tossed his head, breaking branches, and hunkered with his fists punched into the ground—there were hands with horny hairy fingers thick as my arm where he should have had forehooves—bellowed, reared, and sprang away.

Hawk fired his crossbow. The shaft flapped like a darning needle between the timbers of his flank. He was crashing off.

The bark of the tree I'd slammed against chewed on my back as I came away.

"Come on," Hawk hollered, as he ran in the general direction the man-handed bull had.

And I followed that crazy old man, running to kill the beast. We clambered through a cleft of broken rock (it hadn't been broken the last time I'd come wandering down here through the trees—an afternoon full of sun spots and breezes and Friza's hand in mine, on my shoulder, on my cheek). I jumped down on to a stretch of moss-tongued brick that paved the forest here and there. We ran forward and—

Some things are so small you don't notice them. Others are so big you run right into them before you know what they are. It was a hole, in the earth and the side of the mountain, that we almost stumbled into. It was a ragged cave entrance some twenty meters across. I didn't even know it was there till all that sound came out of it.

The bull suddenly roared from the opening in the rock and trees and brick, defining the shape of it with his roaring.

When the echo died, we crept to the crumbled lip and looked over. Below I saw glints of sunlight on hide, turning and turning in the pit. Then he reared, shaking his eyes, his hairy fists.

Hawk jerked back, even though the claws on the brick wall were still fifteen feet below us.

"Doesn't this tunnel go into the source-cave?" I whispered. Before something that grand, one whispers.

Lo Hawk nodded. "Some of the tunnels, they say, are a hundred feet high. Some are ten. This is one of the bigger arterioles."

"Can it get out again?" Stupid question.

On the other side of the hole the horned head, the shoulders emerged. The cave-in had been sloped there. He had climbed out. Now he looked at us, crouched there. He bellowed once with a length of tongue like foamy, red canvas.

Then he leaped at us across the hole.

He didn't make it, but we scurried backward. He caught the lip with the fingers of one hand—I saw black gorges break about those nails—and one arm. The arm slapped around over the earth, searching for a hand-hold.

From behind me I heard Hawk shout (I run faster than he does). I turned to see that hand rise from over him!

He was all crumpled up on the ground. The hand slapped a few more times (*Boom—Boom! Boom!*) and then arm and fingers slipped, pulling a lot of stone and bushes and three small trees, down, down, down.

Lo Hawk wasn't dead. (The next day they discovered he had cracked a rib, but that wasn't till later.) He began to curl up. I thought of an injured bug. I thought of a sick, sick child.

I caught him up by the shoulders just as he started to breathe again. "Hawk! Are you—"

He couldn't hear me because of the roaring from the pit. But he pulled himself up, blinking. Blood began trickling from his nose. The beast had been slapping with cupped palm. Lo Hawk had thrown himself down, and luckily most of the important parts of him, like his head, had suffered more from air-blast than concussion. "Let's get out of here!" and I began to drag him towards the trees.

When we got there, he was shaking his head.

"—no, wait, Lobey—" came over in his hoarse voice during a lull in the roaring.

As I got him propped against a tree, he grabbed my wrist.

"Hurry, Hawk! Can you walk? We've got to get away. Look, I'll carry you—"

"No!" The breath that had been knocked out of him lurched back.

"Oh, come *on,* Hawk! Fun is fun. But you're hurt, and that thing is a lot bigger than either of us figured on. It must have mutated from the radiation in the lower levels of the cave."

He tugged my wrist again. "We have to stay. We have to kill it."

"Do you think it will come up and harm the village? It hasn't gone too far from the cave yet."

"That—" He coughed. "That has nothing to do with it. I'm a hunter, Lobey."

"Now, look—"

"And I have to teach you to hunt." He tried to sit away from the trunk. "Only it looks like you'll have to learn this lesson by yourself."

"Huh?"

"La Dire says you have to get ready for your journey."

"Oh, for goodness—" Then I squinted at him, all the crags and age and assurance and pain in that face. "What I gotta do?"

The bull's roar thundered up from the caved-in roof of the source-cave.

"Go down there; hunt the beast, and kill it."

"No!"

"It's for Friza."

"How?" I demanded.

He shrugged. "La Dire knows. You must learn to hunt, and hunt well." Then he repeated that.

"I'm all for testing my manhood and that sort of thing. But—"

"It's a different reason from that, Lobey."

"But—"

"Lobey." His voice nestled down low and firm in his throat. "I'm older than you, and I know more about this whole business than you do. Take your sword and crossbow and go down into the cave, Lobey. Go on."

I sat there and thought a whole lot of things. Such as: bravery is a very stupid thing. And how surprised I was that so much fear and respect for Lo Hawk had held from my childhood. Also, how many petty things can accompany pith, moment, and enterprise—like fear, confusion, and plain annoyance.

The beast roared again. I pushed the crossbow farther up my arm and settled my machete handle at my hip.

If you're going to do something stupid—and we all do—it might as well be a brave and foolish thing.

I clapped Lo Hawk's shoulder and started for the pit.

On this side the break was sharp and the drop deep. I went around to the sagging side, where there were natural ledges of root, earth, and masonry. I circled the chasm and scrambled down.

Sun struck the wall across from me, glistening with moss. I dropped my hand from the moist rock and stepped across an oily rivulet whose rainbow went out under my shadow. Somewhere up the tunnel, hooves clattered on stone.

I started forward. There were many cracks in the high ceiling, here and there lighting on the floor a branch clawing crisped leaves or the rim of a hole that might go down a few inches, a few feet, or drop to the lowest levels of the source-cave that were thousands of feet below.

I came to a fork, started beneath the vault to the left, and ten feet into the darkness tripped and rolled down a flight of shallow steps, once through a puddle (my hand splatting out in the darkness), once over dry leaves (they roared their own roar beneath my side), and landed at the bottom in a shaft of light, knees and palms on gravel.

Clatter!

Clatter!

Much closer: *Clatter!*

I sprang to my feet and away from the telltale light. Motes cycloned in the slanting illumination where I had been. And the motes stilled.

My stomach felt like a loose bag of water sloshing around on top of my gut. Walking towards that sound—he was quiet now and waiting—was no longer a matter of walking in a direction. Rather: pick that foot up, lean forward, put it down. Good. Now, pick up the other one, lean forward—

A hundred yards ahead I suddenly saw another light because something very large suddenly filled it up. Then it emptied.

Clack! Clack! Clack!

Snort!

And three steps could carry him such a long way.

Then a lot of *clacks!*

I threw myself against the wall, pushing my face into dirt and roots.

But the sound was going off.

I swallowed all the bitter things that had risen into my throat and stepped back from the wall.

With a quick walk that became a slow run I followed him under the crumbling vaults.

His sound came from the right.

So I turned right and into a sloping tunnel so low that ahead of me I heard his horns rasp on the ceiling. Stone and scale and old lichen chittered down at his hulking shoulders, then to the ground.

The gutter on the side of the tunnel had coated the stone with fluorescent slime. The trickle became a stream as the slope increased till the frothing light raced me on the left.

Once his hooves must have crossed a metal floor-plate, because for a half-dozen steps orange sparks glittered where he stepped, lighting him to the waist.

He was only thirty meters ahead of me.

Sparks again as he turned a corner.

I felt stone under the soles of my feet and then cold, smooth metal. I passed some leaves, blown here by what wind, that his hooves had ignited. They writhed with worms of fire, glowing about my toes. And for moments the darkness filled with autumn.

I reached the corner, started around.

Facing me, he bellowed.

His foot struck a meter from my foot and from this close the sparks lit his raw eyes, his polished nostrils.

His hand came between his eyes and me, falling! I rolled backward, grabbing for my machete.

His palm—flat this time, Hawk—clanged on the metal plate where I had been. Then it fell again toward where I was.

I lay on my back with the hilt of the blade on the floor, point up. Very few people, or bulls, can hit a ten penny nail and drive it to the hilt. Fortunately.

He jerked me from the floor, pinioned to his palm, and I got flung around (holding on to the blade with hands and feet and screaming) an awful lot.

He was screaming too, butting the ceiling and lots of things falling. From twenty feet he flung me loose. The blade pulled free, my flute filled with his blood, and I hurled into the wall and rolled down.

His right shoulder struck the right wall. He lurched. His left shoulder struck the left wall. And his shadow flickering on the dripping ceiling was huge.

He came down towards me, as I dragged my knees over a lot of wrought stone beneath me, rocked back to my feet (something was sprained too), and tried to look at him, while he kept going out between steps.

Beside me in the wall was a grating about three feet high, with the bars set askew. It was probably a drain. I fell through. And dropped about four feet to a sloping floor.

It was pitch-black above me and there was a hand grasping and grasping in the dark. I could hear it scrabbling against the wall. I took a swipe overhead, and my blade struck something moving.

Roaaaaaa . . . !

The sound was blunted behind stone. But from my side came the sharp retort of his palm as he started slapping.

I dived forward. The slope increased, and suddenly I slid down a long way, very fast, getting even more scraped up. I came up sharply against pipes.

Eyes closed, I lay there, the tip of the crossbow uncomfortable under my shoulder, the blade handle biting between the bars and my hip. Then the places that were uncomfortable got numb.

If you really relax with your eyes closed, the lids pull slowly open. When I finally relaxed, light filled my eyes from the bottoms up like milk poured in bowls.

Light?

I blinked.

Gray light beyond the grating, the gray that sunlight gets when it comes from around many corners. Only I was at least another two levels down. I lay behind the entrance to another drain like the one I'd leaped through.

Then somewhere, the roar of a bull, echoing through these deep stones.

I pulled myself up on the bars, elbows smarting, shoulders bruised, and something pulled sore in the bulk of my thigh. I gazed into the room below.

At one time there was a floor level with the bottom of this grating, but most of it had fallen in a long and longer time ago. Now the room was double height and the grate was at least fifteen feet above the present floor.

Seventy, eighty meters across, the room was round. The walls were dressed stone, or bare rock, and rose in gray slabs towards the far light. There were many vaulted entrances into dark tunnels.

In the center was a machine.

While I watched it began to hum wistfully to itself and

several banks of lights glittered into a pattern, froze, glittered into another. It was a computer from the old time (when you owned this Earth, you wraiths and memories), a few of which still chuckled and chattered throughout the source-cave. I'd had them described to me, but this was the first I'd seen.

What had wakened me—

(and had I been asleep? And had I dreamed, remembering now with the throbbing image clinging to the back of my eyes, Friza?)

—was the wail of the beast.

Head down, hide bristling over the hunks of his shoulders, gemmed with water from the ceiling, he hunched into the room, dragging the knuckles of one hand, the other—the one I had wounded twice—hugged to his belly.

And on three legs, a four legged animal (even one with hands) limps.

He blinked about the room, and wailed again, his voice leaving pathos quickly and striking against rage. He stopped the sound with a sniff, then looked around and knew that I was there.

And I wanted very much not to be.

I squatted now behind the grating and looked back and up and down and couldn't see any way out. Hunt, Lo Hawk had said.

The hunter can be a pretty pathetic creature.

He swung his head again, tasting the air for me, his injured hand twitching high on his belly.

(The hunted's not so hot either.)

The computer whistled a few notes of one of the ancient tunes, some chorus from *Carmen*. The bull-beast glanced at it uncomprehending.

How was I to hunt him?

I brought the crossbow down and aimed through the

grate. It wouldn't mean anything unless I got him in the eye. And he wasn't looking in the right direction.

I lowered the bow and took up my blade. I brought it to my mouth and blew. Blood bubbled from the holes. Then the note blasted and went reeling through the room.

He raised his head and stared at me.

Up went the bow; I aimed through the bars, pulled the trigger—

Raging forward with horns shaking, he got bigger and bigger and bigger through the frame of stone. I fell back while the roar covered me, closing my eyes against the sight: his eye gushed about my shaft. He grasped the bars behind which I crouched.

Metal grated on stone, stone pulled from stone. And then the frame was a lot bigger than it had been. He hurled the crumpled grate across the room to smash into the wall and send pieces of stone rolling.

Then he reached in and grabbed me, legs and waist, in his fist, and I was being waved high in the air over his bellowing face (left side blind and bloody) and the room arching under me and my head flung from shoulder to shoulder and trying to point the crossbow down—one shaft broke on the stone by his hoof a long way below. Another struck awfully close to the shaft that Lo Hawk had shot into his side. Waiting for a wall of stone to come up and jelly my head, I fumbled another arrow into the slot.

His cheek was sheeted with blood. And suddenly there was more blood. The shaft struck and totally disappeared in the blind well of bone and lymph. I saw the other eye cloud as though someone had overblown the lens with powdered lime.

He dropped me.

Didn't throw me; just dropped. I grabbed the hair on his

wrist. It slipped through my hands, and I slid down his forearms to the crook of his elbow.

Then his arm began to fall. Slowly I turned upside down. The back of his hand hit the floor, and his hind feet were clacking around on the stone.

He snorted, and I began to slide back down his forearm towards his hand, slowing myself by clutching at the bristles with feet and hands. I rolled clear of his palm and staggered away from him.

The thing in my thigh that was sprained throbbed.

I stepped backward and couldn't step any more.

He swayed over me, shook his head, splattering me with his ruined eye. And he was grand. And he was *still* strong, dying above me. And he was huge. Furious, I swayed with him in my fury, my fists clutched against my hips, tongue stifled in my mouth.

He was great and he was handsome and he *still* stood there defying me while dying, scoffing at my bruises. Damn you, beast who would be greater than—

One arm buckled, a hindleg now, and he collapsed away from me, crashing.

Something in the fistful of darkness that were his nostrils thundered and roared—but softer, and softer. His ribs rose to furrow his side, fell to rise again; I took up the bow and limped to the bloody tears of his lips, fitted one final shaft. It followed the other two into his brain.

His hands jerked three feet, then fell (*Boom! Boom!*) relaxing now.

When he was still, I went and sat on the base of the computer and leaned against the metal casing. Somewhere inside it was clicking.

I hurt. Lots.

Breathing was no fun any more. And I had, somewhere

during all this, bitten the inside of my cheek. And when I do that, it gets me so mad I could cry.

I closed my eyes.

"That was very impressive," someone said close to my right ear. "I would love to see you work with a *muleta*. Olé! Olé! First the *verónica,* then the *paso double!*"

I opened my eyes.

"Not that I didn't enjoy your less sophisticated art."

I turned my head. There was a small speaker by my left ear. The computer went on soothingly:

"But you are a dreadfully unsophisticated lot. All of you. Young, but *très charmant.* Well, you've fought through this far. Is there anything you'd like to ask me?"

"Yeah," I said. Then I breathed for a while. "How do I get out of here?" There were a lot of archways in the wall, a lot of choices.

"That is a problem. Let me see." The lights flickered over my lap, the backs of my hands. "Now, of course, had we met before you entered, I could have waved out a piece of computer tape and you would have taken the end and I would have unwound it after you as you made your way into the heart to face your fate. But instead, you have arrived here and found me waiting. What do you desire, hero?"

"I want to go home," I said.

The computer went *tsk-tsk-tsk.* "Other than that."

"You really want to know?"

"I'm nodding sympathetically," it said.

"I want Friza. But she's dead."

"Who was Friza?"

I thought. I tried to say something. With the exhaustion, all that came was a catch in my throat that might have sounded like a sob.

"Oh." After a moment, gently: "You've come into the wrong maze, you know."

"I have? Then what are you doing here?"

"I was set here a long time ago by people who never dreamed that you would come. Psychic Harmony and Entangled Deranged Response Associations, that was my department. And you've come down here hunting through my memories for your lost girl."

Yes, I may have just been talking to myself. I was very tired.

"How do you like it up there?" PHAEDRA asked.

"Where?"

"Up there on the surface. I can remember back when there were humans. They made me. Then they all went away, leaving us alone down here. And now you've come to take their place. It must be rather difficult, walking through their hills, their jungles, battling the mutated shadows of their flora and fauna, haunted by their million-year-old fantasies."

"We try," I said.

"You're basically not equipped for it," PHAEDRA went on. "But I suppose you have to exhaust the old mazes before you can move into the new ones. It's hard."

"If it means fighting off those things—" I jutted my chin towards the carcass on the stone. "Yeah, it is."

"Well, it's been fun. I miss the *revueltas*, the maidens leaping over the horns and spinning in the air to land on the sweating back, then vaulting to the sands! Mankind had style, baby! You may get it yet, but right now your charm is a very young thing."

"Where did they go, PHAEDRA?"

"Where your Friza went, I suppose." Something musical was happening behind my head within the metal. "But you aren't human and you don't appreciate their rules.

You shouldn't try. Down here we try to follow what you're doing for a few generations, and questions get answered we would never have even thought of asking. On the other hand, we sit waiting out centuries for what would seem like the most obvious and basic bits of information about you, like who you are, where you're from and what you're doing here. Has it occurred to you that you might get her back?"

"Friza?" I sat up. "Where? How?" La Dire's cryptic statements came back.

"You're in the wrong maze," PHAEDRA repeated. "And I'm the wrong girl to get you into the right one. Kid Death along for a little while and maybe you can get around him enough to put your foot in the door, finger in the pie, your two cents in, as it were."

I leaned forward on my knees. "PHAEDRA, you baffle me."

"Scoot," PHAEDRA said.

"Which way?"

"Again. You've asked the wrong girl. Wish I could help. But I don't know. But you'd better get started. When the sun goes down and the tide goes out, this place gets dark, and the gillies and ghosties gather 'round, shouting."

I heaved to my feet and looked at the various doorways. Maybe a little logic? The bull-beast had come from the doorway over there. So that's the one I went in.

The long, long dark echoed with my breath and falling water. I tripped over the first stairway. Got up and started climbing. Bruised my shoulder on the landing, groped around and finally realized I had gotten off into a much smaller passage that didn't *seem* like it was going anywhere.

I took up my machete and blew out the last of the blood. The tune now winding with me lay notes over the stone like mica flakes that would do till light came.

Stubbed my toe.

Hopped, cursed, then started walking again alone with the lonely, lovely sounds.

"Hey—"

"—Lobey, is—"

"—is that you?" Young voices came from behind stone.

"Yes! Of course it's me!" I turned to the wall and put my hands against the rock.

"We snuck back—"

"—to watch, and Lo Hawk—"

"—he told us to go down into the cave and find you—"

"—cause he thought you might be lost."

I pushed my machete back into my scabbard. "Fine. Because I am."

"Where are you?"

"Right here on the other side of this—" I was feeling around the stones again, above my head this time. My fingers came on an opening. It was nearly three feet wide. "Hold on!" I hoisted myself up, clambered onto the rim, and saw faint light at the end of a four-foot tunnel. I had to crawl through because there wasn't room to stand.

At the other end I stuck my head out and looked down at the upturned faces of the Bloi triplets. They were standing in a patch of light from the roof.

2-Bloi rubbed his nose with the back of his fist and sniffed.

"Oh," 1-Bloi said. "You were up there."

"More or less." I jumped down beside them.

"Damn!" 3-Bloi said. "What happened to you?" I was speckled with bull's eye, scratched, bruised, and limping.

"Come on," I said. "Which way is out?"

We were only around the corner from the great cave-in. We joined Lo Hawk on the surface.

He stood (remember, he had a cracked rib that nobody

was going to find out about till the next day) against a tree with his arms folded. He raised his eyebrows to ask me the question he was waiting with.

"Yeah," I said. "I killed it. Big deal." I was sort of tired.

Lo Hawk shooed the kids ahead of us back to the village. As we tromped through the long weeds, suddenly we heard stems crash down among themselves.

I almost sat down right there.

It was only a boar. His ear could have brushed my elbow. That's all.

"Come on." Lo Hawk grinned, raising his crossbow.

We didn't say anything else until after we had caught and killed the pig. Lo Hawk's powered shaft stunned it, but I had to hack it nearly in half before it would admit it was dead. After *el toro*? Easy. Bloody to the shoulders, we trudged back finally, through the thorns, the hot evening.

The head of the boar weighed fifty pounds. Lo Hawk lugged it on his back. We'd cut off all four hams, knotted them together, and I carried two on each shoulder, which was another two hundred and seventy pounds. The only way we could have gotten the whole thing back was to have had Easy along. We'd nearly reached the village when he said, "La Dire noticed that business with Friza and the animals. She's seen other things about you and others in the village."

"Huh? Me?" I asked. "What about me?"

"About you, Friza, and Dorik the kage-keeper."

"But that's silly." I'd been walking behind him. Now I drew abreast. He glanced across the tusk. "You were all born the same year."

"But we're all—different."

Lo Hawk squinted ahead, then looked down. Then he looked at the river. He didn't look at me.

"I can't do anything like the animals or the pebble."

"You can do other things. Le Dorik can do still others."

He still wasn't looking at me. The sun was lowering behind copper crested hills. The river was brown. He was silent. As clouds ran the sky, I dropped behind again, placed the meat beside me, and fell on my knees to wash in the silted water.

Back at the village I told Carol if she'd dress the hams she could have half my share. "Sure," but she was dawdling over a bird's nest she'd found. "In a minute."

"And hurry up, huh?"

"All right. All right. Where are you in such a rush to?"

"Look, I will polish the tusks for you and make a spearhead for the kid or something if you will *just keep off my back!*"

"Well, I—look, it's not your kid anyway. It's—"

But I was sprinting towards the trees. I guess I must have still been upset. My legs sprint pretty fast.

It was dark when I reached the kage. There was no sound from behind the fence. Once something blundered against the wire, whined. Sparks and a quick shadow. I don't know which side it came from. No movement from Le Dorik's shack. Maybe Dorik was staying inside the kage on some project. Sometimes they mated in there, even gave birth. Sometimes the offspring were functional. The Bloi triplets had been born in the kage. They didn't have too much neck and their arms were long, but they were quick, bright ten-year-olds now. And 2-Bloi and 3-Bloi are almost as dexterous with their feet as I am. I'd even given Lo 3-Bloi a couple of lessons on my blade, but being a child he preferred to pick fruit with his brothers.

After an hour in the dark, thinking about what went into the kage, what came out, I went back to the village, curled up on the haystack behind the smithy and listened to the hum from the power-shack until it put me to sleep.

At dawn I unraveled, rubbed night's grit out of my eyes, and went to the corral. Easy and Little Jon got there a few minutes after. "Need any help with the goats this morning?"

Little Jon put his tongue in his cheek. "Just a second," he said and went off into the corner.

Easy shuffled uncomfortably.

Little Jon came back. "Yeah," he said. "Sure we need help." Then he grinned. And Easy, seeing his grin, grinned too.

Surprise! Surprise, little ball of fear inside me! They're smiling! Easy hoisted up the first bar of the wooden gate, and the goats bleated forward and put their chins over the second rung. Surprise!

"Sure," Easy said. "Of course we need you. Glad to have you back!" He cuffed the back of my head and I swiped at his hip and missed. Little Jon pulled out the other rung, and we chased the goats across the square, out along the road, and then up the meadow. Just like before. No, not just.

Easy said it first, when the first warmth pried under the dawn chill. "It's not just like before, Lobey. You've lost something."

I struck a dew shower from low willow fronds and wet my face and shoulders. "My appetite," I said. "And maybe a couple of pounds."

"It isn't your appetite," Little Jon said, coming back from a tree stump. "It's something different."

"Different?" I repeated. "Say, Easy, Little Jon, how am I different?"

"Huh?" Little Jon asked. He flung a stick at a goat to get its attention. Missed. I picked up a small stone that happened underfoot. Hit it. The goat turned blue eyes on me and galumphed over to see why, got interested in something else halfway over and tried to eat it. "You got big feet," Little Jon said.

"Naw. Not that," I said. "La Dire had noticed something different about me that's important; something different about me the same way there was about . . . Friza."

"You make music," Easy said.

I looked at the perforated blade. "Naw," I said. "I don't think it's that. I could teach you to play. That's another sort of being different than she's looking for. I think."

Late that afternoon we brought the goats back. Easy invited me to eat and I got some of my ham and we attacked Little Jon's cache of fruit. "You want to cook?"

"Naw," I said.

So Easy walked down to the corner of the power-shack and called towards the square, "Hey, who wants to cook dinner for three hard-working gentlemen who can supply food, entertainment, bright conversation—No, you cooked dinner for me once before. Now don't *push*, girls! Not you either. Whoever taught you how to season? Uh-uh, I remember you, Strychnine Lizzy. O.K. Yeah, you. Come on."

He came back with a cute, bald girl. I'd seen her around but she'd just come to the village. I'd never talked to her and I didn't know her name. "This is Little Jon, Lobey, and I'm Easy. What's your name again?"

"Call me Nativia."

No, I'd never talked to her before. A shame that situation had gone on for twenty-three years. Her voice didn't come from her larynx. I don't think she had one. The sound began a whole lot further down and whispered as out from a cave with bells.

"You can call me anything you like," I said, "as much as you want."

She laughed, and it sounded among the bells. "Where's the food and let's find a fireplace."

We found a circle of rocks down by the stream. We were going to get cookery from the compound but Nativia had a large skillet of her own so all we had to borrow were cinnamon and salt.

"Come on," Little Jon said when he came back from the water's edge. "Lobey, you gotta be entertaining. We'll converse."

"Now, hey—" Then I said to myself *Aw, so what*, lay down on my back, and began to play my machete. She liked that because she kept smiling at me as she worked.

"Don't you got no children?" Easy asked.

Nativia was greasing the skillet with a lump of ham fat.

"One in the kage down at Live Briar. Two with a man in Ko."

"You travel a lot, yeah?" Little Jon asked.

I played a slower tune that came far away, and she smiled at me as she dumped diced meat from a palm frond into the pan. Fat danced on the hot metal.

"I travel." The smile and the wind and the mockery in her voice were delightful.

"You should find a man who travels too," Easy suggested. He has a lot of homey type advice for everybody. Gets on my nerves sometimes.

Nativia shrugged. "Did once. We could never agree on what direction to go in. It's his kid in the kage. Guy's name was Lo Angel. A beautiful man. He could just never make up his mind where he wanted to go. And when he did, it was never where I wanted. No . . ." She pushed the browning meat across the crackling bottom. "I like good, stable, settled men who'll be there when I get back."

I began to play an old hymn—*Bill Bailey Won't You Please Come Home*. I'd learned it from a 45 when I was a kid. Nativia knew it too because she laughed in the middle of slicing a peach.

"That's me," she said. "Bill La Bailey. That's the nickname Lo Angel gave me."

She formed the meat into a ring around the edge of the pan. The nuts and vegetables went in now with a little salt water and the cover clanked on.

"How far have you traveled?" I asked, laying my knife on my stomach and stretching. Overhead, behind maple leaves, the sky was injured in the west with sunset, shadowed by east and night. "I'm going to travel soon. I want to know where there is to go."

She pushed the fruit on to one end of the frond. "I once went as far as the City. And I've even been underground to explore the source-cave."

Easy and Little Jon got very quiet.

"That's some traveling," I said. "La Dire says I have to travel because I'm different."

Nativia nodded. "That's why Lo Angel was traveling," she said, pushing back the lid again. Pungent steam ballooned and dispersed. My mouth got wet. "Most of the ones moving were different. He always said I was different too, but he would never tell me how." She pushed the vegetables into a ring against the meat and filled the center with cut fruit. Cinnamon now over the whole thing. Some of the powdered spice caught the flame that tongued the pan's rim and sparks bloomed. On went the cover.

"Yeah," I said. "La Dire won't tell me either."

Nativia looked surprised. "You mean you don't know?"

I shook my head.

"Oh, but you can—" She stopped. "La Dire is one of this town's elders, isn't she?"

"That's right."

"Maybe she's got a reason not to tell you. I talked to

her just a little while the other day; she's a woman of great wisdom."

"Yeah," I said, rolling on my side. "Come on, if you know, tell me."

Nativia looked confused. "Well, first you tell me. I mean what did La Dire say?"

"She said I would have to go on a journey, to kill whatever killed Friza."

"Friza?"

"Friza was different, too." I began to tell her the story. A minute into it, Easy burped, pounded his chest and complained about being hungry. He obviously didn't like the subject. Little Jon had to get up and when he wandered off into the bushes, Easy went after him, grunting, "Call me when it's finished. Dinner, I mean."

But Nativia listened closely and then asked some questions about Friza's death. When I told her about having to take a trip with Le Dorik, she nodded. "Well, it makes a lot more sense now."

"It does?"

She nodded again. "Hey, you guys, dinner's . . . ready?"

"Then can't you tell me . . . ?"

She shook her head. "You wouldn't understand. I've done a lot more traveling than you. It's just that a lot of different people have died recently, like Friza died. Two down at Live Briar. And I've heard of three more in the past year. Something is going to have to be done. It might as well get started here." She pushed the cover off the pan again: more steam.

Easy and Little Jon, who had been walking back up the stream, began to run.

"Elvis Presley!" Little Jon breathed. "Does that smell good!" He hunkered down by the fire, dribbling.

Easy's adenoids began to rattle. When a cat does it, it's purring.

I wanted to ask more, but I didn't want to annoy Easy and Little Jon; I guess I had acted bad with them, and they were pretty nice about it as long as I let it lie.

A frond full of ham, vegetables, and spiced fruit made me stop thinking about anything except what wasn't in my belly, and I learned that a good deal of my metaphysical melancholia was hunger. Always is.

More conversation, more food, more entertainment. We went to sleep right there by the stream, stretched on the ferns. Towards midnight when it got chilly we rolled into a pile. About an hour before dawn I woke.

I pulled my head from Easy's armpit (and Nativia's bald head moved immediately to take its place) and stood up in the stary dark. Little Jon's head gleamed at my feet. So did my blade. He was using it for a pillow. I slipped it gently from under his cheek. He snorted, scratched himself, was still. I started back through the trees in the direction of the kage.

Once I looked up at the branches, at the wires that ran from the power-shack to the fence. The black lines overhead, or the sound of the stream, or memory took me. Halfway, I started playing. Someone began to whistle along with me. I stopped. The whistle didn't.

Where is he then? In a song?
                                    Jean Genet/*The Screens*

God said to Abraham, "Kill me a son."
Abe said, "God, you must be puttin' me on!"
                                    Bob Dylan/*Highway 61 Revisited*

Love is something which dies and when dead it rots
and becomes soil for a new love . . . Thus in reality
there is no death in love.
                                    Par Lagerkvist/*The Dwarf*

"Le Dorik?" I said. "Dorik?"

"Hi," came a voice from the dark. "Lobey?"

"Lo Lobey," I said. "Where are you?"

"Just inside the kage."

"Oh. What's the smell?"

"Whitey," Dorik said. "Easy's brother. He died. I'm digging a grave. You remember Easy's brother—"

"I remember," I said. "I saw him by the fence yesterday. He looked pretty sick."

"That kind never last long. Come in and help me dig."

"The fence . . ."

"It's off. Climb over."

"I don't like to go in the kage," I said.

"You never used to mind sneaking in here when we

244

were kids. Come on, I've got to move this rock. Lend a foot.''

"That was when we were kids," I said. "We did a lot of things when we were kids we don't have to do now. It's your job. You dig.''

"Friza used to come in here and help me, tell me all about you.''

"Friza used to . . ." Then I said, "Tell?"

"Well, some of us could understand her."

"Yeah," I said. "Some of us could."

I grabbed the wire mesh near the post but didn't start climbing.

"Actually," Dorik said, "I was always sort of sad you never came around. We used to have fun. I'm glad Friza didn't feel the way you did. We used to—"

"—to do a lot of things, Dorik. Yeah, I know. Look, nobody ever bothered to tell me you weren't a girl till I was fourteen, Dorik. If I hurt you, I'm sorry."

"You did. But I'm not. Nobody ever did get around to telling Friza I wasn't a boy. Which I'm sort of glad of. I don't think she would have taken it the same way you did, even so.''

"She came here a lot?"

"All the time she wasn't with you."

I sprang over the wire, swung over the top, and dropped to the other side. "Where's that damn rock you're trying to move?''

"Here—"

"Don't touch me," I said. "Just show me."

"Here," Dorik repeated in the darkness.

I grabbed the edge of the stone shelved in the dirt. Roots broke, dirt whispered down, and I rolled the stone out. "How's the kid, by the way?" I asked.

I had to. And damn, Dorik, why were the next words the ones I was hurting with hoping I wouldn't hear?

"Which one?"

There was a shovel by the post. I jammed it into the grave. Damn Le Dorik.

"Mine and Friza's," Dorik went on after a moment, "will probably be up for review by the doctors in another year. Needs a lot of special training, but she's pretty functional. Probably will never have a La, but at least she won't have to be in here."

"That's not the kid I meant." The shovel clanged on another rock.

"You're not asking about the one that's all mine." There were two or three pieces of ice in that sentence. Dorik flicked them at me, much on purpose. "You mean yours and mine." As if you didn't know, you androgynous bastard. "He's in here for life, but he's happy. Want to go see him—"

"No." Three more shovelsful of dirt. "Let's bury Whitey and get out of here."

"Where are we going?"

"La Dire, she said you and me have to take a trip together to destroy what killed Friza."

"Oh," Dorik said. "Yes." Dorik went over to the fence, bent down. "Help me."

We picked up the bloated, rubbery corpse and carried it to the hole. It rolled over the edge, thumping.

"You were supposed to wait till I came for you," Dorik said.

"Yeah. But I can't wait. I want to go now."

"If I'm going with you, you're waiting."

"Why?"

"Look, Lobey," Dorik said, "I'm kage-keeper and I got a kage to keep."

"I don't care if everything in that kage mildews and
rots. I want to get out and get going!"

"I've got to train a new keeper, check over the education facilities, make sure of the food inventories and special diets, last minute shelter maintenance—"

"Damn it, Dorik, come on."

"Lobey, I've got three kids in here. One's yours, one
belongs to a girl you loved. And one's all mine. Two of
them, if they're loved and taken care of and given a lot of
time and patience may someday come out."

"Two of them, yeah?" My breath suddenly got lost in
my chest and didn't seem to be doing any good. "But not
mine. I'm going."

"Lobey!"

I stopped, straddling the fence.

"Look, Lobey, this is the real world you're living in.
It's come from something; it's going to something: it's
changing. But it's got right and wrong, a way to behave
and a way not to. You never wanted to accept that, even
when you were a kid, but until you do, you won't be very
happy."

"You're talking about me when I was fourteen," I
said.

"I'm talking about you now. Friza told me a lot—"

I jumped over the fence and started through the trees.

"Lobey!"

"What?" I kept walking.

"You're scared of me."

"No."

"I'll show you—"

"You're pretty good at showing people things in the
dark, aren't you? That's how you're different, huh?" I
called over my shoulder.

I crossed the stream and started up the rocks, mad as all Elvis. I didn't go towards the meadow, but around towards the steeper places, slapping leaves and flipping twigs as I barreled through the dark. Then I heard somebody come on through the shadow, whistling.

*There are none here except madmen; and a few there
are who know this world, and who know that he who
tries to act in the ways of others never does anything,
because men never have the same opinions. These do
not know that he who is thought wise by day will
never be held crazy by night.*
       Niccolo Machiavelli/*Letter to Francesco Vittori*

*Experience reveals to him in every object, in every
event, the presence of* something else.
       Jean-Paul Sartre/*Saint Genet, Actor and Martyr*

I stopped. The sound of dry leaves under feet, ferns by a
shoulder, approached me from behind, stopped. The hills'
rim had begun to gray.

"Lobey?"

"You changed your mind about coming?"

A sigh. "Yes."

"Come on, then." We started walking. "Why?"

"Something happened."

Dorik didn't say what. I didn't ask.

"Dorik," I said a little later, "I feel something towards
you very close to hate. It's as close to hate as what I felt
for Friza was close to love."

"Neither's close enough to worry about now. You're
too self-centered, Lobey. I hope you grow up."

"And you're going to show me how?" I asked. "In the dark?"

"I'm showing you now."

Morning, while we walked, leaked up vermilion. With light, my eyes grew surprisingly heavy, stones in my head. "You've been working all night," I volunteered. "I've only had a few hours sleep myself. Why don't we lie down for a few hours?"

"Wait till it gets light enough so you know I'm here." Which was an odd answer. Dorik was a grayed silhouette beside me now.

When there was enough red in the east and the rest of the sky was at least blue, I started looking for a place to fall out. I was exhausted and every time I turned to look at the sun, the world swam with tears of fatigue.

"Here," Dorik said. We'd reached a small stone hollow by the cliff's base. I dropped into it, Dorik too. We lay with the blade between us. I remember a moment of gold light along the arm and back curved towards me before I slept.

I touched the hand touching my face, held it still enough to open my eyes under it. Lids snapped back. "Dorik—?"

Nativia stared down at me.

My fingers intertwined with hers, hammocked by her webs. She looked frightened, and her breath through spread lips stopped my own. "Easy!" she called up the slope. "Little Jon! Here he is!"

I sat up. "Where'd Dorik go . . . ?"

Easy came loping into sight and Little Jon ran after.

"La Dire," Easy said. "La Dire wants to see you . . . before you go. She and Lo Hawk have to talk to you."

"Hey, did anybody see Le Dorik around here? Odd thing to run off—"

Then I saw this expression cracking through Little Jon's miniature features like faults in black rock. "Le Dorik's dead," Little Jon said; "that's what they wanted to tell you."

"Huh?"

"Before sunup, just inside the kage," Easy said. "He was lying by the grave for my brother, Whitey. Remember my brother—"

"Yeah, yeah," I said. "I helped dig it—Before sunup? That's impossible. The sun was up when we went to sleep, right here." Then I said, "Dead?"

Little Jon nodded. "Like Friza. The same way. That's what La Dire said."

I stood up, holding my blade tight. "But that's impossible!" Somebody saying, *Wait till it gets light enough so you'll know I'm here.* "Le Dorik was with me after sunrise. That's when we lay down here to sleep."

"You slept with Le Dorik *after* Le Dorik was dead?" Nativia asked, wonderingly.

Bewildered, I returned to the village. La Dire and Lo Hawk met me at the source-cave. We spoke together a bit; I watched them thinking deeply about things I didn't understand, about my bewilderment.

"You're a good hunter, Lo Lobey," Lo Hawk said at last, "and though a bit outsized below the waist, a fair specimen of a man. You have much danger ahead of you; I've taught you much. Remember it when you wander by the rim of night or the edge of morning." Apparently Le Dorik's death had convinced him there was something to La Dire's suppositions, though I understood neither side of the argument nor the bridge between. They didn't enlighten me. "Use what I have taught you to get where you are going," Lo Hawk went on, "to survive your stay, and make your way back."

"You are different." This is what La Dire said. "You have seen it is dangerous to be so. It is also very important. I have tried to instruct you in a view of the world large enough to encompass the deeds you will do as well as their significance. You have learned much, Lo Lobey. Use what I have taught you too."

With no idea where I was going, I turned and staggered away, still dazed by Dorik's death before sunrise. Apparently the Bloi triplets had been up all night fishing for blind-crabs in the mouth of the source-cave stream. They'd come back while it was still dark, swinging their hand-beams and joking as they walked up from the river—Dorik behind the wire in a net of shadow, circled with their lights, face down at the grave's edge! It must have been just moments after I first left.

I wheeled through the brambles, heading towards the noon, with one thought clearing, as figures on a stream bed clear when you brush back the bubbles a moment: if Le Dorik, dead, had walked with me a while ("I'm showing you now, Lobey."), walked through dawn and gorse, curled on a stone under new sunlight, then Friza too could travel with me. If I could find what killed those of us who were different, but whose difference gave us a reality beyond dying—

A slow song now on my blade to mourn Dorik; and the beat of my feet on earth in journey. After a few hours of such mourning, the heat had polished me with sweat as in some funeral dance.

While day leaned over the hills I passed the first red flowers, blossoms big as my face, like blood bubbles nested in thorns, often resting on the bare rock. No good to stop here. Carnivorous.

I squatted on a broken seat of granite in the yellowing afternoon. A snail the size of my curled forefinger bobbed his eyes at a puddle big as my palm. Half an hour later, climbing down a canyon wall when yellow had died under violet I saw a tear in the rock: another opening into the source-cave. I decided on nighting it there, and ducked in.

Still smells of humans and death. Which is good. Dangerous animals avoid it. I stalked inside, padding on all fours. Loose earth became moss, became cement underfoot. Outside, night, sonic lace of crickets and whining wasps I would not make on my knife, was well into black development.

Soon I touched a metal track, turned, and followed it with my hands . . . over a place where dirt had fallen, across a scattering of twigs and leaves, then down a long slope. I was about to stop, roll against the cave wall where it was drier, and sleep, when the track split.

I stood up.

When I shrilled on my blade, a long echo came from the right: endless passage there. But only a stubby resonance from the left: some sort of chamber. I walked left. My hip brushed a door jamb.

Then a room glowed suddenly before me. The sensor circuits were still sensitive. Grilled walls, blue glass desk, brass light fixtures, cabinets, and a television screen set in the wall. Squinting in the new light I walked over. When they still work, the colors are nice to watch: they make patterns and the patterns make music in me. Several people who had gone exploring the source-cave had told me about them (night fire and freakishly interested children knotted around the flame and the adventurer), and I'd gone to see one in a well explored arm two years back. Which is how I learned about the music.

Color television is certainly a lot more fun than this terribly risky genetic method of reproduction we've taken over. Ah well. It's a lovely world.

I sat on the desk and tried knobs till one clicked. The screen grayed at me, flickered, streamed with colors.

There was static, so I found the volume knob and turned it down . . . so I could hear the music in the colors. Just as I raised my blade to my mouth, something happened.

Laughter.

First I thought it was melody. But it was a voice laughing. And on the screen, in chaotic shimmerings, a face. It wasn't a picture of a face. It was as if I was just looking at the particular dots of melody/hue that formed the face, ignoring the rest. I would have seen those features on any visual riot: Friza's face.

The voice was someone else's.

Friza dissolved. Another face replaced hers: Dorik's. The strange laughter again. Suddenly there was Friza on one side of the screen, and Dorik on the other. Centered: the boy who was laughing at me. The picture cleared, filled, and I lost the rest of the room. Behind him, crumbled streets, beams jutting from the wrecks of walls, weeds writhing; and all lit with flickering green, the sun white on the reticulated sky. On a lamp-post behind him perched a creature with fins and white gills, scraping one red foot on the rust. On the curb was a hydrant laced with light and verdigris.

The boy, a redhead—redder than the Blois, redder than blood gutted blossoms—laughed with downcast eyes. His lashes were gold. Transparent skin caught up the green and fluoresced with it; but I knew that under normal light he would have been as pale as Whitey dying.

"Lobey," in the laughter, and his lips uncurtained small teeth—many too many of them. Like the shark's mouth, maybe, I'd seen in La Dire's book, rank on rank of ivory needles. "Lobey, how you gonna find me, huh?"

"What . . .?" and expected the illusion to end with my voice.

But somewhere that naked, laughing boy still stood with one foot in the gutter filled with waving weeds. Only Friza and Dorik were gone.

"Where are you?"

He looked up and his eyes had no whites, only glittering gold and brown. I'd seen a few like that before, eyes. Unnerving, still, to look at a dog's eyes in a human face. "My mother called me Bonny William. Now they all call me Kid Death." He sat on the curb, hanging his hands over his knees. "You're gonna find me, Lobey, kill me like I killed Friza and Dorik?"

"You? You, Lo Bonny William—"

"Not Lo. Kid Death. Not Lo Kid."

"You *killed* them? But . . . *why?*" Despair unvoiced my words to whispers.

"Because they were different. And I am more different than any of you. You scare me, and when I'm frightened"— laughing again—"I kill." He blinked. "You're not looking for me, you know. I'm looking for you."

"What do you mean?"

He shook shocked crimson from his white brow. "I'm bringing you down here to me. If I didn't want you, you'd never find me. Because I do want you, there's no way you can avoid me. I can see through the eyes of anyone on this world, on any world where our ancestors have ever been: so I know a lot about many things I've never touched or smelled. You've started out not knowing where I am and running towards me. You'll end, Lo Lobey"—he raised his head—"fleeing my green home, scrabbling on the sand like a blind goat trying to keep footing at a chimney edge, and—"

"—how do you know about—"

"—you'll fall and break your neck." He shook a finger at me, clawed like Little Jon's. "Come to me, Lo Lobey."

"If I find you, will you give me back Friza?"

"I've already given you back Le Dorik for a little while."

"*Can* you give me back Friza?"

"Everything I kill I keep. In my own private kage." His moist laughter. Water in a cold pipe, I think.

"Kid Death?"

"What?"

"Where are you?"

The sound snagged on ivory needles.

"Where are you from, Kid Death? Where are you going?"

The long fingers raveled like linen rope snaring gold coins. He pushed weeds away from the gutter grill with his foot. "I broiled away childhood in the sands of an equatorial desert kage with no keeper to love me. Like you, lively in your jungle, I was haunted by the memories of those who homed under this sun before our parents' parents came, took on these bodies, loves, and fears. Most of those around me in the kage died of thirst. At first I saved some of my fellows, bringing water to them the way Friza threw the stone—oh yes, I saw that too. I did that for a while. Then for a while I killed whoever was put in the kage with me, and took the water directly from their bodies. I would go to the fence and stare across the dunes to the palms at the oasis where our tribe worked. I never thought to leave the kage, back then, because like mirages on the glistering I saw through all the worlds' eyes—I saw what you and Friza and Dorik saw, as I see what goes all over this arm of the galaxy. When what I saw frightened me, I closed the eyes seeing. That's what happened to Friza and Dorik. When I am still curious about what's going on through those eyes, more curious than frightened, I open them again. That's what happened with Dorik."

"You're strong," I said.

"That's where I come from, the desert, where death shifts in the gritty bones of the Earth. And now? I am going further and further into the sea." Raising his eyes now, his red hair floated back in the shivering green.

"Kid Death," I called again; he was much further away. "Why were you in the kage? You look more functional than half the Lo and La of my village."

Kid Death turned his head and looked at me from the corner of his eyes. He mocked. "Functional? To be born on a desert, a white-skinned redhead with gills?"

The spreading, drinking, miniature mouth of the shark washed away. I blinked. I couldn't think of anything else so I took papers out of the filing cabinet, spread them under the desk, and lay down, tired and bewildered.

I remember I picked up one page and spelled my way through a paragraph. La Dire had taught me enough to read record labels, when for a while I had foraged about the village archives:

Evacuate upper levels with all due haste. Alarm system will indicate radiation at standard levels. Deeper detection devices are located . . .

Most of the words were beyond me. I halved the paper with toes and quartered it with fingers, let the pieces fall on my stomach before I picked up my machete to play myself to sleep.

What, then, is noble abstraction? It is taking first the essential elements of the thing to be represented, then the rest in the order of importance (so that wherever we pause we shall always have obtained more than we leave behind) and using any expedient to impress what we want upon the mind without caring about the mere literal accuracy of such expedient.

John Ruskin/*The Stones of Venice*

A poem is a machine for making choices.

John Ciardi/*How Does a Poem Mean*

Hours after—I figure it could have been two, it could have been twelve—I rolled from under the desk and came up grunting, yawning, scratching. When I stepped into the hall the light faded.

I didn't go back the way I'd come but headed forward again. There are lots of breakthroughs into the upper levels. I'd go till I saw morning and climb out. About half an hour later I see a three-foot stretch of it (morning) in the ceiling, behind black leaves, and leap for it. Good jumping power in those hams.

I scrambled out on crumbling ground and tame brambles, tripped on a vine, but all in all did pretty well. Which is to avoid saying "on the whole." Outside was cool, misty. Fifty yards by, the lapping edge of a lake flashed. I walked through the tangle to the clear beach. Chunked rock became gravel, became sand. It was a big lake. Down one arm of the beach things faded into reeds and swamp and things. Across, there was a gorse covered plain. I had no idea where I was. But I didn't want to be in a swamp, so I walked up the other way.

Thrash, thrash, *snap!*

I stopped.

Thrash! Just inside the jungle something churned and fought. The fighting was at the point where one opponent was near exhausted: activity came in momentary spurts. (Hissssss!) Curiosity, hunger, devilment sent me forward with high machete. I crept up a slope of rock, looked over into a glade.

Attacked by flowers, a dragon was dying. The blossoms jeweled his scales; thorns tangled his legs. As I watched, he tried again to tear them off with his teeth, but they scurried back, raking briars across his hide, or whipped them at his runny, yellow eyes.

The lizard (twice as big as Easy and man-branded on his left hinder haunch with a crusty cross) was trying to protect the external gill/lung arrangement that fluttered along his neck. The plants had nearly immobilized him, but when a bloom advanced to tear away his breath, he scraped and flailed with one free claw. He'd mauled a good many of the blossoms and their petals scattered the torn earth.

The cross told me he wouldn't hurt me (even crazed, the lizard once used to man becomes pathetic, seldom harmful) so I jumped down from the rock.

A blossom creeping to attack emptied an air-bladder inches from my foot, "Sssssss . . ." in surprise.

I hacked it, and nervous ooze (nervous in the sense that its nerves are composed of the stuff) belched greenly to the ground. Thorns flailed my legs. But I told you about the skin down there. I just have to watch out for my belly and the palms of my hands; feet are fine. With my foot I seized a creeper from the lizard's shoulder and pulled it out far enough—stained teeth go *clik-clik-clik* popping from the dragon's skin where they had been gnawing—to get my blade under, twist . . . and . . . *rip!*

Nerve dribbled the dragon's hide.

Those flowers communicate somehow (differently perhaps) and strove for me, one suddenly rising on its tendrils and leaping, "*Sssssss* . . .." I twiddled my blade in its brain.

I shouted encouragement to the dragon, threw a brave grin. He moaned reptilianly. Lo Hawk should see me do proud his skill.

His mane brushed my arm, his teeth crunched a flower while tendrils curled from the corners of his mouth. He chewed a while, decided he didn't like it, spat thorns. I pried off two more: his foot came free.

"*Sssssss* . . ." I looked to the right.

Which was a mistake because it was coming from the left.

Mistakes like that are a drag. Long and prickly wrapped my ankle and tried to jerk me off my feet. Fortunately you just can't do that. So then it sank lots of teeth into my calf and commenced chewing. I whirled and snatched white petals (this one an albino) which came away gently in my hand. *Crunch, Crunch*, still on my calf. My sword hand was up. I brought it down but it got caught in a net of brambles. Something scratched the back of my neck. Which ain't so tough.

Neither is (come to think): the small of my back, under my chin, between my legs, armpits, behind my ears—I was quickly cataloging all the tender places now. Damn flowers move just slow enough to give you time to think.

Then something long and hot sang by my shins. Petals snapped into the air. The plant stopped chewing and burped nervously down my ankle.

Pinnnnng near my hand, and my hand pulled free. I staggered, hacked another briar away. A bloated rose slithered down the dragon's leg and crawled for cover. They communicate, yes, and the communication was *fear* and *retreat*. The music, though! Lord, the *music!*

I whirled to look up on the rock.

Morning had got far enough along to rouge the sky behind him. He flicked a final encumbering flower from the beast, "*Sssssss* . . . blop!" and coiled his whip. I rubbed my calf. The dragon moaned, off key.

"Yours?" I thumbed over my shoulder at the beast.

"Was." He breathed deeply and the flat, bony chest sagged with his breathing, the ribs opening and closing like blinds. "If you come with us, he's yours—to ride, anyway. If you don't, he's mine again."

The dragon rubbed his gills ingenuously against my hip.

"Can you handle a dragon whip?" the stranger asked me.

I shrugged. "The only time I ever even saw one of these before was when some herders got off their trail six years ago." We'd all climbed up Beryl-Face and watched them drive the herd of lizards back through Green-glass Pass. When Lo Hawk went to talk to them, I went with him, which is where I found out about branding and the gentle monsters.

The stranger grinned. "Well, it's gone and happened again. I judge we're about twenty-five kilometers off. You want a job and a lizard to ride?"

I looked at the broken flowers. "Yeah."

"Well, there's your mount, and your job is to get him up here and back with the herd, first."

"Oh." (Now, lemme see; I remember the herders perched behind the lumps of the beasts' shoulders with their feet sort of tucked into the scaly armpits. My feet? And holding on to the two white whisker type things that grew back from the gills: Gee . . . Haw? Giddiap!)

We floundered in the mud about fifteen minutes with instructions shouted down, and I learned cuss words I hadn't ever heard from that guy. Towards the end we were both sort of laughing. The dragon was up and on the beach now, and he had quite unintentionally thrown me into the water—again.

"Hey, you think I'm going to really learn how to ride that thing?"

With one hand he was helping me up, with the other he was holding my mount by the whiskers, with another he was recoiling his whip, and with the fourth he just scratched his woolly head. "Don't give up. I didn't do too much better when I started. Up you go."

Up I went, and stayed on this time for a staggering run up and down the water's edge. I mean it looks graceful enough from the ground. It *feels* like staggering. On stilts.

"You're getting the hang of it."

"Thanks," I said. "Say, where is the herd; and who are you?"

He stood ankle deep in the lake's lapping. Morning was bright enough now to gem his chest and shoulders with drops from my splashing. He smiled and wiped his face. "Spider," he said. "and I didn't catch your name . . .?"

"Lo Lobey." I rocked happily behind the scaly hump.

"Don't say Lo to nobody herding," said Spider. "No need for it."

"Wouldn't even have thought of it if it weren't for my village ways," I said.

"Herd's off that way." He swung up behind me on the dragon.

Amber haired, four handed, and slightly hump-backed, Spider was seven feet of bone slipped into six feet of skin. Tightly. All tied in with long, narrow muscles. He was burned red, and the red burned brown but still glowing through. And he laughed like dry leaves crushed inside his chest. We circled the lake silently. And, oh man, the music!

The herd, maybe two hundred and fifty dragons moaning about (I was to learn that this was a happy sound), milled in a dell beyond the lake. Youth had romanticized the herders in my memory. They were motley. I see why you don't go around Lo-ing and La-ing and Le-ing herders. Two of them—I *still* don't see how they managed to stay on their dragons. But I came on friendly.

One kid with a real mind: you could tell by the way his green eye glittered at you, as well as his whip skill, and the sure way he handled dragons. Only he was mute. Was it this that upset me and made me think of Friza? You have a job to do. . . .

There was another guy who would have made Whitey look like a total norm. He had some glandular business that made him smell bad too. And he wanted to tell me his life story (no motor control of the mouth so he sort of splattered when he got excited).

I wish Green-eye could have talked instead of Stinky. I wanted to learn where he'd been, what he'd seen—he knew some good songs.

Dragons get lost at night. So you round them up in the morning. I'd been rounded up along with the stray animals. At breakfast I gathered from Stinky that I was a replacement for somebody who had come to a bad, sad, and messy end the previous afternoon.

"Oddest people survive out here," Spider mused. "Oddest ones don't. She looked a lot more 'normal' than you. But she ain't here now. Just goes to show you."

Green-eye blinked at me from under all his black hair, caught me watching him, and went back to splicing his whip.

"When are those dragon eggs gonna finish baking?" Knife asked, pawing at the fireplace stones with gray hands.

Spider kicked at him and the herder scuttled away. "Wait till we all eat." But in a few minutes he crawled back and was rubbing against the stones. "Warm," he muttered apologetically, when Spider started to kick him again. "I like it warm."

"Just keep off the food."

"Where do you take these to?" I indicated the herd. "Where do you bring them from?"

"They breed in the Hot Swamp, about two hundred kilometers west of here. We drive them down this way, across the Great City and on to Branning-at-sea. There the sterile ones are slaughtered; the eggs are removed from the females, inseminated, then we bring the eggs back and plant them in the swamp."

"Branning-at-sea?" I asked. "What do they do with them there?"

"Eat most. Use others for work. It's quite a fantastic place for someone born in the woods, I would imagine. I've been back and forth so many times it's like home.

I've got a house and a wife and three kids there, and another family back in the Swamp."

We ate eggs, fried lizard fat, and thick cereal, hot and filling, with plenty of salt and chopped peppers. When I finished I began to play my blade.

That *music!*

It was a whole lot of tunes at once, many the same, but starting at different times. I had to pick one strand out and play it. A few notes into it, I saw Spider staring at me, surprised. "Where did you hear that?" he asked.

"Just made it up, I guess."

"Don't be silly."

"It was just running around my head. All confused, though."

"Play it again."

I did. This time Spider began to whistle one of the other melodies that went along with it so that they glittered and jumped against each other.

When we finished he said, "You're different, aren't you?"

"So I've been told," I said. "Say, what's the name of that song anyway? It's not like most of the music I know."

"It's Kodaly's 'Sonata for Unaccompanied Cello.' "

Morning wind shook the gorse. "The what?" I asked. Behind us dragons moaned.

"You got it out of my head?" Spider said questioningly. "You couldn't have heard it before unless I was going around humming. And I can't hum a crescendo of triple stops."

"I got it from you?"

"That music's been going through my mind for weeks. Heard it at a concert last summer at Branning-at-sea, the night before I left to take the eggs back to the swamp. Then I discovered an LP of the piece in the music section of the ruins of the ancient library at Haifa.''

"I learned it from you?'' and suddenly all sorts of things cleared up, like how La Dire knew I was different, like how Nativia could tell I was different when I started playing *Bill Bailey*. "Music,'' I said. "So that's where I get my music from.'' I put the blade's tip on the ground and leaned on it.

Spider shrugged.

"I don't think I get all of it from other people,'' I said, frowning. "Different?'' I ran my thumb along the blade's edge and skipped my toes over the holes.

"I'm different too,'' Spider said.

"How?''

"Like this.'' He closed his eyes and all his shoulders knotted.

My machete jerked from my hand, pulled from the ground, and spun in the air. Then it fell point first to quiver in the shank of a log near the fire. Spider opened his eyes and took a breath.

My mouth was open. So I closed it.

Everybody else thought it was very funny.

"And with animals,'' Spider said.

"How?''

"The dragons. To a certain point I can keep them calm, keep them more or less together, and steer dangerous creatures away from us.''

"Friza,'' I said. "You're like Friza.''

"Who's Friza?''

I looked down at my knife. The melody which I had mourned her with was mine. "Nobody,'' I said, "anymore.'' That melody was mine! Then I asked, "Have you ever heard of Kid Death?''

Spider put down his food, brought all his hands in front of him, and tilted his head. His long nostrils flared till they were round. I looked away from his fear. But the others were watching me so I had to look back.

"What about Kid Death?" Spider asked.

"I want to find him and—" I flung my blade in the air and twirled it as Spider had, but my hand propelled. I seized it from its fall with my foot. "—Well, I want to find him. Tell me about him."

They laughed. It started in Spider's mouth, then was coming all sloppy from Stinky, a low hiss from Knife, grunts and cackles from the others, ending in Green-eye's green eye, a light that went out as he looked away. "You're going to have a hard time," Spider said finally, "but"—he rose from the fire—"you're headed in the right direction."

"Tell me about him," I said again.

"There's a time to talk about the impossible, but it's not when there's work to do." He got up, reached into a canvas sack and tossed me a whip.

I caught it mid-length.

"Put your ax away," Spider said. "This sings when it flies." His lash lisped over my head.

Everyone went to his mount, and Spider reeled a bridle and stirrups from the gear sack that fitted those humps and scales neatly, buckling around the forelegs; I see why he'd made me get the feel of things bareback. The semi-saddle and leg-straps make dragon riding almost nice.

"Head them on through that way," he yelled, and I imitated the herders around me as they began the drive.

Dragons swarmed in sunlight.

Oiled whips snapped and glistened over the scales, and the whole world got caught up in the rhythmic rocking of the beast between my legs, trees and hills and gorse and boulders and brambles all taking up the tune and movement as a crowd will begin clapping and stomping to a beat; the jungle, my audience, applauded the beat of surging lizards.

Moaning. Which meant they were happy.

Hissing sometimes. Which meant watch it.

Grunting and cussing and shouting. Which meant the herders were happy too.

I learned an incredible amount of things that morning, lunging back and forth between the creatures: five or six of them were the leaders and the rest followed. Keep the leaders going in the right direction and you had no problem. Dragons tend to go right. You get more response if you slap them on the back haunches. I later learned, nerve clusters there control their rear-end transmissions that're bigger than the brain.

One of the lead dragons kept on wanting to go back and bother an overweight female (ovarian tumor that kept her loaded down with sterile eggs, Spider explained to me) and it was all we could do to keep them apart. I spent a lot of time (imitating Green-eye) scouting the edge of the herd to worry the creatures back together who kept getting curious about things in irrelevant directions.

I began to learn what I was doing when about twenty dragons got stuck in a mintbog (a slushy quicksand *bog* covered with huge bushes of windy *mint,* right? Mintbog). Spider, by himself drove the rest of the herd around in a circle, three whips popping, while the other five of us went sloshing back and forth through the mint to drive the dragons out before they got stuck.

"There shouldn't be too many more of those," Spider shouted when we were charging along again. "We'll be crossing the City in a little while if we're not too far off course. I've been swinging us westward."

My arm was sore.

Once I got twenty seconds of calm riding time beside Green-eye: "Isn't this a pretty stupid way to waste your life, fellow?"

He grinned.

Then two very friendly dragons came galumphing and moaning between us. Sweat slopped into my eyes and my armpits felt oiled. The harness made it a little easier on my inner thighs; they got raw slow 'stead of quick. I could hardly see and was playing it more by ear than eye when Spider called, "Back on course! City up ahead!"

I looked up but fresh sweat flooded my eyes and the heat made everything waver. I drove dragons. The gorse lessened, and we started down.

Earth crumbled under their claws. With no vegetation to blunt the temperature, the sun stuck gold needles in the backs of our necks. Reflected heat from the ground. At last, sand.

The dragons had to slow. Spider paused beside me to thumb sweat from his eyes. "We usually take McClellan Avenue," he told me as he looked across the dunes. "But I think we're closer to Main Street. This hits McClellan a few miles out. We'll stop at the intersection and rest until nightfall." The dragons hissed out across the city sands. Swamp creatures, they were not used to this dryness. As we plowed the ancient place, silent and furious with hundreds of beasts, I remember crossing a moment of untimed horror, when through void buff I imagined myself surrounded of a sudden, crowded by millions, straited by walls, sooty, fuming, roaring with the dread, dead old race of the planet.

I flailed my whip and beat away the notion. The sun ground its light into the sand.

Two dragons began to annoy each other and I flicked them apart. They snatched at my lash indignantly, missed. My breath filed my throat. Yet, as the two moved away, I realized I was grinning. Alone, we toiled through the day, content and terrified.

Slipped from the night waters of the Adriatic and now we skirt down the strait towards Piraeus. At the horizon right and left monstrously beautiful mountains gnaw the sky. The ship is easy on the morning. The speakers give up French, English, and Greek pop music. Sun silvers the hosed deck, burns over the smokestack. Bought deck passage; big and bold last night I walked into a cabin and slept beautifully. Back outside this morning I wonder what effect Greece will have on FFD. The central subject of the book is myth. This music is so appropriate for the world I float on. I was aware how well it fitted the capsulated life of New York. Its torn harmonies are even more congruent with the rest of the world. How can I take Lobey into the center of this bright chaos propelling these sounds? Drank late with the Greek sailors last night; in bad Italian and worse Greek we talked about myths. Taiki learned the story of Orpheus not from school or reading but from his aunt in Eleusis. Where shall I go to learn it? The sailors my age wanted to hear pop English and French music on the portable radio. The older ones wanted to hear the traditional Greek songs. "Demotic songs!" exclaimed Demo. "All the young men in the words want to die as soon as possible because love has treated them badly!"

271

"Not so with Orpheus," Taiki said, *a little myste-*
riously, a little high.

Did Orpheus want to live after he lost Eurydice the
second time? He had a very modern choice to make
when he decided to look back. What is its musical
essence?

*Writer's Journal/*Gulf of Corinth, November 1965

> *I drive fine dragons*
> *for a fine dragon lord,*
> *a lord of fine dragons*
> *and his dragon horde.*

Green-eye sang that silently as we dropped from our mounts.
For the first time in my life I caught words as well as
melody. It surprised me and I turned to stare. But he was
loosening the harness on his beast.

The sky was blue glass. West, clouds smudged the
evening with dirty yellow. The dragons threw long shadows on the sand. Coals glowed in the makeshift fireplace.
Batt was cooking already.

"McClellan and Main," Spider said. "Here we are."

"How can you tell?" I asked.

"I've been here before."

"Oh."

The dragons had more or less decided we were really
stopping. Many lay down.

My mount (whom I had inadvertently named something
unprintable; a day's repetition had stabilized the monicker.
Therefore we must call him: My Mount) nuzzled my neck
affectionately, nearly knocked me down, then dropped his
chin to the sand, folded his forelegs, and let his hinder
parts fall where they might. That's how dragons do it. Sit
down I mean.

Ten steps and I didn't think I would walk again. I tied my whip around my waist, went as close to the food as I could without stepping on anybody, and sat. The exhausted muscles of my legs sagged like water bags. Supplies and equipment were piled to one side. Spider lay down on top of them with one hand hanging down over the edge. I stared at his hand across the fire: because it was in front of me, that's all. And I learned a few things about Spider.

It was large, hung from a knobbly wrist. The skin between thumb and forefinger was cracked like stone, and the ridges of his knuckles were filled with sweat dampened dirt. A bar of callous banded the front of his palm before the abruptness of his fingers—that was all hard dragon work. But also, on the middle finger at the first knuckle was a callous facing the forefinger. That comes from holding a writing tool. La Dire has such a callous and I asked her about it once. Third, on the tips of his fingers (but not his thumb. It was a left hand) there were smooth shiny spots: those you get from playing a stringed instrument, guitar, violin . . . maybe cello? Sometimes when I play with other people I notice them. So Spider herds dragons. And he writes. And he plays music. . . .

While I sat there, it occurred to me how hard breathing was.

I began to think about trees.

I had a momentary nightmare that Batt was going to give us something as difficult to eat as hardshell crabs and steamed artichokes.

I leaned on Green-eye's shoulder and slept.

I think he slept too.

I woke when Batt lifted the cover from the stew pot. The odor pried my mouth open, reached down my throat, took hold of my stomach and twisted. I wasn't sure if it was pleasurable or painful. I just sat, working my jaws, my throat aching. I leaned forward over my knees and clutched sand.

Batt ladled stew into pans, stopping now and then to shake hair out of his eyes. I wondered how much hair was in the stew. I didn't care, mind you. Just curious. He passed the steaming tins and I rested mine in the hollow of my crossed legs. A charred loaf of bread came around. Knife broke open a piece and the fluffy innards popped through a gold streak on the crust. When I twisted some off, I realized the fatigue in my arms and shoulders and almost started laughing. I was too tired to eat, too hungry to sleep. With the paradox both sleeping and eating left the category of pleasure, where I'd always put them, and became duties on this crazy job I'd somehow got into. I sopped gravy on my bread, put it into my mouth, bit, and trembled.

I shoved down half my meal before I realized it was too hot. Hungry like I was hungry, hungry beyond need—it's frightening to be that hungry.

Green-eye was shoving something into his mouth with his thumb.

That was the only other human thing I was aware of during the meal till Stinky spluttered, "Gimme some more!"

When I got my seconds, I managed to slow down enough to look around. You can tell about people from the way they eat. I remember the dinner Nativia had cooked us. Oh, eating were something else back then—a day ago, two days?

"You know," Batt grunted, watching his food go, "you got dessert coming."

"Where?" Knife answered, finishing his second helping and reaching out of the darkness for the bread.

"You have some more food-food first," Batt said,

" 'cause I'm damned if you're gonna eat up my dessert that fast.'' He leaned over, swiped Knife's pan from him, filled it, and those gray hands closed on the tin edge and withdrew into the shadow again. The sound of dogged chewing.

Spider, silent till now, looked with blinking silver eyes. "Good stew, cook."

Batt leered.

Spider who herds dragons; Spider who writes; Spider who has the multiplicated music of Kodaly in his head— good man to receive a compliment from.

I looked from Spider to Batt and back. I wished I had said *Good stew* because it was, and because saying it made Batt grin like that. What I did come out with, the words distorted by that incredible lash of hunger, was: "What's dessert?"

I guess Spider was a bigger person than me. Like I say, that sort of hunger is scary.

Batt took a ceramic dish out of the fire with rags. "Blackberry dumplings. Knife, reach me the rum sauce."

I heard Green-eye's breath change tempo. My mouth got wet all over again. I watched—examined Batt spooning dumplings and berry filling onto the pans.

"Knife, get your fingers out!"

". . . just wanted to taste." But the gray hand retreated. Through the dusk firelight caught on a tongue sliding along a lip.

Batt handed him a plate.

Spider was served last. We waited for him to begin, though, now that the bottom of the pit was lined.

"Night . . . sand . . . and dragons," Stinky muttered. "Yeah." Which was very apt.

I had just taken my blade out to play when Spider said, "You were asking about Kid Death this morning."

"That's right." I lay the blade in my lap. "You had something to say about him?" The others quieted.

"I did the Kid a favor, once," Spider mused.

"When he was in the desert?" I asked, wondering what sort of person you would have to be to be different and doing Kid Death favors.

"When he had just come out of the desert," Spider said. "He was holed up in a town."

"What's a town?" I asked.

"You know what a village is?"

"Yeah. I came from one."

"And you know what a city is." He motioned around at the sand. "Well a village grows bigger and bigger till it becomes a town; then the town grows bigger and bigger till it becomes a city. But this was a ghost town. That means it was from a very old time, from the old people of the planet. It had stopped growing. The buildings had all broken open, sewers caved in, dead leaves fled up the streets, around the stubs of street-lamp bases; an abandoned power station, rats, snakes, department stores—these are the things that are in a town. Also the lowest, dirtiest outcasts of a dozen species who are vicious with a viciousness beyond what intelligence can conceive. Because if there were a brain behind it, they would all be luxuriant, decadent lords of evil over the whole world instead of wallowing in the junk heap of a ghost town. They are creatures you wouldn't put in a kage."

"What did you do for him?" I asked.

"I killed his father."

I frowned.

Spider picked at a tooth. "He was a detestable, three-eyed, three hundred pound worm. I know he'd murdered at least forty-six people. He tried to kill me three times while I was bumming through the town. Once with poison, once with a wrench, once with a grenade. Each time he missed and got somebody else. He'd fathered a couple of dozen, but still a good number less than he'd killed. Once, when I was on fair terms with him, he gave me one of his daughters. Butchered and dressed her himself. Fresh meat is scarce in town. He simply didn't count on one of his various kaged offspring whom he'd abandoned a thousand miles away following him up from the desert. Nor did he count on that child's being a criminal genius, psychotic, and a totally different creature. The Kid and I met up in town there where his father was living high as one could live in that dung pile. The Kid must have been about ten years old.

"I was sitting in a bar, listening to characters brag and boast, while a wrestling match was going in the corner. The loser would be dinner. Then this skinny carrottop wanders in and sits down on a pile of rags. He stared down most of the time so that you looked at those eyes of his through finer veils of gold. His skin was soap white. He watched the fight, listened to the bragging, and once made a design in the dirt with his toe. When the talk got boring, he scratched his elbow and made faces. When the stories got wild and fascinating, he froze, his fingers tied together, and head down. He listens like someone blind. When the stories were through, he walked out. Then someone whispered, *That was Kid Death!* and everybody got quiet. He already had quite a reputation."

Green-eye had moved a little closer to me. There was a chill over the City.

"A little later while I was taking a walk outside," Spider went on, "I saw him swimming in the lake of the Town Park.

Hey, Spiderman, he called me from the water.

I walked over and squatted by the pool's edge. *Hi, kid.*

You gotta kill my old man for me. He reached from the lake and grabbed my ankle. I tried to pull away. The Kid leaned back till his face was under water, and bubbled, *You gotta do me this little favor, Spider. You have to.*

A leaf stuck to his arm. *If you say so, Kid.*

He stood up in the water now, hair lank down his face, scrawny, white, and wet. *I say so.*

Mind if I ask why? I pushed the hair off his forehead. I wanted to see if he was real: cold fingers on my ankle; wet hair under my hand.

He smiled, ingenuous as a corpse. *I don't mind.* His lips, nipples, the cuticles over his claws were shriveled. *There's a whole lot of hate left on this world, Spiderman. The stronger you are, the more receptive you are to the memories that haunt these mountains, these rivers, seas and jungles. And I'm strong! Oh, we're not human, Spider. Life and death, the real and the irrational aren't the same as they were for the poor race who willed us this world. They tell us young people, they even told me, that before our parents' parents came here, we were not concerned with love, life, matter and motion. But we have taken a new home, and we have to exhaust the past before we can finish with the present. We have to live out the human if we are to move on to our own future. The past terrifies me. That's why I must kill it—why you must kill him for me.*

Are you so tied up with their past, Kid?

He nodded. *Untie me, Spider.*

What happens if I don't?

He shrugged. *I'll have to kill you—all.* He sighed. *Under the sea it's so silent . . . so silent, Spider.* He whispered, *Kill him!*

Where is he?

He's waddling along the street while the moonlit gnats make dust around his head, his heel sliding in the trickle of water along the gutter that runs from under the old church wall; he stops and leans, panting, against the moss—

He's dead, I said. I opened my eyes. *I dislodged a slab of concrete from the beams, so that it slid down—*

See you around sometime. The Kid grinned and pushed backward into the pool. *Thanks. Maybe I'll be able to do something for you someday, Spider.*

Maybe you will, I said. He sank in the silvered scum. I went back to the bar. They were roasting dinner."

After a while I said, "You must have lived in town a fair while."

"Longer than I'd like to admit," Spider said. "If you call it living." He sat up and glanced around the fire. "Lobey, Green-eye, you two circle the herd for the first watch. In three hours wake Knife and Stinky. Me and Batt will take the last shift."

Green-eye rose beside me. I stood too as the others made ready to sleep. My Mount was dozing. The moon was up. Ghost lights ran on the humped spines of the beasts. Sore-legged, stiff-armed, I climbed a-back My Mount and with Green-eye began to circle the herd. I swung the whip against my shin as we rode. "How do they look to you?"

I didn't expect an answer. But Green-eye rubbed his stomach with a grimy hand.

"Hungry? Yeah, I guess they are in all this sand." I watched the slender, dirty youngster sway behind the scaled hump. "Where are you from?" I asked.

He smiled quickly at me.

I was born of a lonely mother
with neither father nor sister nor brother.

I looked up surprised.

At the waters she waits for me
my mother, my mother at Branning-at-sea.

"You're from Branning-at-sea?" I asked.

He nodded.

"Then you're going home."

He nodded again.

Silent, we rode on till at last I began to play with tired fingers. Green-eye sang some more as we jogged under the moon.

I learned that his mother was a fine lady in Branning-at-sea, related to many important political leaders. He had been sent away with Spider to herd dragons for a year. He was returning at last to his mother, this year of wandering and work serving as some sort of passage rite. There was a great deal in the thin, bushy haired boy, so skilled with the flock, I didn't understand.

"Me?" I asked when his eye inquired of me in the last of the moonlight. "I don't have any time for the finery of Branning-at-sea as you describe it. I'll be glad to see it, passing. But I got things to do."

Silent inquiry.

"I'm going to Kid Death to get Friza, and stop what's killing all the different ones. That probably means stopping Kid Death."

He nodded.

"You don't know who Friza is," I said. "Why are you nodding?"

He cocked his head oddly, then looked across the herd.

I am different so I bring
words to singers when I sing.

I nodded and thought about Kid Death. "I hate him," I said. "I have to learn to hate him more so I can find him and kill him."

There is no death, only love.

That one arrived sideways.

"What was that again?"

He wouldn't repeat it. Which made me think about it more. He looked sadly out from the work-grime. At the horizon, the fat moon darkened with clouds. Strands of shadow through the thatch of his hair widened over the rest of his face. He blinked; he turned away. We finished our circuit, chased back two dragons. The moon, revealed once more, was a polished bone joint jammed on the sky. We woke Knife and Stinky, who rose and moved to their dragons.

The coals gave the only color. And for one moment when Green-eye crouched to stare at some pattern snaking the ashes, the light cast up on his single-eyed face. He stretched beside the fire.

I slept well, but a movement before dawn roused me. The moon was down. Starlight paled the sand. The coals were dead. One dragon hissed. Two moaned. Silence. Knife and Stinky were returning. Spider and Batt were getting up.

I drifted off and woke again when only one slop of blue lightened the eastern dunes. Batt's dragon came around the fireplace. Spider's lumbered after him. I rose on my elbows.

"Keeping you up?" Spider asked.

"Huh?"

"I was running over the Kodaly again."

"Oh." I could hear it coming across the chill sand. "Naw." I got to my feet. They were about to start around again. "Just a second. I'll go around with you. There's something I want to ask you. I'd have been up in a little while anyway."

He didn't wait but I swung on my dragon and caught up.

He laughed softly when I reached his side. "Wait till you've been out here a few more days. You won't be so ready to give up that last few minutes' sleep."

"I'm too sore to sleep," I said, though the jogging was beginning to loosen stiff me. The coolness had set my joints.

"What did you want to ask me?"

"About Kid Death."

"What about him?"

"You say you knew him. Where can I find him?"

Spider was silent. My Mount slipped in the road and caught his balance again before he answered. "Even if I could tell, even if telling you would do any good, why should I? The Kid could get rid of you like that." He popped his whip on the sand. Grains flew. "I don't think the Kid would appreciate my going around telling people who want to kill him where to find him."

"I don't suppose it would make much difference if he's as strong as you say he is." I ran my thumb over the machete's mouthpiece.

Spider shrugged some of his shoulders. "Maybe not. But, like I say, the Kid's my friend."

"Got you under his thumb too, huh?" It's difficult to be cutting with a cliche. I tried.

"Just about," Spider said.

I flicked my whip at a dragon who looked like he was

thinking of leaving. He yawned, shook his mane, and lay back down. "I guess in a way he's even got me. He said I would try to find him until I had learned enough. Then I'd try to run away."

"He's playing with you," Spider said. He had a mocking smile.

"He's really got us all tied up."

"Just about," Spider said again.

I frowned. "Just about isn't all."

"Well," Spider said in some other direction than mine, "there are a few he can't touch, like his father. That's why he had to get me to kill him."

"Who?"

"Green-eye is one. Green-eye's mother is another."

"Green-eye?" In my repetition of the name I'd asked a question. Perhaps he didn't hear. Perhaps he chose not to answer.

So I asked another. "Why did Green-eye have to leave Branning-at-sea? He half explained to me last night, but I didn't quite get it."

"He has no father," Spider said. He seemed more ready to talk of this.

"Can't they ran a paternity check? The traveling folk-doctors do it all the time in my village."

"I didn't say they didn't know who his father was. I said he had none."

I frowned.

"How are your genetics?"

"I can draw a dominance chart," I said. Most people, even from the tiniest villages, knew their genetics, even if they couldn't add. The human chromosome system was so inefficient in the face of the radiation level that genetics was survival knowledge. I've often wondered why we didn't invent a more compatible method of reproduction to go along with our own three way I-guess-you'd-call-it-sexual devision. Just lazy. "Go on," I said to Spider.

"Green-eye had no father," Spider repeated.

"Parthenogenesis?" I asked. "That's impossible. The sex distinguishing chromosome is carried by the male. Females and androgynes only carry genetic equipment for producing other females. He'd have to be a girl, with haploid chromosomes, and sterile. And he certainly isn't a girl." I thought a moment. "Of course if he were a bird, it would be a different matter. The females carry the sex distinguishing chromosomes there." I looked out over the herd. "Or a lizard."

"But he's not," Spider said.

I agreed. "That's amazing," I said, looking back towards the fire where the amazing boy slept.

Spider nodded. "When he was born, wise men came from all over to examine him. He is haploid. But he's quite potent and quite male, though a rather harried life has made him chaste by temperament."

"Too bad."

Spider nodded. "If he would join actively in the solstice orgies or make some appeasing gesture in the autumnal harvest celebrations, a good deal of the trouble could be avoided."

I raised an eyebrow. "Who's to know if he takes part in the orgies? Don't you hold them in the dark of the moon in Branning?"

Spider laughed. "Yes. But at Branning-at-sea, it's become a rather formal business; it's carried on with artificial insemination. The presentation of the seed—especially by the men of important families—gets quite a bit of publicity."

"Sounds very dry and impersonal."

"It is. But efficient. When a town has more than a million people in it, you can't just turn out the lights and let everybody run wild in the streets the way you can in a small village. They tried it that way a couple of times, back when Branning-at-sea was much smaller, and even then the results were—"

"A million people?" I said. "There are a million people in Branning-at-sea?"

"Last census there were three million six hundred fifty thousand."

I whistled. "That's a lot."

"That's more than you can imagine."

I looked across the herd of dragons; only a couple of hundred.

"Who wants to take part in an orgy of artificial insemination?" I asked.

"In a larger society," Spider said, "things have to be carried on that way. Until there's a general balancing out of the genetic reservoir, the only thing to do is to keep the genes mixing, mixing, mixing. But we have become clannish, more so in places like Branning-at-sea than in the hills. How to keep people from having no more than one child by the same partner. In a backwoods settlement, a few nights of license take care of it, pretty much. In Branning, things have to be assured by mathematical computation. And families have sprung up that would be quite glad to start doubling their children if given half a chance. Anyway, Green-eye just goes about his own business, occasionally saying very upsetting things to the wrong person. The fact that he's different and immune to Kid Death, from a respected family, and rather chary of ritual observances makes him quite controversial. Everybody blames the business on his parthenogenetic birth."

"They frown on that even where I come from," I told Spider. "It means his genetic structure is identical with his mother's. That will never do. If that happens enough, we shall all return to the great rock and the great roll in no time.''

"You sound like one of those pompous fools at Branning." He was annoyed.

"Huh! That's just what I've been taught."

"Think a little more. Every time you say that, you bring Green-eye a little closer to death."

"What?"

"They've tried to kill him before. Why do you think he was sent away?"

"Oh," I said. "Then why is he coming back?"

"He wants to." Spider shrugged. "Can't very well stop him if he wants to."

I grunted. "You don't make Branning-at-sea sound like a very nice place. Too many people, half of them crazy, and they don't even know how to have an orgy." I took up my blade. "I don't have time for nonsense like that."

The music dirged from Spider. I played light piping sounds.

"Lobey."

I looked back at him.

"Something's happening, Lobey, something now that's happened before, before when the others were here. Many of us are worried about it. We have the stories about what went on, what resulted when it happened to the others. It may be very serious. All of us may be hurt."

"I'm tired of the old stories," I said, "their stories. We're not them; we're new, new to this world, this life. I know the stories of Lo Orpheus and Lo Ringo. Those are the only ones I care about. I've got to find Friza."

"Lobey—"

"This other is no concern of mine." I let a shrill note. "Wake your herders, Spider. You have dragons to drive."

I galloped My Mount forward. Spider didn't call again.

* * *

Before the sun hit apogee the edge of the City cleft the horizon. As I swung my whip in the failing heat, I permutated Green-eye's last words, beating out thoughts in time: if there were no death, how might I gain Friza? That love was enough, if wise and articulate and daring. Or thinking of La Dire, who would have amended it (dragons clawed from the warm sand to the leafy hills), there is no death, only rhythm. When the sand reddened behind us, and the foundering beasts, with firmer footing, hastened, I took out my knife and played.

The City was behind us.

Dragons loped easy now across the gorse. A stream ribboned the knolly land and the beasts stopped to slosh their heads in the water, scraping their hind feet on the bank, through grass, through sand, to black soil. The water lapped their knees, grew muddy as they tore the water-weeds. A fly bobbed on a branch, preening the crushed prism of his wing (a wing the size of my foot) and thought a linear, arthropod music. I played it for him, and he turned the red bowl of his eye to me and whispered wondering praise. Dragons threw back their heads, gargling.

There is no death.

Only music.

Whanne, as he strod alonge the shakeynge lee,
The roddie levynne glesterrd on hys headde;
Into hys hearte the azure vapoures spreade;
He wrythde arounde yn drearie dernie payne;—
Whanne from his lyfe-bloode the rodde lemes were
fed,
He felle an hepe of ashes on the playne.

               Thomas Chatterton/*English Metamorphosis*

   "Now there's a quaint taste," said Durcet. "Well,
Curval, what do you think of that one?"
   "Marvelous," the President replied; "there you
have an individual who wishes to make himself famil-
iar with the idea of death and hence unafraid of it,
and who to that end has found no better means than
to associate it with a libertine idea . . ." . . . Sup-
per was served, orgies followed as usual, the house-
hold retired to bed.

               Le Marquis de Sade/*The 120 Days of Sodom*

. . . each bubble contains a complete eye of water.
               Samuel Greenburg/*The Glass Bubbles*

Then to the broken land ("This"—Spider halted his dragon
in the shaly afternoon—"is the broken land." He flung a
small flint over the edge. It chuckled into the canyon.

Around us the dragons were craning curiously at the granite, the veined cliffs, the chasms) slowing our pace now. Clouds dulled the sun. Hot fog flowed around the rocks. I worked one muscle after another against the bone to squeeze out the soreness. Most of the pain (surprise) was gone. We meandered through the fabulous, simple stones.

The dragons made half time here.

Spider said it was perhaps forty kilometers to Branning-at-sea. Wind heated our faces. Glass wound in the rocks. Five dragons began a scuffle on the shale. One was the tumored female. Green-eye and me came at them from opposite sides. Spider was busy at the head of the herd; the scuffle was near the tail. Something had frightened them, and they were plopping up the slope. It didn't occur to us something was wrong; this was the sort of thing that Spider (and Friza) were supposed to be able to prevent. (Oh, Friza, I'll find you through the echo of all mourning stones, all praising trees!) We followed.

They dodged through the boulders. I shouted after them. Our whips chattered. We couldn't outrun them. We hoped they would fall to fighting again. We lost them for a minute, then heard their hissing beyond the rocks, lower down.

Clouds smeared the sky; water varnished the trail ahead. As M. M. crossed the wet rock, he slipped.

I was thrown, scraping hip and shoulder. I heard my blade clatter away on the rock. My whip snarled around my neck. For one moment I thought I'd strangle. I rolled down a slope, trying to flail myself to a halt, got scraped up more. Then I dropped over the edge of something. I grabbed out with both hands and feet. Chest and stomach slapped stone. My breath went off somewhere and wouldn't go back into my lungs for a long time. When it did, it came roaring down my sucking throat, whirled in my bruised chest. Busted ribs? Just pain. And roar again with another breath. Tears flooded my sight.

I was holding on to a rock with my left hand, a vine with my right; my left foot clutched a sapling none too securely by the roots. My right leg dangled. And I just knew it was a long way down.

I rubbed my eye on my shoulder and looked up:

The lip of the trail above me.

Above that, angry sky.

Sound? Wind through gorse somewhere. No music.

While I was looking it started to rain. Sometimes painful catastrophes happen. Then some little or even pleasant thing follows it, and you cry. Like rain. I cried.

"Lobey."

I looked again.

Kneeling on a shelf of stone a few feet above me to the right was Kid Death.

"Kid . . . ?"

"Lobey," he said, shaking wet hair back from his forehead. "I judge you can hold on there twenty-seven minutes before you drop over the edge from exhaustion. So I'm going to wait twenty-six minutes before I do anything about saving your life. O.K.?"

I coughed.

Seeing him close, I guessed he was sixteen or seventeen, or maybe a baby-faced twenty. His skin was wrinkled at his wrists, neck, and under his arms.

Rain kept dribbling in my eyes; my palms stung, and what I was holding on to was getting slippery.

"Ever run into any good westerns?" He shook his head. "Too bad. Nothing I like better than westerns." He rubbed his forefinger under his nose and sniffed. Rain danced on his shoulders as he leaned over to talk to me.

"What is a 'western'?" I asked. My chest still hurt.

"And you mean you're really going to make—" I coughed again "—me hang here twenty-six minutes?"

"It's an art-form the Old Race, the humans, had before we came," Kid Death said. "And yes, I am. Torture is an art-form too. I want to rescue you at the last minute. While I'm waiting, I want to show you something." He pointed up to the rim of the road I'd rolled over.

Friza looked down.

I stopped breathing. The pain in my chest exploded, my wide eyes burned with rain. Dark face, slim wet shoulders, then watch her turn her head (gravel sliding under my belly, the whiplash still around my neck and the handle swinging against my thigh) to catch rain in her mouth. She looked back, and I saw (or did I hear?) her wonder at life returned, and confusion at the rain, these twisted rocks, these clouds. Glory beat behind those eyes above me. Articulate, she would have called my name; saw me, now, impulsively reached her hand to me (did I hear her fear?). "Friza!"

That was a scream.

You and I know the word I shrieked. But nobody else hearing the rough sound my lungs shoved up would have recognized it.

All this, understand, in the instant it takes to open your eyes in the rain, lick a drop from your lip, then focus on what's in front of you and realize it's somebody you love about to die and he tries to scream your name. That's what Friza did there on the road's lip.

And I kept screaming.

What Kid Death did between us was giggle.

Friza began to search right and left for a way to get down to me. She rose, disappeared, was back a moment later, bending a sapling over the edge of the road.

"No, Friza!"

But she started to climb down, dirt and tiny stones shooting out beneath her feet. Then, when she was hanging at the very end, the line of her body arching dark on the rock, she grabbed the whip handle—neither with hands nor feet, but rather as she had once thrown a pebble, as Spider had once pushed over a chunk of cement; she grabbed the handle from where it hung against my thigh, pulled it, lifted it, straining till rain glistened on her sides, knotted the handle around the sapling above the first fork. She started to climb back, jerk of an arm, away a moment, jerk, away, jerk, reaching handhold by handhold towards the road. It kept on going through my head, here she wakes from how many days' death with only a moment to glory before plunging into the rescue of the life running out below her. She was doing it to save me. She wanted me to grab hold of the whip and haul myself to the tree, then by the tree haul myself to the road. I hurt and loved her, held on and didn't fall.

Kid Death was still chuckling. Then he pointed at the apex of the bent tree. "Break!" he whispered.

It did.

She fell, throwing the branch away from her in one instant; clutching at the stone as she fell, snatched at the length of leather dangling from my neck, then let it go.

She let it go because she knew damn well it would have pulled me from the cliff face.

"Baaa—baaa!" Kid Death said. He was imitating a goat. Then he giggled again.

I slammed my face against the shale. *"Friza!"* No, you couldn't understand what I howled.

Her music crashed out with her brains on the rocks of the canyon floor a hundred feet below.

Rock. Stone. I tried to become the rock I hung against. I tried to be stone. Less blasted by her double death I would have dropped. Had she died in any other act than trying to save me, I would have died with her. But I couldn't let her fail.

My heart rocked. My heart rolled.

Numb, I dangled for some timeless time, till my hands began to slip.

"All right. Up you go."

Something seized my wrist and pulled me up, hard. My shoulders rang like gongs of pain under my ears. I was hauled blind over gravel. I blinked and breathed. Somehow Kid Death had pulled me up on the ledge with him.

"Just saved your life," Kid Death said. "Aren't you glad you know me?"

I began to shake. I was going to pass out.

"You're just about to yell at me, 'You killed her!' " Kid Death said. "I killed her again is what really happened. And I may have to do it a third time before you get the idea—"

I lunged, would have gone off and over. But he caught me with one strong, wet hand, and slapped me with the other. The rain had stopped.

Maybe he did more than slap me.

The Kid turned and started scrambling up to the lip of the trail. I started after him.

I climbed.

Dirt ripped under my fingers. It's good about my nail chewing, because otherwise I wouldn't have had any nails left. From the ledge it was possible to get back up. Kid Death leaped and bounded. I crawled.

There's a condition where every action dogs one end. You move/breathe/stop to rest/start again with one thing in mind. That's how I followed. Mostly on my belly. Mostly with my breath held. I'm not too sure where I went. Things didn't clear up till I realized there were two figures in front of me: the moist, white redhead. A black thatch of hair, grimy Green-eye.

I lay on a rock, resting, is how it was, in the fog of fatigue and endeavor, when I saw them.

Kid Death stood with his arm around Green-eye's shoulder at the precipice. The sky in front of them swam violently.

"Look, pardner," Kid Death was saying; "we've got to come to some sort of agreement. I mean, you don't think I came all the way out here just to rustle five dragons from my friend Spider? That's just to let him know I'm still running. But you. You and I have to get together. Haploid? You're totally outside my range. I want you. I want you very much, Green-eye."

The dirty herder shrugged from under the moist fingers.

"Look," Kid Death said and gestured at the crazy sky.

As I had first seen the Kid's face in the glittering screen in the source-cave, I saw in the raveling clouds: a plain surrounded by a wire fence (a kage?) but inside a soaring needle wracked with struts and supports. I got some idea how big it was when I realized the stone blocks by the fence were houses, and the dots moving around were men and women.

"Starprobe," the Kid said. "They're on the verge of discovering the method the humans used to get from planet to planet, star to star. They've been delving in the ruins, tasting the old ideas, licking the bits of metal and wire now for ten years. It's almost finished." He waved his hand. Rolling in place of the scene now was water and water: an ocean. On the water, metal pontoons formed a floating station. Boats plied back and forth. Cranes dropped a metal cabinet towards the ocean floor. "Depthgauge," the Kid explained. "Soon we shall be able to do more than dream across the silt of the ocean floor, but take these bodies to the fond of the world as they did.'' Another wave of the hand and we were looking underground. Segmented worms, driven by women with helmets. ''Rock-drill, going on now in the place they called Chile.'' Then, at a final motion, we were looking at myriad peoples all involved in labor, grinding grain, or toiling with instruments gleaming and baffling and complex. ''There,'' said Kid Death, ''there are the deeds and doings of all the men and women and androgynes on this world to remember the wisdom of the old ones. I can hand you the wealth produced by the hands of them all.'' (Green-eye's green eye widened.) ''I can guarantee it. You know I can. All you have to do is join me.''

The white hand had landed on Green-eye's shoulder. Again he shrugged from under it.

''What power do you have?'' Kid Death demanded. ''What can you do with your difference! Speak to a few deaf men, dead men, pierce the minds of a few idiots?'' I suddenly realized the Kid was very upset. And he wanted Green-eye to agree with him.

Green-eye started to walk away.

''Hey, Green-eye!'' Kid Death bellowed. I saw his stomach sink as the air emptied from his chest. His claws knotted.

Green-eye glanced back.

''That rock!'' The Kid motioned towards a chunk at the cliff's edge. ''Turn that there rock into something to eat.''

Green-eye rubbed his dirty finger behind his ear.

''You've been on this dragon drive now twenty-seven days. You've been away from Branning-at-sea a few days short of a year. Turn that log into a bed, like you used to sleep in at your mother's place. You're a Prince at Branning-at-sea and you smell like lizard droppings. That puddle, make it an onyx bath with water any one of five temperatures controlled by a lever with a copper rat's head on the tip. You've got callouses on your palms and your legs are bowing from straddling a dragon's hump. Where are the dancers who danced for you on the jade tiles of the terrace? Where are the musicians who eased the evenings? Turn this mountain-top into a place worthy of you—''

I think this is when Green-eye looked up and saw me. He started for me, only stopped to pick up my machete that was lying at the foot of the rock, then vaulted up beside me.

On the cliff edge the Kid had gotten furious. He quivered, teeth meshed tight, fists balled against his groin. Suddenly, he whirled and cried something—

Thunder.

It shocked me and I jerked back. Green-eye ignored it and tried to help me sit up. At the cliff's edge, Kid Death shook his arms. Lightning flared down the clouds. The leaves bleached from black to lavender. Green-eye didn't even blink. Thunder again; then someone flung buckets of water.

Herder dirt turned to mud on Green-eye's shoulder as he helped me down the slope. Something wasn't right inside me. Things kept going out inside me. The rain was cold. I was shivering. Somehow it was easier just to relax, not to hold on . . .

Green-eye was shaking my shoulder. I opened my eyes to the rain and the first thing I did was reach out for my blade. Green-eye held it out of reach; he was glaring at me.

"Huh . . . ? Wha . . ." My fingers and toes tingled. "What happened?" Rain stung my ears, my lips.

Green-eye was crying, his lips snarling back from his white teeth. Rain streaked the dirt on his face, sleeked down his hair; he kept shaking my shoulder, desolate and furious.

"What happened?" I asked. "Did I pass out . . . ?"

You died! He stared at me, unbelievingly, angry, and streaming. *God damn it, Lobey! Why did you have to die! You just gave up; you just decided it wasn't worth it, and you let the heart stop and the brain blank! You died, Lobey! You died!*

"But I'm not dead now. . . ."

No. He helped me forward. *The music's going on again. Come on.*

Once more I reached for my blade. He let me have it. There was nothing to hack at. I just felt better holding it. It was raining too hard to play.

We found our mounts moaning in the torrent and flinging their whiskers around happily. Green-eye helped me up. Astride a wet dragon, saddle or no, is as difficult as riding a greasy earthquake. We finally found the herd up ahead, moving slowly through the downpour.

Spider rode up to us. "There you are! I thought we'd lost you! Get over to the other side and keep them out of the prickly pears. Makes them drunk and you can't handle them."

So we rode over to the other side and kept them out of the prickly pears. I kept phrasing sentences in my head to tell Spider about what happened. I chewed over the words, but I couldn't gnaw them into sense. Once, when the pressure of disbelief grew so large I couldn't hold it, I reined my dragon around and dashed across the muddy slope towards Spider. "Boss, Kid Death is riding with—"

I'd make a mistake. The figure who turned wasn't Spider. Red hair slicked the white brow. Needle teeth snagged the thunder that erupted from behind the mountains as he threw back his head in doomed laughter. Naked on his dragon, he waved a black and silver hat over his head. Two ancient guns hung holstered at his hips, with milky handles glimmering. As his dragon reared (and mine danced back) I saw, strapped to his bare, clawed feet, a set of metal cages with revolving barbs that he heeled into his beast's flank, cruelly as a flower.

Dazed, I punched rain from my eyes. But the illusion (with veined temples gleaming with rain) was gone. Gagging on wonder, I rode back to the rim of the herd.

> *Jean Harlow? Christ, Orpheus, Billy the Kid, those*
> *three I can understand. But what's a young spade*
> *writer like you doing all caught up with the Great*
> *White Bitch?!*
> 　*Of course I guess it's pretty obvious.*
> 　　　　　　　　　Gregory Corso/*In conversation*

> *It is not that love sometimes makes mistakes, but that*
> *it is, essentially, a mistake. We fall in love when our*
> *imagination projects nonexistent perfections on to*
> *another person. One day the phantasmagoria vanish-*
> *es, and with it love dies.*
> 　　　　　　　　　Ortega y Gasset/*On Love*

Exhaustion numbed me; routine kaged me. It had stopped
raining almost an hour before I realized it. And the land
had changed.

We had left the rocks. Wet shrubs and briars fell before
the dragons' claws. To our left, a strip of gray ground ran
along with us, just down a small slope. Once I asked
Stinky, "Are we following that funny strip of stone down
there?"

He chuckled and sputtered, "Hey, Lobey, that's the
first paved road I bet you ever seen. Right?"

"I guess so," I said. "What's *paved?*"

Knife, who was riding by, snickered. Stinky went off to

do something else. That was the last I heard of it. Three or four carts trundled by on the road before it struck me what the damn thing was used for. Very clever. When the next one came by, I remembered to stare. It was late afternoon. I was so tired all the world's wonders might have bounced on the balls of my eyes without leaving a picture.

Most of the carts were pulled by four or six legged animals that I was vaguely familiar with. But new animals are not strange sights when your own flock might lamb any monster. One cart made me start, though.

It was low, of black metal, and had no beast at all before or behind. It purred along the road ten times the speed of the others and was gone in smoke before I had time to really see it. A few dragons who had ignored the other vehicles shied now and hissed. Spider called to me as I stared after it, "Just one of the wonders of Branning-at-sea."

I turned back to calm the offended lizards.

The next time I glanced at the road I saw the picture. It was painted on a large stand mounted by the pavement, so that all who passed could see. It was the face of a young woman with cotton white hair, a childish smile, her shoulders shrugged. She had a small chin, and green eyes that looked widened by some pleasant surprise. Her lips were slightly opened over small, shadowed teeth.

THE DOVE SAYS, "ONE IS *nice?* NINE OR TEN ARE SO MUCH *nicer!*"

I spelled out the caption and frowned. Batt was within hollering distance so I hollered. "Hey, who's that?"

"The *Dove!*" he howled, shaking the hair back from his shoulders. "He wants to know who the Dove is!" and the rest of them laughed too. As we got closer and closer to Branning-at-sea I became the butt of more and more jokes. I stuck closer to Green-eye; he didn't make fun of me. The first evening wind blew on the small of my back, the back of my neck and dried the sweat before more sweat rolled. I was staring dutifully at dragon scales when Green-eye stopped and pointed ahead. I looked up. Or rather down.

We had just crested a hill, and the land sloped clear and away to—well, if it were twenty meters away it was a great toy. If it were twenty kilometers away it was just great. Paved roads joined in that white and aluminum confusion at the purple water. Someone had started building it, and it had gotten out of hand and started building itself. There were grand squares where cactuses and palms grew and swayed; occasional hills where trees and lawns ranged about single buildings; many sections of tiny houses shoved and jammed on twisting streets. Beyond, from glazed docks ships plied the watery evening through its harbors.

"Branning-at-sea," Spider said, beside me. "That's it."

I blinked. The sun laid our shadows forward, warmed our necks, and blazed in the high windows. "It's large," I said.

"Right down there"—Spider pointed; I couldn't follow because there was so much to look at, so I listened—"is where we take the herd. This whole side of Branning lives off the herding business. The seaside survives through fishing and trade with the islands."

The others gathered around us. Familiar with the magnificence and squalor below, they grew silent as we went down.

We passed another signboard by the road. This time the Dove was shown from another angle, winking through the twilight.

THE DOVE SAYS, "THOUGH TEN ARE NICE, NINETY-NINE OR A HUNDRED ARE *so* MUCH NICER!"

As I looked, lights came on above the twenty-foot-high face. The huge, insouciant expression leaped at us. I must have looked surprised because Spider thumbed towards it and said, "They keep it lighted all night so passersby can read what the Dove has to say." He smiled as though he were telling me something slightly off-color. Now he coiled his whip. "We'll camp down on the plateau there for the evening and go into Branning at dawn." Twenty minutes later we were circling the herd while Batt fixed dinner. The sky was black beyond the ocean, blue overhead. Branning cast up lights of its own, sparkling like sequins fallen on the shore. Perhaps it was the less violent terrain, perhaps it was Spider's calm, but the dragons were perfectly still.

Afterward, I lay down, but didn't sleep. Along with Knife I had mid-watch. When Green-eye shook my shoulder with his foot, I rolled to standing; anticipatory excitement kept me awake. I would leave the herders; where would I go next?

Knife and I circled the herd in opposite directions. As I rode I reflected: to be turned loose by my lonesome in the woods is a fairly comfortable situation. Turned loose among stone, glass, and a few million people is something else. Four-fifths of the herd slept. A few moaned towards Branning, less bright than before, still a sieve of light on the sea. I reined my mount to gaze at the—

"Hey up there, Dragonman!"

I looked down the bank.

A hunchback had stopped his dog cart on the road.

"Hi down there."

"Taking your lizards into Branning at dawn?" He grinned, then dug beneath the leather flap over the cart and pulled out a melon. "You hungry, herder?" He broke it open and made to hurl me half.

But I slung down from my mount and he held. I scrambled to the road. "Hey, thank you Lo stranger."

He laughed. "No Lo for me."

Just then the dog, looking back and forth between the man and me, began to whine. "Me. Me. Me hungry. Me."

The hunchback handed me my half, then ruffled the dog's ears. "You had your dinner."

"I'll share mine," I said.

The hunchback shook his head. "He works for me and I feed him."

He broke apart his piece and tossed the piece to the animal, who drove his snout into it, champing. As I bit into my melon, the stranger asked me, "Where are you from, Dragonman?"

I gave him the name of my village.

"And this is your first time to Branning-at-sea?"

"It is. How could you tell?"

"Oh." He grinned over a crowd of yellow teeth. "I came to Branning-at-sea a first time myself. There are a few things that set you off from the natives down there, a couple of points that make you different—"

"Different?"

He raised his hand. "No offense meant."

"None taken."

The hunchback chuckled once more as I took a sweet wet mouthful.

"What's diamond here is dung there," he pronounced sagely. "No doubt the Dove said that at one time or another."

"The Dove," I said. "She's La Dove, isn't she?"

He looked surprised. "The Lo, La, and Le is confusing here. No." He scraped the rind with his front teeth and spun it away. "Diamond and dung. I gather it worked in your town like it did in mine. Lo and La and Le titles reserved for potent normals and eventually bestowed on potent functionals?"

"That's the way it is."

"Was. It was that way in Branning-at-sea. It's not the way it is now. So little is known about difference in the villages that nobody gets angry at being called such."

"But I am different," I said. "Why should I be angry? That's the way it is."

"Again, that's the way it was in Branning. Not the way it is now. A third time: diamond and dung. I just hope your backwoods ways don't get you into trouble. Mine got me half a dozen thrashings when I first got to Branning-at-sea, fifteen years ago. And even then the place was much smaller than it is now." He looked down the road.

I recalled what Spider had said about titling herders. "How does it work now?" I asked. "I mean here? At Branning-at-sea?"

"Well"—the hunchback hooked his thumbs under his belt—"there are about five families that control everything that goes on in Branning-at-sea, own all the ships, take in rent on half the houses, will probably pay your salary and buy up those dragons. They, along with fifteen or twenty celebrities, like the Dove, take Lo or La when you address them in person. And you'll find some pretty non-functional people with those titles."

"Well, how am I to know them then, if their obvious functionality doesn't matter?"

"You'll know them if you run into them—but it's not very likely you will. You can spend a lifetime at Branning-at-sea and never have to Lo or La once. But if you go about titling everyone you meet, or bridling when someone doesn't use a title to you, you'll be taken for a fool, or crazy, or at best recognized as a village lout."

"I'm not ashamed of my village!"

He shrugged. "I didn't suggest you were. Only trying to answer your questions."

"Yes. I understand. But what about difference?"

The hunchback put his tongue in his cheek, then took it out. "At Branning-at-sea difference is a private matter. Difference is the foundation of those buildings, the pilings beneath the docks, tangled in the roots of the trees. Half the place was built on it. The other half couldn't live without it. But to talk about it in public reveals you to be ill-mannered and vulgar."

"They talk about it." I pointed back to the herd. "I mean the other dragon drivers."

"And they are vulgar. Now if you hang with herders all the time—and you can spend your life that way if you want—you can talk about it all you want."

"But I am different—" I began again.

Having told me once, his patience with me and the subject ended.

"—but I guess I better keep it to myself," I finished.

"Not a bad idea." He spoke sternly.

But how could I tell him about Friza? How could I search if our differences were secret? "You," I said after embarrassed silence. "What do you do at Branning-at-sea?"

The question pleased him. "Oh, I run a little meeting place where the tired can sit, the hungry can eat, the thirsty can drink, and the bored can find entertainment." He ended his pronouncement by flinging his red cape back over his misshapen shoulder.

"I'll come and visit you," I said.

"Well," mused the hunchback, "not many herders come to my place; it's a bit refined. But after you've been in Branning-at-sea for a while and you think you can behave yourself, come around with some silver in your wallet.

Though I'll take most of it away from you, you'll have a good time."

"I'll be sure to come," I said. I was thinking of Kid Death. I was journeying down the long night. I was searching out Friza. "What's your name and where can I find you?"

"My name is Pistol, but you can forget that. You'll find me at *The Pearl*—the name of my place of business."

"It sounds fascinating."

"The most fascinating thing the likes of you have ever seen," he said modestly.

"Can't pass that up. What are you doing out on the paved road this late?"

"Same as yourself; going to Branning-at-sea."

"Where are you going from?"

"My outland friend, your manners are incredible. Since you ask, I come from friends who live outside Branning. I brought them gifts; they gave me gifts in return. But since they are not friends of yours, you shouldn't inquire after them."

"I'm sorry." I felt slightly rankled at this formality I didn't understand.

"You don't understand all this, do you?" He softened a little. "But when you've worn shoes a while and kept your navel covered, it will make more sense. I tell you all this now, but a year in Branning-at-sea will jack up my jabber with meaning."

"I don't intend to stay a year."

"You may not. Then, you may stay the rest of your life. It's that sort of place. It holds many wonders and the wonders may hold you."

"I'm passing," I insisted. "The death of Kid Death is at the end of my trip."

He got the oddest look. "I tell you, woodsboy," he

admonished, "forget rough herders' talk. Don't swear by
nightmares to your betters."

"I'm not swearing. The redheaded pest rides with this
herd to plague Green-eye and me."

Hunched Pistol decided that the oaf (who was me) was
beyond tutoring. He laughed and clapped my shoulder.
That vulgar streak in him that had first prompted him to
open conversation came out again. "Then good luck to
you, Lo Dirty-face and may the different devil die soon
and by your hand."

"By my knife," I corrected, drawing my machete for
him to see. "Think of a song."

"What?"

"Think of some song. What music do they play at your
pearl?"

He frowned, and I played.

His eyes widened, then he laughed. He leaned against
his wagon, slapped his stomach. The thing inside me that
laughs or cries laughed with him a while. I played. But
when his humor was past my understanding, I sheathed my
machete.

"Dragon driver," he explained through his laughter, "I
have only two choices, to mock your ignorance, or assume
that you mock me."

"As you said to me, no offense meant. But I wish you'd
explain the joke."

"I have, several times. You persist." He examined my
puzzlement. "Keep your differences to *yourself*. They are
your affair, nobody else's."

"But it's only music."

"Friend, what would you think of a man you just met
who, three minutes into the conversation, announced the
depth of his navel?"

"I don't see the point."

He beat his forehead with his fingers. "I must remember my own origins. Once I was as ignorant as you; I swear, though, I can't remember when." He pendulumed between humor and exasperation faster than I followed.

"Look," I said. "I don't see the pattern in your formality. What I do see I don't like—"

"It's not for you to judge," Pistol said. "You can accept it, or you can go away. But you can't go around disregarding other people's customs, joking with the profane, and flaunting the damned."

"Will you *please* tell me what customs I've disregarded, what I've flaunted? I've just said what was on my mind."

His country face hardened again (hard country faces I was to become used to in Branning). "You talk about Lo Green-eye as if he rode by you among the lizards and you hail Kid Death as though you yourself have looked down his six-gun."

"And where"—I was angry—"do you think Green-eye is? He's sleeping by the coals up there." I pointed up the rise. "And Kid Death—"

Fire surprised us and we whirled. Behind us in flame, he stood up and smiled. As he pushed back the brim of his hat with the barrel of his gun, red hair fell. "Howdy, pardners," he snickered. Shadow from grass and rock jogged on the ground. Where flame slapped his wet skin, steam curled away.

"Ahhhhhh-ahhhh—*ahhhh*-eeeee!" That was Pistol. He fell against his cart, his jaw flopped down. He closed it to swallow, but it fell open again. The dog growled. I stared.

The fire flared, flickered, dimmed. Then only the smell of leaves. My eyes pulsed with the afterimage and rage. I looked around me. Pulsing darkness moved with my eyes. Behind it, on the rise by the road, the light from the road lamp brushing his knees, was Green-eye. He rubbed the tiredness out of his face with his fist. Kid Death had gone to wherever he goes.

The cart started behind me.

Pistol was still trying to get seated and at the same time guide the dog. I thought he was going to fall. He didn't. They trundled away. I climbed up to Green-eye's side. He looked at me . . . sadly?

In the light up from the road, his sharp cheekbones were only slightly softened by wisps of adolescent beard. His shadowed socket was huge.

We went back to the fire. I lay down. Sleep pawed my eyes down and the balls beneath my lids exploded till dawn with amazing dreams of Friza.

The Dove has torn her wing so no more songs of love.
We are not here to sing: we're here to kill the Dove.

Jacques Brel/*La Colombe*

It is in the lightning and the thunder of the elements
that warm him so that he takes time to pause and to
reflect. There is a dragon there. They do not hear,
nor he. The elements have rendered voice inaudible.
There is a dragon there.

Hunce Voelker/*The Hart Crane Voyages*

I
think of people sighing over poetry, using it,
I
    don't know what it's for . . .
"Oh, I'll give your bores back!"

Joanne Kyger/*The Pigs for Circe in May*

She is with me evenings.

My ear is a funnel for all voice and trill and warble you can conceive this day.

She is with me mornings.

310

Came back to the house early. They have brought wine for New Year. There were musicians down in the white city. I remember a year and a half ago when I finished The Fall of The Towers, *saying to myself, you are twenty-one years old, going on twenty-two: you are too old to get by as a child prodigy: your accomplishments are more important than the age at which they were done; still, the images of youth plague me, Chatterton, Greenburg, Radiguet. By the end of FFD I hope to have excised them. Billy the Kid is the last to go. He staggers through this abstracted novel like one of the mad children in Crete's hills. Lobey will hunt you down, Billy. Tomorrow, weather permitting, I will return to Delos to explore the ruins around the Throne of Death in the center of the island that faces the necropolis across the water on Rhenia.*

Writer's Journal/Mykonos, December 1965

Throughout most of the history of man the importance of ritual has been clearly recognized, for it is through the ritual acts that man establishes his identity with the restorative powers of nature or makes and helps effect his passage into higher stages of personal development and experience.

Masters & Houston/*The Varieties of Psychedelic Experience*

The lights of Branning were yellow behind mist and brambles as night made blue, wounded retreat through the chill. Sun streaked the east while there were still stars in the west. Batt blew up the fire. Three dragons had strolled down to the pavement, so I rode down and ran them back. We ate with grunts and silences.

This close to the sea morning was damp. Beyond Branning, boats floated like papers towards the islands. To My Mount then, and the jerky, gentle trail down. Hisses left and right as we prodded them, but soon they were stomping and pawing in easy convergence.

Spider saw them first. "Up ahead. Who are they?"

People were running along the road; behind them, people walked. The road lights, tuned to an earlier month and longer night, went out.

Loosely curious, I rode to the head of the herd. "They're singing," I called back.

Spider looked uncomfortable. "You can hear the music?"

I nodded.

His head was still; the rest of his body swayed under his face. He switched his whip handle from hand to hand to hand; it was a quiet, beautiful way to be nervous, I thought. I played the melody for him because the sound hadn't reached us yet.

"They're singing together?"

"Yes," I told him. "They're chanting."

"Green-eye," Spider called. "Stay by me."

I put down my blade. "Is there anything wrong?"

"Maybe," Spider said. "That's the family anthem of Green-eye's line. They know he's here."

I looked questioningly.

"We wanted to get him back to Branning quietly." He flapped his dragon on the gills. "I just wonder how they found out he was coming in this morning."

I looked at Green-eye. Green-eye didn't look at me. He was watching the people along the road. I couldn't think of anything else to do, so I started to play. I didn't want to tell Spider about the man in the dog cart last night.

The voices reached us.

At which point I decided I better tell him anyway. He didn't say anything.

Suddenly Green-eye urged his dragon ahead. Spider tried to restrain him. But he slipped beneath one hand after the other. Worry perched on his amber eyebrows. Green-eye's mount stomped ahead.

"You don't think he should go to them?" I asked.

"He knows what he's doing." The people were thick on the road. "I hope."

I watched them come, remembering Pistol. His terror must have spread over nighttime Branning like harbor oil. Dragons herded down the road; people herded up.

"What will happen?"

"They'll praise him," Spider said, "now. Later, who knows?"

"To me," I said. "I mean what's going to happen to me."

He was surprised.

"I've got to find Friza. Nothing changes. I've got to destroy the Kid. It's still the same."

I recalled the look on Pistol's face when he'd fled the Kid. Spider's face—I was shocked at the recognition—twisted under the same fear. But there was so much more in the face: strength rode the same muscles as terror. Yes, Spider was a large man.

"I don't care about Green-eye, or anyone else." My words were carapaced with belligerence. "I'm going down to get Friza; and I'm going to come up with her again."

"You—" he began. Then his width accepted me. "I

wish you good luck." He looked again after Green-eyes, swaying ahead of us towards the crowds. So much of him rode ahead with the boy. I didn't realize how much of him lingered with me. "You've done your job, then, Lobey. When we turn the herd in, you'll be paid—" He stopped. Some other thought. "Come to my house for your pay."

"Your house?"

"Yes. My home in Branning-at-sea." He coiled his whip and kneed his dragon.

We passed another signboard. The white-haired woman with the cool lips and warm eyes looked moodily at me as I rode by.

THE DOVE SAYS, "WHY HAVE NINETY-NINE WHEN NINE THOUSAND ARE THERE?"

I turned away from her mocking and wondered how many people swarmed up through the morning. They lined the road. As they recognized the young herder, their song crumbled into cheering. We entered the crowd.

A jungle is a myriad of individual trees, vines, bushes; passing through, you see it, however, as one green mass. Perceiving a crowd works the same way: first the single face here (the old woman twisting her green shawl), there (the blinking boy smiling over a missing tooth) and following (three gaping girls protecting one another with their shoulders). Then the swarms of elbows and ears, tongues scraping words from the floor of the mouth and flinging them out "—move!" "Ouch! Get your—" "—I can't see—" "Where is he? Is that him—" "No!" "Yes—" while the backs of the dragons undulated through the clumps of heads. They cheered. They waved their fists in the air before the gate. My job is over, I thought. People jostled My Mount. "Is that him? Is that—" The dragons were unhappy. Only Spider's calming kept them peacefully heading forward. We crowded through the gate at Branning-at-sea. At which point a lot of things happened.

I don't understand all of them. In the first few hours a lot were things that would happen to anybody who had never seen more than fifty people together at once thrust into alleys, avenues and squares that trafficked thousands. The dragon herd left me (or I left it) to stumble about with my mouth open and my head up. People kept bumping into me and telling me to "Watch it!" which is exactly what I was trying to do; only I was trying to watch it all at the same time. Which would be difficult even if it kept still. While I watched one part, another would sneak up behind me and nearly run me down. Here's fragmenting for you:

The million's music melded to a hymn like when your ears ring and you're trying to sleep. In a village you see a face and you know it—its mother, its father, its work, how it curses, laughs, lingers on one expression, avoids another. Here one face yawns, another bulges with food; one scarred, one longing with what could be love, one screaming: each among a thousand, none seen more than once. You start to arrange the furniture in your head to find a place for these faces, someplace to dump all these quarter emotions. When you go through the gate at Branning-at-sea and leave the country, you retreat to the country for your vocabulary to describe it: rivers of men and torrents of women, storms of voices, rains of fingers and jungles of arms. But it's not fair to Branning. It's not fair to the country either.

I stalked the streets of Branning-at-sea dangling my unplayable knife, gawking at the five-story buildings till I saw the buildings with twenty-five stories. Gawked at them till I saw a building with so many stories I couldn't count, because halfway up (around ninety) I kept losing myself while people jostled me.

There were a few beautiful streets where trees rubbed their leaves over the walls. There were many filthy ones where garbage banked the sidewalk, where the houses were boxes pushed together, without room for movement of air or people. The people stayed, the air stayed; both grew foul.

On the walls were flayed posters of the Dove. Here there were others also. I passed some kids elbowing each other around one such poster that wrinkled over a fence. I squeezed among them to see what they looked at.

Two women gazed idiotically from swirling colors. The caption: "THESE TWO IDENTICAL TWINS ARE NOT THE SAME."

The youngsters giggled and shoved another. Obviously I missed something about the sign. I turned to one boy. "I don't get it."

"Huh?" He had freckles and a prosthetic arm. He scratched his head with plastic fingers. "What do you mean?"

"What's so funny about that picture?"

First disbelief: then he grinned. "If they're not the same," he blurted, *"they're different!"* They all laughed. Their laughter was filigreed with the snicker that let you know when laughter's rotten.

I pushed away from them. I searched for music; heard none. After the listening stops, after the searching—when these sidewalks and multitudes will not bear your questions any more: that's what lonely is, Friza. Clutching my knife, I made my headlong way through evening, isolated as if I had been lost in a City.

The shingled tones of the Kodaly cello sonata! I swung around on my heels. The flags were clean and unbroken.

There were trees on the corner. The buildings slanted high behind brass gates. The music unraveled in my head. Blinking, I looked from gate to gate. I chose. Faltering, I walked up the short marble steps and struck my machete hilt on the bars.

The clang leaped down the street. The sound scared me but I struck again.

Behind the gate the brass studded door swung in. Then there was a click in the lock and the gate itself rattled loose. Cautiously, I started the walk that led to the open door. I squinted in the shadow at the doorway, then went inside, blind from the sun and alone with the music.

My eyes accustomed to the dimmer light: far ahead was a window. High in dark stone, a dragon twisted through lead tesselations.

"Lobey?"

But I have this *against thee, that thou didst leave thy first love.*

            The Revelation of John/Chapter 2, verse 4

My trouble is, such a subject cannot be seriously looked at without intensifying itself towards a center which is beyond what I, or anyone else, is capable of writing of . . . Trying to write it in terms of moral problems alone is more than I can possibly do. My main hope is to state the central subject and my ignorance from the start.

            James Agee/*Letter to Father Flye*

Where is this country? How does one get there? If one is born lover with an innate philosophic bent, one will get there.

            Plotinus/*The Intelligence, the Idea, and Being*

Spider looked up from the desk where he'd been reading. "I thought that would be you."

In shadow behind him I saw the books. La Dire had owned some hundred. But the shelves behind him went from floor to ceiling.

"I want . . . my money." My eyes came back to the desk.

"Sit down," Spider said. "I want to talk to you."

"About what?" I asked. Our voices echoed. The music was nearly silent. "I have to be on my way to get Friza, to find Kid Death."

Spider nodded. "That's why I suggest you sit down." He pressed a button, and dust motes in the air defined a long cone of light that dropped to an onyx stool. I sat slowly, holding my blade. As he had once shifted the handle of his dragon whip from hand to hand, now he played with the bleached, fragile skull of some rodent. "What do you know about mythology, Lobey?"

"Only the stories that La Dire, one of the elders of my village, used to tell me. She told all the young people stories, some of them many times. And we told them to each other till they sank into memory. But then there were other children for her to tell."

"Again, what do you know about mythology?—I'm not asking you what myths you know, nor even where they came from, but why we have them, what we use them for."

"I . . . don't know," I said. "When I left my village, La Dire told me the myth of Orpheus."

Spider held up the skull and leaned forward. "Why?"

"I don't . . ." Then I thought. "To guide me?"

I could offer nothing else. Spider asked, "Was La Dire different?"

"She was—" The prurience that had riddled the laughter of the young people gaping at the poster came back to me; I did not understand it, still I felt the rims of my ears grow hot. I remembered the way Easy, Little Jon, and Lo Hawk had tried to brake my brooding over Friza; and how La Dire had tried, her attempt like theirs—yet different. "Yes," I confessed, "she was."

Spider nodded and rapped his rough knuckles on the desk. "Do you understand difference, Lobey?"

"I live in a different world, where many have it and many do not. I just discovered it in myself weeks ago. I know the world moves towards it with every pulse of the great rock and the great roll. But I don't understand it."

Through the eagerness on his drawn face Spider smiled. "In that you're like the rest of us. All any of us knows is what it is not."

"What isn't it?" I asked.

"It isn't telepathy; it's not telekinesis—though both are chance phenomena that increase as difference increases. Lobey, Earth, the world, fifth planet from the sun—the species that stands on two legs and roams this thin wet crust: it's changing, Lobey. It's not the same. Some people walk under the sun and accept that change, others close their eyes, clap their hands to their ears, and deny the world with their tongues. Most snicker, giggle, jeer and point when they think no one else is looking—that's how the humans acted throughout their history. We have taken over their abandoned world, and something new is happening to the fragments, something we can't even define with mankind's leftover vocabulary. You must take its importance exactly as that: it is indefinable; you are involved in it; it is wonderful, fearful, deep, ineffable to your explanations, opaque to your efforts to see through it; yet it demands you take journeys, defines your stopping and starting points, can propel you with love and hate, even to seek death for Kid Death—"

"—or make me make music," I finished for him. "What are you talking about, Spider?"

"If I could tell you, or you could understand from my inferences, Lobey, it would lose all value. Wars and chaoses and paradoxes ago, two mathematicians between them ended an age and began another for our hosts, our ghosts called Man. One was Einstein, who with his Theory of Relativity defined the limits of man's perception by expressing mathematically just how far the condition of the observer influences the thing he perceives."

"I'm familiar with it," I said.

"The other was Gödel, a contemporary of Einstein, who was the first to bring back a mathematically precise statement about the vaster realm beyond the limits Einstein had defined: *In any closed mathematical system*—you may read 'the real world with its immutable laws of logic'—*there are an infinite number of true theorems*—you may read 'perceivable, measurable phenomena'—*which, though contained in the original system, can not be deduced from it*—read 'proven with ordinary or extraordinary logic.' Which is to say, there are more things in heaven and Earth than are dreamed of in your philosophy, Lo Lobey-o. There are an infinite number of true things in the world with no way of ascertaining their truth. Einstein defined the extent of the rational. Gödel stuck a pin into the irrational and fixed it to the wall of the universe so that it held still long enough for people to know it was there. And the world and humanity began to change. And from the other side of the universe, we were drawn slowly here. The visible effects of Einstein's theory leaped up on a convex curve, its productions huge in the first century after its discovery, then leveling off. The productions of Gödel's law crept up on a concave curve, microscopic at first, then leaping to equal the Einsteinian curve, cross it, outstrip it. At the point of intersection, humanity was able to reach the limits of the known universe with ships and projection forces that are still available to anyone who wants to use them—"

"Lo Hawk," I said. "Lo Hawk went on a journey to the other worlds—"

"—and when the line of Gödel's law eagled over Einstein's, its shadow fell on a deserted Earth. The humans had gone somewhere else, to no world in this continuum. We came, took their bodies, their souls—both husks abandoned here for any wanderer's taking. The cities, once bustling centers of interstellar commerce, were crumbled to the sands you see today. And they were once greater than Branning-at-sea.''

I thought a moment. "That must have taken a long time," I said slowly.

"It has," Spider said. "The City we crossed is perhaps thirty thousand years old. The sun has captured two more planets since the Old People began here."

"And the source-cave?" I suddenly asked. "What was the source-cave?"

"Didn't you ever ask your elders?"

"Never thought to," I said.

"It's a net of caves that wanders beneath most of the planet, and the lower levels contain the source of the radiation by which the villages, when their populations become too stagnant, can set up a controlled random jumbling of genes and chromosomes. Though we have not used that for almost a thousand years. Though the radiation is still there. As we, templated on man, become more complicated creatures, the harder it is for us to remain perfect: there is more variation among the normals and the kages fill with rejects. And here you are, now, Lobey."

"What does this all have to do with mythology?" I was weary of his monologue.

"Recall my first question."

"What do I know of mythology?"

"And I want a Gödelian, not an Einsteinian answer. I don't want to know what's inside the myths, nor how they clang and set one another ringing, their glittering focuses, their limits and genesis. I want their shape, their texture, how they feel when you brush by them on a dark road, when you see them receding into the fog, their weight as they leap your shoulder from behind; I want to know how you take to the idea of carrying three when you already bear two. Who are you, Lobey?"

"I'm . . . Lobey?" I asked. "La Dire once called me Ringo and Orpheus."

Spider's chin rose. His fingers, caging the bone face, came together: "Yes, I thought so. Do you know who I am?"

"No."

"I'm Green-eye's Iscariot. I'm Kid Death's Pat Garrett. I'm Judge Minos at the gate, whom you must charm with your music before you can even go on to petition the Kid. I'm every traitor you've ever imagined. And I'm a baron of dragons, trying to support two wives and ten children."

"You're a big man, Spider."

He nodded. "What do you know of mythology?"

"Now that's the third time you've asked me." I picked up my blade. From the grinding love that wanted to serenade his silences—the music had all stopped—I leaned the blade against my teeth.

"Bite through the shells of my meanings, Lobey. I know so much more than you. The guilty have the relief of knowledge." He held the skull over the table. I thought he was offering it to me. "I know where you can find Friza. I can let you through the gate. Though Kid Death may kill me, I want you to know that. He is younger, crueler, and much stronger. Do you want to go on?"

I dropped my blade. "It's fixed!" I said. "I'll fail! La Dire said Orpheus failed. You're trying to tell me that these stories tell us just what is going to happen. You've been telling me we're so much older than we think we are;

this is all schematic for a reality I can't change! You're telling me right now that I've failed as soon as I start."

"Do you believe that?"

"That's what you've said."

"As we are able to retain more and more of our past, it takes us longer and longer to become old; Lobey, everything changes. The labyrinth today does not follow the same path it did at Knossos fifty thousand years ago. You may be Orpheus; you may be someone else, who dares death and succeeds. Green-eye may go to the tree this evening, hang there, rot, and never come down. The world is not the same. That's what I've been trying to tell you. It's different."

"But—"

"There's just as much suspense today as there was when the first singer woke from his song to discover the worth of the concomitant sacrifice. You don't know, Lobey. This all may be a false note, at best a passing dissonance in the harmonies of the great rock and the great roll."

I thought for a while. Then I said, "I want to run away."

Spider nodded. "Some mason set the double-headed labrys on the stones at Pheistos. You carry a two edge knife that sings. One wonders if Theseus built the maze as he wandered through it."

"I don't think so," I said, defensive and dry. "The stories give you a law to follow—"

"—that you can either break or obey."

"They set you a goal—"

"—and you can either fail that goal, succeed, or surpass it."

"Why?" I demanded. "Why can't you just ignore the old stories? I'll go on plumb the sea, find the Kid without your help. I can ignore those tales!"

"You're living in the real world now," Spider said sadly. "It's come from something. It's going to something. Myths always lie in the most difficult places to ignore. They confound all family love and hate. You shy at them on entering or exiting any endeavor." He put the skull on the table. "Do you know why the Kid needs you as much as he needs Green-eye?"

I shook my head.

"I do."

"The Kid needs me?"

"Why do you think you're here?"

"Is the reason . . . different?"

"Primarily. Sit back and listen." Spider himself leaned back in his chair. I stayed where I was. "The Kid can change anything in the range of his intelligence. He can make a rock into a tree, a mouse into a handful of moss. But he cannot create something from nothing. He cannot take this skull and leave a vacuum. Green-eye can. And that is why the Kid needs Green-eye."

I remembered the encounter on the mountain where the malicious redhead had tried to tempt the depthless vision of the herder-prince.

"The other thing he needs is music, Lobey."

"Music?"

"This is why he is chasing you—or making you chase him. He needs order. He needs patterning, relation, the knowledge that comes when six notes predict a seventh, when three notes beat against one another and define a mode, a melody defines a scale. Music is the pure language of temporal and co-temporal relation. He knows nothing of this, Lobey. Kid Death can control, but he cannot create, which is why he needs Green-eye. He can control, but he cannot order. And that is why he needs you."

"But how—?"

"Not in any way your village vocabulary or my urban refinement can state. Differently, Lobey. Things passing in a world of difference have their surrealistic corollaries in the present. Green-eye creates, but it is an oblique side effect of something else. You receive and conceive music; again only an oblique characteristic of who you are—"

"*Who* am I?"

"You're . . . something else."

My question had contained a demand. His answer held a chuckle.

"But he needs you both," Spider went on. "What are you going to give him?"

"My knife in his belly till blood floods the holes and leaks out the mouthpiece. I'll chase the sea-floor till we both fall on sand. I—" My mouth opened; I suddenly sucked in dark air so hard it hurt my chest. "I'm afraid," I whispered. "Spider, I'm afraid."

"Why?"

I looked at him behind the evenly blinking lids of his black eyes. "Because I didn't realize I'm alone in this." I slid my hands together on the hilt. "If I'm to get Friza, I have to go alone—not with her love, but without it. You're not on my side." I felt my voice roughen, not with fear. It was the sadness that starts in the back of the throat and makes you cough before you start crying. "If I reach Friza, I don't know what I'll have, even if I get her."

Spider waited for my crying. I wouldn't give him the satisfaction. So after a while he said, "Then I guess I can let you through, if you really know that."

I looked up.

He nodded to my silent question.

"There's someone you must go to see. Here." He stood

up. In his other hand was a small sack. He shook it. Inside coins clinked. He flung the sack towards me. I caught it.

"Who?"

"The Dove."

"The one whose pictures I've seen? But who—"

"Who is the Dove?" asked Spider. "The Dove is Helen of Troy, Star Anthim, Mario Montez, Jean Harlow." He waited.

"And you?" I asked. "You're Judas and Minos and Pat Garrett? Who are you to her?"

His snort was contemptuous and amused. "If the Dove is Jean Harlow I'm Paul Burn."

"But why—?"

"Come on, Lobey. Get going."

"I'm going," I said. "I'm going." I was confused. For much the same reasons you are. Though not *exactly* the same. As I walked to the door I kept glancing back at Spider. Suddenly he tossed the skull gently. It passed me, hovered a moment, then smashed on the stones; and Spider laughed. It was a friendly laugh, without the malicious flickering of fish scales and flies' wings that dazzled the laughter of the Kid. But it nearly scared me to death. I ran out of the door. For one step bone fragments chewed at my instep. The door slammed behind me. The sun slapped my face.

Leave Crete and come to this holy temple.

Sappho/*Fragment*

This morning I took refuge from the thin rain in a tea-house with the dock workers. Yellow clouds moiled outside above the Bosphorus. Found one man who spoke French, two others who spoke Greek. We talked of voyages and warmed our fingers on glasses of tea. Between the four of us we had girdled the globe. The radio over the stove alternated repetitive Turkish modulations with Aznavour and the Beatles. Lobey starts the last leg of his journey. I cannot follow him here. When the rain stopped, I walked through the waterfront fish market where the silver fish had their gills pulled out and looped over their jaws so that each head was crowned with a bloody flower. A street of wooden houses wound up the hill into the city. A fire had recently raged here. Few houses had actually burned down, but high slabs of glittering carbon leaned over the cobbles where the children played with an orange peel in the mud. I watched some others chase a redheaded boy. His face was wet; he tripped in the mud, then fled before me. The backs had been trod down on his shoes. Perhaps on rewriting I shall change Kid Death's hair from black to red. Followed the wall of Topkapi palace, kicking away

*wet leaves from the pavement. I stopped in the
Sultanahmet Jammi. The blue designs rose on the
dome above me. It was restful. In a week another
birthday, and I can start the meticulous process of over-
laying another filigree across the novel's palimpsest.
The stones were cold under my bare feet. The designs
keep going, taking your eyes up and out of yourself.
Outside I put on my boots and started across the
courtyard. In the second story of the old teahouse
across the park I sat in a corner away from the stove
and tried to wrestle my characters towards their endings. Soon I shall start again. Endings to be useful
must be inconclusive.*

                    Writer's Journal/Istanbul, March 1966

*What are your qualifications? Dare you dwell in the
East where we dwell? Are you afraid of the sun?
When you hear the new violet sucking her way among
the clods, shall you be resolute?*

                    Emily Dickinson/*Letter to K. S. Turner*

The Pearl surprised me. A million people is too many to
sort an individual from a slum. But the established classes
are all the more centralized. There in the furious evening I
saw the sign down the street. I looked in my purse. But
Spider would have given me enough.

Black doors broke under a crimson sunburst. I went up
the stairs beneath the orange lights. There was perfume.
There was noise. I held my sword tight. Tack-heads had
worn away the nap of the carpet with the tugging of how
many feet. Someone had painted a *trompe l'oeil* still life
on the left wall: fruit, feathers, and surveying instruments
on crumpled leather. Voices, yes. Still, at the place where

the auditory nerve connects to the brain and sound becomes music, there was silence.

"Lo?" inquired the dog at the head of the steps.

I was baffled. "Lo Lobey," I told his cold face, and grinned at it. It stayed cold.

And on the balcony across the crowded room where her party was, she stood up, leaned over the railing, called, "Who are you?" with contralto laughter spilling her words.

She was pretty. She wore silver, a sheath V'd deeply between small breasts. Her mouth seemed used to emotions, mostly laughter I guessed. Her hair was riotous and bright as Little Jon's. The person she was calling to was me. "Um-hm. You, silly. Who are you?"

It had slipped my mind that when somebody speaks to you, you answer. The dog coughed, then announced. "Eh . . . Lo Lobey is here." At which point everyone in the room silenced. With the silence I learned how noisy it had been. Glasses, whispers, laughter, talk, feet on the floor, chair legs squeaking after them: I wished it would start again. In a doorway on the side of the room where two serpents twined over the transom, I saw the fat, familiar figure of the hunchback Pistol. He was obviously coming from somewhere to see what was wrong; he saw me, closed his eyes, took a breath, and leaned on the door jamb.

Then the Dove said, "Well, it's about time, Lo Lobey. I thought you'd never get here. Pistol, bring a chair."

I was surprised. Pistol was astounded. But after he got his mouth closed, he got the chair. With drawn machete I stalked the Dove among the tables, the flowers, the candles and cut goblets; the men with gold chained dogs crouching at their sandals; the women with jeweled eyelids, their breasts propped in cages of brass mesh or silver wire. They all turned to watch me as I went.

I mounted the stairway to the Dove's balcony. One hip against the railing, she held out her hand to me. "You're Spider's friend," she beamed. She made you feel very good when she talked. "Pistol"—she twisted around; wrinkles of light slid over her dress—"put the seat by mine." He did and we sat on the brocade cushions.

With the Dove in front of me it was a little difficult to look at anyone else. She leaned towards me, breathing. I guess that's what she was doing. "We're supposed to talk. What do you want to talk about?"

Breathing is a fascinating thing to watch in a woman. "Eh . . . ah . . . well . . ." I pulled my attention forcefully back to her face. "Are nine thousand really that much better than ninety-nine?" (You think I knew what I was talking about?) She began to laugh without making any sound. Which is even more fascinating.

"Ah!" she responded, "you must try it and find out."

At which point everybody started talking again. The Dove still watched me. "What do you do?" I asked. "Spider says you're supposed to help me find Friza."

"I don't know who Friza is."

"She was—" The Dove was breathing again. "—beautiful too."

Her face passed down to deeper emotion. "Yes," she said.

"I don't think we can talk about it here." I glanced at Pistol, who was still hovering. "The problem isn't exactly the same as you might think."

She raised a darkened eyebrow.

"It's a bit . . ."

"Oh," she said, and her chin went up.

"But you?" I said. "What do you do? Who are you?"

Her eyebrow arch grew more acute. "Are you serious?"

I nodded.

In confusion she looked to the people around her. When no one offered to explain for her, she looked back at me. Her lips opened, touched; her lashes dipped and leaped. "They say I'm the thing that allows them all to go on loving."

"How?" I asked.

Someone beside her said, "He really doesn't know?"

From the other side: "Doesn't he know about keeping confusion in the trails fertile?"

She placed a finger perpendicular to her lips. They quieted at the sound of her sigh. "I'll have to tell him. Lobey—this is your . . . name."

"Spider told me to talk to you . . ." I offered. I wanted to fix myself by informative hooks to her world.

Her smile cut guys. "You try to make things too simple. Spider. The great Lord Lo Spider? The traitor, the false friend, the one who has already signed Green-eye's death decree. Don't concern yourself with that doomed man. Look to yourself, Lobey. What do you want to know—"

"Death decree—"

She touched my cheek. "Be selfish. What do you want?"

"Friza!" I half stood in my seat.

She sat back. "Now I'll ask you a question, having not answered yours. Who is Friza?"

"She answered yours. Who is Friza?"

"She . . ." Then I said, "She was almost as beautiful as you."

Her chin came down. Light, light eyes darkened and came down too. "Yes." That word came with the sound of only the breath I had been watching, without voice. So much questioning in her face now made her remembered expression caustic.

"I . . ." The wrong word. "She . . ." A fist started

to beat my ribs. Then it stopped, opened, reached up into my head, and scratched down the inside of my face: forehead and cheeks burned. My eyes stung.

She caught her breath. "I see."

"No you don't," I got out. "You don't."

They were watching again. She glanced right, left, bit her lip as she looked back. "You and I are . . . well, not quite the same."

"Huh? . . . oh. But—Dove—"

"Yes, Lobey?"

"Where am I? I've come from a village, from the wilds of nowhere, through dragons and flowers. I've thrown my Lo, searching out my dead girl, hunting a naked cowboy mean as Spider's whip. And somewhere a dirty, one-eyed prince is going to . . . die while I go on. Where am I, Dove?"

"This close to an old place called Hell." She spoke quickly. "You can enter it through death or song. But you may need some help to find your way out."

"I look for my dark girl and find you silver."

She stood, and blades of light struck at me from her dress. Her smooth hand swung by her hip. I grabbed it with my rough one. "Come," she said.

I came.

As we descended from the balcony she leaned on my arm. "We are going to walk once around the room. I suppose you have the choice either of listening, or watching. I doubt if you can do both. I couldn't, but try." As we started to circuit the room, I beat my shin with the flat of my sword.

"We are worn out with trying to be human, Lobey. To survive even a dozen more generations we must keep the genes mixing, mixing, mixing."

An old man leaned his belly on the edge of his table,

gaping at the girl across from him. She licked the corner of
her mouth, her eyes wondrous and blue and beautiful.
Her cheekbones mocked him.

"You can't force people to have children with many
people. But we can make the idea as attractive"—she
dropped her eyes—"as possible."

At the next table the woman's face was too loose for the
framing bone beneath. But she laughed. Her hand wrinkled over the smooth fingers of the young man across from
her. She gazed enviously from lined eyes at his quick lids,
dark as olives when he blinked, his hair shinier than hers,
wild where hers was coiffed in high lacquer.

"Who am I, Lobey?" she suggested—rather than asked—
rhetorically. "I'm the key image in an advertising cam-
paign. I'm the good/bad wild thing whom everybody wants,
wants to be like—who prefers ninety-nine instead of one.
I'm the one whom men search out from seeding to seeding. I'm the one whom all the women style their hair after,
raise and lower their hems and necklines as mine raise and
lower. The world steals my witticisms, my gestures, even
my mistakes, to try out on each new lover."

The couple at the next table had probably forgotten most
of what it was like to be forty. They looked happy,
wealthy and content. I was envious.

"There was a time," the Dove went on, pressing the
back of my hand with her forefinger, "when orgies and
artificial insemination did the trick. But we still have a
jelling attitude to melt. So, that's what I do. Which leaves
you, I gather, with another question."

The youngsters across from us clutched each other's
hands and giggled. Once I thought that twenty-one was the
responsible age; it had to be, it was so far away. Those
kids could do anything and were just learning how, and

were hurt and astounded and deliriously happy at once with the prospects.

"The answer"—and I looked back at the Dove—"lies with the particular talent I have that facilitates my job."

The finger that had pressed my hand now touched my lips. She pouted for silence. With her other hand she lifted my sword. "Play, Lobey?"

"For you?"

She swept her hand around the room. "For them." She turned to the people. "Everybody! I want you to be quiet. I want you to hear. You must be still—"

They stilled.

"—and listen."

They listened. Many leaned their elbows on the table. The Dove turned to me and nodded. I looked at my machete.

Across the room Pistol was holding his head. I smiled at him. Then I sat down on the edge of an empty table, toed the holes, fingered them.

I blew a note. I looked at the people. I blew another one. I laughed after that one.

The youngsters laughed too.

I blew two notes, down, then shrill.

I started to clap my hands, a hard, slow rhythm. I made the melody with feet alone. The kids thought that was pretty funny too. I rocked on the table edge, closed my eyes, and clapped and played. In the back somebody began to clap with me. I grinned into the flute (difficult) and the sound brightened. I remembered the music I'd got from Spider. So I tried something I'd never done before. I let one melody go on without my playing it, and played another instead. Tones tugged each other into harmony as they swooped from clap to clap. I let those two continue and threaded a third above them. I pushed the music into a body swayer, a food shaker, till fingers upon the tablecloth pounced on the pattern. I played, looking hard at them, weighing the weight of music in them, and when there was enough, I danced. Movements repeated themselves; making dances is the opposite of taking them. I danced on the table. Hard. I whipped them with music. Sound peeled from sound. Chords fell open like sated flowers. People called out. I shrilled my rhythms at them down the hollow knife, gouged notes down their spines the way you pith a frog. They shook in their seats. I put into the music a fourth line, dissonant to lots and lots of others. Three people had started dancing with me. I made the music make them. Rhythm buoyed their jerking. The old man was shaking his shoulders at the blue-eyed girl. Clap. The youngsters shook shoulder—Clap—to shoulder. The older couple held hands very tightly. Clap. Sound banked behind—Clap—itself. Silence a moment. Clap. Then loosed through the room; like dragons in the gorse, wild, they moaned together, beat their thighs and bellies to four melodies.

On the raised dais, where the Dove's table had been, somebody opened the wide windows. The wind on my sweaty back made me cough. The cough growled in the flute. A breeze in a closed room lets you know how hot it is. The dancers moved to the balcony. I followed them. The tiles were red and blue. The gold evening streamed with blue wounds. One or two dancers rested on the railing. My sword fell from my lips as I gazed around the—

It caught me across the eyes. The silver dress rippled in the wind. But it wasn't the Dove. She raised dark knuckles to her brown cheek, her full mouth parting in a sigh. She blinked, brushed her hand across her hair, searching through the dancers. One and another of them hid her a moment, stepped away.

Dark Friza—

Friza returned and turning among the dancers—

Beautiful and longed for Friza, found—

Once I was so hungry that when I ate I was frightened. The same fear now. Only more. The music played itself. The blade hung in my hand. Once Friza had thrown a pebble—

I began to run the maze of dancers.

She saw me. I caught her shoulders; she clutched me, cheek on my neck, breast on my breast, her arms hard across my back. Her name swam in my head. I know I hurt her. Her fists on my back hurt me. My eyes were wide and tearing. I wanted to be open to everything about her. Nothing shook in her. I held all her slim strength. My arms tightened, relaxed, tightened again.

Across the park below was a single tree, wintered by the insane sun. Roped from the crotch, one arm to each fork, head so far forward the neck had to be broken, dangled Green-eye. Blood from a rope cut glittered along his arm.

She twisted in my arms, looked at me, at what I was looking at; quickly she put her hands over my eyes. Alone in her dark hands, I recognized the music. Polyphonized and danced by strangers, it was the mourning song of the girl who shielded my eyes now, played for the garroted prince.

Under the music, a voice whispered, "Lobey, be careful." It was the Dove's voice. "Do you want to look that closely?"

The fingers stayed over my face.

"I can look down your head like a hall. You died, Lobey. Somewhere in the rocks and rain, you died. Do you want to look at that closely—"

"I'm no ghost!"

"Oh, you're real, Lobey! But perhaps—"

I twisted my head again, but darkness followed.

"Do you want to know about the Kid?"

"I want to know anything that'll help me kill him."

"Then listen. Kid Death can bring back to life only the ones he himself takes from it. He can only keep the belly buttons he harvests. But do you know who brought you back from—"

"Take your hands away."

"You've got a choice to make, Lobey, quick!" the Dove whispered. "Do you want to see what's in front of you? Or do you want to see only what you saw before?"

"Your hands. I can't see anything with your hands in front of my . . ." I stopped, horrified at what I had just said.

"I'm very talented, Lobey, in what I do." Light seeped in, as gently the pressure released. "I've had to perfect that talent to survive. You can't ignore the laws of the world you've chosen—"

I took the wrists and pulled the hands down. The Dove's hands resisted just a moment, then fell. Green-eye was still roped to the tree below me.

I grabbed the Dove's arms. "Where *is* she?" I looked about the terrace. I shook her and she pulled back against the rail.

"I become the thing you love, Lobey. That's part of my talent. That's how I can be the Dove."

I shook my head. "But you—"

She rubbed her shoulder. Her hand slid under the silver cloth. It shifted with her fingers.

"And they—" I gestured towards the dancers. The youngsters, still holding hands, were pointing into the park and giggling. "They call you La Dove."

She cocked her head, brushing back silver hair. "No, Lobey." She shook her head. "Who told you that, Lobey? Who told you that? I'm Le Dove."

I got chills. The Dove extended a slim hand. "Didn't you know? Lobey, you mean you didn't—"

I backed away, raising my sword.

"Lobey, we're not human! We live on their planet, because they destroyed it. We've tried to take their form, their memories, their myths. But they don't fit. It's illusion, Lobey. So much of it. He brought you back: Greeneye. He's the one who could have brought back, really brought back your Friza."

"Green-eye . . . ?"

"But we're just not the same as they were, Lobey. We're—"

I turned and ran from the balcony.

Inside, I overturned a table, whirled at the barking dog. "Lo Lobey!" He sat on the dais where the Dove's party had been. "Come. Have you been enjoying the floor show here at the Pearl?"

Before I could say anything, he nosed a switch in the wall.

The floor began to rotate. Through my hysteria I realized what was happening. The floor was two panes of polarized plastic, one above the other. The top one turned; the lower one was still. As they reached transparency, I saw figures moving below in the crevices of the stone, down below the chair and table legs.

"The *Pearl* is built over one of the corridors for the kage at Branning-at-sea. Look: they weave there among the crags, that one falling, that other, clinging to the wall, chewing his tongue and drooling blood. We have no kage-keeper here. The old computer system the humans used for Psychic Harmony and Entangled Deranged Response Associations takes care of their illusions. Down there is a whole hell full of gratified desire—"

I flung myself on the floor, pressing my face against the transparency. "PHAEDRA!" I screamed. "PHAEDRA, where is she?"

"Hi, baby!" Lights glittered below me from the shadow. A couple with many too many arms stood in a quiet embrace beneath the flickering machine.

"PHAEDRA—"

"It's still the wrong maze, baby. You can find another illusion down here. She'll follow you all the way to the door, but when you turn around to make sure she's there, you'll see through it all again, and you'll leave alone. Why even bother to go through with it?" The voice was thinned through the plastic floor. "Mother is in charge of everything down here. Don't come playing your bloody knife around me. You've got to try and get her back some other way. You're a bunch of psychic manifestations, multi-sexed and incorporeal, and you—you're all trying to put on the limiting mask of humanity. Turn again, Lobey. Seek somewhere outside the frame of the mirror—"

"Where—"

"Have you begged at the tree?"

Below me the lost drooled and lurched and jabbered in the depths of the kage beneath PHAEDRA's flickering. I pushed away. The dog barked as I reached the door.

I missed a stair and grabbed the banister four steps down. The building hurled me into the park. I caught my balance. Around the plaza metal towers roared with spectators dancing on the terraces, singing from crowded windows.

I stood before the tree and played to him, pleading. I hung chords on a run of sevenths that begged his resolution. I began humbly, and the song emptied me, till there was only the pit. I plunged. There was rage. It was mine, so I gave him that. There was love. That shrilled beneath the singing in the windows.

Where his forearm had been lashed to the branch, the bone had broken. His hand sagged away from the bark and—

—and nothing. I shrieked, as outrage broke. With the hilt in both hands, I plunged the point in his thigh, sank it to the wood. I screamed again and wrenched away, quivering.

In pity for man's darkening thought
He walked that room and issued thence
In Galilean turbulence;
The Babylonian starlight brought
a fabulous, formless darkness in.

William Butler Yeats/*Song from a Play*

I have heard that you will give 1000 dollars for my
body which as I understand, it means as a witness
. . . if it was so as I could appear in court, I would
give the desired information, but I have indictments
against me for things that happened in the Lincoln
County War, and am afraid to give myself up because
my enemies would kill me.

Willaim H. Bonney (Billy the Kid)/
Letter to Lt.-Gov. Lew Wallace

I seek with garlands to redress that wrong.

Andrew Marvell/*The Coronet*

The sea broke. Morning ran over the water. I walked along
the beach alone. There were a lot of shells around. I kept
on thinking, just a day before we rode into Branning on
dragons. Now his life and my illusions were gone. Behind
me Branning-at-sea diminished on the dawn. The point of
my machete scarred the sand again and again as I walked.

I was not tired. I'd walked all night. But something had wound the ends of fatigue so tight I couldn't stop. The dawn beach was beautiful. I climbed a dune crested with long, lisping grasses.

"Hey, Lobey."

Whatever it was unwound and shook like sprung clockworks.

"How you been?"

He was sitting on a log jammed into the moist sand at the bottom of the dune. He squinted up at me, brushed back his hair. The sun flamed the crystals on his shoulder, his arm: salt.

"I been waiting a long, long time." He scratched his knee. "How are you?"

"I don't know," I said. "Tired."

"Are you going to play?" He pointed up at my sword. "Come on down."

"I don't want to," I said.

Sand trickled from the soles of my feet. I looked down, just as a piece of dune fell away beneath me. I staggered. Fear jogged loose. I fell, and began to claw at the ground. While the Kid chuckled, I slipped down the slope. At the bottom, I whirled. The Kid, still sitting on the log, looked down at me.

"What do you want?" I whispered. "You've lost Green-eye. What do you want from me?"

The Kid rubbed his ear, smiling over many small teeth. "I need that." He pointed to my machete. "Do you think Spider would really—" He stopped. "Spider decided Green-eye, you, and me couldn't stay alive in the same world; it was too dangerous. So he signed the death decree and had Green-eye strung up while you played him out, and I cried beneath the sea where you can't see tears; is that what you believe?"

"I don't . . . I don't know."

"I believe that Green-eye lives. I don't know. I can't follow him like I can the rest of you. He could be dead." He leaned forward and bared his teeth. "But he's not."

I pushed my back against the sand.

"Give me your sword."

I pulled back my arm. Suddenly I swung forward and hacked at him. He dodged. Wood splintered.

"If you hit me," he said, "I suppose it would be unpleasant. I do bleed. But if I can tell what you're thinking, well then, attempts to get rid of me like that are really fruitless." He shrugged, smiling, reached out, and touched the blade.

My hand jumped. He took the machete, fingered the holes. "No," he sighed. "No, that doesn't do me any good." He held it out to me again. "Show me how?"

I took it from him because it was mine and I didn't like him holding it.

He scratched his right heel with his left foot, "Come on. Show me. I don't need the knife. I need the music inside. Play, Lobey." He nodded.

Terrified, I put the handle to my mouth.

"Go on."

A note quavered.

He leaned forward, gold lashes low. "Now I'm gonna take everything that's left." His fingers snared one another. He curled his toes, tearing earth.

Another note.

I began a third—

It was a sound and a motion and a feeling all at once. It was a loud *snap*: the Kid arched his back and grabbed his neck; the feeling was terror going a few degrees further than I thought it could. Spider, from the top of the dune shouted, "Keep playing, damn it!"

I squawked through the blade.

"As long as you make music, he can't use his mind for anything else!"

The Kid was standing. The dragon whip lashed over my head. Blood lanced down his chest. He stumbled back over the driftwood, fell. I scrambled aside, managing to keep my feet under me—a trifle easier for me than most other people. I was still getting some sort of noise out of the knife.

Spider, his whip singing, came crabwise down the dune.

The Kid flipped to his belly under the lash and tried to crawl. The gills under the hair falling over his neck spread. Spider cut his back open, then yelled at me, "Don't stop playing!"

The Kid hissed and bit the ground. He rolled to his side, sand on his mouth and chin. "Spider . . . aw, Spider. Stop it! Don't, please . . . don—" The whip opened his cheek and he clutched his face.

"Keep playing, Lobey! Damn it, or he'll kill me!"

Overblown at the octave, my notes jabbed the morning.

"Ahhhhh . . . no, Spider-man. Don't hurt me no more!" His speech slurred on his bloody tongue. "Don't—ahhh*hhh*— it hurts. It hurts! You're supposed to be my friend, Spider!—naw, you're supposed to be my . . ." Sobs for a while. The whip cut the Kid again and again.

Spider's shoulders ran with sweat. "Okay," he said. He coiled his lash, breathing hard.

My tongue was sore, my hands numb. Spider looked from me to the Kid. "It's over," he said.

"Was it . . . necessary?" I asked.

Spider just looked at the ground.

There was a thrashing in the bush. A length of thorn coiled over the sand, dragging a blossom.

Spider started up the slope. "Come on," he said. I

followed him. At the top I looked back. A bouquet clustered over the corpse's head, jostling for eyes and tongue. I followed Spider down.

At the bottom he turned to me. Then he frowned. "Snap out of it, boy. I just saved your life. That's all."

"Spider . . . ?"

"What?"

"Green-eye . . . I think I've figured something out."

"What? . . . Come on, we have to get back."

"Like the Kid; I can bring back the ones I've killed myself."

"Like in the broken land," Spider said. "You brought yourself back. You let yourself die, and you came back. Green-eye is the only one who can bring your Friza back—now."

"Green-eye," I said again. "He's dead."

Spider nodded. "You killed him. It was that last stroke of your . . ." He gestured towards my machete.

"Oh," I said. "What's going on back at Branning-at-sea?"

"Riots."

"Why?"

"They're hungry for their own future." For a moment I pictured the garden of the Kid's face. It made me ill.

"I'm going back," he said. "Are you coming?"

The sea receded and froth spiraled the sand.

I thought for a while. "Yes. But not now."

"Green-eye will"—Spider mashed something into the sand with his foot—"wait, I suppose. And the Dove too. The Dove leads them in the dance, now, and won't be so ready to forgive you for the choice you made."

"What was it?"

"Between the real and—the rest."

"Which did I choose?"

Spider pushed my shoulder, grinning. "Maybe you'll know when you get back. Where you off to?" He started to turn.

"Spider?"

He looked back.

"In my village there was a man who grew dissatisfied. So he left this world, worked for a while on the moon, on the outer planets, then on worlds that were stars and stars away. I might go there."

Spider nodded. "I did that once. It was all waiting for me when I got back."

"What's it going to be like?"

"It's not going to be what you expect." He grinned, then turned away.

"It's going to be . . . different?"

He kept walking down the sand.

As morning branded the sea, darkness fell away at the far side of the beach. I turned to follow it.

—September 1965
—November 1966

AYE, AND GOMORRAH . . .

And came down in Paris:

Where we raced along the Rue de Médicis with Bo and Lou and Muse inside the fence, Kelly and me outside, making faces through the bars, making noise, making the Luxembourg Gardens roar at two in the morning. Then climbed out and down to the square in front of St. Sulpice where Bo tried to knock me into the fountain.

At which point Kelly noticed what was going on around us, got an ashcan cover, and ran into the pissoir, banging the walls. Five guys scooted out: even a big pissoir only holds four.

A very blond young man put his hand on my arm and smiled. "Don't you think, Spacer, that you . . . people should leave?"

I looked at his hand on my blue uniform. *"Est-ce que tu es un frelk?"*

His eyebrows rose, then he shook his head. "Une *frelk*," he corrected. "No. I am not. Sadly for me. You look as though you might once have been a man. But now . . ." He smiled. "You have nothing for me now. The police." He nodded across the street where I noticed the gendarmerie for the first time. "They don't bother us. You are strangers, though . . ."

But Muse was already yelling: "Hey, come on! Let's get out of here, huh?" And left. And went up again.

And came down in Houston:

"God damn!" Muse said. "Gemini Flight Control—you mean, this is where it all started? Let's get *out* of here, *please!*"

So took a bus out through Pasadena, then the monoline to Galveston, and were going to take it down the Gulf, but Lou found a couple with a pickup truck—

"Glad to give you a ride, Spacers. You people up there on them planets and things, doing all that good work for the government."

—who were going south, them and the baby, so we rode in the back for two hundred and fifty miles of sun and wind.

"You think they're frelks?" Lou asked, elbowing me.

351

"I bet they're frelks. They're just waiting for us to give 'em the come-on."

"Cut it out. They're a nice, stupid pair of country kids."

"That don't mean they ain't frelks!"

"You don't trust anybody, do you?"

"No."

And finally a bus again that rattled us through Brownsville and across the border into Matamoros where we staggered down the steps into the dust and the scorched evening with a lot of Mexicans and chickens and Texas Gulf shrimp fishermen—who smelled worst—and *we* shouted the loudest. Forty-three whores—I counted—had turned out for the shrimp fishermen, and by the time we had broken two of the windows in the bus station, they were all laughing. The shrimp fishermen said they wouldn't buy us no food but would get us drunk if we wanted 'cause that was the custom with shrimp fishermen. But we yelled, broke another window; then, while I was lying on my back on the telegraph office steps, singing, a woman with dark lips bent over and put her hands on my cheeks. "You are very sweet." Her rough hair fell forward. "But the men, they are standing around and watching *you*. And that is taking up *time*. Sadly, their time is our *money*. Spacer, do you not think you . . . people should leave?"

I grabbed her wrist. *"¡Usted!"* I whispered. *"¿Usted es una frelka?"*

"Frelko en español." She smiled and patted the sunburst that hung from my belt buckle. "Sorry. But you have nothing that . . . would be useful to me. It is too bad for you look like you were once a woman, no? And I like women, too . . ."

I rolled off the porch.

"Is this a drag or is this a drag!" Muse was shouting. "Come *on*! Let's *go*!"

We managed to get back to Houston before dawn, somehow. And went up.

And came down in Istanbul:

That morning it rained in Istanbul.

At the commissary we drank our tea from pear-shaped glasses, looking out across the Bosphorus. The Princes Islands lay like trash heaps before the prickly city.

"Who knows their way in this town?" Kelly asked.

"Aren't we going around together?" Muse demanded. "I thought we were going around together."

"They held up my check at the purser's office," Kelly explained. "I'm flat broke. I think the purser's got it in for me," and shrugged. "Don't want to, but I'm going to have to hunt up a rich frelk and come on friendly—" went back to the tea; *then* noticed how heavy the silence had become. "Aw, come *on*, now! You gape at me like that and I'll bust every bone in that carefully-conditioned-from-puberty body of yours. Hey, you!" meaning me. "Don't give me that holier-than-thou gawk like you never went with no frelk!"

It was starting.

"I'm not gawking," I said and got quietly mad.

The longing, the old longing.

Bo laughed to break tensions. "Say, last time I was in Istanbul—about a year before I joined up with this platoon—I remember we were coming out of Taksim Square down Istiqlal. Just past all the cheap movies we found a little passage lined with flowers. Ahead of us were two other spacers. It's a market in there, and farther down they got fish and then a courtyard with oranges and candy and sea urchins and cabbages. But flowers in front. Anyway, we noticed something funny about the spacers. It wasn't their uniforms: they were perfect. The haircuts: fine. It wasn't till we heard them talking—they were a man and woman, dressed up like spacers, trying to pick up frelks! Imagine, queer for frelks!"

"Yeah," Lou said. "I seen that before. There were a lot of them in Rio."

"We beat hell out of them two," Bo concluded. "We got them in a side street and went to *town*!"

Muse's tea glass clicked on the counter. "From Taksim down Istiqlal till you get to the flowers? Now why didn't you say that's where the frelks were, huh?" A smile on Kelly's face would have made that okay. There was no smile.

"Hell," Lou said, "nobody ever had to tell me where to look. I go out in the street and frelks smell me coming. I can spot 'em halfway along Piccadilly. Don't they have nothing but tea in this place? Where can you get a drink?"

Bo grinned. "Moslem country, remember? But down at the end of the Flower Passage, there's a lot of little bars with green doors and marble counters where you can get a liter of beer for about fifteen cents in lira. And there're all these stands selling deep-fat-fried bugs and pig's gut sandwiches—''

"You ever notice how frelks can put it away? I mean liquor, not . . . pig's guts.''

And launched off into a lot of appeasing stories. We ended with the one about the frelk some spacer tried to roll who announced: "There are two things I go for. One is spacers; the other is a good fight . . .''

But they only allay. They cure nothing. Even Muse knew we would spend the day apart now.

The rain had stopped so we took the ferry up the Golden Horn. Kelly straight off asked for Taksim Square and Istiqlal and was directed to a dolmush, which we discovered was a taxicab, only it just goes one place and picks up lots and lots of people on the way. And it's cheap.

Lou headed off over Ataturk Bridge to see the sights of New City. Bo decided to find out what the Dolma Boche really was; and when Muse discovered you could go to Asia for fifteen cents—one lira and fifty krush—well, Muse decided to go to Asia.

I turned through the confusion of traffic at the head of the bridge and up past the gray, dripping walls of Old City, beneath the trolley wires. There are times when yelling and helling won't fill the lack. There are times when you must walk by yourself because it hurts so much to be alone.

I walked up a lot of little streets with wet donkeys and wet camels and women in veils; and down a lot of big streets with buses and trash baskets and men in business suits.

Some people stare at spacers; some people don't. Some people stare or don't stare in a way a spacer gets to recognize within a week after coming out of training school at sixteen. I was walking in the park when I caught her watching. She saw me see and looked away.

I ambled down the wet asphalt. She was standing under the arch of a small, empty mosque shell. As I passed, she walked out into the courtyard among the cannons.

"Excuse me."

I stopped.

"Do you know whether or not this is the shrine of St. Irene?" Her English was charmingly accented. "I've left my guidebook home."

"Sorry. I'm a tourist, too."

"Oh." She smiled. "I am Greek. I thought you might be Turkish because you are so dark."

"American red Indian." I nodded. Her turn to curtsy.

"I see. I have just started at the university here in Istanbul. Your uniform, it tells me that you are . . ."—and in the pause, all speculations resolved—"a spacer."

I was uncomfortable. "Yeah." I put my hands in my pockets, moved my feet around on the soles of my boots, licked my third from the rear left molar—did all the things you do when you're uncomfortable. *You're so* exciting *when you look like that,* a frelk told me once. "Yeah, I am." I said it too sharply, too loudly, and she jumped a little.

So now she knew I knew she knew I knew, and I wondered how we would play out the Proust bit.

"I'm Turkish," she said. "I'm not Greek. I'm not just starting. I'm a graduate in art history here at the university. These little lies one makes for strangers to protect one's ego . . . why? Sometimes I think my ego is very small."

That's one strategy.

"How far away do you live?" I asked. "And what's the going rate in Turkish lira?" That's another.

"I can't pay you." She pulled her raincoat around her hips. She was very pretty. "I would like to." She shrugged and smiled. "But I am . . . a poor student. Not a rich one. If you want to turn around and walk away, there will be no hard feelings. I shall be sad, though."

I stayed on the path. I thought she'd suggest a price after a little while. She didn't.

And that's another.

I was asking myself, *What do you want the damn money for anyway?* when a breeze upset water from one of the park's great cypresses.

"I think the whole business is sad." She wiped drops from her face. There had been a break in her voice, and for a moment I looked too closely at the water streaks. "I think it's sad that they have to alter you to make you a spacer. If they hadn't, then *we* . . . If spacers had never been, then we could not be . . . the way we are. Did you start out male or female?"

Another shower. I was looking at the ground, and droplets went down my collar.

"Male," I said. "It doesn't matter."

"How old are you? Twenty-three, twenty-four?"

"Twenty-three," I lied. It's reflex. I'm twenty-five, but the younger they think you are, the more they pay you. But I didn't want her damned money—

"I guessed right, then." She nodded. "Most of us are experts on spacers. Do you find that? I suppose we have to be." She looked at me with wide black eyes. At the end of the stare, she blinked rapidly. "You would have been a fine man. But now you are a spacer, building water-conservation units on Mars, programming mining computers on Ganymede, servicing communication relay towers on the moon. The alteration . . ." Frelks are the only people I've ever heard say "the alteration" with so much fascination and regret. "You'd think they'd have found some other solution. They could have found another way than neutering you, turning you into creatures not even androgynous; things that are—"

I put my hand on her shoulder, and she stopped like I'd hit her. She looked to see if anyone was near. Lightly, so lightly then, she raised her hand to mine.

I pulled my hand away. "That are what?"

"They could have found another way." Both hands in her pockets now.

"They could have. Yes. Up beyond the ionosphere, there's too much radiation for those precious gonads to work right anywhere you might want to do something that would keep you there over twenty-four hours, like the moon, or Mars, or the satellites of Jupiter—"

"They could have made protective shields. They could have done more research into biological adjustment—"

"Population Explosion time," I said. "No, they were hunting for any excuse to cut down kids back then—especially deformed ones."

"Ah, yes." She nodded. "We're still fighting our way up from the neo-puritan reaction to the sexual freedom of the twentieth century."

"It was a fine solution." I grinned and hung my hand over my crotch. "I'm happy with it." I've never known why that's so much more obscene when a spacer does it.

"Stop it," she snapped, moving away.

"What's the matter?"

"Stop it," she repeated. "Don't do that! You're a child."

"But they choose us from children whose sexual responses are hopelessly retarded at puberty."

"And your childish, violent substitutes for love? I suppose that's one of the things that's attractive. Yes, I know you're a child."

"Yeah? What about frelks?"

She thought a while. "I think they are the sexually retarded ones they miss. Perhaps it was the right solution. You really don't regret you have no sex?"

"We've got you," I said.

"Yes." She looked down. I glanced to see the expression she was hiding. It was a smile. "You have your glorious, soaring life, *and* you have us." Her face came up. She glowed. "You spin in the sky, the world spins under you, and you step from land to land, while we . . ." She turned her head right, left, and her black hair curled and uncurled on the shoulder of her coat. "We have our dull, circled lives, bound in gravity, *worshipping* you!" She looked back at me. "Perverted, yes? In love with a bunch of corpses in free fall!" Suddenly she hunched her shoulders. "I don't like having a free-fall-sexual-displacement complex."

"That always sounded like too much to say."

She looked away. "I don't like being a frelk. Better?"

"I wouldn't like it either. Be something else."

"You don't choose your perversions. *You* have no perversions at all. You're free of the whole business. I love you for that, spacer. My love starts with the fear of love. Isn't that beautiful? A pervert substitutes something unattainable for 'normal' love: the homosexual, a mirror, the fetishist, a shoe, or a watch, or a girdle. Those with free-fall-sexual-dis—"

"Frelks."

"Frelks substitute"—she looked at me sharply again—"loose, swinging meat."

"That doesn't offend me."

"I wanted it to."

"Why?"

"You don't have desires. You wouldn't understand."

"Go on."

"I want you because you can't want me. That's the pleasure. If someone really had a sexual reaction to . . . us, we'd be scared away. I wonder how many people there were before there were you, waiting for your creation. We're necrophiles. I'm sure grave robbing has fallen off since you started going up. But you don't understand . . ." She paused. "If you did, then I wouldn't be scuffing leaves now and trying to think from whom I could borrow sixty lira." She stepped over the knuckles of a root that had cracked the pavement. "And that, incidentally, is the going rate in Istanbul."

I calculated. "Things still get cheaper as you go east."

"You know," and she let her raincoat fall open, "you're different from the others. You at least *want* to know—"

I said, "If I spat on you for every time you'd said that to a spacer, you'd drown."

"Go back to the moon, loose meat." She closed her eyes. "Swing on up to Mars. There are satellites around Jupiter where you might do some good. Go up and come down in some other city."

"Where do you live?"

"You want to come with me?"

"Give me something," I said. "Give me *some*thing—it doesn't have to be worth sixty lira. Give me something that you like, anything of yours that means something to you."

"No!"

"Why not?"

"Because I—"

"—don't want to give up part of that ego. None of you frelks do!"

"You really don't understand I just don't want to *buy* you?"

"You have nothing to buy me with."

"You are a child," she said. "I love you."

We reached the gate of the park. She stopped, and we stood time enough for a breeze to rise and die in the grass. "I . . ." she offered tentatively, pointing without taking her hand from her coat pocket. "I live right down there."

"All right," I said. "Let's go."

*   *   *

A gas main had once exploded along the street, she explained to me, a gushing road of fire as far as the docks, overhot and overquick. It had been put out within minutes, no building had fallen, but the charred facias glittered. "This is sort of an artist and student quarter." We crossed the cobbles. "Yuri Pasha, number fourteen. In case you're ever in Istanbul again." Her door was covered with black scales: the gutter was thick with garbage.

"A lot of artists and professional people are frelks," I said, trying to be inane.

"So are lots of other people." She walked inside and held the door. "We're just more flamboyant about it."

On the landing there was a portrait of Ataturk. Her room was on the second floor. "Just a moment while I get my key—"

Marsscapes! Moonscapes! On her easel was a six-foot canvas showing the sunrise flaring on a crater's rim! There were copies of the original Observer pictures of the moon pinned to the wall, and pictures of every smooth-faced general in the International Spacer Corps.

On one corner of her desk was a pile of those photo magazines about spacers that you can find in most kiosks all over the world: I've seriously heard people say they were printed for adventurous-minded high school students. They've never seen the Danish ones. She had a few of those, too. There was a shelf of art books, art history texts. Above them were six feet of cheap paper-covered space operas: *Sin on Space Station #12, Rocket, Rake, Savage Orbit.*

"Arrack?" she asked. "Ouzo, or pernod? You've got your choice. But I may pour them all from the same bottle." She set out glasses on the desk, then opened a waist-high cabinet that turned out to be an icebox. She stood up with a tray of lovelies: fruit puddings, Turkish delight, braised meats . . .

"What's this?"

"Dolmades. Grape leaves filled with rice and pignolias."

"Say it again?"

"Dolmades. Comes from the same Turkish word as 'dolmush.' They both mean 'stuffed.' " She put the tray beside the glasses. "Sit down."

I sat on the studio couch-that-becomes-bed. Under the

brocade I felt the deep, fluid resilience of a glycogel mattress. (They've got the idea that it approximates the feeling of free fall.) "Comfortable? Would you excuse me for a moment? I have some friends down the hall. I want to see them for a moment." She winked. "They like spacers."

"Are you going to take up a collection for me?" I asked. "Or do you want them to line up outside the door and wait their turn?"

She sucked a breath. "Actually I was going to suggest both." Suddenly she shook her head. "Oh, what do you want!"

"What will you give me? I want something," I said. "That's why I came. I'm lonely. Maybe I want to find out how far it goes. I don't know yet."

"It goes as far as you will. Me? I study, I read, paint, talk with my friends"—she came over to the bed, sat down on the floor—"go to the theater, look at spacers who pass me on the street, till one looks back; I am lonely, too." She put her head on my knee. "I want something. But," and after a minute neither of us had moved, "you are not the one who will give it to me."

"You're not going to pay me for it," I countered. "You're not, are you?"

On my knee her head shook. After a while she said, all breath and no voice: "Don't you think you . . . should leave?"

"Okay," I said and stood up.

She sat back on the hem of her coat. She hadn't taken it off yet.

I went to the door.

"Incidentally." She folded her hands in her lap. "There is a place in New City you might find what you're looking for. It's called the Flower Passage—"

I turned toward her, angry. "The frelk hangout? Look, I don't *need* money! I said *any*thing would do! I don't want—"

She had begun to shake her head again, laughing quietly. Now she lay her cheek on the wrinkled place where I had sat. "Do you persist in misunderstanding? You said you were lonely. It is a spacer hangout. When you leave, I am going to visit my friends and talk about . . . ah, yes, the beautiful one that got away. I thought you might find . . . perhaps someone you knew."

With anger, it ended.

"Oh," I said. "Oh, it's a spacer hangout. Yeah. Well, thanks."

And went out. And found the Flower Passage, and Kelly and Lou and Bo and Muse. Kelly was buying beer so we all got drunk, and ate fried fish and fried clams and fried sausage, and Kelly was waving the money around, saying, "You should have seen him! The changes I put that frelk through, you should have *seen* him! Eighty lira is the going rate here, and he gave me a hundred and fifty!" and drank more beer.

And went up.

—Milford
September
1966

TIME CONSIDERED AS A HELIX OF SEMI-PRECIOUS STONES

Lay ordinate and abscíssa on the century. Now cut me a quadrant. Third quadrant if you please. I was born in 'fifty. Here it's 'seventy-five.

At sixteen they let me leave the orphanage. Dragging the name they'd hung me with (Harold Clancy Everet, and me a mere lad—how many monickers have I had since? But don't worry, you'll recognize my smoke) over the hills of East Vermont, I came to a decision:

Me and Pa Michaels, who had belligerently given me a job at the request of *The Official* looking *Document* with which the orphanage sends you packing, were running Pa Michaels' dairy farm, i.e., thirteen thousand three hundred sixty-two piebald Guernseys all asleep in their stainless coffins, nourished and drugged by pink liquid flowing in clear plastic veins (stuff is sticky and messes up your hands), exercised with electric pulsers that make their muscles quiver, them not half-awake, and the milk just a-pouring down into stainless cisterns. Anyway. The Decision (as I stood there in the fields one afternoon like the Man with a Hoe, exhausted with three hard hours of physical labor, contemplating the machinery of the universe through the fog of fatigue): With all of Earth, and Mars, and the Outer Satellites filled up with people and what-all, there had to be something more than this. I decided to get some.

So I stole a couple of Pa's credit cards, one of his helicopters, and a bottle of white lightning the geezer made himself, and took off. Ever try to land a stolen helicopter on the roof of the Pan Am building, drunk? Jail, schmail, and some hard knocks later I had attained to wisdom. But remember this o best beloved: I have done three honest hours on a dairy farm less than ten years back. And nobody has ever called me Harold Clancy Everet again.

Hank Culafroy Eckles (red-headed, a bit vague, six-foot-two) strolled out of the baggage room at the spaceport, carrying a lot of things that weren't his in a small briefcase.

Beside him the Business Man was saying, "You young fellows today upset me. Go back to Bellona, I say. Just

365

because you got into trouble with that little blonde you were telling me about is no reason to leap worlds, come on all glum. Even quit your job!''

Hank stops and grins weakly: ''Well . . .''

''Now I admit, you have your real needs, which maybe we older folks don't understand, but you have to show some responsibility toward . . .'' He notices Hank has stopped in front of a door marked MEN. ''Oh. Well. Eh.'' He grins strongly. ''I've enjoyed meeting you, Hank. It's always nice when you meet somebody worth talking to on these damned crossings. So long.''

Out same door, ten minutes later, comes Harmony C. Eventide, six-foot even (one of the false heels was cracked, so I stuck both of them under a lot of paper towels), brown hair (not even my hairdresser knows for sure), oh so dapper and of his time, attired in the bad taste that is oh so tasteful, the sort of man with whom no Business Men would start a conversation. Took the regulation 'copter from the 'port over to the Pan Am building (Yeah. Really. Drunk), came out of Grand Central Station, and strode along Forty-second towards Eighth Avenue, with a lot of things that weren't mine in a small briefcase.

The evening is carved from light.

Crossed the plastiplex pavement of the Great White Way— I think it makes people look weird, all that white light under their chins—and skirted the crowds coming up in elevators from the subway, the sub-sub-way, and the sub-sub-sub (eighteen and first week out of jail, I hung around here, snatching stuff from people—but daintily, daintily, so they never knew they'd been snatched), bulled my way through a crowd of giggling, goo-chewing school girls with flashing lights in their hair, all very embarrassed at wearing transparent plastic blouses which had just been made legal again (I hear the breast has been scene [as opposed to obscene] on and off since the seventeenth century), so I stared appreciatively; they giggled some more. I thought, Christ, when I was that age, I was on a Goddamn dairy farm, and took the thought no further.

The ribbon of news lights looping the triangular structure of Communication, Inc., explained in Basic English how Senator Regina Abolafia was preparing to begin her investigation of Organized Crime in the City. Days I'm so happy I'm disorganized I couldn't begin to tell.

Near Ninth Avenue I took my briefcase into a long, crowded bar. I hadn't been in New York for two years, but on my last trip through ofttimes a man used to hang out here who had real talent for getting rid of things that weren't mine profitably, safely, fast. No idea what the chances were I'd find him. I pushed among a lot of guys drinking beer. Here and there were a number of well-escorted old bags wearing last month's latest. Scarfs of smoke gentled through the noise. I don't like such places. Those there younger than me were all morphadine heads or feeble-minded. Those older only wished more younger ones would come. I pried my way to the bar and tried to get the attention of one of the little men in white coats.

The lack of noise behind me made me glance back.

She wore a sheath of veiling closed at the neck and wrists with huge brass pins (oh so tastefully on the border of taste); her left arm was bare, her right covered with chiffon like wine. She had it down a lot better than I did. But such an ostentatious demonstration of one's understanding of the fine points was absolutely out of place in a place like this. People were making a great show of not noticing.

She pointed to her wrist, blood-colored nail indexing a yellow-orange fragment in the brass claw of her wristlet. "Do you know what this is, Mr. Eldrich?" she asked; at the same time the veil across her face cleared, and her eyes were ice; her brows, black.

Three thoughts: (One) She is a lady of fashion, because coming in from Bellona I'd read the *Delta* coverage of the "fading fabrics" whose hue and opacity were controlled by cunning jewels at the wrist. (Two) During my last trip through, when I was younger and Harry Calamine Eldrich, I didn't do anything *too* illegal (though one loses track of these things); still I didn't believe I could be dragged off to the calaboose for anything more than thirty days under the name. (Three) The stone she pointed to. . . .

". . . Jasper?" I asked.

She waited for me to say more; I waited for her to give me reason to let on I knew what she was waiting for (when I was in jail, Henry James was my favorite author. He really was).

"Jasper," she confirmed.

"—Jasper . . ." I reopened the ambiguity she had tried so hard to dispel.

". . . Jasper—" But she was already faltering, suspecting I suspected her certainty to be ill-founded.

"Okay. Jasper." But from her face I knew she had seen in my face a look that had finally revealed I knew she knew I knew.

"Just whom have you got me confused with, ma'am?"

Jasper, this month, is the Word.

Jasper is the pass/code/warning that the Singers of the Cities (who last month sang "Opal" from their divine injuries; and on Mars I'd heard the Word and used it thrice, along with devious imitations, to fix possession of what was not rightfully my own; and even there I pondered Singers and their wounds) relay by word of mouth for that loose and roguish fraternity with which I have been involved (in various guises) these nine years. It goes out new every thirty days; and within hours every brother knows it, throughout six worlds and worldlets. Usually it's grunted at you by some blood-soaked bastard staggering into your arms from a dark doorway; hissed at you as you pass a shadowed alley; scrawled on a paper scrap pressed into your palm by some nasty-grimy moving too fast through the crowd. And this month, it was: Jasper.

Here are some alternate translations:

Help!

or

I need help!

or

I can help you!

or

You are being watched!

or

They're not watching now, so *move*!

Final point of syntax: If the Word is used properly, you should never have to think twice about what it means in a given situation. Fine point of usage: Never trust anyone who uses it improperly.

I waited for her to finish waiting.

She opened a wallet in front of me. "Chief of Special

Services Department Maudline Hinkle," she read without looking at what it said below the silver badge.

"You have that very well," I said, "Maud." Then I frowned. 'Hinkle?"

"Me."

"I know you're not going to believe this, Maud. You look like a woman who has no patience with her mistakes. But my name is Eventide. Not Eldrich. Harmony C. Eventide. And isn't it lucky for all and sundry that the Word changes tonight?" Passed the way it is, the Word is no big secret to the cops. But I've met policemen up to a week after change date who were not privy.

"Well, then: Harmony. I want to talk to you."

I raised an eyebrow.

She raised one back and said, "Look, if you want to be called Henrietta, it's all right by me. But you listen."

"What do you want to talk about?"

"Crime, Mr. . . .?"

"Eventide. I'm going to call you Maud, so you might as well call me Harmony. It really is my name."

Maud smiled. She wasn't a young woman. I think she even had a few years on Business Man. But she used make-up better than he did. "I probably know more about crime than you do," she said. "In fact I wouldn't be surprised if you hadn't even heard of my branch of the police department. What does Special Services mean to you?"

"That's right, I've never heard of it."

"You've been more or less avoiding the Regular Service with alacrity for the past seven years."

"Oh, Maud, really—"

"Special Services is reserved for people whose nuisance value has suddenly taken a sharp rise . . . a sharp enough rise to make our little lights start blinking."

"Surely I haven't done anything so dreadful that—"

"We don't look at what you do. A computer does that for us. We simply keep checking the first derivative of the graphed-out curve that bears your number. Your slope is rising sharply."

"Not even the dignity of a name—"

"We're the most efficient department in the Police Organization. Take it as bragging if you wish. Or just a piece of information.''

"Well, well, well," I said. "Have a drink?" The little man in the white coat left us two, looked puzzled at Maud's finery, then went to do something else.

"Thanks." She downed half her glass like someone stauncher than that wrist would indicate. "It doesn't pay to go after most criminals. Take your big-time racketeers, Farnesworth, The Hawk, Blavatskia. Take your little snatch-purses, small-time pushers, housebreakers, or vice-impresarios. Both at the top and the bottom of the scale, their incomes are pretty stable. They don't really upset the social boat. Regular Services handles them both. They think they do a good job. We're not going to argue. But say a little pusher starts to become a big-time pusher; a medium-sized vice-impresario sets his sights on becoming a full-fledged racketeer; that's when you get problems with socially unpleasant repercussions. That's when Special Services arrive. We have a couple of techniques that work remarkably well.''

"You're going to tell me about them, aren't you."

"They work better that way," she said. "One of them is hologramic information storage. Do you know what happens when you cut a hologram plate in half?"

"The three dimensional image is . . . cut in half?"

She shook her head. "You get the whole image, only fuzzier, slightly out of focus.''

"Now I didn't know that."

"And if you cut it in half again, it just gets fuzzier still. But even if you have a square centimeter of the original hologram, you still have the whole image—unrecognizable but complete.''

I mumbled some appreciative *m*'s.

"Each pinpoint of photographic emulsion on a hologram plate, unlike a photograph, gives information about the entire scene being hologrammed. By analogy, hologramic information storage simply means that each bit of information we have—about you, let us say—relates to your entire career, your overall situation, the complete set of tensions between you and your environment. Specific facts about specific misdemeanors or felonies we leave to Regular Services. As soon as we have enough of our kind of data, our method is vastly more efficient for keeping track—even predicting—where you are or what you may be up to.''

"Fascinating," I said. "One of the most amazing paranoid syndromes I've ever run up against. I mean just starting a conversation with someone in a bar. Often, in a hospital situation, I've encountered stranger—"

"In your past," she said matter-of-factly, "I see cows and helicopters. In your not too distant future, there are helicopters and hawks.''

"And tell me, Oh Good Witch of the West, just how—" Then I got all upset inside. Because nobody is supposed to know about that stint with Pa Michaels save thee and me. Even the Regular Service, who pulled me, out of my mind, from that whirlibird bouncing towards the edge of the Pan Am, never got that one from me. I'd eaten the credit cards when I saw them waiting, and the serial numbers had been filed off everything that could have had a serial number on it by someone more competent than I: good Master Michaels had boasted to me, my first lonely, drunken night at the farm, how he'd gotten the thing in hot from New Hampshire.

"But why"—it appalls me the clichés to which anxiety will drive us—"are you telling me all this?"

She smiled, and her smile faded behind her veil. "Information is only meaningful when shared," said a voice that was hers from the place of her face.

"Hey, look, I—"

"You may be coming into quite a bit of money soon. If I can calculate right, I will have a helicopter full of the city's finest arriving to take you away as you accept it into your hot little hands. That is a piece of information . . ." She stepped back. Someone stepped between us.

"Say, Maud—"

"You can do whatever you want with it."

The bar was crowded enough so that to move quickly was to make enemies. I don't know—I lost her and made enemies. Some weird characters there: with greasy hair that hung in spikes, and three of them had dragons tattooed on their scrawny shoulders, still another with an eye patch, and yet another raked nails black with pitch at my cheek (we're two minutes into a vicious free-for-all, case you missed the transition. I did) and some of the women were screaming. I hit and ducked, and then the tenor of the brouhaha changed. Somebody sang, "Jasper!" the way she is supposed to be sung. And it meant the heat (the ordinary, bungling Regular Service I had been eluding these seven years) were on their way. The brawl spilled into the street. I got between two nasty-grimies who were doing things appropriate with one another, but made the edge of the crowd with no more wounds than could be racked up to shaving. The fight had broken into sections. I left one and ran into another that, I realized a moment later, was merely a ring of people standing around somebody who had apparently gotten really messed.

Someone was holding people back.

Somebody else was turning him over.

Curled up in a puddle of blood was the little guy I hadn't seen in two years who used to be so good at getting rid of things not mine.

Trying not to hit people with my briefcase, I ducked between the hub and the bub. When I saw my first ordinary policeman, I tried very hard to look like somebody who had just stepped up to see what the rumpus was.

It worked.

I turned down Ninth Avenue and got three steps into an inconspicuous but rapid lope—

"Hey, wait! Wait up there . . ."

I recognized the voice (after two years, coming at me just like that, I recognized it) but kept going.

"Wait! It's me, Hawk!"

And I stopped.

You haven't heard his name before in this story; Maud mentioned *the* Hawk, who is a multi-millionaire racketeer basing his operations on a part of Mars I've never been (though he has his claws sunk to the spurs in illegalities throughout the system) and somebody else entirely.

I took three steps back towards the doorway.

A boy's laugh there: "Oh, man. You look like you just did something you shouldn't."

"Hawk?" I asked the shadow.

He was still the age when two years' absence means an inch or so taller.

"You're still hanging out around here?" I asked.

"Sometimes."

He was an amazing kid.

"Look, Hawk, I got to get out of here." I glanced back at the rumpus.

"Get." He stepped down. "Can I come, too?"

Funny. "Yeah." It makes me feel very funny, him asking that. "Come on."

By the street lamp half a block along, I saw his hair was still pale as split pine. He could have been a nasty-grimy: very dirty black denim jacket, no shirt beneath; very ripe pair of black-jeans—I mean in the dark you could tell. He went barefoot; and the only way you can tell on a dark street someone's been going barefoot for days in New York is to know already. As we reached the corner, he grinned up at me under the street lamp and shrugged his jacket together over the welts and furrows marring his chest and belly. His eyes were very green. Do you recognize him? If by some failure of information dispersal throughout the worlds and wordlets you haven't, walking beside me beside the Hudson was Hawk the Singer.

"Hey, how long have you been back?"

"A few hours," I told him.

"What'd you bring?"

"Really want to know?"

He shoved his hands into his pockets and cocked his head. "Sure."

I made the sound of an adult exasperated by a child. "All right." We had been walking the waterfront for a block now; there was nobody about. "Sit down." So he straddled the beam along the siding, one filthy foot dangling above the flashing black Hudson. I sat in front of him and ran my thumb around the edge of the briefcase.

Hawk hunched his shoulders and leaned. "Hey . . ." He flashed green questioning at me. "Can I touch?"

I shrugged. "Go ahead."

He grabbed among them with fingers that were all knuckle and bitten nail. He picked two up, put them down, picked up three others. "Hey!" he whispered. "How much are all these worth?"

"About ten times more than I hope to get. I have to get rid of them fast."

He glanced down past his toes. "You could always throw them in the river."

"Don't be dense. I was looking for a guy who used to hang around that bar. He was pretty efficient." And half the Hudson away a water-bound foil skimmed above the foam. On her deck were parked a dozen helicopters—being ferried up to the Patrol Field near Verrazano, no doubt. But for moments I looked back and forth between the boy and the transport, getting all paranoid about Maud. But the boat *mmmm*ed into the darkness. "My man got a little cut up this evening."

Hawk put the tips of his fingers in his pockets and shifted his position.

"Which leaves me up tight. I didn't think he'd take them all, but at least he could have turned me on to some other people who might."

"I'm going to a party later on this evening—" he paused to gnaw on the wreck of his little fingernail—"where you might be able to sell them. Alexis Spinnel is having a party for Regina Abolafia at Tower Top."

"Tower Top . . .?" It had been a while since I palled around with Hawk. Hell's Kitchen at ten; Tower Top at midnight—

"I'm just going because Edna Silem will be there."

Edna Silem is New York's eldest Singer.

Senator Abolafia's name had ribboned above me in lights once that evening. And somewhere among the endless magazines I'd perused coming in from Mars, I remember Alexis Spinnel's name sharing a paragraph with an awful lot of money.

"I'd like to see Edna again," I said offhandedly. "But she wouldn't remember me." Folk like Spinnel and his social ilk have a little game, I'd discovered during the first leg of my acquaintance with Hawk. He who can get the most Singers of the City under one roof wins. There are five Singers of New York (a tie for second place with Lux on Iapetus). Tokyo leads with seven. "It's a two Singer party?"

"More likely four . . . if I go."

The inaugural ball for the mayor gets four.

I raised the appropriate eyebrow.

"I have to pick up the Word from Edna. It changes tonight."

"All right," I said. "I don't know what you have in mind, but I'm game." I closed the case.

We walked back towards Times Square. When we got to Eighth Avenue and the first of the plastiplex, Hawk stopped. "Wait a minute," he said. Then he buttoned his jacket up to his neck. "Okay."

Strolling through the streets of New York with a Singer (two years back I'd spent much time wondering if that were wise for a man of my profession) is probably the best camouflage possible for a man of my profession. Think of the last time you glimpsed your favorite Tri-D star turning the corner of Fifty-seventh. Now be honest. Would you really recognize the little guy in the tweed jacket half a pace behind him?

Half the people we passed in Times Square recognized him. With his youth, funereal garb, black feet and ash pale hair, he was easily the most colorful of Singers. Smiles; narrowed eyes; very few actually pointed or stared.

"Just exactly who is going to be there who might be able to take this stuff off my hands?"

"Well, Alexis prides himself on being something of an adventurer. They might just take his fancy. And he can give you more than you can get peddling them in the street."

"You'll tell him they're all hot?"

"It will probably make the idea that much more intriguing. He's a creep."

"You say so, friend."

We went down in the sub-sub. The man at the change booth started to take Hawk's coin, then looked up. He began three or four words that were unintelligible through his grin, then just gestured us through.

"Oh," Hawk said, "thank you," with ingenuous surprise, as though this were the first, delightful time such a thing had happened. (Two years ago he had told me sagely, "As soon as I start looking like I expect it, it'll stop happening." I was still impressed by the way he wore his notoriety. The time I'd met Edna Silem, and I'd mentioned this, she said with the same ingenuousness, "But that's what we're chosen for.")

In the bright car we sat on the long seat; Hawk's hands were beside him, one foot rested on the other. Down from us a gaggle of bright-bloused goo-chewers giggled and pointed and tried not to be noticed at it. Hawk didn't look at all, and I tried not to be noticed looking.

Dark patterns rushed the window.

Things below the gray floor hummed.

Once a lurch.

Leaning once, we came out of the ground.

Outside, the city tried on its thousand sequins, then threw them away behind the trees of Ft. Tryon. Suddenly the windows across from us grew bright scales. Behind them girders reeled by. We got out on the platform under a light rain. The sign said TWELVE TOWERS STATION.

By the time we reached the street, however, the shower had stopped. Leaves above the wall shed water down the brick. "If I'd known I was bringing someone, I'd have had Alex send a car. I told him it was fifty-fifty I'd come."

"Are you sure it's all right for me to tag along?"

"Didn't you come up here with me once before?"

"I've even been up here once before that," I said. "Do you still think it's . . ."

He gave me a withering look. Well; Spinnel would be delighted to have Hawk even if he dragged along a whole gang of real nasty-grimies—Singers are famous for that sort of thing. With one more or less presentable thief, Spinnel was getting off light. Beside us rocks broke away into the city. Behind the gate to our left the gardens rolled up towards the first of the towers. The twelve immense, luxury apartment buildings menaced the lower clouds.

"Hawk the Singer," Hawk the Singer said into the speaker at the side of the gate. *Clang* and tic-tic-tic and *Clang*. We walked up the path to the doors and doors of glass.

A cluster of men and women in evening dress were coming out. Three tiers of doors away they saw us. You could see them frowning at the guttersnipe who'd somehow gotten into the lobby. (For a moment I thought one of them was Maud because she wore a sheath of the fading fabric, but she turned: beneath her veil her face was dark as roasted coffee.) One of the men recognized him, said something to the others. When they passed us, they were smiling. Hawk paid about as much attention to them as he had to the girls on the subway. But when they'd passed, he said, "One of those guys was looking at you."

"Yeah. I saw."

"Do you know why?"

"He was trying to figure out whether we'd met before."

"Had you?"

I nodded. "Right about where I met you, only back when I'd just gotten out of jail. I told you I'd been here once before."

"Oh."

Blue carpet covered three-quarters of the lobby. A great pool filled the rest in which a row of twelve-foot trellises stood, crowned with flaming braziers. The lobby itself was three stories high, domed and mirror-tiled.

Twisting smoke curled towards the ornate grill. Broken reflections sagged and recovered on the walls.

The elevator door folded about us its foil petals. There was the distinct feeling of not moving while seventy-five stories shucked down around us.

We got out on the landscaped roof garden. A very tanned, very blond man wearing an apricot jump-suit, from the collar of which emerged a black turtleneck dicky, came down the rocks (artificial) between the ferns (real) growing along the stream (real water; phony current).

"Hello! Hello!" Pause. "I'm terribly glad you decided to come after all." Pause. "For a while I thought you weren't going to make it." The Pauses were to allow Hawk to introduce me. I was dressed so that Spinnel had no way of telling whether I was a miscellaneous Nobel laureate that Hawk happened to have been dining with, or a varlet whose manners and morals were even lower than mine happen to be.

"Shall I take your jacket?" Alexis offered.

Which meant he didn't know Hawk as well as he would like people to think. But I guess he was sensitive enough to realize, from the hard little things that happened in the boy's face, that he should forget his offer.

He nodded to me, smiling—about all he could do—and we strolled towards the gathering.

Edna Silem was sitting on a transparent inflated hassock. She leaned forward, holding her drink in both hands, arguing politics with the people sitting on the grass before her. She was the first person I recognized (hair of tarnished silver; voice of scrap brass). Jutting from the cuffs of her mannish suit, her wrinkled hands about her goblet, shaking with the intensity of her pronouncements, were heavy with stones and silver. As I ran my eyes back to Hawk, I saw half a dozen whose names/faces sold magazines, music, sent people to the theater (the drama critic for *Delta*, wouldn't you know), and even the mathematician from Princeton I'd read about a few months ago who'd come up with the "quasar/quark" explanation.

There was one woman my eyes kept returning to. On glance three I recognized her as the New Fascistas' most promising candidate for president, Senator Abolafia. Her arms were folded, and she was listening intently to the discussion that had narrowed to Edna and an overly gregarious younger man whose eyes were puffy from what could have been the recent acquisition of contact lenses.

"But don't you feel, Mrs. Silem, that—"

"You must remember when you make predictions like that—"

"Mrs. Silem, I've seen statistics that—"

"You *must* remember"—her voice tensed, lowered till the silence between the words was as rich as the voice was sparse and metallic—"that if everything, *everything* were known, statistical estimates would be unnecessary. The science of probability gives mathematical expression to our ignorance, not to our wisdom," which I was thinking was an interesting second installment to Maud's lecture when Edna looked up and exclaimed, "Why, Hawk!"

Everyone turned.

"I *am* glad to see you. Lewis, Ann," she called: there were two other Singers there already (he dark, she pale, both tree-slender; their faces made you think of pools without drain or tribute come upon in the forest, clear and very still; husband and wife, they had been made Singers together the day before their marriage seven years ago), "he hasn't deserted us after all!" Edna stood, extended her arms over the heads of the people sitting, and barked across her knuckles as though her voice were a pool cue. "Hawk, there are people here arguing with me who don't know nearly as much as you about the subject. You'd be on my side, now wouldn't you—"

"Mrs. Silem, I didn't mean to—" from the floor.

Then her arms swung six degrees, her fingers, eyes, and mouth opened. "You!" Me. "My dear, if there's anyone I never expected to see here! Why it's been almost two years, hasn't it?" Bless Edna; the place where she and Hawk and I had spent a long, beery evening together had more resembled that bar than Tower Top. "Where have you been keeping yourself?"

"Mars, mostly," I admitted. "Actually I just came back today." It's so much fun to be able to say things like that in a place like this.

"Hawk—both of you—" (which meant either she had forgotten my name, or she remembered me well enough not to abuse it) "come over here and help me drink up Alexis' good liquor." I tried not to grin as we walked towards her. If she remembered anything, she certainly recalled my line of business and must have been enjoying this as much as I was.

Relief spread Alexis' face: he knew now I was *someone* if not *which* someone I was.

As we passed Lewis and Ann, Hawk gave the two Singers one of his luminous grins. They returned shadowed smiles. Lewis nodded. Ann made a move to touch his arm, but left the motion unconcluded; and the company noted the interchange.

Having found out what we wanted, Alex was preparing large glasses of it over crushed ice when the puffy-eyed gentleman stepped up for a refill. "But, Mrs. Silem, then what do you feel validly opposes such political abuses?"

Regina Abolafia wore a white silk suit. Nails, lips and hair were one color; and on her breast was a worked copper pin. It's always fascinated me to watch people used to being the center thrust to the side. She swirled her glass, listening.

"I oppose them," Edna said. "Hawk opposes them. Lewis and Ann oppose them. We, ultimately, are what you have." And her voice had taken on that authoritative resonance only Singers can assume.

Then Hawk's laugh snarled through the conversational fabric.

We turned.

He'd sat cross-legged near the hedge. "Look . . ." he whispered.

Now people's gazes followed his. He was looking at Lewis and Ann. She, tall and blonde, he, dark and taller, were standing very quietly, a little nervously, eyes closed (Lewis' lips were apart).

"Oh," whispered someone who should have known better, "they're going to . . ."

I watched Hawk because I'd never had a chance to observe one Singer at another's performance. He put the soles of his feet together, grasped his toes, and leaned forward, veins making blue rivers on his neck. The top button of his jacket had come loose. Two scar ends showed over his collarbone. Maybe nobody noticed but me.

I saw Edna put her glass down with a look of beaming anticipatory pride. Alex, who had pressed the autobar (odd how automation has become the upper crust's way of flaunting the labor surplus) for more crushed ice, looked up, saw what was about to happen, and pushed the cut-off button. The autobar hummed to silence. A breeze (artificial or real, I couldn't tell you) came by, and the trees gave a final *shush*.

One at a time, then in duet, then singly again, Lewis and Ann sang.

Singers are people who look at things, then go and tell people what they've seen. What makes them Singers is their ability to make people listen. That is the most magnificent over-simplification I can give. Eighty-six-year-old El Posado in Rio de Janeiro saw a block of tenements collapse, ran to the Avenida del Sol and began improvising, in rhyme and meter (not all that hard in rhyme-rich Portuguese), tears runneling his dusty cheeks, his voice clashing with the palm swards above the sunny street. Hundreds of people stopped to listen; a hundred more; and another hundred. And they told hundreds more what they had heard. Three hours later, hundreds from among them had arrived at the scene with blankets, food, money, shovels, and more incredibly, the willingness and ability to organize themselves and work within that organization. No Tri-D report of a disaster has ever produced that sort of reaction. El Posado is historically considered the first Singer. The second was Miriamne in the roofed city of Lux, who for thirty years walked through the metal street, singing the glories of the rings of Saturn—the colonists can't look at them without aid because of the ultraviolet the rings set up. But Miriamne, with her strange cataracts, each dawn walked to the edge of the city, looked, saw, and came back to sing of what she saw. All of which would have meant nothing except that during the days she did not sing—through illness, or once she was on a visit to another city to which her fame had spread—the Lux Stock Exchange would go down, the number of violent crimes rise. Nobody could explain it. All they could do was proclaim her Singer. Why did the institution of Singers come about, springing up in just about every urban center throughout the system? Some have speculated that it was a spontaneous reaction to the mass media which blanket our lives. While Tri-D and radio and news-tapes disperse information all over the worlds, they also spread a sense of alienation from first-hand experience. (How many people still go to sports events or a political rally with their little receivers plugged to their ears to let them know that what they see is really happening?) The first Singers were proclaimed by the people around them. Then, there was a period where anyone could proclaim himself who wanted to, and people either responded to him or laughed him into oblivion. But by the time I was left on the doorstep of somebody who didn't want me, most cities had more or less established an unofficial quota. When a position is left open today, the remaining Singers choose who is going to fill it. The required talents are poetic, theatrical, as well as a certain charisma that is generated in the tensions between the personality and the publicity web a Singer is immediately snared in. Before he became a Singer, Hawk had gained something of a prodigious reputation with a book of poems published when he was fifteen. He was touring universities and giving readings, but the reputation was still small enough so that he was amazed that I had ever heard of him, that evening we encountered in Central Park (I had just spent a pleasant thirty days as a guest of the city and it's amazing what you find in the Tombs Library). It was a few weeks after his sixteenth birthday. His Singership was to be announced in four days, though he had been informed already. We sat by the lake till dawn while he weighed and pondered and agonized over the coming responsibility. Two years later, he's still the youngest Singer in six worlds by half a dozen years. Before becoming a Singer, a person need not have been a poet, but most are either that or actors. But the roster through the system includes a long-shoreman, two university professors, an heiress to the Silitax millions (Tack it down with Silitax), and at least two persons of such dubious background that the ever-hungry-for-sensation Publicity Machine itself has agreed not to let any of it past the copy editors. But wherever their origins, these diverse and flamboyant living myths sang of love, of death, of the changing of seasons, social classes, governments, and the palace guard. They sang before large crowds, small ones, to an individual laborer coming home from the city's docks, on slum street corners, in club cars of commuter trains, in the elegant gardens atop Twelve Towers, to Alex Spinnel's select soireé. But it has been illegal to reproduce the ''Songs'' of the Singers by mechanical means (including publishing the lyrics) since the institution arose, and I respect the law, I do, as only a man in my profession can. I offer this explanation then in place of Lewis' and Ann's song.

They finished, opened their eyes, stared about with expressions that could have been embarrassment, could have been contempt.

Hawk was leaning forward with a look of rapt approval. Edna was smiling politely. I had the sort of grin on my face that breaks out when you've been vastly moved and vastly pleased. Lewis and Ann had sung superbly.

Alex began to breath again, glancing around to see what state everybody else was in, saw, and pressed the autobar, which began to hum and crush ice. No clapping, but the appreciative sounds began; people were nodding, commenting, whispering. Regina Abolafia went over to Lewis to say something. I tried to listen until Alex shoved a glass into my elbow.

''Oh, I'm sorry . . .''

I transferred my briefcase to the other hand and took the drink smiling. When Senator Abolafia left the two Singers, they were holding hands and looking at one another a little sheepishly. They sat down again.

The party drifted in conversational groups through the gardens, through the groves. Overhead clouds the color of old chamois folded and unfolded across the moon.

For a while I stood alone in a circle of trees, listening to the music: a de Lassus two-part canon programmed for audio-generators. Recalled: an article in one of last week's large-circulation literaries, stating that it was the only way to remove the feel of the bar lines imposed by five centuries of meter on modern musicians. For another two weeks this would be acceptable entertainment. The trees circled a rock pool; but no water. Below the plastic surface, abstract lights wove and threaded in a shifting lumia.

"Excuse me . . . ?"

I turned to see Alexis, who had no drink now or idea what to do with his hands. He *was* nervous.

". . . but our young friend has told me you have some-thing I might be interested in."

I started to lift my briefcase, but Alex's hand came down from his ear (it had gone to belt to hair to collar already) to halt me. Nouveau riche.

"That's all right. I don't need to see them yet. In fact, I'd rather not. I have something to propose to you. I would certainly be interested in what you have if they are, indeed, as Hawk has described them. But I have a guest here who would be even more curious."

That sounded odd.

"I know that sounds odd," Alexis assessed, "but I thought you might be interested simply because of the fi-nances involved. I am an eccentric collector who would offer you a price concomitant with what I would use them for: eccentric conversation pieces—and because of the nature of the purchase I would have to limit severely the people with whom I could converse."

I nodded.

"My guest, however, would have a great deal more use for them."

"Could you tell me who this guest is?"

"I asked Hawk, finally, who you were, and he led me to believe I was on the verge of a grave social indiscretion. It would be equally indiscreet to reveal my guest's name to you." He smiled. "But indiscretion is the better part of the fuel that keeps the social machine turning, Mr. Harvey Cadwaliter-Erickson . . ." He smiled knowingly.

I have *never* been Harvey Cadwaliter-Erickson, but Hawk

was always an inventive child. Then a second thought went by, viz., the tungsten magnates, the Cadwaliter-Ericksons of Tythis on Triton. Hawk was not only inventive, he was as brilliant as all the magazines and newspapers are always saying he is.

"I assume your second indiscretion will be to tell me who this mysterious guest is?"

"Well," Alex said with the smile of the canary-fattened cat, "Hawk agreed with me that *the* Hawk might well be curious as to what you have in there," (he pointed) "as indeed he is."

I frowned. Then I thought lots of small, rapid thoughts I'll articulate in due time. "*The* Hawk?"

Alex nodded.

I don't think I was actually scowling. "Would you send our young friend up here for a moment?"

"If you'd like." Alex bowed, turned. Perhaps a minute later, Hawk came up over the rocks and through the trees, grinning. When I didn't grin back, he stopped.

"Mmmm . . ." I began.

His head cocked.

I scratched my chin with a knuckle. ". . . Hawk," I said, "are you aware of a department of the police called Special Services?"

"I've heard of them."

"They've suddenly gotten very interested in me."

"Gee," he said with honest amazement. "They're supposed to be pretty effective."

"Mmmm," I reiterated.

"Say," Hawk announced, "how do you like that? My namesake is here tonight. Wouldn't you know."

"Alex doesn't miss a trick. Have you any idea *why* he's here?"

"Probably trying to make some deal with Abolafia. Her investigation starts tomorrow."

"Oh." I thought over some of those things I had thought before. "Do you know a Maud Hinkle?"

His puzzled look said "no" pretty convincingly.

"She bills herself as one of the upper echelon in the arcane organization of which I spoke."

"Yeah?"

"She ended our interview earlier this evening with a little homily about hawks and helicopters. I took our subsequent encounter as a fillip of coincidence. But now I discover that the evening has confirmed her intimations of plurality." I shook my head. "Hawk, I am suddenly catapulted into a paranoid world where the walls not only have ears, but probably eyes and long, claw-tipped fingers. Anyone about me—yea, even very you—could turn out to be a spy. I suspect every sewer grating and second-story window conceals binoculars, a tommygun, or worse. What I just can't figure out is how these insidious forces, ubiquitous and omnipresent though they be, induced you to lure me into this intricate and diabolical—"

"Oh, cut it out!" He shook back his hair. "I didn't lure—"

"Perhaps not consciously, but Special Services has Hologramic Information Storage, and their methods are insidious and cruel—"

"I said cut it out!" And all sorts of hard little things happened again. "So you think I'd—" Then he realized how scared I was, I guess. "Look, the Hawk isn't some small-time snatch-purse. He lives in just as paranoid a world as you do now; only all the time. If he's here, you can be sure there are just as many of his men—eyes and ears and fingers—as there are of Maud Hickenlooper's."

"Hinkle."

"Anyway, it works both ways. No Singer's going to—Look, do you really think *I* would—"

And even though I knew all those hard little things were scabs over pain, I said: "Yes."

"You did something for me once, and I—"

"I gave you some more welts. That's all."

All the scabs pulled off.

"Hawk," I said. "Let me see."

He took a breath. Then he began to open the brass buttons. The flaps of his jacket fell back. The lumia colored his chest with pastel shiftings.

I felt my face wrinkle. I didn't want to look away. I drew a hissing breath instead, which was just as bad.

He looked up. "There're a lot more than when you were here last, aren't there?"

"You're going to kill yourself, Hawk."

He shrugged.

"I can't even tell which are the ones I put there anymore."

He started to point them out.

"Oh, come on," I said too sharply. And for the length of three breaths, he grew more and more uncomfortable till I saw him start to reach for the bottom button. "Boy," I said, trying to keep despair out of my voice, "why do you do it?" and ended up keeping out everything. There is nothing more despairing than a voice empty.

He shrugged, saw I didn't want that, and for a moment anger flickered in his green eyes. I didn't want that either. So he said: "Look . . . you touch a person softly, gently, and maybe you even do it with love. And, well, I guess a piece of information goes on up to the brain where something interpets it as pleasure. Maybe something up there in my head interprets the information all wrong . . ."

I shook my head. "You're a Singer. Singers are supposed to be eccentric, sure; but—"

Now he was shaking his head. Then the anger opened up. And I saw an expression move from all those spots that had communicated pain through the rest of his features and vanish without ever becoming a word. Once more he looked down at the wounds that webbed his thin body.

"Button it up, boy. I'm sorry I said anything."

Halfway up the lapels, his hands stopped. "You really think I'd turn you in?"

"Button it up."

He did. Then he said, "Oh." And then, "You know, it's midnight."

"So?"

"Edna just gave me the Word."

"Which is?"

"Agate."

I nodded.

He finished closing his collar. "What are you thinking about?"

"Cows."

"Cows?" Hawk asked. "What about them?"

"You ever been on a dairy farm?"

He shook his head.

"To get the most milk, you keep the cows practically in suspended animation. They're fed intravenously from a big tank that pipes nutrients out and down, branching into smaller and smaller pipes until it gets to all those high-yield semi-corpses."

"I've seen pictures."

"People."

" . . . and cows?"

"You've given me the Word. And now it begins to funnel down, branching out, with me telling others and them telling still others, till by midnight tomorrow . . ."

"I'll go get the—"

"Hawk?"

He turned back. "What?"

"You say you don't think I'm going to be the victim of any hanky-panky with the mysterious forces that know more than we. Okay, that's your opinion. But as soon as I get rid of this stuff, I'm going to make the most distracting exit you've ever seen."

Two little lines bit down Hawk's forehead. "Are you sure I haven't seen this one before?"

"As a matter of fact I think you have." Now I grinned.

"Oh," Hawk said, then made a sound that had the structure of laughter but was all breath. "I'll get the Hawk."

He ducked out between the trees.

I glanced up at lozenges of moonlight in the leaves.

I looked down at my briefcase.

Up between the rocks, stepping around the long grass, came the Hawk. He wore a gray evening suit, a gray silk turtleneck. Above his craggy face, his head was completely shaved.

"Mr. Cadwaliter-Erickson?" He held out his hand.

I shook: small sharp bones in loose skin. "Does one call you Mr. . . . ?"

"Arty."

"Arty the Hawk?" I tried to look like I wasn't giving his gray attire the once-over.

He smiled. "Arty the Hawk. Yeah, I picked that name up when I was younger than our friend down there. Alex says you got . . . well, some things that are not exactly yours. That don't belong to you.''

I nodded.

"Show them to me."

"You were told what—"

He brushed away the end of my sentence. "Come on, let me see." He extended his hand, smiling affably as a bank clerk.

I ran my thumb around the pressure-zip. The cover went *tsk*. "Tell me," I said, looking up at his head still lowered to see what I had, "what does one do about Special Services? They seem to be after me."

The head came up. Surprise changed slowly to a craggy leer. "Why, Mr. Cadwaliter-Erickson!" He gave me the up and down openly. "Keep your income steady. Keep it steady, that's one thing you can do."

"If you buy these for anything like what they're worth, that's going to be a little difficult."

"I would imagine. I could always give you less money—"

The cover went *tsk* again.

"—or, barring that, you could try to use your head and outwit them."

"You must have outwitted them at one time or another. You may be on an even keel now, but you had to get there from somewhere else."

Arty the Hawk's nod was downright sly. "I guess you've had a run-in with Maud. Well, I suppose congratulations are in order. And condolences. I always like to do what's in order."

"You seem to know how to take care of yourself. I mean I notice you're not out there mingling with the guests."

"There are two parties going on here tonight," Arty said. "Where do you think Alex disappears off to every five minutes?"

I frowned.

"That lumia down in the rocks"—he pointed towards my feet—"is a mandala of shifting hues on our ceiling. "Alex," he chuckled, "goes scuttling off under the rocks where there is a pavilion of Oriental splendor—"

"—and a separate guest list at the door?"

"Regina is on both. I'm on both. So's the kid, Edna, Lewis, Ann—"

"Am I supposed to know all this?"

"Well, you came with a person on both lists. I just thought . . ." He paused.

I was coming on wrong. Well. A quick change artist learns fairly quick that the verisimilitude factor in imitating someone up the scale is your confidence in your unalienable right to come on wrong. "I'll tell you," I said. "How about exchanging these"—I held out the briefcase—"for some information."

"You want to know how to stay out of Maud's clutches?" He shook his head. "It would be pretty stupid of me to tell you, even if I could. Besides, you've got your family fortunes to fall back on." He beat the front of his shirt with this thumb. "Believe me, boy. Arty the Hawk didn't have that. I didn't have anything like that." His hands dropped into his pockets. "Let's see what you got."

I opened the case again.

The Hawk looked for a while. After a few moments he picked a couple up, turned them around, put them back down, put his hands back in his pockets. "I'll give you sixty thousand for them, approved credit tablets."

"What about the information I wanted?"

"I wouldn't tell you a thing." He smiled. "I wouldn't tell you the time of day."

There are very few successful thieves in this world. Still less on the other five. The will to steal is an impulse towards the absurd and the tasteless. (The talents are poetic, theatrical, a certain reverse charisma. . . .) But it is a will, as the will to order, power, love.

"All right," I said.

Somewhere overhead I heard a faint humming.

Arty looked at me fondly. He reached under the lapel of his jacket and took out a handful of credit tablets—the scarlet-banded tablets whose slips were ten thousand apiece. He pulled off one. Two. Three. Four.

"You can deposit this much safely—?"

"Why do you think Maud is after me?"

Five. Six.

"Fine," I said.

"How about throwing in the briefcase?" Arty asked.

"Ask Alex for a paper bag. If you want, I can send them—"

"Give them here."

The humming was coming closer.

I held up the open case. Arty went in with both hands. He shoved them into his coat pockets, his pants pockets; the gray cloth was distended by angular bulges. He looked left, right. "Thanks," he said. "Thanks." Then he turned and hurried down the slope with all sorts of things in his pockets that weren't his now.

I looked up through the leaves for the noise, but I couldn't see anything.

I stooped down now and laid my case open. I pulled out the back compartment where I kept the things that did belong to me and rummaged hurriedly through.

Alex was just offering Puffy-eyes another Scotch, while that gentleman was saying, "Has anyone seen Mrs. Silem? What's that humming overhead—?" when a large woman wrapped in a veil of fading fabric tottered across the rocks, screaming.

Her hands were clawing at her covered face.

Alex sloshed soda over his sleeve, and the man said, "Oh, my God! Who's that?"

"No!" the woman shrieked. "Oh, no! Help me!" waving her wrinkled fingers, brilliant with rings.

"Don't you recognize her?" That was Hawk whispering confidentially to someone else. "It's Henrietta, Countess of Effingham."

And Alex, overhearing, went hurrying to her assistance. The Countess, however, ducked between two cacti and disappeared into the high grass. But the entire party followed. They were beating about the underbrush when a balding gentleman in a black tux, bow tie, and cummerbund coughed and said in a very worried voice, "Excuse me, Mr. Spinnel?"

Alex whirled.

"Mr. Spinnel, my mother . . ."

"Who are *you*?" The interruption upset Alex terribly.

The gentleman drew himself up to announce: "The Honorable Clement Effingham," and his pants leg shook for all the world as if he had started to click his heels. But articulation failed. The expression melted on his face. "Oh, I . . . my mother, Mr. Spinnel. We were downstairs at the other half of your party when she got very upset. She ran up here—oh, I told her not to! I knew you'd be upset. But you must help me!" and then looked up.

The others looked, too.

The helicopter blacked the moon, doffing and settling below its hazy twin parasols.

"Oh, please . . ." the Honorable Clement said, "You look over there! Perhaps she's gone back down. I've got to"—looking quickly both ways—"find her." He hurried in one direction while everyone else hurried in others.

The humming was suddenly syncopated with a crash. Roaring now, as plastic fragments from the transparent roof clattered down through the branches, cracked on the rocks. . . .

I made it into the elevator and had already thumbed the edge of my briefcase clasp, when Hawk drove between the unfolding foils. The electric-eye began to swing them open. I hit DOOR CLOSE full fist.

The boy staggered, banged shoulders on two walls, then got back breath and balance. "Hey, there's police getting out of that helicopter!"

"Hand-picked by Maud Hinkle herself, no doubt." I pulled the other tuft of white hair from my temple. It went into the case on top of the plastiderm gloves (wrinkled, thick blue veins, long carnelian nails) that had been Henrietta's hands, lying in the chiffon folds of her sari.

Then there was the downward tug of stopping. The Honorable Clement was still half on my face when the door opened.

Gray and gray, with an absolutely dismal expression on his face, the Hawk swung through the doors. Behind him people were dancing in an elaborate pavilion festooned with Oriental magnificence (and a mandala of shifting hues on the ceiling). Arty beat me to DOOR CLOSE. Then he gave me an odd look.

I just sighed and finished peeling off Clem.

"The police are up there?" the Hawk reiterated.

"Arty," I said, buckling my pants, "it certainly looks

that way.'' The car gained momentum. "You look almost as upset as Alex." I shrugged the tux jacket down my arms, turning the sleeves inside out, pulled one wrist free, and jerked off the white starched dicky with the black bow tie and stuffed it into the briefcase with all my other dickies; swung the coat around and slipped on Howard Calvin Evingston's good gray herringbone. Howard (like Hank) is a red head (but not as curly).

The Hawk raised his bare brows when I peeled off Clement's bald pate and shook out my hair.

"I noticed you aren't carrying around all those bulky things in your pocket any more."

"Oh, those have been taken care of," he said gruffly. "They're all right."

"Arty," I said, adjusting my voice down to Howard's security-provoking, ingenuous baritone, "it must have been my unabashed conceit that made me think that those Regular Service police were here just for me—"

The Hawk actually snarled. "They wouldn't be that unhappy if they got me, too."

And from his corner Hawk demanded: "You've got security here with you, don't you, Arty?"

"So what?"   .

"There's one way you can get out of this," Hawk hissed at me. His jacket had come half-open down his wrecked chest. "That's if Arty takes you out with him."

"Brilliant idea," I concluded. "You want a couple of thousand back for the service?"

The idea didn't amuse him. "I don't want anything from you." He turned to Hawk. "I need something from you, kid. Not him. Look, I wasn't prepared for Maud. If you want me to get your friend out, then you've got to do something for me."

The boy looked confused.

I thought I saw smugness on Arty's face, but the expression resolved into concern. "You've got to figure out some way to fill the lobby up with people, and fast."

I was going to ask why, but then I didn't know the extent of Arty's security. I was going to ask how, but the floor pushed up at my feet and the doors swung open. "If you can't do it," the Hawk growled to Hawk, "none of us will get out of here. None of us!"

I had no idea what the kid was going to do, but when I started to follow him out into the lobby, the Hawk grabbed my arm and hissed, "Stay here, you idiot!"

I stepped back. Arty was leaning on DOOR OPEN.

Hawk sprinted towards the pool. And splashed in.

He reached the braziers on their twelve-foot tripods and began to climb.

"He's going to hurt himself!" the Hawk whispered.

"Yeah," I said, but I don't think my cynicism got through. Below the great dish of fire, Hawk was fiddling. Then something under there came loose. Something else went *Clang!* And something else spurted out across the water. The fire raced along it and hit the pool, churning and roaring like hell.

A black arrow with a golden head: Hawk dove.

I bit the inside of my cheek as the alarm sounded. Four people in uniforms were coming across the blue carpet. Another group were crossing in the other direction, saw the flames, and one of the women screamed. I let out my breath, thinking carpet and walls and ceiling would be flame-proof. But I kept losing focus on the idea before the sixty-odd infernal feet.

Hawk surfaced on the edge of the pool in the only clear spot left, rolled over on to the carpet, clutching his face. And rolled. And rolled. Then, came to his feet.

Another elevator spilled out a load of passengers who gaped and gasped. A crew came through the doors now with fire-fighting equipment. The alarm was still sounding.

Hawk turned to look at the dozen-odd people in the lobby. Water puddled the carpet about his drenched and shiny pants legs. Flame turned the drops on his cheek and hair to flickering copper and blood.

He banged his fists against his wet thighs, took a deep breath, and against the roar and the bells and the whispering, he Sang.

Two people ducked back into two elevators. From a doorway half a dozen more emerged. The elevators returned half a minute later with a dozen people each. I realized the message was going through the building, there's a Singer singing in the lobby.

The lobby filled. The flames growled. The fire fighters stood around shuffling; and Hawk, feet apart on the blue rug by the burning pool, sang, and sang of a bar off Times Square full of thieves, morphandine-heads, brawlers, drunkards, women too old to trade what they still held out for barter, and trade just too nasty-grimy; where earlier in the evening, a brawl had broken out, and an old man had been critically hurt in the fray.

Arty tugged at my sleeve.

"What . . . ?"

"Come on," he hissed.

The elevator door closed behind us.

We ambled through the attentive listeners, stopping to watch, stopping to hear. I couldn't really do Hawk justice. A lot of that slow amble I spent wondering what sort of security Arty had:

Standing behind a couple in a bathrobe who were squinting into the heat, I decided it was all very simple. Arty wanted simply to drift away through a crowd; so he'd conveniently gotten Hawk to manufacture one.

To get to the door we had to pass through practically a cordon of Regular Service policemen, who I don't think had anything to do with what might have been going on in the roof garden; they'd just collected to see the fire and stayed for the Song. When Arty tapped one on the shoulder—"Excuse me please—" to get by, the policeman glanced at him, glanced away, then did a Mack Sennet double-take. But another policeman caught the whole interchange, touched the first on the arm, and gave him a frantic little headshake. Then both men turned very deliberately back to watch the Singer. While the earthquake in my chest stilled, I decided that the Hawk's security complex of agents and counter-agents, maneuvering and machinating through the flaming lobby, must be of such finesse and intricacy that to attempt understanding was to condemn oneself to total paranoia.

Arty opened the final door.

I stepped from the last of the air-conditioning into the night.

We hurried down the ramp.

"Hey, Arty . . . ?"

"You go that way." He pointed down the street. "I go this way."

"Eh . . . what's that way?" I pointed in my direction.

"Twelve Towers sub-sub-subway station. Look. I got you out of there. Believe me, you're safe for the time being. Now go take a train someplace interesting. Goodbye. Go on now." Then Arty the Hawk put his fists in his pockets and hurried up the street.

I started down, keeping near the wall, expecting someone to get me with a blow-dart from a passing car, a deathray from the shrubbery.

I reached the sub.

And still nothing had happened.

Agate gave way to Malachite:

Tourmaline:

Beryl (during which month I turned twenty-six):

Porphyry:

Sapphire (that month I took the ten thousand I hadn't frittered away and invested it in The Glacier, a perfectly legitimate ice cream palace on Triton—the first and only ice cream palace on Triton—which took off like fireworks; all investors were returned eight-hundred percent, no kidding. Two weeks later I'd lost half of those earnings on another set of preposterous illegalities and was feeling quite depressed, but The Glacier kept pulling them in. The new Word came by):

Cinnabar:

Turquoise:

Tiger's Eye:

Hector Calhoun Eisenhower finally buckled down and spent three months learning how to be a respectable member of the upper middle class underworld. That is a long novel in itself. High finance; corporate law; how to hire help: Whew! But the complexities of life have always intrigued me. I got through it. The basic rule is still the same: observe carefully, imitate effectively.

Garnet:

Topaz (I whispered that word on the roof of the Trans-Satellite Power Station, and caused my hirelings to commit two murders. And you know? I didn't feel a thing):

Taafite:

We were nearing the end of Taafite. I'd come back to Triton on strictly Glacial business. A bright pleasant morning it was: the business went fine. I decided to take off the afternoon and go sight-seeing in the Torrents.

". . . two hundred and thirty yards high," the guide announced, and everyone around me leaned on the rail and gazed up through the plastic corridor at the cliffs at frozen methane that soared through Neptune's cold green glare.

"Just a few yards down the catwalk, ladies and gentlemen, you can catch your first glimpse of the Well of This World, where over a million years ago, a mysterious force science still cannot explain caused twenty-five square miles of frozen methane to liquefy for no more than a few hours during which time a whirlpool twice the depth of Earth's Grand Canyon was caught for the ages when the temperature dropped once more to . . ."

People were moving down the corridor when I saw her smiling. My hair was black and nappy, and my skin was chestnut dark today.

I was just feeling overconfident, I guess; so I kept standing around next to her. I even contemplated coming on. Then she broke the whole thing up by suddenly turning to me and saying perfectly deadpan: "Why, if it isn't Hamlet Caliban Enobarbus!"

Old reflexes realigned my features to couple the frown of confusion with the smile of indulgence. *Pardon me, but I think you must have mistaken . . .* No, I didn't say it. "Maud," I said, "have you come here to tell me that my time has come?"

She wore several shades of blue with a large blue brooch at her shoulder, obviously glass. Still, I realized as I looked about the other tourists, she was more inconspicuous amidst their finery than I was. "No," she said. "Actually I'm on vacation. Just like you."

"No kidding?" We had dropped behind the crowd. "You are kidding."

"Special Services of Earth, while we cooperate with Special Services on other worlds, has no official jurisdiction on Triton. And since you came here with money, and most of your recorded gain in income has been through The Glacier, while Regular Service on Triton might be glad to get you, Special Services is not after you as yet.'' She smiled. ''I haven't been to The Glacier. It would really be nice to say I'd been taken there by one of the owners. Could we go for a soda, do you think?''

The swirled sides of the Well of This World dropped away in opalescent grandeur. Tourists gazed, and the guide went on about indices of refraction, angles of incline.

''I don't think you trust me,'' Maud said.

My look said she was right.

''Have you ever been involved with narcotics?'' she asked suddenly.

I frowned.

''No, I'm serious. I want to try and explain something . . . a point of information that may make both our lives easier.''

''Peripherally,'' I said. ''I'm sure you've got down all the information in your dossiers.''

''I was involved with them a good deal more than peripherally for several years,'' Maud said. ''Before I got into Special Services, I was in the Narcotics Division of the regular force. And the people we dealt with twenty-four hours a day were drug users, drug pushers. To catch the big ones we had to make friends with the little ones. To catch the bigger ones, we had to make friends with the big. We had to keep the same hours they kept, talk the same language, for months at a time live on the same streets, in the same buildings.'' She stepped back from the rail to let a youngster ahead. ''I had to be sent away to take the morphadine detoxification cure twice while I was on the narco squad. And I had a better record than most.''

''What's your point?''

''Just this. You and I are traveling in the same circles now, if only because of our respective chosen professions. You'd be surprised how many people we already know in common. Don't be shocked when we run into each other crossing Sovereign Plaza in Bellona one day, then two weeks later wind up at the same restaurant for lunch at Lux on Iapetus. Though the circles we move in cover worlds, they *are* the same, and not that big.''

''Come on.'' I don't think I sounded happy. ''Let me

treat you to that ice cream." We started back down the walkway.

"You know," Maud said, "if you do stay out of Special Services' hands here and on Earth long enough, eventually you'll be up there with a huge income growing on a steady slope. It might be a few years, but it's possible. There's no reason now for us to be *personal* enemies. You just may, someday, reach that point where Special Services loses interest in you as quarry. Oh, we'd still see each other, run into each other. We get a great deal of our information from people up there. We're in a position to help you, too, you see."

"You've been casting holograms again."

She shrugged. Her face looked positively ghostly under the pale planet. She said, when we reached the artificial lights of the city, "I did meet two friends of yours recently, Lewis and Ann."

"The Singers?"

She nodded.

"Oh, I don't really know them well."

"They seem to know a lot about you. Perhaps through that other Singer, Hawk."

"Oh," I said again. "Did they say how he was?"

"I read that he was recovering about two months back. But nothing since then."

"That's about all I know too," I said.

"The only time I've ever seen him," Maud said, "was right after I pulled him out."

Arty and I had gotten out of the lobby before Hawk actually finished. The next day on the news-tapes I learned that when his Song was over, he shrugged out of his jacket, dropped his pants, and walked back into the pool.

The fire-fighter crew suddenly woke up; people began running around and screaming: he'd been rescued, seventy percent of his body covered with second- and third-degree burns. I'd been trying hard not to think about it.

"*You* pulled him out?"

"Yes. I was in the helicopter that landed on the roof," Maud said. "I thought you'd be impressed to see me."

"Oh," I said. "How did you get to pull him out?"

"Once you got going, Arty's security managed to jam the elevator service above the seventy-first floor, so we didn't get to the lobby till after you were out of the building. That's when Hawk tried to—''

"But it was you who actually saved him, though?"

"The firemen in that neighborhood hadn't had a fire in twelve years! I don't think they even knew how to operate the equipment. I had my boys foam the pool, then I waded in and dragged him—''

"Oh," I said again. I had been trying hard, almost succeeding these eleven months. I wasn't there when it happened. It wasn't my affair. Maud was saying:

"We thought we might have gotten a lead on you from him, but when I got him to the shore, he was completely out; just a mass of open, running—''

"I should have known the Special Services uses Singers, too," I said. "Everyone else does. The Word changes today, doesn't it? Lewis and Ann didn't pass on what the new one is?"

"I saw them yesterday, and the Word doesn't change for another eight hours. Besides, they wouldn't tell me anyway." She glanced at me and frowned. "They really wouldn't."

"Let's go have some sodas," I said. "We'll make small talk and listen carefully to each other while we affect an air of nonchalance; you will try to pick up things that will make it easier to catch me; I will listen for things you let slip that might make it easier for me to avoid you."

"Um-hm." She nodded.

"Why did you contact me in that bar, anyway?"

Eyes of ice: "I told you, we simply travel in the same circles. We're quite likely to be in the same bar on the same night."

"I guess that's just one of the things I'm not supposed to understand, huh?"

Her smile was appropriately ambiguous. I didn't push it.

It was a very dull afternoon. I couldn't repeat one exchange from the nonsense we babbled over the cherry-peaked mountains of whipped cream. We both exerted so much energy to keep up the appearance of being amused, I doubt either one of us could see our way to picking up anything meaningful; if anything meaningful was said.

She left. I brooded some more on the charred phoenix.

The Steward of The Glacier called me into the kitchen to ask about a shipment of contraband milk (The Glacier makes all its own ice cream) that I had been able to wangle on my last trip to Earth (it's amazing how little progress there has been in dairy farming over the last ten years; it was depressingly easy to hornswoggle that bumbling Vermonter) and under the white lights and great plastic churning vats, while I tried to get things straightened out, he made some comment about the Heist Cream Emperor; that didn't do *any* good.

By the time the evening crowd got there, and the moog was making music, and the crystal walls were blazing; and the floor show—a new addition that week—had been cajoled into going on anyway (a trunk of costumes had gotten lost in shipment [or swiped, but I wasn't about to tell them that]), and wandering through the tables I, personally, had caught a very grimy little girl, obviously out of her head on morph, trying to pick up a customer's pocketbook from the back of a chair—I just caught her by the wrist, made her let go, and led her to the door daintily, while she blinked at me with dilated eyes and the customer never even knew—and the floor show, having decided what the hell, were doing their act *au naturel*, and everyone was having just a high old time, I was feeling really bad.

I went outside, sat on the wide steps, and growled when I had to move aside to let people in or out. About the seventy-fifth growl, the person I growled at stopped and boomed down at me: "I thought I'd find you, if I looked hard enough! I mean if I really looked."

I looked at the hand that was flapping at my shoulder, followed the arm up to the black turtleneck where there was a beefy, bald, grinning head. "Arty," I said, "what are . . . ?" But he was still flapping and laughing with impervious *gemütlicheit*.

"You wouldn't believe the time I had getting a picture of you, boy. Had to bribe one out of the Triton Special Services Department. That quick change bit. Great gimmick. Just great!" The Hawk sat down next to me and dropped his hand on my knee. "Wonderful place you got here. I like it, like it a lot." Small bones in veined dough. "But not enough to make you an offer on it yet. You're learning fast there, though. I can tell you're learning fast. I'm going to be proud to be able to say I was the one who gave you your first big break.'' His hand came away, and he began to knead it into the other. ''If you're going to move into the big time, you have to have at least one foot planted firmly on the right side of the law. The whole idea is to make yourself indispensable to the good people; once that's done, a good crook has the keys to all the treasure houses in the system. But I'm not telling you anything you don't already know.''

''Arty,'' I said, ''do you think the two of us should be seen together here . . . ?''

The Hawk held his hand above his lap and joggled it with a deprecating motion. ''Nobody can get a picture of us. I got my men all around. I never go anywhere in public without my security. Heard you've been looking into the security business yourself,'' which was true. ''Good idea. Very good. I like the way you're handling yourself.''

''Thanks. Arty, I'm not feeling too hot this evening. I came out here to get some air . . .''

Arty's hand fluttered again. ''Don't worry, I won't hang around. You're right. We shouldn't be seen. Just passing by and wanted to say hello. Just hello.'' He got up. ''That's all.'' He started down the steps.

''Arty?''

He looked back.

''Sometimes soon you will come back; and that time you will want to buy out my share of The Glacier, because I'll have gotten too big; and I won't want to sell because I'll think I'm big enough to fight you. So we'll be enemies for a while. You'll try to kill me. I'll try to kill you.''

On his face, first the frown of confusion; then the indulgent smile. ''I see you've caught on to the idea of hologramic information. Very good. Good. It's the only way to outwit Maud. Make sure all your information relates to the whole scope of the situation. It's the only way to outwit me, too.'' He smiled, started to turn, but thought of something else. ''If you can fight me off long enough and keep growing, keep your security in tiptop shape, eventually, we'll get to the point where it'll be worth both our whiles to work together again. If you can just hold out, we'll be friends again. Someday. You just watch. Just wait.''

''Thanks for telling me.''

The Hawk looked at his watch. "Well, Goodbye." I thought he was going to leave finally. But he glanced up again. "Have you got the new Word?"

"That's right," I said. "It went out tonight. What is it?"

The Hawk waited till the people coming down the steps were gone. He looked hastily about, then leaned towards me with hands cupped at his mouth, rasped, "Pyrite," and winked hugely. "I just got it from a gal who got it direct from Colette," (one of the three Singers of Triton). Then he turned, jounced down the steps, and shouldered his way into the crowds passing on the strip.

I sat there mulling through the year till I had to get up and walk. All walking does to my depressive moods is add the reinforcing rhythm of paranoia. By the time I was coming back, I had worked out a dilly of a delusional system: The Hawk had already begun to weave some security ridden plot about me, which ended when we were all trapped in some dead end alley, and trying to get aid I called out, "Pyrite!" which would turn out not to be the Word at all but would serve to identify me for the man in the dark gloves with the gun/grenade/gas.

There was a cafeteria on the corner. In the light from the window, clustered over the wreck by the curb was a bunch of nasty-grimies (á la Triton: chains around the wrist, bumble-bee tattoo on cheek, high-heel boots on those who could afford them). Straddling the smashed headlight was the little morph-head I had ejected earlier from The Glacier.

On a whim I went up to her. "Hey?"

She looked at me from under hair like trampled hay, eyes all pupil.

"You get the new Word yet?"

She rubbed her nose, already scratch red. "Pyrite," she said. "It just came down about an hour ago."

"Who told you?"

She considered my question. "I got it from a guy, who says he got it from a guy, who came in this evening from New York, who picked it up there from a Singer named Hawk."

The three grimies nearest made a point of not looking at me. Those further away let themselves glance.

"Oh," I said. "Oh. Thanks."

Occam's Razor, along with any real information on how security works, hones away most such paranoia. Pyrite. At a certain level in my line of work, paranoia's just an occupational disease. At least I was certain that Arty (and Maud) probably suffered from it as much as I did.

The lights were out on The Glacier's marquee. Then I remembered what I had left inside and ran up the stairs.

The door was locked. I pounded on the glass a couple of times, but everyone had gone home. And the thing that made it worse was that I could see it sitting on the counter of the coatcheck alcove under the orange bulb. The steward had probably put it there, thinking I might arrive before everybody left. Tomorrow at noon Ho Chi Eng had to pick up his reservation for the Marigold Suite on the interplanetary liner *The Platinum Swan*, which left at one-thirty for Bellona. And there behind the glass doors of The Glacier, it waited with the proper wig, as well as the epicanthic folds that would halve Mr. Eng's sloe eyes of jet .

I actually thought of breaking in. But the more practical solution was to get the hotel to wake me at nine and come in with the cleaning man. I turned around and started down the steps; and the thought struck me, and made me terribly sad, so that I blinked and smiled just from reflex: it was probably just as well to leave it there till morning because there was nothing in it that wasn't mine anyway.

—*Milford*
July
1968

Forward to an Afterword

Why do you write a novel about language?

Why do you write a novel about myth?

In the middle sixties, when the two SF novels here were written, I suspect it was because everybody around me was saying how profound and important the topics were, and though I was ready to believe them, I didn't fully understand why. As a young science fiction writer, I told myself: Maybe if you dream and doodle and tell yourself stories about them both, and submit those stories to the rigors that will make them coherent for other people, perhaps you'll understand a bit better what the fuss is about.

There's a lot in *Babel-17* to suggest that the form of language directly controls thought, which then directly molds society. That, indeed, is one of the stories everyone has been telling each other throughout the twentieth century. Among linguists, that particular story often bears the title The Whorf-Sapir hypotheses—though I wasn't to hear it referred to by that name for several years after *Babel-17* was written. But the fact that this particular tale had escaped its title—had, in fact, preceded it in many quarters—to be told, now in pieces, now completely, and at least in part by practically everyone who was thinking about language with any sophistication at all is merely, an emblem of how widespread the tales were. But because it was among the most popular stories of its day, it's understandable that a twenty-three-year-old SF writer (my age when I finished *Babel-17* and started *A Fabulous, Formless Darkness*) might begin by telling that same story, unaware it was not his own.

As for myths, the popular story about *them* was that they were deep wells of therapeutic wisdom. You had only to rub up against them to begin to be radically healed by their mystical glow of concealed richness. . . .

Let me state it here:

Experiences directly generate thought. Language is simply the most important tool for stabilizing thinking. And

405

"stabilizing thinking" is *very* different from "generating thought." The stabilizing process feeds back, of course, to affect the nature of the experiences as we have them: stabilizing one's thoughts with language is, after all, an experience too. But, once again, stabilizing is *still* different from generating. And to get lost in the ambiguities of the word "control," as it fails to specify the differences between "generate" and "stabilize," is to court endless mistakes and mystifications in the notions that come under the rubric, "language controls thought."

As to the radical wisdom of myth? Well, as Ernst Cassirer noted so many years back, the committee nature of their composition assures that myths will be conservative. Should we study them? Of course; but we must remember that myths are the stories a society can bear to tell about itself. Their significance only comes clear when we realize that around any myth there always hovers the unstated, the repressed, the socially unendurable truths, truths frequently in direct contradiction to what the myth declares, truths that the society is terrified of and bewildered by. Rubbing up against them may reassure; but reassurance alone marks the extent of their healing power. There is nothing radical in their stated portions. And to learn truly and deeply from them requires an active, skeptical, and informed reading that takes into account not only the mythic narrative but the social conditions the narrative was responding to, both by its statements *and* by its silences.

In short, the positive stories of language and myth are, themselves, both myths. Both, expressed in their positive form, are specious bits of language. For me, then, these novels were part of my own process of working away from the language of myth, the myth of language—a process not completed in either book; indeed, a process that, in terms of any given society, must always remain partial.

But it is those old, positive stories that stabilize my early SF novels and tales' popularity, even today, even winning them the awards that, today, justify this omnibus volume.

Yet the process of working away was still going on. Its traces are visible, I hope, here and there throughout. But if there is any enduring interest to these texts, it is where, in terms of the old stories, they fight with themselves, where they come up against the contradictions, where they stall at some moment of metaphor or within some narrative aporia or allegorical ambiguity—where, as science fiction, the world of the story organizes itself in some way in which the fictive subject becomes, momentarily, ambiguously objective. These are what, twenty years after the elusive fact of writing, I would alert any lingering reader to.

With each of these texts, I had very recently gone through some period of great happiness and pleasure—periods which, even as I began to write, were slipping away. To say that the memory of the happiness allowed me to hold on to the contradictions of a more recent pain (or, better, numbness) as long as I could (and express the tension in the text) is only, I suspect, to tell another old story, to retell another myth.

Still, in the case of *Babel–17*, I had lived for a few ideal months with my then-wife, Marilyn Hacker, ex–Quiz Kid, superb poet, and fine friend, and a young man from Florida, Bob Folsom, who, in his twenty-four years, had had what could only be called a "checkered" career, ranging from captaining shrimp boats off the gulf coast of Texas to scuffling and hustling in the more depraved sections of our big cities, a life that had already encompassed both prison and the sea. During the best of that time, Marilyn was going off every morning to edit an engineering magazine. Bob was going up each spring day to work in a tool-and-die shop in the Bronx. And I stayed home and wrote science fiction. The dull and numbing ending of that time is chronicled in Marilyn's poem "The Navigators" (included in her first collection, *Presentation Piece*, by Marilyn Hacker, New York: Viking, 1975), written largely in the same months in which I, now and again in *Babel–17*, was memorializing some of its glories.

But such autobiographical nostalgias as these invariably flirt with just the old tales one tries to work away from. For when one does anything new, whether pleasurable or painful, whatever is in it that is truly unusual—and possibly radical—is precisely what, at least at first, escapes language, just as it generates feeling and thought; is precisely what requires the carefullest stabilization.

Let me give you here, then, some notes I put together from journals I kept between New Year's of 1966 and New Year's of 1967. They commence after Bob had returned south, and I (after writing two more long SF stories, "Empire

Star" and "The Star-Pit") had gone to Europe, and Marilyn had remained in New York: they overlap both the writing of *A Fabulous, Formless Darkness* and "Aye, and Gomorrah . . ." and originally appeared in Terry Carr's fanzine *Lighthouse,* for 1968. They cover a year that saw me move from Europe back to the States and to Europe again. Their original title was:

Afterword:

A Fictional Architecture that Manages Only with Great Difficulty Not Once to Mention Harlan Ellison

. . . and the light.

"It's almost solid here." John's hand reverses to a claw. And much white wrist from the cuff of his sweater. "It's almost . . ." He looks up the rocks, across the cactus (the isles of Greece, the isles of Greece? Um-hm), the grass, at the geometric lime-washed buildings. "Chip, it's almost as if each object were *sunk* in light!" It's late December, five in the afternoon, and golden. "Marvelous!" exclaims John.

"You are a silly romantic," I say.

Gold light sheds on his sweater as he faces me. "But it's true! You can see things at the horizon as clearly as if they were a hundred or so yards away."

"No, look, John—" Down through the windmills the white village sickles the bay. "The clarity is a function of the landscape. We're used to a horizon five miles away. In these hills, these rocks, it's impossible to have a horizon more than a mile off. But your eye doesn't know this. That church over there is not miles distant; even though it's just before the edge of things, it's much smaller and nearer than you think, which is why it's so sharply in focus."

Behind the church the sky is lemon; above us, a blue I cannot name. Over the sea a wall of salmon and gold is blurred with blood behind the hulking ghost of Syros.

"I prefer the clarity to the explanations." John puts his

hands in his jeans. "But that's probably why *you* write science fiction."

"Which reminds me," say I, "did you finish those serials I asked you to read?"

"The first one was *very* long." He adds, "I finished it."

"What did you think?"

"Remember, I told you I don't like science fiction as a rule—"

"You told me you'd never read any. That's not the same thing."

He looks down at his sandals slapping the tarmac. *"Bene disserere est finis logics,"* he intones.

"Is that where the *Bene Gesserit* comes from?"

(John is an English writer, English teacher, twenty-five— two years my senior—with a degree from London University.)

"Eh . . . what's that a quote from?" I ask.

"Your Mr. Herbert probably took it from Act I, Scene I of Marlowe's *Dr. Faustus*. It's a mistranslation of Aristotle into Latin."

" 'To argue well is the end of logic' . . .?" I translate off the cuff I wear to impress. "But did you like the book—"

"You must understand the Greek original has all the multiple ironies of the English. In Latin, 'end,' in this sense, can only mean 'purpose'—diametrically opposed to the ironical Greek intention. To judge the validity of the total statement *The Prophet of Dune* makes as a novel, you must decide whether you hold with the Greek or the Latin sense of this statement. If you hold with the Roman, then the book must ultimately be a failure. If you hold with the Greek, then it's a success."

"Did you *like* it, John? I want to know if you . . . which sense do you hold with?"

"Greece seems to be so 'in' right now." He glances around. "Witness ourselves. Always obliged to rebel, I'll take the Roman."

"Oh," I say. "I'm afraid to ask you what you thought of the other one."

John throws back his head, laughing. "It was perfectly delightful! Now *there's* a book it's no embarrassment to commit yourself to. If you could assure me there were some dozen writers who could word as well as your Mr. Zelazny, you might make me a 'fan,' as you call them.''

The first science fiction I had given John to read was my battered September 1962 edition of *F&SF*. (I had bought it, a couple months after it came out, from a newsstand chary of returns, on the same day I received author's copies of *The Jewels of Aptor*—running along Fourth Street, stopping outside Gerde's, Folk City panting, and flinging the six books high into December [another year, another latitude]; and a brilliant contemporary poet clapped her hands and laughed as the books flopped to the sidewalk.) I suspect John enjoyed *When You Care, When You Love* immensely. But he refused to comment because it was unfinished. On the strength of it, however, he read the other things I gave him. His comment on the Merril article included in the *F&SF* Sturgeon issue, which begins: ''The man has *style*,'' was to narrow his eyes, smile, nod, and murmur: ''*So* has the lady.''

''Come on,'' says John. ''I want to get to Petraiki's before he closes. I refuse to have a dry New Year's. Christmas was bad enough.'' He laughs again. ''I'll never forget you and Costas running around killing turkeys Christmas Eve.''

''Don't knock it,'' I say. ''It's paying for the New Year's wine.''

A number of the internationals wintering on the island had ordered turkeys for Christmas and had been quite chagrined when the birds arrived live. Costas, an auto mechanic who worked in Anó Merá, the island's other town, found out from the butcher to whom the birds had gone; we marched up the island road Christmas Eve ringing doorbells and necks. ''If you'd boil up a pot of water, ma'am (monsieur, signora, Fräulein), we'll pluck it for you.'' My father used to raise turkeys near Poughkeepsie; Costa's father, in Sarconia. We were tipped five to ten drachmas per bird.

''How did you manage it?'' John asks. ''Costas speaks Arabic, German, and Greek. All you've got is French, Spanish, and English. It must have been terribly complicated to set up.''

''We spent most of the time laughing at one another. That made it easier. Speak three languages and you speak 'em all.'' Forget cognate vocabularies. Monoglots (and even diglots) tend to get caught up in metaphorical extensions of meaning. Suspect, depend, expect: literally, look under, hang from, look out for. It's easier to communicate (by charade if necessary) the concrete meanings, letting the "foreigner" intuit by the corresponding mental states implied (suspicion, dependence, expectation), than to try to indicate directly the state of mind itself. "I wrote a novel all about that sort of thing," I tell John. "It should be out by spring. Hope you get a chance to read it."

John asks, "Do you find technical-mindedness conflicts with artistic expression?" Really. We are passing the wooden gate before the art school. Behind, the mosaics of the winter gardens, the empty dorms with hot and cold running water (sigh!).

"A man once asked me," profoundly say I, "why I wanted to be a creative artist in this age of science; I told him—quoting a brilliant contemporary poet—that I saw no dichotomy between art and science, as both were based on precise observation of inner and outer worlds. And that's why I write science fiction." Then I look up. "Hey! *Ya su*, Andreas!"

Andreas the Sandy is an eighteen-year-old fisherman, with baggy pants, a basket enameled blue; his toes and the backs of his hands and his hair glitter with grains.

We go through hello, how are you, what have you been doing, fishing, writing, have you finished your book, no but come up to the house for dinner, come down to the port for ouzo, and Andreas wraps half a kilo of *maridas* from his basket in newspaper and gives them to me for a New Year's present, thank you, you know how to fry them in oil, yes? yes, thank you again, Andreas.

John waits. He can quote hunks of the Iliad in the original, but speaks no Modern Greek. The turkey venture with Costas forced me to begin learning (Costas, and the Greek for all those damn auto parts), and soon I will overhear John boasting about his clever little American who learned Greek in three weeks. Andreas waves good-bye.

We stroll down from the terraced outcropping that falls by the bloody doors of the slaughterhouse into the Aegean. This daily trip from the house to buy wine, oil, oranges, fish, and little papers of dun-colored coffee should take only twenty minutes or so. Often it becomes a full afternoon.

K. Cumbani is having a snack outside the laiki taverna on the port. Punch, beneath the chair, paws and nuzzles a shell. An old man, a big man, K. Cumbani wears a bulky, white wool jacket—looks like a pudgy Hemingway. His grandmother's bust sits on a pedestal in the town square. She was a heroine of the Greek Civil War. His family is the cultural quintessence of the island. He lets us borrow freely among his French and English books. Once a week he will contrive to say, *"C'est terrible! Vraiment je crois que je parle français mieux que grecque!"* As French is the language of the older internationals with whom he mostly associates (English is very markedly the language of the younger), this could be true.

We discuss the effect of Romantic music on post-Wagnerian opera. Tactfully politic, John and I try a few witty remarks on the Chopin-Sand affair so as to maneuver onto the correspondence between Sand and Flaubert, ultimately to change the topic to Flaubert's style (about which we *know* something). Cumbani won't bite. This sort of afternoon, vermilion on the empty winter sea, can be taxing.

"And your own book, how is that coming?" Cumbani asks.

"Slowly," I say.

"You have a very strange way of writing a novel," he muses.

Last week, on a walk at three in the morning, Cumbani saw me sitting in the moonlight on the prow of Andreas's boat, barefeet shoved beneath the sleeping pelican, singing loudly and tearing pages from my notebook, balling them up and flinging them on the water or on the concrete walk, jumping up to chase a page, retrieve a word or phrase and rescrawl it on another page. "Young man, *what* are you doing?"

"Deploying images of Orpheus by the Greek and midnight sea!"

"It's past midnight and much too cold for you to be out like this."

"Oh, look, I'm really all right—"

Cumbani made me come home with him, have some brandy and borrow a sweater, then sent me home.

Now he asks me: "Will you finish your book here?"

I shrug.

"You must send me a copy when it is published."

Cumbani's guest book, glorious upon the walnut low-boy, contains names like de Beauvoir, Menhuin, Kazantzakis, Max Ernst: His shelves are filled with their books; their paintings are on his walls.

"Yes, I will want to see this book—that you say is about mythology?"

"I'll send you a copy."

Damn Ace Books covers!

"I'm taking the boat to Delos again, I think," I say. "I want to explore the ruins some more. Out from the central excavations, there's a strange rock formation facing the necropolis on Rhenia. Do you know what it is, K. Cumbani?"

He smiles. "You are friendly with some of the fishermen. Ask them."

We return to the house early. Just before we leave the port the musicians come down, practicing for the New Year, and I am cast back to my first night on the island, when I ran up from the launch that took us in from the boat, running through the narrow streets of the white city at midnight, white, white, and white around each tiny corner; then a window: inside a man in a brown sweater gazed at an abstraction in orange on his easel under a brass lamp.

Artemus has already brought a rafia-covered bottle of wine and left it on the porch. I pace the garden, remembering a year and a half back when I finished *The Fall of the Towers* and saying to myself, you are twenty-one, going on twenty-two: You are too old to be a child prodigy. Your accomplishments are more important than the age at which you did them. Still, the images of youth plague me. Chatterton, suiciding on arsenic in his London garret at seventeen; Samuel Greenburg, dead of tuberculosis at twenty-four; Radiguet, hallucinating through the delirium of typhus that killed the poet/novelist/chess prodigy at twenty. By the end of this book I hope to exorcise them. Billy the Kid is the last to go. He staggers through this abstracted novel like one of the mad children in Crete's hills. Lobey will hunt you down, Billy. Tomorrow, weather permitting, I will go to Delos.

New Year's itself is party at the house with Susan and Peter and Bill and Ron, and Costas, and John. Costas dances for us, picking the table up in his teeth, his brown hair shaking as his boot heels clatter on the floor, teeth gritting on the wood, and the wine in the glasses shaking too, but none spills. This is also sort of a birthday party for Costas, who was twenty-one last week.

Then Susan calls us to the balcony. The musicians have come up the road, with drums and clarinets, and hammers rattling on the siduri, and another playing bagpipes made from a goat's belly. And later I sit on the ladder, eating fried chicken and hush-puppies (deep-fried in pure olive oil), and talk with John till morning bleaches the air above the garden wall near the cactus by the cistern.

"Watch out with that book of yours," he tells me jokingly. "I'd like to see you finish it."

Then, a sudden depression. I am overcome with how little I have done this past year, how much there is to do.

The first days of January will be warm enough for us to wear bathing suits in the garden, read, write, swat flies against the shutters. Orion will straddle the night, and hold the flaps of darkness tight above the cold roads.

Some fragments of the year following?

Athens: An incredible month in the Plaka, playing guitar in the clubs at the foot of the Acropolis; watching Easter from the roofs of Anaphiotika's stone houses, at the top of the spiral stairs, while the parishioners gather with their candles at the church to march down through the city saddled between the double hills, as lines of light worm the streets toward the monastery. We made Easter eggs that night, with various leaves and flowers—poppies picked at the bottom of the Parthenon's east porch—pressed to the shells and dipped in boiling onion skins: polished floral tracery over the maghogany ovoids. *"Chrónia polá! Chrónia polá!"* and have a bright, red egg.

Istanbul: Four days' hitchhiking from Athens by the road that took me past Mt. Olympus, her twinned and hairy peaks on the left, the sea all gray to Eboiea on the right. I arrived in The City (*Eis Ton Polis—this the city*—Istanbul) with forty lepta, which is less than 1¢. A month of muddy streets and snow and gorgeous stone walls alive with carved leaves and flowers, the men stopping to wash their feet at the troughs, and mild nights on Galata bridge, the iron scrollwork, the octagonal panes of the streetlamps, and the Queen of Cities glittering under the smokey night among her domes and minarets across the water as I returned at midnight to The Old City over the Golden Horn. Reconnoitering, T. described the "bay fire" to me: "A Russian tanker broke up in the harbor, sheeting the yellow water wth a rainbow slick. Then, some-how, a spark! Miles of docks roared and spat at the sky. We stayed in our room, the lights out, the windows flickering. Then, *splat*, and the pane was beaded with blood—the fire-trucks were wetting down all the houses near the bay." (T. is a Swiss painter with a heavy black beard.) Rooms laced with sweet smoke, and oil reeking through the muddy streets; the Turkish bath where steam drifts through the high marble arches as you walk into the dark stalls with white stone basins and metal dipping pans; days of begging with the Danes whose hair was even longer than mine, and the strange girl dying of cancer and abandoned by her German lover in the rain, in spring, in Istanbul.

I hitched out of The City with six and a half feet of Kentuckian called Jerry, I trying to explain about love, he trying to explain about pain. He made hexes in the dirt beside the road and I fixed them on all the cars that passed and wouldn't pick us up—till a road-building machine run by Turkish soldiers stopped for us. "Get up, get up quick! We must not stop for hitchhikers, and our Commander will be up soon in his jeep! But get on quick, and crouch down—" (I had enough Turkish to figure that one out by now) at which point said jeep with said Commander arrived and he told us to get off, and the soldiers looked embarrassed, and we put the most powerful hex possible on that surplus U.S. Army jeep. Forty minutes later, when a truck hauling rock had given us a lift, we passed the jeep in flames, overturned on the road's edge. The road-building machine had pulled off beside it, and soldiers were standing around scratching their heads.

Crete: Cocooned in a sleeping bag against the cabin wall of the *Herakleon*, the wind frosting the top of my head, though it was summer; Heracleon, another dusty island city, where the "k" sounds of Northern Greek are replaced by an Italianate "ch." The two youth hostels here were op-art fantasias, one run by a madman who wouldn't let you use the toilet. I wandered down by the Venitian fountain of the lions, then past the police box to the raucous markets of the city. I made no attempt to resist the pull that forces a visitor to focus his life about the neolithic palaces. In broiling noon, I visited Knossos, descending the lustral basins, roaming through this bizarre construction, comparing the impression of ten years' reading with the reality.

Sir Arthur Evans' reconstructions are not brilliant. They are laudable for what they have preserved of the architecture. Praise him for the Great Staircase. But the Piet de Jong drawings and recreations of the frescoes (literally *everything* you have seen of Minoan graphic art is a de Jong interpretation of what *may* have been there) are a good deal more influenced by Art Nouveau, current when the reconstructions were done, than by anything Minoan. But the work of neither man is harmful, only incredibly misleading for the lay public. The single stone chair found in the palace is as likely to be a footstool for a palace guard as it is to be "Minos' Throne." The bare court that was labeled "Ariadne's Dancing Floor" is pure invention, as with the labeling of "King's room," "Queen's room," etc. The Queen's W.C. probably *is* a W.C. But to whom it belonged is total supposition. The entire wing of the palace which has been labeled the Domestic Wing, with all the charming, personalized anecdotes that have become attached to it: these are all the fantasies of a blind old English eccentric. I sat for an hour on "Minos' Throne," making notes for the book, and feeling for the labyrinth's bottom. Where would you put a computer among these stones?

Strolling with Fred near the sea by the red ruins of the palace at Malia, I asked him what he knew of the Alter Stones. (Fred is an Austrian archeologist.) "The theory seems to be they put a different plant or piece of grain in each little cup around the edge and prayed to it in some religious ceremony."

"Is this what they think, or what they know?"

He smiled. "What they think. They have to give it some explanation and it's as good as any other. Minoan archeology, even in 1966, is mostly guesswork, though they try to make it look documented."

Around the edges of the circular stones—some are thirty

inches across, some several feet in diameter—there are thirty-four evenly spaced indentations, then a thirty-fifth twice as wide as the others, making thirty-six divisions in all. To me this suggests either a compass or a calendar.

Below Phaestos, the gray palace on the cliff, the shrieking children hid in the time-drunk caves of Matla. Peacocks and monkeys played by the bay of Agia Nickoláos, and in the mountains, in the dark hut, I toasted Saint George (passing and stopping at his shrine on the tortuous cliff road, walking the edge and gazing into the foaming ravine, and further at the true Mediterranean Sea) and moved on into the central ridge of stone that bursts Crete's back. I paused, crouched beneath the curtained stones at the great cave of Dicte overlooking the mills of Lasithi in the navel of the island, after having hitched six hours into the island's high core, on the rocks, past fields so loud with bees you couldn't hear your own voice, past poppies, past black orchids wild at the road's edge with purple pistils long as my forearm and blossoms big as my head: at Dicte, birth cave of Zeus, miles deep, more likely the true labyrinth than Knossos, I constructed the great rent in the source-cave for the bull-god to stalk out into my novel. The high rocks were veiled with wet moss. And later, I returned on the windy ship *Heracleon* to Piraeus, with its yacht harbors and its bawdy district and its markets where sea urchin and octopus are sold with shrimp and tomatoes and white cheese under the glass awnings.

New York? My home city, new now this trip, is the slow, blond young man who ran away from his wife in Alabama and who talked and talked and talked for nine days straight with the radio erupting pop music that became translated under the sound of his drawl. He told of his childhood suicide attempts, some dozen before he was nine, trying to drown self, drink iodine, jump out window, till he was put in a mental hospital: At five a drowning, at eight a hanging, at twelve threw himself under a car and broke his back and arm, at fifteen he drank a bottle of rubbing alcohol but had his stomach pumped in time, at eighteen he cut his wrists, at twenty-one he drank rat poison because his wife wouldn't go to bed with him, and here he was pushing twenty-four and the three years were almost up and what if he succeeded this time? and got drunk, and sick, and lay on the floor urinating all over himself, and talked about the mental hospital some more, and then about the year he spent in jail (at eighteen, where he cut his wrists) and how he tried to break open a trustee's head with a scrub brush because the man had kicked him, and the trustee had him tied to a metal bed frame and nearly cut his tongue out with a spoon; talked of how he had stood under the tree, shouting while his drunken twin brother hacked at himself with a piece of broken glass: "Cut it deeper! That's right, Alfred, cut it *deeper*! Now cut it *again*!" A northern Negro, I am as cut off from understanding the white southerner's fascination with pain as the northern white is from understanding the mental matrix in which the southern black lives.

In Cleveland: Sitting at the end of the hall of the Sheraton playing the guitar while Roger Z (at the announcement of his presence at the convention opening, the standing ovation went on, and on, and on . . .), crosslegged on the carpet, played the harmonica and the others listened. Or that same evening, gardenias floating in rums and rums, and Judith and Roger beneath plaster rocks while I tried to break the inarticulate webs, and water washed the blue lights of the stream that wound the restaurant floor. And the inarticulateness becoming, suddenly, pages and pages in an attempt to catch the forms in Roger's linguistic webbing. New and terrible, they do not answer if you call them by old names. (In this year between endings, the Judiths, Zelazny, Merril, and Blish all ceased to be names and became people.) And New York became Bob Silverberg's cats, roaming the halls and steps of Silver Mountain Castle, beneath the trees of Fieldstone.

This whole flow, fixed now by Jim Sallis's letters, contorting silences by those things unsaid, out of Iowa, out of Iowa City—RFD 3, which for me now has become part of his name. Very few things are more important than these.

The novel I was afraid might kill me is finished now, has achieved cover, print, and the multiple production and distribution that creates myth. (The book, McLuhan reminds us, was the first mass-produced object. Before that, story repeated by word of mouth: creating the mass sensibility.) That which totally occupied a year is fallible and subjected to the whims of whoever will pay 40¢. How strange—did I really write it for that? But a new book has taken its place, as different from

it as it was from the one before: the new one exacts responses
from such dissimilar sensibilities . . . even the work method
is totally different. Am I at all the same person?

Another New Year's staggers towards us over the temporal horizon.

After Christmas, I take a seventy mile drive in the back
seat of an open sports car through the English December to a
house of dark and solid furniture, with a stuffed giraffe in the
hall, a Christmas ball hanging from its lower lip.

Every day I have risen in the dark, dressed, pulled back
the blue drapes and sat down to work. Outside the window
the street lamps shine up to diamond the water on the high
panes. Then night drifts away from morning behind the peaked
roofs across the street. The arbitrary measurements man im-
poses on his existence force me to consider the year, ending
now. The two books I discussed in their magazine serial
versions with John on the golden rocks a year ago have now
been released in paperback book form. One of my dawn
labors is to compare the magazine versions with the books.
The first pages of *And Call Me Conrad*, as far as words and
word order go, are the same, without any cutting. But let me
compare the editing:

Magazine:

". . . *you once told me that your birthday . . .*"

"*All right!*"

Book:

". . . *you once told me that your birthday—*"

"*All right!*"

Interruption is signified by a dash, whereas three dots
signifies that the voice trails off; I approve of the book
editing.

But, in the magazine:

After a time I explained:

"*Back when I was a brat . . .*"

While for some inexplicable reason in the book this has been
edited to:

After a time I explained, "Back when I was a brat . . ."

The first is precise; the luminous generality of "explained"
is focused through the colon on the statement that follows.
The second is diffused, unfocused, and clumsy.

And the first line of the body of the text of the paperback edition of *Dune* explodes over a typographical blunder. (And these people are publishing the book this year has garnered?

(Damn Ace Books proofreading!

(Has anything really changed over this year?)

Later on in the day, the color of gas-fire through a glass of sherry recalls the light on late Greek afternoons.

Time magazine this week has done an article on the "generation under twenty-five" and the subject floats about London, conversations on the surface of wine glasses, over pints of bitter, and coffee cups: How is the "pop" (as opposed to the "popular") image propagated? Again Marshall McLuhan has provided the vocabulary. Trying to define the relationship of the pop image to this younger generation, I am brought up short by Jim Ballard. "You know"—he smiles, and the fire is coke this time and the distorting lens scotch—"you're not going to be under twenty-five forever." (Voice of draining time.)

(Passing thought, looking at the portrait of James Pringle, red nosed, high hatted, leering from the lobby wall: If you haven't had opportunity to use the public health facilities of a city, you haven't really been there. Briefly I go over the cities in which I have been . . .)

In Pam Zoline's apartment above the butcher's, Tom Disch and Pam and I drink much wine and turn the sound off on the telly while BBC-2 presents the life story of Eleanor Roosevelt. *Revolver* is playing on the gramophone. Her despairing and ravaged face:

"Well, well, well. He'll make you—Dr. Roberts!" the voices warn her. The correspondences that the music and the mosaic film-clips force from you, each image changing in time to the music, words and music incessantly commenting on one another, is exhausting and staggering. It becomes apparent that this will work only with shows that are planned to utilize the incredibly high participation that TV demands, whereas films—created for a different medium—shown on TV fall very flat. Yet a TV newscast or a TV documentary is perfect for this.

"Please! Please, for God's sake," Pam, her head on Tom's knee, "it's the most exhausting thing I've ever done!" against our hysteria.

Amid white masonite and mushroom salad, the evening winds toward sleep. And later Pam and I discuss how Jim's letters from over the sea have so managed to fix the rush of colored nights to the solid structure of time. There is a soup then, sensuous, with water chestnuts, and apricots, and grapes, and chicken, and mushrooms, that orders the whole sensory mandala of the evening. And the *Heracleon, Life* suddenly informs me as I pick up a stray copy, is sunk with 240 people.

The next day I try to explain the soup, at least, to Mike Moorcock. Futile.

There is a poem by the late Jack Spicer, not one of his best, but it contains the following example:

> *Colorblind people can still drive because the red light is*
>   *on the top and the green green light is on the bottom.*
> *(Or is it the other way around? I don't know because*
>   *I'm not colorblind.)*

How much more economical that would have been:

> *Colorblind people can still drive because the red light is*
>   *on the top and the green light is on the bottom.*
> *(I think.)*

"Style," say I to Mike, quoting B.C.P. (brilliant contemporary poet), "is when the writer forces the reader to supply all the ugly parts of the sentence."

Mike towers over me, face framed in hair, as we move from the rugs, cushions, and clouded and flowered glass of the pub. Later, Mike ponders: "If we don't write what we seriously consider worthwhile, why bother writing?" (This is the only man I have ever met in an editorial capacity whom I can leave and not spend the next two days seriously considering giving up writing as a profession.)

These blue-draped dawns, Gloria and I battle each other as to who will get the first cup of coffee while the Brunners are still asleep. New Year's Eve morning I report at eight o'clock to Judy Merril's basement flat on Portland Street.

"I've been up since four o'clock this morning. I was just (yawn) taking a nap."

where, in a white bowl, the whisky and sugar have been soaking overnight by the stove

"And I want you to know, sir, that whisky is seven dollars a bottle over here."

and we start to play with cream.

"You see, they have single and double cream here, instead of light and heavy. But the single cream is as thick as American heavy."

which is true. It still doesn't whip. It takes me twenty minutes to discover this.

"There's a little grocery around the corner. Dear me; perhaps you'd better try double . . ."

The proper combination (after a phone call to Hilary Moorcock) seems to be half and half.

"Mmmmm—butter, eh?"

Then we play with eggs.

"Look, you and your old family recipes; *why* don't you separate the yolks from the whites?"

It takes much less time to whip twelve eggs

"Watch it—!"

and one egg shell than it does to whip one pint of light/single cream

"Are you sure you need six more eggs?"

—or eighteen eggs, for that matter. Alcohol (proof increased considerably by 24 hours in sugar) cooks eggs.

"Wouldn't you say this is a terribly expensive way to make an omelette?"

The rotary beater makes like an outboard through the froth of sugar and booze as drop by drop the eggs are spooned down.

"I'd like to understand a little further what you mean by the distinctions between the generation under twenty-five and—woooooops!"

It is much easier to mix two gallons of whisky & egg mixture into two quarts of English whipped cream

"It's *very* yellow, isn't it?"

than it is to mix two quarts of English whipped cream into two gallons of egg & whisky.

"Well, it *looks* like butter."

Then we lug the plastic wash tub, covered with tinfoil, into the back yard and place it under a box, in the rain.

New Year's Eve, and the party erupts in much mauve and gold corduroy mod. Tom Disch greets me at the bottom of the steps (another American science-fiction writer) in evening dress (John Sladek in military maroon, and Chris Priest, face shattered and beautiful, in jeans and blue turtleneck); Tom is handing out masks. Pam has made some umpty of them, one the size of a postage stamp, razored from a photograph and mounted on a stick to be held up in front of the eye; another three feet across, the sleeping face of the sun rayed with red, and floppy. Some of the masks are drawn, some are collage with features grafted from magazines (one gasping mouth, with crayoned lips, disgorging flowers from some *House Beautiful* advertisement) and the false faces turn, laugh, fall and rise again—"I want you to know your eggnog is a total success! I had to save a glass behind the steps so you'd have some!"—glowing among these faces: Some have two eyeholes, some have one. There is one with three, and the sleeping sun, which eventually comes to me, as people pass them to one another, has none. The music pinions us to the instant. And later, talking to Tom (he stands by the door, his hands in the pockets of his tuxedo pants, yellow hair falling to the black silk collar of his jacket, trying to comprehend this moment past midnight), I insist: "This year, I've actually done so little, written so little, so few of the millions of impressions have been fixed by anything resembling art—I'm going to lose them,"

He laughs. "Why? Because you won't have another first night in Paris? It's not lost, Chip—"

I try to explain this way: "Some time between a year ago and now I was standing on the steps of the Blue Mosque in Istanbul, looking across the courtyard, and suddenly I realized that I could be *anywhere* within a year; there was as much chance of my being in Bombay or Tokyo, or some city or town I don't even know the name of today, as there was of my being in New York, Paris or London. There's this insane, unfixed energy—"

But it isn't explaining.

And the New Year deliquesces about our images. (How much of the noise is to convince ourselves that we can still hear? There is so much death in the "younger generation"

. . .) Cherry colored nigas with the Aldisse's on a brittle Oxford afternoon—

A few days later Tom and I go to the British Museum. It is cold, and January is still brittle on the streets.

"The gold on those gray pediment statues is really incredible," Tom says as we pass the gates and cross the sprawling pink tiles of the plaza before the steps.

The archaic statuary room is closed.

"I won't feel my trip to Greece is complete until I've seen the Elgin Marbles. Come on."

In the neoclassic hall the ruined frieze occupies and mutes us. Tom moves slowly from panel to panel, hands sunk in his overcoat.

Through reproduction, the most familiar of the panels have been erased of all freshness. Still, moments of drapery and musculature explode with the energy of a people caught in the transition from conceptual to representational art. (Passing thought: science fiction at its best takes literature back along this same route, starting at the representational as defined by Materialism, and pushes us toward the conceptual, its energy comes from the reserve latent in the gap.)

> *This panel depicts the battle between the*
> *Centaurs and the Lapiths. The head of the*
> *Centaur is in the Louvre. An unimportant*
> *fragment of the panel is still in Athens.*

I don't suppose assassinating Harold Wilson would get them back to Greece.

Upstairs the museum has arranged a display of fifteenth and sixteenth century Mogul prints from India.

I walk across the polished wood (ice skating through the King's Library, pulling back the purple drapes from the autographs of Keats, Byron, Shelley, Macaulay—and Tom looking at the massed volumes behind the glass doors of the two-story hall, panicking; "What are you and I making more *books* for!") toward the cases.

"Look! Look at the light!"

On their ivory mattes, sixteenth century India quivers in distorted perspective, the blacks, vermilions, chartreuses, the gold so vivid that in some prints it takes a full minute for a landscape to clear while the colors tear my eyes.

"It's as though . . ." I begin. "It's as though each object were *sunk* in light!"

No figure among the prints casts a shadow, yet each is modeled and shaded in three dimensions; each has a halo of shadow about it. Brilliant elephants cross blinding rivers. Soldiers glitter across landscapes where no discernible sun shines.

"It's incredible. The things at the horizon are painted just as clearly as . . ."

I stop.

Tom looks from me to the prints and back. "The whole scheme of color values is something that I guess we just don't understand anymore. Did they really do these? You couldn't possibly reproduce them with modern printing methods. Hey, what's the matter?"

"Nothing . . ." We spend nearly two hours in the room, wandering among the prints.

And the light . . .

Mykonos, London, New York
January 1966–January 1967

ABOUT THE AUTHOR

"SAMUEL R. DELANY is the most interesting author of science fiction writing in English today," said *The New York Times Book Review*. He was born in New York City in 1942. His acclaimed science fiction novels include *Babel-17* and *The Einstein Intersection*, both winners of the Nebula Award for best science fiction novel. He has also written *Nova*, *Triton*, the best selling *Dhalgren* and the Nevèrÿon fantasy series, *Tales of Nevèrÿon*, *Neveryóna* and *Flight from Nevèrÿon*. *Stars in My Pocket Like Grains of Sand* is the first volume of a science fiction diptych which will conclude with *The Splendor and Misery of Bodies, of Cities*, to be published by Bantam Spectra Books in 1986. Also a critic of science fiction, he has published two essay collections on the field, *The Jewel-Hinged Jaw* and *Starboard Wine*, as well as *The American Shore*, a book-length semiotic study of the science fiction short story "Angouleme" by Thomas M. Disch.